Praise for *The Eng*

'*The Engraver's Secret* is an inspired bl
braiding two stories of fathers and daughters and family secrets
across time. Lisa Medved conjures Rubens' house and his world so
vividly that Antwerp and this wonderful debut novel will inhabit
your dreams.' **Dominic Smith**, *New York Times* **bestselling
author of** *The Last Painting of Sara de Vos* **and** *Return to Valetto*

'Perfect for fans of dark academia, *The Engraver's Secret* is a richly
woven tale of intrigue, with two very determined women at its
heart. A captivating debut that brings the art and history of the
Baroque era to life on the page.' **Evie Woods, author of the
#1** *Wall Street Journal* **and Amazon Kindle bestseller** *The
Lost Bookshop*

'*The Engraver's Secret* enthralled me from its first lush sentence. Set
in seventeenth-century and modern-day Antwerp, the search to
uncover the secrets of Rubens' mysterious engraver transported
me into the deliciously ruthless world of art history academia.
Medved's knowledge of the architecture, art and culture of Rubens'
era is breathtaking in scope and masterfully rendered. I was utterly
taken by this stunning debut, a riveting and perfectly paced tale
of betrayal, secrets, theft, ambition, danger, and desire.' **Melissa
Ashley, bestselling author of** *The Birdman's Wife*, *The Bee and
the Orange Tree* **and** *The Naturalist of Amsterdam*

'A beautifully told tale about the strength of familial bonds, and
a centuries-old mystery that holds the key to a young woman's
future.' **Lauren Chater, bestselling author of** *The Lace Weaver*,
Gulliver's Wife, *The Winter Dress* **and** *The Beauties*

'A skilful and passionate writer, Lisa Medved lured me into
seventeenth-century Antwerp and held me captive there. I
was engrossed by this tale of art and intrigue, love and betrayal,
friendship and loss.' **Suzanne Leal, bestselling author of** *The
Teacher's Secret* **and** *The Watchful Wife*

'Art and history collide in this sumptuous novel of dark secrets, family, violence and treachery. Two extraordinary women, set apart by time, are beholden to a past and the men who shaped it. For the talented Antonia, it's the conflict between the magnificent artist, Peter Paul Rubens, and her frustrated engraver father that tears her life apart. Then, there's Charlotte, the brilliant Rubens' scholar, who stumbles upon a mystery protected for centuries – a mystery that will either augment her career or destroy it. This atmospheric, suspenseful tale, where the streets of seventeenth-century and modern Antwerp come alive, is as gorgeously and deftly crafted as a Rubens masterpiece.' **Karen Brooks, bestselling author of** *The Good Wife of Bath*, *The Brewer's Tale* **and** *The Escapades of Tribulation Johnson*

'Trust, betrayal, and the painful lessons of the past: these interweave in the connected stories of two women centuries apart, both seeking truth, and a way to build independent lives. At the heart of each woman's story are family secrets and the risks of ambition and failure. Lisa Medved's meticulous research plummets us into the fascinating creative world of Antwerp's Golden Age, while a compelling modern mystery propels the novel through twists, feuds, and intrigues to its thrilling conclusion.' **Kelly Gardiner, critically acclaimed, bestselling author of** *Goddess*

'The exotic mystery and brutal treachery of art and academia across eras binds two women to both their ambition and each other in Lisa Medved's expertly researched and tenderly wrought debut novel. Crafted with care and delivered with fervour through the hearts and minds of Antonia and Charlotte, *The Engraver's Secret* will reignite a passion for perseverance and commitment to self-belief and reveal that our impulses to unravel the past can make or break who we are in the present.' **Sally Colin-James, author of** *One Illumined Thread*, **winner of the Colleen McCullough Fellowship Award**

Lisa Medved is an Australian author who divides
her time between Melbourne and The Hague.
After completing a Bachelor of Arts in history and
fine art from the University of Melbourne, Lisa
went on to work in public relations and event
management, honing her writing skills for various
corporate publications and several magazines in
the UK and the Netherlands. *The Engraver's Secret*
is her first novel, and was born out of a passion
for history and art.

The
ENGRAVER'S
Secret

The
ENGRAVER'S
Secret

LISA MEDVED

HarperCollins*Publishers*

HarperCollins*Publishers*
Australia • Brazil • Canada • France • Germany • Holland • India
Italy • Japan • Mexico • New Zealand • Poland • Spain • Sweden
Switzerland • United Kingdom • United States of America

HarperCollins acknowledges the Traditional Custodians
of the lands upon which we live and work, and pays respect
to Elders past and present.

First published on Gadigal Country in Australia in 2024
by HarperCollins*Publishers* Australia Pty Limited
ABN 36 009 913 517
harpercollins.com.au

A catalogue record for this book is available from the National Library of Australia

ISBN 978 1 4607 6427 5 (paperback)
ISBN 978 1 4607 1632 8 (ebook)
ISBN 978 1 4607 3698 2 (audio book)

Cover design by Louisa Maggio, HarperCollins Design Studio
Cover images: Woman © Dmytro Baev / Trevillion Images; Flowers, butterflies, skull and quill by
Europeana/Unsplash; all other images by shutterstock.com
Author photograph by Vinita Salomé
Typeset in Hoefler Text and Bembo Std by Kirby Jones
Printed and bound in Australia by McPherson's Printing Group

MIX
Paper from
responsible sources
FSC® C001695
www.fsc.org

For Stan, Natasha and Alex

PART ONE

'Do you not know that there comes a midnight hour
when everyone has to throw off his mask?'

– Søren Kierkegaard

1

July 22, 1675 – Antwerpen, Spanish Hapsburg Empire

I buried a fragment of my heart today. It lies forever in the dark, hidden within the folds of my father's shroud, beneath a massive slab of marble in the south aisle of Sint-Jacobskerk.

We arrived at church as dawn was breaking. Hendrik and his wife, with my nephews and nieces, stood close at my side, all eyes turned to the pit. Early morning of high summer was the most practical time for an internment, yet the air was already ripe with the sun's warmth and the press of the crowd. Over a hundred mourners thronged to observe the burial rites, even envoys from the Hapsburg court, ostentatious in their velvet, ribbons and lace. Most were mere onlookers, hiding whispers behind pomanders pressed to their nostrils. They understood nothing of my grief, of the secret that bound my lips to silence.

The sprigs of lemon balm and hyssop slipped within the shroud did little to mask the fetid smell emanating from the pit. I held a kerchief to my nose and breathed in the scent of cloves and cinnamon. As the priest intoned the liturgy, I stared into the blackness, tracing the curves of my father's wrapped body. There lay Papa: Lucas Vorsterman, renowned engraver of Antwerpen, who immortalised hundreds with burin on copper, charcoal on paper. There he lay in his many guises: guild member, scholar, linguist, devout Catholic, dutiful husband, loving father, deceiver. Nine decades wrapped in the shroud. Nine decades of joy, sorrow, regret and life-crippling shame.

Grief is made even more severe when you adore someone with such intensity and that adoration turns sour, nay, even rancid. Worse, too, is the fact that he is gone and I am unable to ask the questions that beg to be answered. They linger, afloat like the wind, leaving me to forever speculate. His final words carried a loathsome burden and shifted its weight to me. Like a lodestone, his confession sits in the cavity of my chest, shaming me into silence.

Standing near the burial pit, I closed my eyes to force away the tears. Take this encumbrance back, I silently whispered, and let it be buried with you. It is not mine. Give me oblivion. Give me ignorance. Let me drink from the waters of Lethe.

I adored my father until the day he died. On that day, a transformation took place deep within me. Beginning as a flutter in my chest, it settled in my gut, turning my adoration into sorrow and disbelief. This burden lay heavy within me as I sat by his side, waiting for him to pass from this world into the next. The sweet scent of beeswax wafted in the air; no cheap tallow for his deathbed. The vein on his temple pulsed with the merest tremble. Candlelight shadows flickered over his closed lids and parted lips, across the blanket rising and falling with each breath, to his hand resting in mine. His fingers were limp, his skin a map of protruding veins, age spots and creases.

He stared at me with such intensity, I forgot for a moment that he saw little but shadows through his cloudy irises. He struggled with his last words, pausing often to draw breath. Each word, every utterance of my name – 'Antonia, *mijn liefje*' – although whispered with tenderness, felt like a stone, heavy and cold.

I am not your confessor, Papa, I longed to say. But I stilled my lips and caressed his hand, soothing away his agitation. Ever the dutiful daughter.

He implored for understanding and forgiveness, and whispered his insistence that I preserve his secret. Soon after his final plea, with a gentle exhalation, his chest stilled. My father, suddenly a stranger, was gone.

2

Charlotte scans the room, hungry for clues, committing images to memory. Despite knowing he is absent, she still hesitates, struggling to push away the anxiety.

She moves to a display cabinet. Three squat stone statues glare out from behind the glass. Pockmarked, teeth bared, ferocious but powerless.

'Sixteenth-century Aztec,' his assistant tells her. 'He's been collecting them for years. Makes an interesting contrast to his area of expertise.'

They are the ugliest creatures Charlotte has ever seen: obscene gargoyles with splayed limbs and distended bellies, loincloths hiding priapic bulges. She nods, feigning interest, but all she can think about is the man who belongs to this room. Breathing in, she tries to identify his scent – lingering aftershave, perhaps a hint of tobacco – but there's nothing.

'Would you like a coffee while you wait?' asks his assistant.

'Thank you, but no.' Charlotte moves to another cabinet, this one displaying ancient masks. Skeletal features with sunken cheeks, empty eye sockets, grotesque protruding teeth. The skin on the back of her neck prickles.

The assistant retreats to the outer office, sitting at a desk bearing a nameplate: *Miss Ulrika Beulen*. The woman's eyebrows are pencilled with a distinct arch, her grey hair pulled into a chignon; all precision and control.

Glancing around the office, Charlotte takes in the neatly arranged bookshelves, slick chrome armchairs, the monstrous antique desk, a Gallé lamp on a side table. Eclectic. Classics paired with the macabre. The inventory continues, her eyes furtive, taking in every detail. Art

Nouveau desk set with an obsolete inkwell and a not-so-obsolete letter opener with a polished six-inch blade. Blue Murano bowl holding business cards. She slips a card into her pocket; talisman for luck or amulet to fend off the unwanted. Either will do.

On the wall hangs a huge map of the Lowlands, displaying the early sixteenth-century dominions of the Hapsburg Empire and Duchy of Guelders. Surrounding the map are framed degrees, certificates and photographs.

His name is everywhere. Master's degree, doctorate in history, professor of the history department, all written with cursive swirls. A framed title page of his doctorate dissertation on the 1543 conclusion of the Guelders Wars. Certificates and citations, all bearing his name: *Sébastien Sterck*.

Since discovering his name five weeks ago, she has spoken it aloud dozens of times. Repeating his name while pacing her apartment, echoing it while in the shower, trying to wash away the heaviness in her limbs, soothe the turmoil, make sense of it all. Today, finally, she has entered his domain, desperate to search his world, unfold secrets, understand a past that has been a dark cloud for so long. She whispers his name, each syllable hissing, a sibyllic snake, coiled within.

The past is all around her, yet it remains a mystery. She peers at framed photographs, searching for a resemblance. Most are posed: shaking hands, staring at the camera, standing before banners denoting faculty symposiums and history conferences. A suited figure sandwiched among rows of well-dressed no-names, his face partially obscured by tortoiseshell frames, greying hair combed back to reveal a widow's peak, neatly clipped beard and moustache. Demeanour neutral, nothing hinting at his personality.

On a side table she spies a photo of the same man with a younger face. Sprawled on the deck of a boat, he smiles into the sun, the wind ruffling his hair. Another photo, this one a grainy black-and-white, shows two teenage boys resting against a tiller. Is this him as a boy? Does he have a brother?

Charlotte moves to the window, which offers a perfect bird's-eye view over the courtyard. Cobblestones arranged in geometric patterns: central star, overlapping Venn circles, balanced and precise.

Will she spot him walking across the courtyard? Would she recognise him from this distance? More importantly, despite all she has been told, is there a chance, once they come face-to-face, that he will recognise her? Her mind is a jumble of conflicting stories gathered over the years. Truth and falsehood blurring at the seams of a carefully constructed past.

The phone in the outer office rings. Miss Beulen's voice is intermittent: '... someone waiting ... delayed with campus police ... the investigation ...'

Frowning, Charlotte looks at the wall clock. Is he always this late?

Her phone vibrates. She pulls it from her pocket.

The voice on the other end is unfamiliar, male, with a Belgian accent. 'This is Willem from Acquisitions. I hear you're the new Rubens specialist in the art history department.'

The unexpected title takes her by surprise, a warm thrill surging through her. 'Yes. I've just arrived.'

'Welcome.' Willem rushes on. 'I've been examining a map folio that was donated to the university. Seventeenth century, made in Amsterdam, seven maps bound together. There's something unusual about it, related to Rubens, which you may find interesting.'

She turns from the window. A map with a link to Rubens, created in the same century as the artist? She's instantly intrigued. 'What have you found?'

'A crest with his name.'

She frowns at the clock. She's been here fifteen minutes; still no sign of the professor. She'd rather be examining this new find.

'I could take a look, but it'll have to be quick. I'm presenting my first lecture at twelve.'

Miss Beulen's mouth drops open when Charlotte explains she's leaving.

'But this is your induction,' says the assistant.

Charlotte recalls the email from the University of Antwerp, her surprise at discovering the induction meeting would be with the head of history rather than her own department. Surprise changed to anxiety when she realised the meeting was with Sébastien Sterck. Of all the professors for her to meet on her first day.

'I'm sorry. I have another appointment and ... I can't be late,' she finishes lamely. Her emotions are mixed: relieved she doesn't have to meet him, disappointed her curiosity must wait to be resolved.

Miss Beulen's eyebrows arch upwards as she stands and smooths her black pencil skirt. 'Professor Sterck isn't normally late.'

'We can make a new time. Please give the professor my apologies.'

The assistant picks up a folder from the desk, her mouth opening and closing like a trout.

'Is that for me?' Charlotte spots her name, upside-down on the folder's cover: *Dr Charlotte Hubert*.

The assistant hugs the folder to her chest. More aquatic facial twitches. 'Professor Sterck was going to explain everything.'

'Why don't I read it first? If I have any questions, I can ask.' She holds out her hand, smiling.

'It has your timetable, research guidelines, assessment protocols' – Miss Beulen finally, reluctantly, hands over the folder – 'and there's a leaflet about campus safety. We've had several incidents recently, with students threatened. Everyone needs to be extra careful.'

Charlotte nods to show she's listening, but in truth, she's picturing devilish statues behind glass and a Rubens self-portrait in a wide-brimmed hat. She hurries along the corridor, trying to ignore the fluttering sensation in her stomach.

3

'It's a labyrinth,' Willem calls over his shoulder, and pushes open the stairwell door. He's tall and thin, with legs like a stick insect, and climbs the steps two at a time.

Charlotte hurries to keep up, breathless as they emerge into a corridor. Grey linoleum floor, drab walls, a dozen closed doors: a palette of monotony.

'Stairwell for the basement archive and conservation room is that way.' He waves at a door as they continue along the corridor. 'It's easy to get lost, so best not wander down there on your own.'

She follows closely, almost immediately losing track of the route they've taken.

Willem slows his pace until they are walking abreast. 'I read about you in the faculty newsletter under new appointments. Rubens specialist from the University of Toronto. Impressive. Are you related to Dr Rachael Hubert?'

The question stretches into silence. When she finally speaks, her voice catches. 'Yes … my mother.' They are the only words she can manage. She clears her throat, hoping there will be no further questions.

She knew the topic would arise when she arrived in Antwerp. After all, her mother was a recipient of the Prix d'Histoire, lauded by academics across North America and Europe. But the reality comes as a shock. Hearing the name *Dr Rachael Hubert* spoken in the context of her role as a pre-eminent historian fills Charlotte with a warmth in her chest, a light-headedness. Pleasure and pride merge. Yet, knowing this remarkable woman was also a devoted single mother, *her* audacious, fun-loving mother, fills her with an ache so profound she falters mid-stride, desperate to lean against the wall to catch her breath, to release a sliver of built-up pain in a low gasp. It has only been five weeks since her mother's death, yet it could have been five days ago. Her anguish feels no less raw, no less fresh.

Willem chatters about his work in Acquisitions. Despite her mother's renown in academic circles, he appears to be unaware of her death. He ushers her into an office, bright with fluorescent light. 'You're giving a lecture soon, so I'll be quick.'

She focuses on Willem's voice. Now is not the time to become overwhelmed.

He points at a stack of cartons against the wall. 'The university's always receiving donations. Individuals and organisations clear out their attics and send their forgotten treasures here. Every so often we get something exceptional. During the summer term we received donations from Sister Anna, Mother Superior of Begijnhof Sint-Catharina, one of Antwerp's oldest orders.' He indicates a table, spread with yellowed journals wrapped in clear archive plastic.

'What did she send?' asks Charlotte.

'Almanacs and religious journals from the 1800s.'

'And the map folio?'

'It's stunning.' He points at the leather-bound folio lying on a felt mat. 'It's not related to the other items, but it's similar in size to the almanacs.'

'How old is it?'

'1686.'

'Where is it dated?' She's already done the calculations; the folio was created forty-six years after Rubens' death.

'Three places. Title cartouche and printer's mark on the first page.' He passes her a pair of nitrile gloves and wriggles into his own pair, snapping the thin rubber around his wrists.

'And the third?'

'The Rubens Crest.' Willem looks sheepish. 'Didn't know what else to call it.'

She smiles at him, recognising the historian's need to identify, categorise and label. She wonders if the crest is the family's coat-of-arms, used for the first time in the fifteenth century, comprising a shield with fleur-de-lis, bugle and flowers. It only appeared on legal documents, never on his artworks and, as far as she knows, never on a map.

Willem touches the folio's corners. 'The crest is on the first map.'

The folio is covered in shabby green leather the colour of overcooked spinach. The edges are tatty, sections of green having worn away to reveal a layer of brown underneath. Remnants of gold embossed letters speckle the cover.

As he opens the folio, Charlotte moves in for a closer look. Cursive Latin is centred on the title page: *Nova Europae Descriptio*. The name is surrounded by a border of organic curlicues, shaded in olive green and twisted in folds, reminding her of the thick seaweed on Pocologan Beach in New Brunswick, where she holidayed as a child.

'There's Europa,' Willem says, 'daughter of a Phoenician king.'

Charlotte is mesmerised by the finely detailed figure of a woman pictured above the title. Seated on a throne, the woman is bare-breasted and crowned, dressed in robes of Madonna blue with a hem of frothing sea foam.

Willem points at rows of tiny script. 'Date and name of the printer, Frederik de Wit. The numerals indicate it's a first state printing, equivalent to a first edition. Incredibly rare. Only a handful of De Wits in the world are first states.'

Using a metal spatula, he turns the delicate page. The intensity of the double-paged map is startling, coloured like a handful of gemstones. Splashes of sapphire highlight rivers, lakes and seas. Flatlands and mountains are painted in tones of emerald and malachite. Borders are marked with snaking lines of garnet. The map shows Western Europe, stretching from *Hispania* and *Anglia* in the west, to *Italia* and *Germania* in the east, overlaid with faint grid lines indicating geographical coordinates.

Willem continues: 'De Wit was a cartographer and printer, working in Amsterdam from the 1650s until his death in 1706 ...'

She leans in to study the detail. The map lines and place names are uniform, suggesting the page was printed on a press. But several patches of colour are uneven, blues and greens seeping over borders, suggesting the colours were added by hand – and not always a steady one. The grid lines, although ruler-straight, have uneven darker spots, indicating the printer used a nib to draw the lines by hand, rather than have them printed.

'… colouring is typical of late seventeenth-century maps from the Dutch Republic,' says Willem, 'which were printed, then embellished by hand.' He points out the blurred colours along the edge of France where the colourist's hand had trembled while shading the water's edge in ultramarine.

A series of rounded horizontal lozenges run along the top and bottom of the double-page spread, forming a decorative frieze. Each one is filled with a small drawing of a city, its Latin name included beneath. She recognises *Roma* with ancient buildings perched on multiple hills, bridges across the river in *Londinium*, boats on the canals of *Venetia*, step-gabled façades in *Antwerpen*.

'First state maps by De Wit are in libraries in Brussels, Amsterdam, Utrecht, Munich, Vienna and Yale,' says Willem. 'Incredible that our library now has its own. The decorative details and colours are remarkable. It's been kept in the optimum environment … cool, dry, dark.'

The frieze continues along the left and right sides of the map with more lozenges, these ones stretched into vertical shapes. Each is filled with a miniature figure and a Latin title. She identifies *Papa Romanorum* wearing a triple crown, *Rex Hispaniae* in doublet and hose, *Rex Anglia* draped in ermine, *Regina Franciae* with a laurel crown. The miniature cityscapes and figures are vibrant: russet rooftops and honey-hued stone walls, magenta robes and mint leggings, cerulean rivers snaking through lush hills.

'De Wit made multiple copies of his maps, but not this one,' says Willem. 'I've searched online and haven't found another one like it anywhere in the world. No copies from this first state survived. Maybe they were never made in the first place.'

'But printers made numerous copies to maximise their revenue.'

'Not this one. It's unique.'

'But–'

'I've checked.' Willem unfurls to his full height. 'There's no other De Wit map with exactly the same decorative frieze, hand-drawn markings or Rubens Crest.'

She lets his words register. A tingle of excitement grows. 'Where's the crest?'

He passes her a magnifying glass, pointing to southern Portugal. Peering through the glass, a crest comes into focus. It bears no resemblance to the Rubens family coat-of-arms. No fleur-de-lis, bugle or flowers.

Perfectly camouflaged within Portugal, it is the size of a postage stamp. Tilted on its side, its top edge mimics the Portuguese coast. Its remaining edges follow the southern coast of the Mediterranean, then turn north to trail the Spanish border before turning west to the coast. The words in the crest are printed in Old Flemish: *Frederik de Wit voor Antonia Vorsterman, Antwerpen, 1686.*

'... for Antonia Vorsterman,' translates Charlotte. Why did a renowned cartographer from Amsterdam's Dutch Republic inscribe a map folio for a woman in Spanish-ruled Antwerp in 1686 at a time when the two nations were quarrelling over borders and trading rights? Communications and commerce between Amsterdam and Antwerp were fraught with conflict during this period.

'Who's Antonia?' Willem asks.

'Lucas Vorsterman worked for Rubens as his engraver from 1618,' she says, 'but Antonia ... I'm not sure.'

'Maybe she commissioned the folio.'

Charlotte adjusts the magnifying glass, and the words at the top of the crest come into focus: *In de voetsporen van Peter Paul Rubens.*

'In the footsteps of Peter Paul Rubens,' she translates. A shiver begins at the nape of her neck and creeps down her spine.

'Peter Paul,' she repeats, enjoying the alliteration. She recalls her first year at university. Fresh-faced and eager, she'd signed up for a unit called *The Seductive Power of Rubens.* By the end of the first lecture, the seduction was complete, leaving her captivated by the artist's opulent style, theatrical play of light and movement, supersized goddesses and warriors writhing across canvases.

The more Charlotte studied his art, the more she became fascinated by the man: diplomat, scholar, master of a prolific studio, expert in all genres, devout family man and Catholic, loyal to the Spanish Hapsburg princes who ruled his hometown of Antwerp. The multifaceted genius was far too intriguing to relegate to a minor position in her studies, and by the completion of her Master's degree, she was a highly accomplished Rubens scholar. Toronto offered her a position. Her academic star shone brightly.

Hungry to learn about the physical properties of paintings, she worked for a year in a conservation studio. Later, enrolling for a doctorate, she happily allowed it to take over her life: the all-consuming research, writing journal articles, delivering lectures, the irritation of supervising first-year students more interested in Jägerbombs than Brueghels. Moving from one cramped inner-city apartment to the next, forgoing romantic relationships for another weekend at work, summer breaks spent completing her doctorate. Transferring from Toronto to Chicago then a two-year sojourn at Dartmouth, back to Toronto before reaching the pinnacle of every Rubens academic: at the age of thirty-four, finally, a position in the art history department in Antwerp. No matter that it is only for two terms. If she makes an impact, it may be extended. Better, she may be offered a permanent place. A dream come true.

For two terms, Antwerp will become her home. She will follow the ghost of Rubens along the same streets he walked, gaze up at the same Stadhuis façade he admired, explore his studio and his home. His view from long ago will become her view. A fragment of his vision will become hers.

Charlotte rummages in her satchel, pulls out a notebook and pen, opens to a fresh page. Her fingers prickle with excitement. Energy she hasn't felt in weeks.

Thrilling as it is to be in Rubens' hometown, she's pragmatic enough to realise not everything about her new position is a dream come true. She had learnt about the Antwerp opportunity at a time when her mother's health had deteriorated rapidly. Despite serious misgivings, she had accepted the job on the encouragement of her mother. Now, at long last, she is in Antwerp, but her mother is no longer a phone call away to share the excitement of this new adventure, to offer encouragement and advice. And, of course, now she must contend with *him*.

She tries to ignore the anxiety of having to share the campus, attend the same faculty meetings, run the risk of seeing *him* around every corner. She won't let his presence detract from this incredible experience. She's worked too hard to let this opportunity be marred by his presence. *Concentrate on the job*, she tells herself. *Relish the experience. Don't let him get under your skin.*

Charlotte trains the magnifying glass on the Rubens Crest, scribbles in her notebook: *In the footsteps of Peter Paul Rubens.*

Walking in the footsteps of a renowned person is something she is familiar with. As a child, she sat in her mother's office and listened to students debate theories, cementing her passion for history and academic research at an early age. By fifteen, she had decided to become an historian like her mother, albeit in a different field. Her mother's specialisation in the sixteenth-century border wars of the Low Countries was drawn from her curiosity about her Belgian roots. Charlotte's specialisation in Rubens was based on her interest in Flemish history and art, and a desire to strike out on a different academic pathway from her mother's.

'... Antonia Vorsterman, whoever she is, could have commissioned the folio for a Rubens-inspired Grand Tour,' says Willem.

She realises that while she's been lost in reflection, Willem has continued talking.

He adjusts a desk lamp, focusing the light on the centre of the map: an aurora of blues and greens.

'Every word is Latin,' she murmurs, 'except the Rubens Crest, which is Old Flemish.'

'Perhaps it commemorates the fiftieth anniversary of his death.'

'Rubens died in 1640, while the folio was made in 1686.' She speaks gently, careful not to curb Willem's enthusiasm.

She taps the pen on the table edge. 'I don't think it's commemorative. The mapmaker has gone to a lot of effort to hide the crest within Portugal, placing it on its side. If the intention was to celebrate the most successful artist of his time, why not proclaim it on the title page in bold letters? Why camouflage it?'

Willem beams. 'Knew you'd find it interesting.'

'What can you tell me about Begijnhof Sint-Catharina? How did they come by the folio? Is Sister Anna the best person for me to contact for more information?'

'Professor Sterck knows Sister Anna quite well. They met at a symposium during the summer, which is how the Begijnhof came to donate material to the university.'

'I'll call her to make an appointment.'

'It'll be tricky contacting anyone at the Begijnhof.'

'Don't tell me they've taken vows of silence.' She smiles at her own joke.

His brow furrows. 'There was a major incident at the Begijnhof last week …'

Charlotte is only half-listening, realising she needs to locate the lecture hall and check the audio-visual equipment. She discards the gloves on the desk, shoves her notebook and pen into her satchel.

Willem is still talking as she moves to the door. '… piece of masonry came loose from the belfry and injured a visitor. Professor Sterck said the local authorities are investigating.'

4

Charlotte stands in the middle of a vast stage, surrounded by darkness, and adjusts the lectern's reading light. She has attended enough lectures to know that from this angle, her face is bizarrely shadowed like a Cubist portrait. Distorted nose and jaw, eyes sunk into deep sockets, mouth askew.

'Rubens spent ten years in Italy,' her voice rings out, 'learning from the masters of the Venetian school.' Clicking to the next picture, an image of a drunk titan surrounded by nymphs and satyrs flashes onto the screen behind her. 'He painted *Drunken Hercules* in 1613, two years after returning to Antwerp.'

The mute faces of a hundred people loom out of the half-light. As each row ascends into blackness, the faces blur into obscurity. By the last rows, they're little more than androgynous shapes.

She clicks to a picture of a satyr with a leering face and twin horns sprouting through curls. Another click, and the image zooms to a nymph with golden braids and wild eyes. 'Classical myths were a constant source of inspiration for Rubens.'

When the image of a fleshy nude, wrapped in fur, appears on the screen, Charlotte leans into the microphone. 'The grandiose style of his early paintings set the groundwork for his later works, such as this erotic portrait of his second wife, Hélène Fourment.' Pausing, she scans the audience and smiles. She still can't quite believe she is finally delivering a lecture in Antwerp, only a ten-minute walk from the Rubenshuis where her artistic hero lived.

'You can hear more about Hélène at next week's lecture.' She shuffles her notes together, taps a switch on the lectern, and Hélène fades into a blanched apparition as light floods the front of the auditorium. Amid squeaking seats and shuffling footsteps, students file to the door.

A dreadlocked woman in the second row continues writing in a notebook. Something about her reminds Charlotte of herself as a student. Not the scraggy hair or multiple piercings, of course, but the intensity of her manner. The woman is totally captivated. Hungry to burrow inside the artist's mind, understand the vortex of colours and movement, discover his thought process and his muse.

Charlotte glances at the cluster of well-dressed people congregating at the bottom of the steps. Here to listen to her first lecture, they now wait to meet her. Polished and self-assured, they stand in a circle, talking among themselves. Men wearing jackets and ties. Women with tailored blazers, slicks of lipstick, hair in chic up-dos. No hint of the slouchy raggedness of semi-impoverished students. Charlotte recalls her own transition, over ten years ago, from student to teacher. Does she look like these people now? Is the uncertainty of her youth finally gone, replaced with the self-assurance of her thirty-something self?

She tucks in a stray curl from her braided bun, squares her shoulders and walks towards them.

The group opens their circle, ushering her inside, some speaking Dutch, others English. She responds in both.

'Excellent debut lecture, Dr Hubert.'

'High time the department had a Rubens specialist.'

'Welcome to the Arts Faculty, Dr Hubert.'

She shakes hands and accepts business cards, caught in a ritualistic head-bobbing, hand-shaking dance. She uses a memory game to anchor names to faces. Arnold Blauwmann's steel-framed glasses are bright blue. Karl Joosten reminds her of a Toronto colleague with a similar towering frame. Jeanette Chevalier has a whinnying laugh like a horse. By the time a lanky man with a goatee introduces himself, the names and titles are blurring. One after another, they say farewell and move to the door in a slow-motion conga line.

Alone at last, her footsteps echo as she returns to the stage. Closing her laptop, she smiles. She'd met the dean of the Arts Faculty and several senior lecturers, including Professor Chevalier, the head of the art history department and no doubt her new supervisor. Seems friendly enough. Pity about the laugh.

A flash of movement makes Charlotte stop. Up the steep incline of seats, a man sidesteps along the back row, holding a mobile phone to his ear. Pocketing the phone, he comes down the stairs towards her. He's impeccably groomed: tailored jacket and silk necktie, knife-edge creases down his trousers. She tries to make out his features, but his face remains in shadow.

The man steps closer, clears his throat with a patter of soft coughs. 'My apologies for missing our meeting earlier today, Dr Hubert. I was unavoidably delayed.' His English is excellent, the merest hint of a Belgian accent. 'Professor Sébastien Sterck, head of the history department. Pleased to meet you.'

He offers his hand. She's unaware of reaching out to accept it, but somehow it's in her palm, cool and firm, in stark contrast to the clamminess of her own. Releasing his hand, she steps back. Her cheeks are warm, yet coldness prickles her skin.

His eyes are a surprise – green with flecks of amber. The same eyes she sees every time she looks in a mirror.

God, it's really him.

He holds her gaze for a moment, then glances at the stage. 'This is the oldest lecture hall on campus, although Antwerp is young compared to the likes of Bologna and Oxford.'

She opens her mouth to speak, but no sound comes out. A fog clouds her mind. His voice sounds far off, fragmented words crackling like an untuned radio.

'I delivered my first lecture here years ago.' His hand covers his mouth, overcome by a paroxysm of coughing. 'Excuse me.' He walks to a water cooler by the door, tugs out a paper cup and fills it, keeping his back to her as he drinks.

The water cooler gurgles as he refills the cup. He tilts his head, taking slow sips. Staring at his back, Charlotte concentrates on staying calm. He's more fastidious than she imagined. There's a restraint about him, indiscernible from the handful of pictures she'd found online. There were no videos, otherwise she might have expected his meticulous way of talking, his restrained gestures and expressions, the coolness of those eyes. He looks older and thinner than the pictures.

He pivots to face her, tweaks his cufflinks. 'Our facilities are a little cramped at the moment as we're renovating, so I'm afraid you'll have to share an office with Dr Miles Thornton from the history department.'

'Share?' Her voice is scratchy.

'Your timetables mean you'll have the office to yourself for much of the time.'

'I'm sure it will be fine,' she replies, wanting to sound amenable.

'You've heard about Professor Chevalier?' His eyebrows lift, green eyes stare.

'My supervisor ...'

'Professor Chevalier is leaving on sabbatical next week, so I will be your supervisor.' He fiddles with a signet ring on his little finger. 'You'll find the history and art history departments work as a close-knit team, given we're both under the Arts Faculty.'

She keeps her expression neutral, but her jaw tightens. Why *him*?

'The art history department is short-staffed at the moment. Professor Chevalier's sabbatical was approved earlier this year, and since then, they've had several senior lecturers pull out from teaching due to illness.'

He straightens his tie. All this fiddling suggests he's uncomfortable, but his face remains composed. Unreadable.

She would have been fine having a supervisor below the rank of professor. All she needs is someone to explain the Antwerp system, confirm she's on the right path with her research or suggest a different tack. She's experienced enough to know how to develop a premise, formulate research, ensure lectures follow the curriculum.

'Given your academic experience,' he continues, 'I'm sure you won't require close supervision. But I'm here if you need me.'

'Thank you.' Keeping her voice light, she pretends to be unfazed. She wants to talk about lectures and research – to sound competent at least – but her mind is blank. *Narrow your focus*, she tells herself. *Breathe*.

She stares at his shoes. Brogues, navy suede, with perforations punched in the leather. His trousers end in crisp turn-ups. And those creases, neat and precise, so very formal. Everything about him is formal. Everything shouts starched and stuffy and conventional, absolutely, smackingly dead-centre. Does he run his life in the same way? Does he manage his staff with the same control?

She's imagined this moment, played it over in her mind so many times, anticipating what she would say, how she would feel, how he would react. But this, *this moment*, is different from anything she could have imagined. A muffled beat echoes in her ears. *I am your daughter*, she wants to say, to shout, to scream.

She bites her bottom lip. He doesn't know.

5

February 26, 1621 – Antwerpen, Spanish Hapsburg Empire

Papa presented me with a journal on the morning of my name day, handing it across the breakfast table as he recounted a dull little anecdote about Blessed Antonia of Florence.

'You can look to her for inspiration in your own life, *mijn liefje*,' he said. 'She was a devout follower of Our Lord, and displayed humility and obedience to the family of nuns to whom she belonged.'

I cared little for an obscure Tuscan nun from a distant land two centuries past. The journal, however, was beautiful: tooled in calfskin, the colour of onions, with a leather tie holding the cover in place. Niels looked on with envy, reaching out a sticky finger, but I held it close to my chest, wise in the ways of little brothers. Being the firstborn came with the privilege of occasionally receiving gifts that were mine and mine alone.

My father, Lucas Vorsterman, and mother, Anne Franckx, had me baptised Antonia Lijsbeth at Antwerpen's Sint-Jacobskerk following my birth on March 15, 1609. My brother Hendrik arrived three years later, then two years after, Niels appeared, all pudgy fists, mewling mouth, as bald as a potato. Two boys followed, their muted cries heard for mere seconds before departing this world as placidly as they arrived. A shame, but 'tis life. The next babe, named Lucas after my father, was born on a winter's morning. The sun was just appearing when his first lusty howls filled the house.

'Here be a child who wants to stay,' said Janneke, bustling into the kitchen with an armload of blood-soaked linens.

'How is Mama?' I sat in the corner of the kitchen, observing the maids' activities. Mama's cries had awoken me during the night, reminding me how her previous confinements had ended in misery. During the darkest hours, I clasped my rosary and prayed to the patron saint of childbirth, Margaret of Antioch, imploring her to let this confinement result in happiness.

'Your mama is strong and has a hearty babe. She be restin' now.' Janneke placed the linens on the steps leading to the yard, then poked some stray curls under my cap, her roughened fingertips stroking my cheek. 'Tomorrow, your papa will lead us to Sint-Jacobskerk for Lucas to be baptised, then we will come home to feast.'

Whenever a new babe arrived, we celebrated, our house brimming with visitors and sideboards groaning with food. Rooms overflowed with the goodwill of family, friends, neighbours and Papa's work fellows. During times of sorrow, when loved ones breathed their last, those same visitors were just as quick to arrive on our doorstop, but with mournful faces and words of compassion. News spread quickly. Secrets were rare.

Our house sits tall and proud on Eikenstraat, a few blocks from Sint-Jacobskerk. It is a narrow, three-storey, red-brick townhouse in a cobblestoned street named after the oak trees lining the canal. The house once belonged to my *opa*, but I have no memory of him, only vague recollections of my *oma*, who died when I was barely five. I recall hugging a bony woman who smelt of sweet Castile soap, which Spanish merchants brought from their homeland to the market.

My father is an engraver and a member of the Sint-Lucas Guild. A towering man with a broad chest and large hands, he is quick to embrace me and tickle my face with his beard. He stands large in a room, not only for his height but also his deep voice and expressive hands, which he flourishes whenever he speaks. He is the axis on which our household turns.

Whenever we sit together in his workroom, I marvel at the way his thick fingers wield the delicate engraver's burin with such ease. I love watching him work, his head bent over the desk, the tassel at the end of his red felt cap swaying as he moves. We converse on all manner of topics, me peppering him with questions, him encouraging my curiosity, reminding me that my knowledge and conversation are mature for my tender years.

'Why are the northern provinces revolting against the Spanish?'

'How long did Meneer Rubens take to paint the ceiling of Sint-Carolus Borromeuskerk?'

'How did the oysters make the pearls in Mama's necklace?'

'Is the Sint-Lucas Guild named after you, Papa?'

He rumpled my curls. 'The guild has existed since 1382. It's not only a building, but a group of people united in their artistic skill and training. All of us create items of beauty' – he paused with a smile – 'some with more skill than others.'

'Do you have the most skill?'

Laying down his charcoal pencil, he nudged the drawing towards me. It showed a gentleman wearing a floppy-brimmed hat. 'You have seen me labour over this drawing for the past half-hour, yes?'

I peered at the face of the gentleman, recognising him as a frequent caller. Count Alvaro González wore the most elaborately plumed hats and widest ruffs, had the loudest laugh, told the bawdiest jokes. My Spanish vocabulary expanded with new words at each visit – words I could never speak aloud.

'It is a passable likeness of the Count and will suffice for his needs.' Papa waved his hand at the drawing, his gesture dismissive. 'But the artist for whom I now work has skills unmatched by any other in the Guild. He could make a likeness of the Count in a few minutes and it would be superior to this.' Looking at me, he winked. 'But I am a better engraver than he.'

'But Meneer Rubens is not an engraver like you, Papa. He is a painter.'

'Yes indeed, but he dabbles in engraving. He is also a scholar, a court diplomat and speaks five languages.'

'So do you, Papa.'

His laugh unfurled from deep within his belly. 'Indeed I do, but not with the same prowess as Meneer Rubens.'

When I was seven, Papa took me to visit the Plantijnhuis and showed me the desk where he created engravings for the Plantijn Press. But that was years ago. He now works exclusively for Antwerpen's most revered artist, Meneer Peter Paul Rubens. I have yet to visit Papa's workspace at the Rubenshuis.

I have glimpsed Meneer Rubens on several occasions about town – doffing his wide-brimmed hat as he enters Sint-Jacobskerk, striding across Grote Markt while deep in conversation with a *burgemeester*. Late one afternoon, as Janneke and I returned from the market,

I spied him emerging from Gulick Inn, all ruddy cheeked and hat askew, his arm thrown around the shoulder of a friend. He always appears amiable, unaffected by his widespread fame, at ease in the company of all, be they servant, apprentice, merchant or nobleman.

Naturally, this was only my impression from a distance. One can never understand a person's true nature until you meet them face-to-face, spend time with them. As the daughter of an employee, there is little chance I will ever meet the great man myself.

6

Charlotte checks the nameplate on the door a second time: *Dr Miles Thornton*. Her shoulders slump.

She steps into the room and closes the door behind her. There's mess everywhere: floor-to-ceiling shelves crammed with books, papers spilling from folders, textbooks lying open, binders jammed onto shelves. Two desks face one another, butted together like an island in the centre of the room. One desk is bare, except for a chipped marmalade pot stuffed with pens. The other is crowded with books and folders, heaped in teetering piles. Papers covered in scrawly writing, vivid doodles in margins. Dirty mugs, shrivelled apple cores, empty crisp packets. A plastic pot with a near-dead orchid, petals translucent as old skin.

It's reminiscent of the disorder of her mother's study. Except that room had comfy armchairs to curl into, soft light to diminish the chaos, maidenhair ferns to freshen the air. Dr Thornton's office is a time-travel back to Charlotte's early university days, when she shared with roommates who dumped sweaty gym gear on the floor, could never find the right textbook, and spent more time cultivating dope in the bathtub than attending lectures.

The room is silent. Stacked on the floor are two cartons. Reading the shipping label, she pauses at her name and pick-up address – *Dr Charlotte I. Hubert, University of Toronto, Ontario* – its formality making it real, even the *I* for her quaint middle name of Irma. Being in Antwerp is no longer a dream.

She tears the packing tape from the cartons with a screeching rip, pulls out books, and stacks them in piles: artist biographies, European rulers, foreign dictionaries. Balancing a volume on Rubens in one hand and a tome on the Antwerp School in the other, she carries them to an empty section of shelving. She paces from desk to wall, arranging books according to topic. The second carton contains books on Rubens' mentors, collaborators and students. Next, colour-coded folders: red for lectures, blue for tutorials, green for research. The shelves are starting to look familiar, everything in its place. But the sense of calm she is seeking is absent; the anxiety from the auditorium still lingers.

A phrase plays on loop in her mind: *he doesn't know me, he doesn't know me.* Although relieved he didn't recognise her as his daughter, she's still filled with intense, warring emotions. Tears sting her eyes, and she brushes them away. She can't let herself fall apart; Dr Thornton could arrive at any moment. Charlotte wraps her arms tightly across her chest, wishing she could squeeze the jumble of emotions into a tight ball, lodge it deep within her, deal with it later.

The hollowness of her grief is constant. Her mother's illness, diagnosis and death all occurred so quickly, giving her little time to comprehend the prognosis, cope with the swift advance of symptoms, prepare for end-of-life care. Sitting at her mother's bedside, she had wished the hours would slow long enough for her to fathom the enormity of what was happening, give her a moment to catch her breath. But time marched resolutely onwards.

Charlotte pulls a paper-wrapped bundle from the bottom of the carton. Free from its wrapping, a framed photo of her darling mama smiles at her. Wearing a peasant blouse with intricate embroidery around the neckline, Rachael Hubert stands before a turquoise sea, head thrown back, laughing, dark curls falling over her shoulders. It was taken two summers ago in Corfu, when she'd urged Charlotte to set aside her research for ten days to share an impromptu trip.

'Imagine the island is going to float away next year and this is your last opportunity to visit,' her mother had said.

'Don't be ridiculous,' Charlotte had replied.

'If all you do is work, work, work …' Rachael waggled her finger.

Rachael was the most spontaneous person Charlotte had ever known. The trip to Corfu had been their last overseas vacation together. Re-wrapping the photograph, she slips it into her satchel, wipes away tears. Her grief is still so raw.

She longs to hear her mother's voice: her laughter as she tells a joke, her banter around the dinner table. Even her raised voice, tight with anger, would be preferable to this quiet. Anything would be better than the fragile whispers of regret that filled her mother's final hours. Rachael's deathbed confession is just as vivid and heartbreaking as it was five weeks ago.

Overlaying the grief is anger, multifaceted. Anger over the death of someone so vibrant, intelligent and beloved, felled at least two decades too soon. Anger at her mother, for the years of lies. How is it possible to love someone so deeply, to suffer their loss so acutely, yet also feel such anger towards them?

Her mother's duplicity still stings. Charlotte recalls one scene after another, played out throughout her childhood, culminating in her mother's dying revelation. More than thirty years of certainty, dissolved in an instant. A foundation of trust, crumbled.

Looking back on her childhood, Charlotte recalls the hints of disquiet whenever she'd asked about her father. *Tell me more*, she'd begged. *Where are the photos of him holding me as a baby? Where did we go on vacation?*

Questions were redirected, stories romanticised, anecdotes woven to placate a young child. Fabrications of happiness, love and contentment – which Charlotte now recognised as a deterrent to further questions – preceded her mother's announcement of his sudden passing, followed by inexplicable tight-lipped silence. As she grew into adulthood, Charlotte and Rachael had maintained a tacit agreement to not broach the subject, allowing fantasy to fill the unspoken world between them. But, upon learning the truth at Rachael's deathbed, a lifetime of trust disintegrated. Decades of half-truths and silence, laid bare. All this time, her mother had been concealing the fact he was alive.

In the days they had left, Charlotte had tried to glean more information about her mother's relationship with her father, the decision to invent his death, the possibility he knew of his daughter's existence.

'He knows nothing about you,' Rachael had reassured her. 'You're going to Antwerp to work. Don't get distracted with a past you can't change or control.'

'He'll probably work out you're my mother from my surname, but is there any chance he knows he's my father?'

'He never knew I was expecting. It ended horribly. We focused too much on our careers. He was too controlling. He offered to help with a theory I was researching, and before I had finalised it, *my* idea – the exact same theory – appeared in an article written by his supervisor. When I confronted him, he rambled on, made excuses, but I knew he was responsible. After that, I couldn't trust him. We argued constantly. Said things we couldn't unsay, couldn't forgive, couldn't move on from.' Rachael balled the blanket into her fists. 'You and I were better off without him. That's why I told you he was dead. He doesn't know about you.' She looked away, the past dismissed with clenched jaw and flinty eyes.

'Perhaps he'll work it out,' Charlotte insisted, wondering if she should still go to Antwerp. Enduring Mama's death was hard enough; how could she cope with a long-lost father now alive, secrets about him exposed? The animosity in her heart was so severe it frightened her.

'You've worked too hard to give up on Antwerp. Keep your distance from him. You'll be fine.' These were her mother's final words on the subject.

With misgivings, Charlotte boarded the Belgium-bound aircraft. *Avoid him*, became her mantra as the plane touched down in Brussels. *Ignore him*, she chanted to herself as she caught the train to Antwerp. *Don't let him get under your skin*, she told herself as she crossed the university courtyard for the first time.

But now she's here and forced to face him every day, she knows avoiding him, ignoring him, will be impossible. Since their first meeting in the auditorium, her mind has been filled with doubts. Why was *he* scheduled to hold her induction? Why is *he* her supervisor? Why did he attend her first lecture? Despite what Mama told her, is it possible Sébastien Sterck knows the truth?

Worse than the anger over Mama's lies is the anger she feels towards this man over his abhorrent treatment of her mother. How can someone profess their love and then betray their lover?

She remembers the pain of betrayal on her mother's face whenever Sébastien Sterck's name was mentioned. Charlotte had been better off without this man. Her time in Antwerp would be better off without acknowledging him as her father. Let him, and everyone else, remain ignorant of the truth. Besides, she earned this job on her merits; she won't let anyone assume nepotism played a part in her appointment.

Charlotte blinks rapidly, forcing her thoughts aside. Taking in the neat array of her books and folders amid Dr Thornton's clutter, she realises her mother was correct. She has worked too hard to give up the Antwerp position. Her personal life will not detract from this incredible opportunity. Sébastien Sterck could throw anything in her direction and she would rise above it. Hell, the cosmos had already thrown heartbreak at her and she had not caved, nor would she. She would triumph. Let her mother's past remain buried. It cannot be changed. But the present and future, Charlotte has some control over. The best way to begin this new chapter is to immerse herself in her research and teaching, and what better subject to focus on than the intriguing map folio? Uncover its mysteries. Discover its link to Rubens.

After flattening the cartons, she slides them into a narrow space between a filing cabinet and the wall. The office is small, but hopefully she'll have the office to herself for a reasonable amount of time.

She scans the spines on Dr Thornton's shelves. Mostly English, several Dutch, all focusing on the European Age of Discovery. *Thornton, an English name*, she muses – which doesn't necessarily mean he's English.

Taking a step back, her heel bumps a desk leg. She turns in time to see the orchid topple. Clumps of dry dirt spill over Dr Thornton's desk, covering books, folders and papers.

'Bloody hell.'

The soil is everywhere, across pages, wedged in open books. The desk has to be cleared. Working quickly, she lifts each item, sweeps soil into the rubbish bin, wipes away dirt with her sleeve. A loose paper flutters to the floor. She scoops it up, places it on the desk and, oblivious to what she's doing, automatically scans it. It's a note, written in neat handwriting: *Miles, It's taken care of … don't be worried … she's gone. Sébastien.*

Although alone, she glances about the room guiltily, afraid her inadvertent snooping might be detected. He could arrive at any moment – how would she explain this? She replaces items on the desk in precise disarray. Stepping back, she surveys her work. Just as chaotic as before, folders and apple cores haphazardly arranged. Bruised petals, leaves and tangled roots are all that remain in the orchid pot.

'The dirt.' She snatches up the bin and tips dry soil back into the pot.

Finally settling into a chair, she's about to study her new timetable when the office door clicks open a crack. She sits up, alert.

The door remains ajar, as if someone had begun to open it but stopped. Through the frosted glass, she sees the blurred silhouette of two people facing one another. Voices, muffled at first, grow louder.

'... nobody knows the details, so let's keep it that way.' Professor Sterck's tone climbs.

'I should never have dragged you into this,' says another voice. Male. English.

'What's done is done,' says Sterck tersely. 'She's gone.'

'It's still a mess,' says the other man, his voice rising with tension.

The office door bangs open, the glass panel rattling. A man in his mid-thirties stands in the doorway, blond fringe falling across his forehead. Sterck is behind him.

The man steps into the room, his face a parody of bewilderment, open-mouthed and staring. 'You must be … the Canadian … the Rubens expert …'

Rising, she extends her hand. 'Charlotte Hubert.' She offers a smile, suggesting professional warmth and candour without, she hopes, any hint that she's overheard their conversation.

'Miles Thornton.' He continues staring, then turns to the professor. 'Have you–'

'We've already met.' Charlotte cuts him off smoothly. *Everything will be fine*, she tells herself. *Uncomplicated and manageable.*

She smiles broadly, looks into familiar green eyes. 'A pleasure to see you again, Professor Sterck.'

He leans forward as if ready to take another step, yet remains rooted to the spot. 'Sébastien,' he says. 'Please call me Sébastien.'

7

March 15, 1621

On the morning of my twelfth birthday, Hendrik, Niels and I sat in the kitchen eating bread dipped in warm milk.

Papa came through the doorway and called out the customary birthday greeting – *Gefeliciteerd* – and announced that today marked the beginning of a new family tradition.

'You will encounter challenges throughout your lives, requiring all your skills to solve. Do not assume all challenges are tiresome. Many can be enjoyable.' He kissed me on the forehead, handed me a note and then, smiling, walked from the room.

Unfolding the note, I read aloud a phrase, stumbling over unfamiliar Latin words. *'Torquent et vertas, quae revelabitur.'* I looked from Hendrik to Janneke. 'What does it mean?'

'You know I don't read,' said Janneke, 'nor understand Latin.' She turned back to the fireplace and continued stirring the broth.

Hendrik giggled, hinting at collusion. I begged him for help, but he scampered off. Grumbling to myself, I fetched my Latin grammar. My progress was slowed by interruptions to join Mama in her bedchamber for birthday well-wishes, play chase with Hendrik and Niels, rock baby Lucas to sleep in the cradle, and pour batter as Janneke held the waffle iron. By midday, I finally finished the translation.

'What does it say?' Hendrik hopped from one foot to the other with excitement.

With all the dignity I could muster, I cleared my throat and read my translation: 'Twist and turn, all will be revealed.'

Hendrik laughed so hard he fell to the floor, rolling around clutching his belly. Janneke shooed him away with a broom.

'What shall I do?' I wailed to Janneke.

'Our Lord blessed you with a clever mind, Miss Antonia. You best use it.' She sliced the head off a fish and dropped it into the pot. 'Off you go. Don't pester me with yer puzzle or I'll find work for you in the kitchen.'

I scurried to the attic, where spring sunshine spilled its warmth through the dormer windows. Curling up in the sun, I waited for inspiration to arrive. Alas, it wasn't until late afternoon that the puzzle was solved. Elated, I rushed down the stairs and knocked on the door to Papa's workroom.

'Enter.' Papa sat at his desk, burin in hand. 'Well?'

I waved the note in the air. 'I am required to look within your cabinet.'

His eyebrows rose. 'Is that so?'

I rushed to his side and wrapped my arms around him. 'I translated the Latin into Flemish, then placed the letters in a different order. When rearranged, it says: *look within workroom cabinet*.' I watched his face.

Smiling, he adjusted the red felt cap on his head, which I had knocked askew.

I turned to the massive oak cabinet, which filled the width of the room, and eyed the thick doors, each panel intricately carved with foliage and fruit. In the centre of the top moulding, carved in sinuous loops, was the year of my parents' marriage: 1608.

'Try the door in the middle,' said Papa.

On the lowest shelf, I spied a little pile of gifts and scooped them into my lap: a grey velvet hair ribbon, tortoiseshell comb, feather quill, cup-and-ball toy made of wood. The last gift was a small book, covered in green leather the colour of springtime oak leaves. Printed on the central pages were a dozen engravings, depicting works by famous artists from Italy. The remaining pages were filled with Latin. I sighed. More translating.

'This book is an excerpt from a much larger work by Florentine historian Giorgio Vasari. His original book was published more than seventy years ago.' Papa touched the leather cover. 'I know you do not like Latin, Antonia.'

I looked glumly at the little book.

'When you are older, you will be pleased I had you study languages. Scholarship is one of the most powerful tools granted to men.'

'To men?' I was puzzled that Papa was encouraging my academic education when he had just declared it to be an enterprise solely for men.

'You misunderstand me. I am referring to the general term of man as human, which you know in Latin is ...' He paused, eyebrows raised.

'*Humano*,' I replied.

'... and *humano* includes both the male and female of the species.'

I opened the book, curious to know if Vasari had included women artists.

'Although you may never have the opportunity to study at university,' said Papa, 'there is no reason why you cannot study at home. I want my daughter to speak French and Spanish, to know Latin, to understand history and geography. I don't want people thinking my children are dim-witted and dull; I want my children to be seen as intelligent, and just as distinguished as those from the families of Sweerts, Coudenberg and Roodenbeke.'

I nodded with enthusiasm, pleased that Papa believed me bright enough for such an education, although surprised he had mentioned our humble family alongside such noble ones.

'Treasure this book, Antonia. It has crossed the Alps to be in your hands.'

As I nestled in bed that evening, I recalled Vasari's engravings. My dreams took me from my snug Antwerpen bedchamber, across the Alps to the waterways of Venice, along the peninsula to Florence then Rome. Beneath my closed lids I saw Brunelleschi's Duomo and Bramante's Tempietto.

Papa always knows how best to stir my imagination, to inspire me to master new skills. I am excited that my next birthday, and each one to follow, will include new cryptic puzzles with which I can test my knowledge and demonstrate my willingness to learn. Perhaps one day I will prove to Papa I am as clever as Hendrik and Niels, even though I am a girl.

8

'You'll find Antwerp easy to navigate,' says Miles. 'Might want to get yourself a bike – just be careful when it's icy …' He flits from one topic to the next. Pubs with the best Trappist beer, the tedium of faculty meetings, social club activities. He laughs, a sudden burst of delight. 'Not sure the club's latest activity of a pub crawl using bikes was the safest, but sure was fun. If you want some company while you look around, I'm happy to play tour guide.'

'Thank you, I'd like that. I've been to Antwerp once before, but I spent most of my time inside museums, libraries and the Rubenianum Institute, so didn't get to know the city like a resident.' Charlotte rotates the ceramic pot on her desk. Stamped on its front is an inky blue crest: *Dundee Marmalade 1862.*

'I'm collecting.' He points to the highest shelf behind her, where twenty or more chipped ceramic pots are arranged, each with a navy crest denoting its maker and variety: *James Keiller and Son, Dundee and Glasgow, Golden Shred, Rough Cut, Seville.*

She squints at the faded print. 'Scottish, aren't they? But your accent …'

He grins, his smile crooked, his teeth even and white. 'I'm English, but lived in Edinburgh for a while. Developed my fetish for marmalade pots while I was there. S'pose it's natural for historians to collect old things. I've managed to find a few in the vintage markets here. Not marmalade, mind, more confiture. You'll find all sorts of interesting stuff in the markets.' Crossing one leg over the other, he jiggles his foot. 'Do you collect?'

'Collect?' She's jet-lagged and fuzzy-brained. All she can think about are the collections of masterpieces adorning the walls of museums.

'Bric-a-brac? Antiques? The odd Rubens masterpiece?' That grin again.

'Wouldn't that be amazing? Buried at the bottom of an old crate at a market in a Belgian village.' For the first time in weeks, the muscles in her face and shoulders begin to relax; her limbs feel lighter.

His enthusiasm is contagious. With energy and humour like this, he'll be the perfect antidote to the stress she's been facing. Her concerns about moving to the other side of the world, away from everyone familiar, begin to ease.

Leaning back in his chair, he taps his hands on his knees, unable to keep still. 'If you'd like to visit the markets, let me know, and I'll also give you a tour of the campus. Bit of a rabbit warren, but you'll get the hang of it.'

He leans forward so suddenly the armrests of his chair slam into the desk. Piles of books teeter as he jumps up. 'Let's go to the staff lounge now. Introduce you to some of the other inmates. No time like the present.'

He's still laughing at his own joke and at the door before she has a chance to respond. Within seconds, he's guiding her along the corridor, pointing out the photocopier and meeting rooms, pulling a look of mock horror at the staff kitchen. 'Watch out for the coffee machine. Comes out like weak mud. Doesn't taste much better. Café across the road is safer.'

Stopping at a set of double doors, he ushers her into a large room with armchairs arranged around low tables.

'Gets crowded during lunchtime,' he says, 'but it's great for impromptu meetings.'

Groups of people sit around talking, some reading, others thumbing phones. Charlotte spies the university's organisation chart hanging on the nearest wall. She makes out the names and titles beneath each photograph. The university's rector is at the apex of the pyramid and below her, nine faculties, each represented by a dean. She recognises Mulder, dean of the Arts Faculty, remembering his firm handshake after her lecture. Below the dean is a row of ten photographs, beginning with Jeanette Chevalier and ending with Sébastien Sterck. Chevalier is smiling, toothpaste-white teeth contrasting with her brunette helmet bob. Sterck is serious, his mouth a narrow line, eyes partially concealed behind his glasses. Eyebrows lifted slightly, either in disdain or surprise, she can't tell.

'I heard Professor Sterck is going to be your supervisor,' says Miles.

'He's your supervisor, too, isn't he? What's he like?'

'Doesn't give as many lectures these days. Busy with admin, I guess. But he's highly accomplished, writes a huge number of journal articles, has a phenomenal memory. I'm sure he doesn't sleep, just stays awake, thinking about his next article or planning a topic for a post-grad student to develop.'

'Sounds a bit … obsessive.' She's curious to hear Miles' reaction to her rash appraisal.

Miles speaks with his hands, gesturing to make a point. 'Sterck's okay. Bit of a stuffed shirt, but he manages the budget fairly, which is no mean feat given the latest cutbacks. There was the usual scramble for resources, everyone vying for their share. Only three new positions for this term, including yours, were approved. Several senior lecturers missed out on funding for new research, so there's a bit of tension …'

Research sidelined due to budget constraints, co-workers scrabbling for acknowledgement, resentment over projects. Not an ideal situation to walk into, but she's dealt with similar challenges before. All academic institutions have power struggles.

'… always teething issues at the beginning of a new term,' he continues, 'but the tension will ease.' He lowers his voice. 'Word around campus is Dean Mulder has been offered a position elsewhere and Sterck is favourite to replace him.'

She's about to ask whether anyone was dealt a particularly harsh blow with the cutbacks, perhaps a colleague adversely affected by her own appointment, when a hand touches her shoulder. She jumps. A man with sandy hair and bright blue glasses stands behind her, smiling.

'Charlotte,' says Miles, 'have you met Arnold?'

'Sorry. Didn't mean to make you jump.' The man offers his hand. 'I'm Arnold Blauwmann. We met after your lecture.'

'Yes, I remember.'

He leans in, smiling. 'I've had an idea for a joint lecture series. You. Me. Diplomacy and Art in the Spanish Hapsburg Court. Ties in brilliantly with your man Rubens, artist and diplomat. Whaddaya think?'

She's flustered, reluctant to commit to lectures with someone she's only just met.

'We can discuss it over lunch at Grand Café Horta next Tuesday,' he says.

'I have back-to-backs that day,' she counters, 'but could meet in the office on Wednesday.'

Arnold pouts. 'Lunch is much more civilised. Why not Grand Café Horta on Wednesday?'

'I have a tutorial at midday, but the morning is free for a quick meeting.'

He frowns. 'Guess it'll have to do. We'll need to write a plan and get it approved; can't drag our heels. You know what it's like in academic institutions. Need to stand out if you wanna get anywhere.' Offers a toothy smile.

'I'll call you to set up a time,' she says, before exchanging farewells. He seems friendly enough, if a little intense. Still, she'd prefer to work with a confident go-getter than someone who spends more time daydreaming about ideas.

A man with a goatee has cornered Miles and they are deep in conversation.

Charlotte turns back to the organisation chart, browsing names and faces, wondering if there are any kindred spirits among them. Everyone she has met so far has been welcoming, but perhaps there will be one or two people she'll grow close to. Not a fling or, good grief, a romance – she's only here for six months. Besides, her success with long-term relationships is mediocre. Her first serious college boyfriend cheated on her with her alleged best friend. Years later, her two-year relationship with a fellow lecturer at Toronto ended when she confronted him about his patronising manner towards her at work. Her reluctance to trust others became a factor in every broken relationship that followed. She had learnt the hard way that trust was easy to lose, difficult to re-establish, and workplace relationships were fraught with difficulty. Her parents were a case in point.

Scanning the notices tacked to a board, she reads about the renovation of Building A, programs for career planning, advice about campus safety, activities for the staff social club. Her gaze is drawn to an article emblazoned with the heading *Stop Intellectual Theft*.

Years ago, her mother had warned her about the prevalence of intellectual theft in academic circles, explaining that it occurred on multiple levels, peer against peer, senior versus junior.

'Early in my academic career,' her mother cautioned, 'I had a professor who insisted his name be included as co-author on all his students' research papers, even though his only contribution was a cursory read-through and the occasional grammatical tweak. I'd always wondered how he was able to write so many articles. Turned out he was taking credit for the work of his students. Don't let it happen to you.'

'But if they insist—'

'If your supervisor offers only insignificant suggestions, they shouldn't be acknowledged as having made a contribution.'

Buoyed by her mother's advice, Charlotte earned a reputation for being shrewd and uncompromising when working with her supervisors, insisting they only received credit when it was due. She became wary of peers asking complex questions about her research, worried one of her ideas would be stolen. Her mother's personal experience of intellectual theft, which had led to the breakdown of her relationship with Sterck, had been at the forefront of Charlotte's mind as she prepared to relocate to Antwerp. *Be cautious*, she warned herself. *Trust others only once they've earned that trust.*

In the days following her mother's funeral, as she absorbed the betrayal and hurt her mother had experienced at Sterck's hands, a lump of wariness and resentment began to grow within her. By the time she arrived in Antwerp, her grief over her mother's death was blanketed with an intense suspicion, directed at this man.

The babble of voices in the staff lounge breaks through her thoughts. The words *Stop Intellectual Theft* on the noticeboard could be a neon sign. She tells herself it's the grief talking. She's too emotional, irrational. Shouldn't overthink a past that belongs to others. It's impossible for her to fully understand, let alone change.

But it's no use. Standing in the staff lounge, glaring at the photo of this man who is her father, she knows she will never trust him.

9

'Staff kitchen is here,' says Miles, ushering Charlotte into a cubbyhole with mugs crammed on shelves, a counter sticky with coffee rings and sugar crystals.

A tall man stands in front of a built-in coffee machine, stooping to avoid a low-hanging light.

'Every day,' says Miles, 'Karl risks his life by drinking coffee from this machine.'

As if in protest, the machine lets out a burble.

Grinning, the man turns to Charlotte. He looks familiar. 'Karl Joosten. I teach the Renaissance art history course. I enjoyed your lecture. We met afterwards … briefly.'

'It was great giving my first Antwerp lecture to a full auditorium,' she says. 'Thanks for attending.'

'All *Sinjoren* are proud of their local hero Rubens,' says Karl.

She recalls the nickname for local inhabitants, related to the Spanish Hapsburg noblemen who ruled the city centuries ago. Guess she's an honorary *Sinjoren* now, she realises.

Miles indicates a poster on a small noticeboard. 'Karl organises the staff social club.'

'We're visiting the Sablon market in Brussels next weekend,' says Karl. 'You should join us.'

The conversation moves to a bike ride along the Scheldt, beer tasting at De Koninck, a concert in Sint-Jacobskerk. Charlotte recalls the posters displayed around Toronto, Chicago and Dartmouth universities promoting social events, many of which she avoided because putting the finishing touches on an article seemed preferable to downing pints in a beer garden. She'll make more of an effort this time, she tells herself, rather than hyper-focusing on work. When she finishes her six-month stint in Antwerp – assuming it hasn't been extended – she wants to remember the people she's met, not just the inside of auditoriums.

She pictures the envelope she was handed when she visited the administrative services office yesterday. Inside were a set of keys and details of the one-bedroom furnished apartment reserved for short-term university appointees. Not fancy, but comfortable, and centrally located. She'd unpacked her suitcases within an hour. Her portable speaker filled the apartment with Gershwin's whimsical harmonies, followed by the voices of George Ezra and Melody Gardot. Her mother's opaque glass frog was given pride of place on the coffee table. She'd surveyed it from all angles, making sure its iridescent green haunches were positioned to catch the light. She'd forgotten how her mother had come by the frog, but it was always on her desk, weighing down papers, its comical bulging eyes making Charlotte smile. The frog was the smallest object from her mother's glass collection; easy to bring to Antwerp, perfect for helping her focus on happy memories, ease her heartache.

During the eulogy, her mother's only sibling, Francine, had reflected on her older sister's penchant for collecting, '… copper pots in all sizes, the larger ones holding plants, the smaller ones filled with seed pods, river pebbles, ammonites … and her collection of crystal and glass. Rachael collected these objects in the same way she gathered fellow academics around her. They were drawn to her creativity and openness, her kindness and empathy, her willingness to encourage, listen and debate.'

Charlotte had welled up at Aunt Francine's reminder of the regular academic gatherings in her mother's sunroom. They would sit around the kitchen table with chai tea, debating topics, reviewing dissertations. The shelves around the room were filled with handblown glass and faceted crystal in myriad shimmering greens; mementoes from travelling, collected from a bric-a-brac shop or vintage market, some gifted by family and friends over the years. An apple-green *millefiori* perfume bottle Charlotte had brought back from Venice for her mother's sixtieth birthday. The lime-green Fenton glass candlesticks she gave her mother for Christmas last year.

In the weeks following the funeral, Charlotte had pushed aside her grief and worked long hours, tidying and sorting, preparing her mother's house as a furnished rental. A week before her departure, she signed the lease and handed the keys to a newly arrived professor and his young family, pleased her childhood home would be filled with the laughter of children. The day before her flight to Europe, she brushed away her tears as she locked the storage unit brimming with her mother's possessions.

Only a small number of mementoes accompanied her to the apartment on Antwerp's Kloosterstraat. Some personal photos, her mother's treasured anthologies by Sylvia Plath, a half-dozen of Rachael's silk scarves wrapped around the glass frog. Those silly bulbous eyes and absurd wavy mouth would help her smile on the days she sat alone with her pain, reliving memories.

Startled by voices, Charlotte's attention returns to the staffroom, aware the conversation between the men has continued around her. They are talking about the social club's plan to attend a Baroque concert at Sint-Jacobskerk.

'Your hero Rubens is buried in a side chapel,' says Karl.

Miles laughs at Karl. 'Are you reminding a Rubens expert where Rubens is buried?'

'I know it well,' she replies, enjoying the banter. 'The altar painting is by him.'

'Wasn't his crypt opened in 2018 by forensic experts?' asks Karl.

'Yes, they wanted to learn more about his cause of death,' she replies, 'and whether it was related to lead poisoning from paint.'

Miles grimaces. 'Imagine climbing into a crypt to study old bones.'

She doesn't like the turn the conversation has taken. Burials and decaying bones are not topics she wants to contemplate. Scanning the noticeboard, her gaze stops at a poster with a photo of a smiling group of students. She reads the heading – *Antwerp University is committed to providing a safe campus community for students, staff and visitors* – and remembers the same poster in the staff lounge, the same wording on a leaflet in her induction folder.

The advice is always the same, no matter which university: walk in well-populated areas at night; avoid alleyways and deserted streets; be cautious of strangers who approach you; report anything suspicious to police. She recalls her two years in the Windy City, triple-locking her apartment door when home and carrying pepper spray when out. Holding the cylinder in the palm of her hand was enough to steel her nerves as she walked to the 'L' along 59th Street after evening lectures. But surely Antwerp is not as socio-economically depressed as Chicago. Are attacks over valuables common?

She indicates the safety poster. 'Is personal safety an issue here?'

Karl shrugs. 'No worse than any city.'

'Miss Beulen mentioned there have been several incidents with students threatened on campus,' she says.

'Last term,' says Karl, 'a post-grad student left the library late one evening and was followed by a man. She was threatened, and valuables were stolen.'

'There was a second incident involving a female student who was accosted while returning to her car,' says Miles. 'She opened the boot to place her laptop bag inside and the attacker threatened her with a tyre iron and snatched her bag.'

'Is it only women being attacked?'

'A male student was attacked last February,' says Karl. 'He had his backpack stolen, containing his laptop and research notes.'

'It sounds like personal safety *is* an issue here,' says Charlotte, looking from Miles to Karl, baffled. Their tone and demeanour are calm, as if describing something petty. But these are serious crimes involving violence and theft. Laptops worth several thousand dollars. Research notes representing months of valuable work.

'Campus police are still investigating,' says Karl. 'Campus security have increased their awareness campaign. Leaflets have been distributed and posters put up.'

'Do you know the victims?' she asks. 'Are they okay?'

'They were all post-grad students in the Arts Faculty,' says Karl. 'They ended up transferring to other universities. One went to Maastricht, another to Stockholm and the other ...'

Miles stares at the floor. 'She went to Edinburgh.'

Charlotte is shocked into silence. Appalled that the victims were so traumatised they abandoned their work, withdrew from familiar surroundings, choosing to start afresh in a new city. All victims were post-graduate students, which meant they had a support network of tutors, students and friends in Antwerp. As post-grads, they probably conducted tutorials, which meant that in leaving, they had given up an income, albeit a small one.

The coffee machine makes a high-pitched whirr followed by a clunk. Karl slides a mug beneath the dispenser. 'Who'd like coffee? Charlotte?' His finger pauses above the touchpad screen.

'No, thank you.' Her mind is whirring like the coffee machine.

'Hope we haven't scared you.' Karl presses the screen. The machine grinds, clunks and roars, spitting out frothy brew. 'We're all being extra cautious, making sure to stick with others after dark.'

She wants to ask whether there is anything else she needs to be aware of, perhaps inter-departmental tensions or a faculty head with eccentricities, but it all seems trivial compared to an attacker on the loose.

After farewelling Karl, they return to the office, with Miles chatting about the upcoming Sint-Jacobskerk concert. Charlotte is distracted, thinking about the victims.

As they follow the hallway, she spots another safety poster on the door of the photocopy room. Do campus police think it's a lone perpetrator or multiple attackers? Either way, police will need to do more than put up posters to keep everyone safe. Students shouldn't be scared off, forced to abandon their work. Avoiding a tough situation isn't the answer. Be proactive, she wants to shout at the nameless victims. Don't run away.

The hypocrisy hits her swiftly, a blunt force trauma of memories.

'Stand up for yourself, Charlotte,' her mother had said to her years ago, having come home to find her daughter sobbing into the sofa cushions, vowing to transfer to a new course. 'You hit a little snag two months into your first year and already you want to give up.'

'Being bullied by one of the men in my tutor group is not a little snag,' she retorted. 'We have to work together on a joint project and he's being a tyrant.'

'Sidestepping the problem isn't going to fix it,' her mother insisted. 'This won't be the last bully or difficult situation you encounter. You need to face the problem, Charlotte. Be assertive. Show some backbone.'

Hollow words, realises Charlotte, from her mother who fled Belgium because of a disastrous relationship, choosing to give up her career in Europe and instead become a single mother in Toronto.

A fluttery sensation starts in her chest, building to an unpleasant awareness that she's following a path of avoidance in her own life. Her plan to avoid Sterck, pretend he isn't her father, is no better than running away, refusing to face the truth.

Miles holds their door open for her. She's suddenly relieved to be sharing an office, grateful for the companionship. She barely knows him, but senses he's the sort of person who can lighten an awkward moment, lift the mood with an upbeat story.

A dried orchid petal lies on the floor. She stoops to pick it up then twirls the petal between her fingers, spinning it until it blurs. Something jars her memory. Her mother's garden, the gravel pathway leading to a wall of sweet-smelling jasmine, peonies as big as teacups, delphiniums faded to denim. She remembers. Miles' eyes are the same blue as the delphiniums in her mother's garden.

10

March 19, 1621

My chest swells with pride when I recall Papa's announcement this morning. We were discussing the rumour of King Felipe's failing health and the impact on the ongoing war against the united northern provinces should the King die during the campaign.

Papa pointed to the table set against the wall. Natural light spilled from the lead-paned window above, casting a diamond-pattern across my workbook. 'Time for you to practise Latin so you, too, can add to the number of languages you will one day master.' As much as Papa enjoyed our conversations, he would never allow them to detract from my studies.

Sighing, I picked up my quill. 'The Van Helst girls don't have to sit for hours conjugating Latin verbs,' I murmured to myself as I dipped the quill, forgetting his sense of hearing was acute.

'Your mind is too bright to be filled with the trifling pursuits of your playmates. Focus on your work, Antonia, and no more grumbling.' His voice was brusque.

My quill scratched across the page as I translated verbs: *scribo, scribam, scripsi, scripseram*. I bit my lower lip as an ugly ink blot appeared. This will never become easy.

'Papa, what use will I have for Latin?'

'Latin will help you read your prayer book without having to rely on others to explain it to you.'

'I can already read my prayer book.' Another blot, this one bleeding through to the next page. Oh, dear.

'Reciting the words is not the same as understanding them.' Papa walked over and scrutinised my work. 'On Monday, you will join your brothers with their tutor.'

I picked up a rag and wiped ink from my fingers. 'Am I to help Hendrik and Niels with their studies?'

'You will further your own studies under the guidance of the tutor. Despite your gender, you are just as capable as your brothers in academic work. When you reach marriageable age, a pre-eminent man, perhaps a court official or *burgemeester*, will be captivated by your intelligence, wit and charm, your ability to converse in numerous languages, and your devotion to Our Lord, and you will make a favourable marriage. Indeed, distinguished men will vie for the honour of being married to the clever daughter of Antwerpen's most famous engraver.' Papa picked up the end of one of my long curls and used it to tickle my nose. 'Latin, French, Spanish, mathematics, geography and history ... what say you?'

'I shall work my hardest, Papa.' I beamed and sat tall, thinking only of the pride in my papa's voice, not of the long hours I would need to labour, nor of the marriage I was expected to achieve. I was only twelve and, for me, marriage was too many years away to consider. All I could think about was Papa's declaration that I was clever and worthy of tutorship. My playmates danced with greater skill and produced finer embroidery, but they couldn't speak in near-fluent Spanish and French as I, nor did they understand our city's struggles with the Spanish Hapsburg administrators. I would gladly toil, even over Latin verbs, to please my papa.

'Does this mean I no longer need to practise the *spinetten*?' I crossed my fingers for luck.

'A young lady's education needs to include mastery of a musical instrument. The *spinetten* is the one your mama has chosen for you.'

'Perhaps–'

'Along with mastery of needlework.'

'But–'

'You must apply yourself with diligence to every task, even the ones you don't enjoy.' He waggled his forefinger in front of my nose. 'No more hiding in the attic to avoid pressing the linen or helping with your baby brother. Such behaviour is unacceptable.'

I lowered my eyes for a second before my boldness took hold. 'Do you have tasks you don't enjoy?'

He pinched the ends of his moustache into a bushy smile. 'We must all endure less pleasurable tasks, completing them to the best of our ability.'

'Which tasks do you dislike?'

'Nothing that need concern you.'

Ah, a smile. I knew it was there, lurking beneath his moustache. His tenderness is never far away, his love everlasting. Honesty, diligence, kindness, courage and following Our Lord's commandments – these are the foundations of our family.

11

The library atrium is crowded, people clustered in groups, the buzz of conversation filling the air. Charlotte scans the room, craning to see him. Karl Joosten ambles through the main door, engrossed in his mobile phone. Arnold Blauwmann leans against the wall, chatting to a young man holding an armload of books. Neither is the person she's looking for.

'You look lost.'

She turns and finds Miles, that lopsided grin on his face.

'I can't find Willem.'

'Seriously? He's a walking skyscraper.'

'He was taking me to Acquisitions – I couldn't remember how to get there. But we got separated in the crowd.'

Stretching on tiptoe, she peers across a sea of heads, spots Willem in a doorway. He waves at her, arms swinging like a palm tree in the wind. She turns to Miles – 'Found him' – and catches a glimpse of tweed jacket and widow's peak on the far side of the room. She'd seen Professor Sterck only briefly since her first day. At a meeting last week, she hastily joined a group of colleagues by the window when she noticed him at the front of the room. Last Thursday, they nearly collided in the corridor, shuffling from side to side in an awkward dance, exchanging mumbled apologies. There'd been several other sightings over the past weeks, but Charlotte had kept her distance, intent on work, busy delivering lectures, supervising tutorials, refusing to be distracted. When the time is right, she tells herself, she'll approach him about their shared history.

Now, seeing him walk towards her, the familiar tightness fills her chest. She's not ready to confront the past. Not yet.

'Willem's waiting. I have to go,' she says, watching the tweed jacket edge through a cluster of students. 'By the way, Sterck's heading our way.'

Miles grimaces. 'How's he look? Annoyed? Pleased?'

'Can't tell.'

'Probably chasing a report I owe him. Or chasing you ...'

She stops.

'He asked after you the other day.'

'He did?' She glances at the approaching tweed. Thirty metres.

'Wanted to know how you were settling in.'

'And?'

'I said you were keeping busy ... lectures, tutorials, usual stuff.'

She takes a step backwards. 'I need to go.'

'What is it between you two?'

'Nothing.'

'You freeze whenever he's around –'

'Nonsense.' She laughs, but it comes out forced, more gruff than jovial.

'– like a deer caught in headlights.'

She manages another laugh, this one light-hearted. 'Willem's waiting.' Sterck is twenty metres away.

Miles shoos her. 'I'll deal with him.'

She offers a grateful smile – 'I'll get coffees tomorrow morning' – then turns and flees, sidestepping around students. *Escape, escape,* her feet beat upon the linoleum floor. *Poor Miles. I'll make it up to him: perhaps one of those cinnamon scrolls he likes.*

She follows Willem along corridors, trying to keep track of the left and right turns. Pushing aside images of a tweed jacket and green eyes, she concentrates on the inch of daffodil sock showing at Willem's spindly ankles.

He stops at a blank door. 'Familiar?'

Rows of identical doors line the corridor. 'I'll get the hang of it,' she lies, silently cursing her inept sense of direction.

Inside the room, the map folio is open on the table. She's at work within minutes, tugging on nitrile gloves, picking up a magnifying glass, wondering about the link between Antonia Vorsterman and Rubens. This is the best part of research: pulling apart the layers of history, searching for clues, deciphering a symbol, translating an old letter. Examining one obscure pathway, looking for more clues, then finally the joy of discovering a fragment of the puzzle. Vague ideas coalescing into certainties.

Willem is talking, '... finished cataloguing the Begijnhof's almanacs ...'

Charlotte hovers the magnifying glass above the lozenges. Miniature cityscapes and Lilliputian figures pop into focus, details and colours vivid. Church spires and cobblestones, feathered hats and brass-buckled shoes.

Willem leans against a nearby cabinet, watching her.

She stares at the picture of London, muttering aloud to herself. 'Interesting ...'

'What?'

'*Londinium* is printed in black, except for the letter *D*, which is dark blue and thicker.' She scans another lozenge. '*Franciae* is black except *N*, which is blue. *A* in *Antwerpen*, *P* in *Paris*, *R* in *Romanorum* – all blue – also an *A* and *O*.'

'Let's see.'

Handing Willem the magnifying glass, she writes in a notebook. Seven letters in dark blue: D-N-A-P-R-A-O.

'Maybe the ink's faded,' he says.

'Possibly.' Using the spatula, she flips to the next page, showing a map of the Low Countries. 'Have you found any other references to Rubens?' she asks, turning to a map of the Germanic states.

'No.'

'What about other hidden crests?' She turns the pages: Italy's boot, Iberia, the British Isles, France looking thinner than its modern-day self.

'Nothing.'

She taps the magnifying glass. 'Have you got anything stronger?'

'The conservation room has stronger equipment.'

'I'd love to get a closer look at all these details.' She uses the spatula to return to the title page. 'Why don't I take the folio to the conservation room?'

His brow furrows. He speaks haltingly. 'I should check with ... the conservation room ...'

She imagines he's about to list the forms needing completion, the approvals required. Procedures can be so tedious.

'… and my supervisor … and …'

Holding the corners between gloved fingertips, Charlotte closes the cover. 'I'm just taking it to the basement. Won't take it off-site. Promise.'

He frowns at the green leather cover.

She holds up her gloved hands, a surgeon preparing to operate. 'We could wrap it in archive plastic. Perhaps you could call the conservator to let him know I'm bringing it downstairs? I tried meeting him last week, but he wasn't available. I've forgotten his name. Is it Thomas?'

'Theo.'

She slips the strap of her satchel across her body, leaving her hands free. She smiles at him. Within minutes she's standing at the door, holding the wrapped folio in her outstretched hands as if carrying a pizza box.

He holds the door open. 'Do you know how to get there?'

'I'll be fine. Thanks.' Another smile. At the end of the corridor, she turns left. Using her shoulder, she pushes through the door, careful to hold the folio away from walls, remembering its fragile cover. What a stunning collection of maps, vibrant colours and precise Latin print. She must call the Begijnhof and speak to the mother superior. Sister Anna, wasn't it? She'll ask Willem if he knows of anyone else with contacts at the Begijnhof who could help with an introduction. Are the inhabitants called nuns, or is the more accurate term *begijnen*?

She takes another turn. It doesn't look right; perhaps she should've turned left back there. No matter, there's sure to be a route to the basement this way.

Pushing through a second door, she finds herself in the periodicals section. Metal shelving stretches the length of the room. At the far end, a grey door. She glimpses figures browsing journals in the side aisles. The library is enormous, she fumes, like the Library of Congress.

She walks along the central aisle, focusing on the grey door. This'll lead to the stairwell, she's sure. Ten paces from the door, she hears his voice. Distant, behind her, from an aisle to the right.

'Charlotte?'

She curses under her breath. The sensible thing to do would be to stop, say hello. But what if he wants to gab on about mundane departmental issues? Or worse, something personal? She doesn't feel confident enough to easily excuse herself. In his presence, she's awkward. Tongue-tied.

Concentrating on the door ahead, she increases her stride. She doesn't have time to stop. Must deliver the folio, have a quick chat with Thomas or Theo or whatever his name is, then get to her lecture. He'll just slow her down. *Just ignore him*, she tells herself.

'Charlotte?' Sterck calls a second time.

Balancing the map folio in one hand, she twists the handle and pushes her shoulder into the door. It opens suddenly, catapulting her through the doorway. She lurches over the doorstep, struggles to right herself, steadying the map folio. Before she can register her mistake, the door closes behind her with a heavy clunk. She's standing on an outside terrace with a stone balustrade. A privet hedge flutters in the wind.

She turns around. Emblazoned across the door are the words: *Fire exit*. She jiggles the handle, but it's locked so people can't enter from the outside. The terrace extends over thirty metres, ending in a flight of stairs to the courtyard. Clenching her jaw, she heads along it. She'll need to walk through the main entrance, find the stairs to the basement. This was supposed to be a quick trip to the conservation room, not a circumnavigation of the entire bloody library.

A dozen people are grouped on the stairs, lounging, chatting, smoking.

Pausing at the top, Charlotte frowns. Clouds the colour of granite roll in from the west. A gust of wind grabs a corner of the plastic sheet and flicks it open. Another gust brings on a crazed flapping of the plastic, like an ungainly bird trying to launch itself. As Charlotte struggles to tuck in the loose plastic, a raindrop splatters her cheek. People gather their belongings and scurry for cover. Clasping the folio to her chest, she rushes down the stairs.

She stumbles on the third step, then her body slams against stone. She jolts to the bottom where she lies in a heap, motionless. Stunned.

The folio hits the ground with a muffled thump. It's split along its spine, its cover severed from its body. They lie together, she clutching her head, the book fractured in two.

The pain is a distant thrum, arcing from shoulder to head, tightening around her skull. Gravel presses into her cheek. Flakes of leather shift, snatched by the wind and then gone. The inside cover is torn, forming a gaping pouch. Tucked inside, a sheet of paper flutters in the wind. She curls her fingers around it, drawing it to her chest.

Voices call out, footsteps approach, a hand touches her shoulder. Shadows waver around the edges of her vision. Blackness.

12

Trolley wheels squeak, a clatter of stainless-steel instruments, the sharp smell of antiseptic. Charlotte opens her eyes. A pillow, soft against her cheek. Blue curtains billow around her like the undulating surface of a pond. A pair of white plastic clogs appear below the curtain then walk away. Voices call out, the language foreign yet familiar.

'You're awake.' It's the professor's voice.

She turns her head towards him.

He stands at the foot of the bed, fiddling with the ring on his finger. 'How do you feel?'

As she lifts her head from the pillow, tears flood her eyes. Closing them, she squeezes the tears away. Licking her lips, she tastes bitterness, like metal or antiseptic. Memories come back in disconnected waves: raindrops on her cheek, flapping plastic, stone steps, white hot pain. The fragments begin to coalesce, but not him. Why is he here?

His voice again. 'I'll drive you home once you've been discharged.'

She turns onto her side. *Don't want that. Need to be alone, away from noise, smells, lights, fuss.* Too many unexplained sensations: rushing down steps, jostling, pressure of a hand, uncertain if it was reaching out to shove or save. Is she the latest victim of the campus attacker? Where's her satchel, containing all her work?

Get up and leave, she tells herself. Leaning into the mattress, she pushes herself into a seated position. A groan escapes through clenched teeth. Swinging her legs off the bed, she keeps her back to him, stretches her toes, searching for the floor. As she stands, a wave of nausea rolls from her stomach to the back of her throat. She sits back down.

'Do you need some help?'

She shakes her head, then flinches. God, it hurts. Marbles rattling around inside her skull. Floor pitching, room spinning.

She stands slowly, tasting acid. Waits for the dizziness to pass. *Stay calm and they'll let you go.* Away from lights, noise, questions. Away from him hovering in the background.

Using her toes, she nudges her ankle boots from under the bedside cabinet.

'I can get those.' He takes a step forward.

'It's okay. I'm fine.' Her voice is husky. Easing her feet into the boots, she turns to face the curtain as it flutters apart. A man dressed in medical scrubs pushes through the gap, blue against blue, camouflaged so well Charlotte blinks as if seeing an illusion.

'Good to see you awake, Miss Hubert. Please sit down.' His voice is smooth like butter. She sits on the edge of the bed. Her legs are heavy and pendulous. The medic takes her wrist between his fingers, glances at his watch. A faint waft of peppermint. Perhaps he has a spare mint to get rid of this awful metallic taste. And the dryness. Did they put cotton wool in her mouth?

'You're doing well, Miss Hubert.' He releases her wrist. 'How do you feel?'

'Queasy … sore,' she whispers.

He picks up a clipboard and scribbles notes. 'It's to be expected with concussion. We'll give you some pain relief. You've got some nasty bruises, but nothing's broken. Take it easy. Don't overdo it. You should feel better within a few days …'

Her mind wanders, lost to the medic's smooth voice. Discharge documents and a bottle of pills are slipped into her hands. She focuses on the stethoscope around his neck, the blue of his scrubs. His voice is reassuring. Mentions her satchel in the bedside cabinet, and the letter she was holding when the paramedics arrived.

She flicks open the door of the bedside cabinet and is relieved to see her satchel. Resting on top is a loose sheet of paper, yellowed and crumpled, curled at the edges, oddly familiar.

Sensations and images flash in her mind: a yellowed page fluttering, reaching out to grab it. *Oh god, no, the map folio.* She remembers everything now. The map folio, over three hundred years old, its spine broken, the inside cover torn, a page nearly escaping in the wind. What has she done?

'Do you have someone at home who can keep an eye on you?' asks the medic.

'Yes ... yes. It's all good.'

'It's important to rest when you have a concussion. How are you getting home?'

'Taxi.' The word comes out louder than she intends.

The medic writes on the clipboard, tells her to come back if the symptoms get worse. He searches for the opening in the curtains.

The professor moves closer. 'How can I help, Charlotte?'

'I'm feeling better,' she lies, dragging her satchel onto the bed. Her hands fumble with the clasp, heartbeat skipping, fighting a growing sense of dismay. *Don't leave me alone with this man*, she wants to shout to the retreating medic.

The curtains swish closed. The medic is gone.

'Let me drive you home,' says the professor.

'Thank you, but there's no need. I'll catch a taxi.' She slides the yellowed page into the satchel. Forces a smile. 'Not sure why the hospital called you.'

'My business card was in your pocket.'

She exhales with a soft hiss. So much for his business card becoming a talisman. It was stupid for her to think it would keep him distant, like a necklace of garlic keeping vampires away.

Easing the satchel onto her shoulder, she smiles again, warmer this time. 'There's no need to trouble yourself.'

'It's no trouble.'

She pushes at the wall of blue, searching for the exit. Finding a gap, she looks over her shoulder where he stands fixed to the spot, his mouth an *Oh* of bewilderment. 'Thanks for the offer. I'm sorry for wasting your time.' She manages another smile, then shoves through the blue, the curtain swirling behind her.

She dodges laundry trolleys and staff pushing wheelchairs. A set of automatic doors swing open, spewing her into a waiting room with people seated in plastic chairs. She lurches to a stop, her mind flashing back to an earlier time: sitting in a similar room, her name called, the harsh smell of antiseptic, thin plastic tubes, her mother's face white against the pillow. The memories come in waves, tightening her chest, dragging the air out of her lungs. Mouth numb, fingers tingling. On the verge of retching.

She forces herself to place one foot in front of the other, propelling herself through another set of doors. Standing outside the emergency department, she draws in lungfuls of frigid night air, forces the memories away. The panic subsides.

A taxi disgorges a passenger. Charlotte slides into the solitude of the back seat. As the car pulls away from the kerb, she leans against the headrest, breathing in the fustiness of the overheated interior. How long was she in the hospital bed? Who found her at the bottom of the steps? Was she unconscious or babbling incoherently? Who searched her pockets and found Sterck's card?

Wincing as the taxi bumps from smooth bitumen to cobblestone, she turns on her phone. A flurry of beeps indicates several incoming messages. Everyone will be asking about the map folio. How could she have been so reckless? Bossing around poor Willem as if she knew better. She's only been at the university a short time, hardly knows her way around, and now she's damaged a valuable document through her carelessness. How will she explain herself? And where is the map folio? Can it be mended, or is the damage irreparable?

One after another, three disembodied voices fill her ear.

Willem's hesitant voice is first. 'Hope you're okay. Don't worry about the map folio. Theo will look after it.'

Relief surges. Thank goodness it's safe. Hopefully it can be repaired.

The second voice is unfamiliar. Male with a French accent. 'Hello, Dr Hubert. This is Theodore Giroux, the conservator. I heard about your accident. Willem showed me the Rubens Crest. There's something else in the folio which may be related to Rubens. Please call me.' The voice is brusque, then softens. 'Hope you recover quickly.'

She manages a faint smile while listening to the final message. 'Miles here. I heard from Theo you took a tumble, ended up in hospital with Sterck keeping you company. Theo told me about the map folio. I'm sure it'll be fine. Call me when you can. I'll bring over chicken soup or whatever's recommended for people taking nosedives, okay?'

The taxi stops in a line of traffic, bathing the back seat in the rosy glow of brake lights. The heater purrs. Her eyelids grow heavy and the vice-like grip around her skull eases; the pain relief pills beginning their work. Has Theo spotted the blue letters and solved their mystery? Or has he found a new puzzle? 'Curiouser and curiouser,' she mumbles, her eyes closing.

13

April 18, 1621

'The most important gift a parent can bestow on their child is knowledge,' said Papa, following evening prayers.

'What about love?' I dared question him.

He stroked his moustache. 'Love is God's gift to mankind and reveals itself through the virtues of diligence, patience, kindness, humility and trust. But knowledge is a privilege we can nurture ourselves. It will help you withstand whatever comes your way in life.'

It was all very well for Papa to extol the virtues of diligence and patience, but he did not have to endure lessons with the frightful Meneer Terhoeven.

Our tutor was thin, gaunt and wore his hair in lank, unwashed strands. He paced the classroom, glaring at the walls as if equations and foreign verbs were inscribed upon the plaster.

Hendrik could do no wrong. Ink blots were ignored, inaccurate conjugations smoothly corrected. Niels was pampered as if he was King Felipe's favourite spaniel, indulged with the easiest sums and verbs. I was not so fortunate. No matter how carefully I worked, Meneer Terhoeven's wooden ruler slammed upon my desk with regularity.

'Take more care with your penmanship, Miss Antonia.'

'Henry the Third is not the father of the current French king.'

'The future tense is *ouvrirai*, Miss Antonia, not *ouvrais*.'

I clenched my teeth each time he spoke my name in his loathsome drawl. We sighed with relief when Meneer Turdhoeven – as we had secretly nicknamed him – bundled his books together and departed at the close of lessons, always with a scowl upon his face.

'The old fart,' whispered Hendrik.

Six mornings a week, I underwent lessons with Meneer Terhoeven. Hendrik and Niels suffered additional lessons three afternoons a week because – as our tutor explained – a boy's mind has greater capacity for learning than a girl's. This was said with a sneer in my direction.

While my brothers attended additional lessons, I was burdened with mastering the *spinetten*, completing needlework and practising the necessary skills for the efficient running of a household. Mama assigned me the responsibility of caring for baby Lucas in the late afternoon as the servants prepared the evening meal. Although there were moments I was charmed with his dimples and toothless smile, I often felt irritated that I had so little time to do as I pleased. Maintaining high levels of industry was essential, according to Mama, lest I fall into idleness. Apparently idleness leads to wickedness and self-importance.

Every Saturday afternoon, I stood in Papa's workroom, waiting as he checked my writing and equations. If pleased with my progress, he granted me a reward – sometimes an afternoon at leisure with the Van Helst girls or a drawing lesson in his workroom. If he felt my progress had lapsed, I was tasked with pressing the linen, polishing pewter or – the worst punishment of all – additional practice on the *spinetten*. Our entire household secretly celebrated when my studies were successful, relieved that they did not have to endure the disharmony I forced from those ivory keys.

Nearly a month after I began studying under Meneer Terhoeven, I presented myself at the door of Papa's workroom with my books in hand.

Papa laid down a charcoal stub. 'Have you made steady progress this week?'

'I have mastered the Latin verbs *consuendi* and *coquere*, the French verbs *polir* and *balayer*, the Spanish verbs *cantar* and *sonreír*.' I opened my notebooks and laid them on the desk.

Papa's brow furrowed, his smile absent.

'I also learnt how the French king's mother, Marie de' Medici, is related to the Spanish Hapsburgs.'

Papa tugged on his lower lip, staring at me with an expression I could not fathom.

My cheeks flushed. Had I displeased him in some way? Meneer Terhoeven had been especially relentless that week, goading me to quit academic studies and focus on needlepoint and music, insisting my attempts in the classroom amounted to nothing and that I should accept my limitation as a female.

'I will have a word with your tutor about broadening your vocabulary. Being female is no reason to restrict your learning to such verbs as sew, cook, polish, sweep and ... what were the other verbs?' Papa scanned the page. 'Sing and smile.'

I silently sang with joy at Papa's wisdom.

'I am pleased with your progress, Antonia. You show yourself to be advanced beyond your twelve years. Next Monday, you will accompany me to my work at the studio of Meneer Rubens.'

At last, a visit to the Master's studio. I skipped from the room.

14

Pain radiates from the base of her skull, dull and throbbing. She longs for it to splinter, float through the air like dust motes, evaporate into nothingness. Grimacing, she eases herself from the sofa and walks to the window. The slate rooftops of the Old Town blur behind a wall of drizzle. She rests her forehead on the glass, its coolness soothing. Muffled sounds float up from the street to the third-floor apartment. Early morning, Saturday, and most of Antwerp is still asleep.

Her limbs and mind are sluggish. She'd slept fitfully since arriving home from hospital, overcome with nausea whenever she sat up. Even the lilting melody of Debussy's 'Arabesque' was too much. Beneath the nausea and throbbing head is the hollow ache in her heart, suffused with grief over Mama, anger over secrets released and years of deceit.

Snippets of the past twenty-four hours trickle back: fluorescent lights, blue curtains, her father watching from the end of the hospital bed. Her father, a total stranger yet strangely familiar, long-believed dead, brought back to life with mere words.

'I'm sorry,' Mama had said, pausing often to draw breath. 'Thought it was for the best ... Telling you he was dead meant he'd be gone for good. Forget the past ... focus on the future. We never needed him.'

'Why, after all these years, are you telling me?'

Rachael blinked away tears. 'Guilt ... atonement ... tie up loose ends ...'

Charlotte had sat by her bedside, dozing when Mama fell into a morphine-induced sleep, startled awake by her cries. Rachael plucked at the blankets, calling out, memories surfacing, random phrases making little sense. During her lucid moments, she clutched Charlotte's hand, apologised for her mistakes. When the pain swelled, she released tirades of fury directed at her former lover, hurling recriminations as if he stood before her.

Days later, when the end came, questions remained unanswered, secrets cremated. Charlotte was left with Rachael's anger ringing in her ears, most of it directed at Sébastien Sterck. In the days that followed, as she organised the funeral and prepared to move to Antwerp, the bitterness sat inside her like a dead weight. His figure hovered like a shadow in the background as she packed boxes, cancelled utilities.

Charlotte turns away from the window. Her feet lead her to the bathroom, as if of their own volition. Staring into the mirror, she runs her fingers over the raised bruise on her forehead, the grazes along her jaw. She recalls stirring in the hospital bed, aware Sterck had stood, watching her as she lay unconscious. The hospital staff should never have allowed him to stay by her bedside. He had no right to be there. Had he followed her to the stone steps, seen her fall?

She glares at her reflection, forces the paranoia away. The tension on campus with an attacker on the loose has unsettled her. Sébastien has been polite and professional since she arrived in Antwerp. He came to the hospital to offer his help, seemed genuinely concerned. One knock to the head and she's imagining the worst. Idiotic.

Filling the sink with warm soapy water, she submerges her hands, watches the dried blood on her knuckles dissolve. Details come rushing back. A loose page fluttering in the wind. A paramedic had placed the page in her satchel, assuming it belonged to her.

She dries her hands, locates the satchel, carefully slides out the page, retrieved from the inside cover of a map folio over three hundred years old.

The yellowed paper is thick, covered in delicate veins, peppered with follicles. Vellum. The animal skin had been soaked in lime, scraped and stretched, pumiced until smooth. Looks as if a mouse has nibbled along the edges, pausing occasionally to take larger bites. The page is filled with cursive handwriting, faded to sepia. The language, Old Flemish. A date in elegant script at the top: *5 November 1686.*

'Same year as the map folio,' she murmurs. If the paper is over three hundred years old, it will be fragile.

From a nearby shelf, she grabs an acid-free plastic sleeve, magnifying glass, lexicon of Old Flemish words. Slipping the page into the protective sleeve, she settles on the sofa and begins to translate, the medic's order to rest forgotten.

After more than ten years of studying the life of Rubens, Charlotte has developed her own unique language skills. Her written understanding of Old Flemish is nearly as fluent as her modern-day Dutch. She recognises Latin and Spanish, two languages favoured by the polyglot Rubens. Her Québécois French helps her translate the French often used in the artist's correspondence. Raised in Toronto by a mother who spoke to her in English, French and Dutch – the latter language thanks to her mother's grandmother, born in Belgium – Charlotte can flit from one language to another.

Translating the historic document, she is re-energised.

My dear nephew Gerard,

You and I have long shared a bond, from the time I tended you as a babe in arms and as you grew into adulthood. The loyalty and devotion you have demonstrated within our family is stronger than that of anyone else. For this reason, I turn to you.

The unrest in our city gives credence to my decision to keep my plans hidden from all but you. The closure of the Scheldt, soldiers marching to battle the French at Namur, the burgemeesters' duplicitous dealings with the merchants' guild, such dissension makes us suspicious of even lifelong friends. Protecting our loved ones is my strongest desire. It should be yours, too. Focus your efforts on the protection of our family, for the sake of those who have gone before and those who come after.

Soon after my passing, you will receive a map folio entitled 'Nova Europae Descriptio', with the name of the famed cartographer and printer of Amsterdam, Frederik de Wit, –

Charlotte's pulse quickens. The seventeenth-century map folio! The mystery behind its provenance is revealed.

*– comprising seven maps, each map and picture wrought with
infinite detail.*

*This folio is no mere object to assist you in your travels. Each
map conceals words, verses and directions in foreign languages to
guide your path. Every picture tells the story of the pride that
overtook your grandpapa Lucas.*

*I trust your skills will help you find the answers. You have
prepared for this since you were a youngster, although you knew
nought of this until now. Remember the puzzles of your youth,
taught to you by your father and to me by mine, a tradition passed
down from one generation to the next? Having no children of my
own, I turn to you, dear nephew, to fulfil my plan.*

*Be eager to unravel the secrets, for they will provide you with a
deeper understanding of our family. You will discover what I heard
eleven years ago, and you will comprehend the wrong that must be
set right. I learnt how the treasures were removed, concealed within
a roll of waxed cloth, carried home beneath a cloak, remaining
hidden for at least sixty-five years. Find them, Gerard, and restore
them to their rightful owner. The descendants of the Master have
long awaited their return.*

*Accept this calling, as I have accepted my promise to my papa,
which I pledged at his deathbed, to never speak the whereabouts of
his secret to another soul while I lived. There are miscreants who
would seek these treasures for their own gain, so guard my words
and trust your heart.*

*Along with the folio, I have arranged for you to receive your
grandpapa Lucas' red felt tasselled cap. It was always on his head
as he toiled in his workroom, keeping him warm on chill evenings.
Look upon it often and do not dwell on his mistakes. Remember
him for his goodness.*

Your loving aunt,
Antonia

Charlotte paces across the room, headache forgotten. Here is the
woman whose name appears on the Rubens Crest, the daughter of
the engraver. An amazing find: an undiscovered letter about Lucas
Vorsterman, one of Rubens' closest collaborators, which alludes to a

family shame. Antonia includes the term *treasures* twice in her letter, suggests they were stolen, declares they belonged to the *descendants of the Master*. Although Antonia doesn't name the Master, surely it is Rubens. He was known as the Master of Antwerp.

'Who are you, Antonia Vorsterman?' murmurs Charlotte.

Someone had stowed the letter and re-adhered the endpaper to make a perfect hiding place. Did Antonia hide it in 1686? Is this the first time it has been read? Or did Gerard read his aunt's letter and then return it to the map folio?

Charlotte re-reads the letter. Why is Antonia so desperate to protect a family secret? Was she completely loyal to her father? Was Lucas Vorsterman as devoted in return? If so, their relationship is the polar opposite to the one Charlotte has with her own father. Antonia's appears to be based on respect and love, while her own is based on ignorance and contempt – he is ignorant of her existence and, to her, he is contemptible.

She picks up a notepad and pen, and begins writing a list of questions. Is the letter genuine? How did the map folio come to be at the Begijnhof? Why was it donated to the university? Does the Begijnhof have any related documents? Is there another document concealed inside the folio's back cover?

The doorbell chimes. She glares at Antonia's letter, as if blaming the inanimate object for being mute.

Another chime. She opens the door, irked by the interruption. Miles stands in the hallway, holding a bag of takeaway food. The aroma of stir-fried noodles enters the room.

15

Pausing at a street corner, Miles pushes a pedestrian button. 'Theo told me about the damage to the map folio. He knows a colleague who may be able to repair it.'

'Thank goodness,' says Charlotte, wrapping her arms tightly across her chest.

The throbbing in her temples has increased and coupled with an empty stomach, a sensation of nausea grows. She had barely touched the Thai takeaway Miles had brought over earlier, her mind reeling from Antonia's letter, and still filled with concern over her role in damaging the map folio. As she nibbled on a spring roll, her concussed brain suddenly remembered the conservator's message on her phone: *something else in the folio which may be related to Rubens*. Antonia had written about the folio containing hidden words, verses and puzzles. Perhaps Theo had found something in the folio related to Antonia's letter. When Charlotte said she planned to meet with Theo, Miles had shoved the leftover chicken satays in the fridge and announced he would accompany her.

Miles thrusts his hands into the pockets of his coat. 'Theo also said there was an attempted break-in at the conservation room.'

Her insides twist with alarm. 'That's awful. When did it happen?'

'This afternoon,' he replies. 'The thief, or thieves, didn't manage to get inside, but the security keypad was damaged.'

The pedestrian signal flickers from red to green. They cross the road.

'Does Theo know what was targeted?' She wonders if someone was trying to steal De Wit's folio.

'Not sure, but there was no risk of the map folio being stolen. After your accident, someone placed it in Acquisitions. It wasn't in the conservation room at the time of the attempted break-in.' He indicates an alleyway. 'Let's take a shortcut.'

They skirt around revellers, loud with laughter, who have spilled out of a bar and gathered on the pavement. Street lights cast an orange glow into the alleyway.

'Is this the first time someone has tried to break in to the conservation room?' she asks.

'No. Last year, someone jemmied the door and stole an eighteenth-century Dutch manuscript.'

'Did they catch the thief?'

'No, and the manuscript was never recovered.'

Charlotte slows her pace, gingerly stepping over cobblestones slippery from rain. 'It's kind of you to keep me company, Miles, but I could've walked to the university on my own.'

'Wouldn't be chivalrous of me to let a concussed newcomer wander the streets alone at dusk.' His tone is light, but his expression serious. 'Besides, I want to see how Theo's faring. He's annoyed the conservation room was targeted.'

She casts him a sidelong glance. A part of her is relieved he's escorting her, but she also wishes she could study the map folio without others hovering around. She wants time alone to search for clues, determine the authenticity of Antonia's letter, formulate a plan. Putting her trust in colleagues she barely knows is too risky, especially given the atmosphere of unrest around campus with budget cutbacks and an attacker on the loose. If Antonia's statements have any merit and Charlotte finds herself on the verge of discovering something remarkable, her next move will be critical. One poor decision could see the project wrested from her control, handed to someone else to reap the rewards.

'Projects aren't bestowed simply for performance, no matter how exceptional,' Rachael had told Charlotte when she grumbled about her Toronto supervisor's penchant for favouritism. 'It often comes down to funding and who can provide the greatest benefit to the university as a whole.'

Charlotte remembers feeling crestfallen, hearing such advice from her mother, who had worked in academia for nearly forty years. 'So, no matter how hard I work,' said Charlotte, fuming at the unfairness. 'I'm at the mercy of the higher-ups, is that it? I should be grateful for any crumbs thrown my way?'

'Don't show your full hand,' said Rachael. 'Only reveal it when you're ready.'

Charlotte pictures the document box concealed inside a cupboard in her Antwerp apartment. Tucked inside is Antonia's letter, safe within its acid-free sleeve. It will remain there until she's decided on her next step.

After exiting the alleyway, they follow the road until they emerge into the cobblestoned expanse of Grote Markt. A massive statue, as large as a bus, looms in the middle of the square. A Roman soldier is poised, ready to fling a giant's severed hand across the square. Arcs of water squirt from the wrist stump and the mouths of the surrounding sea creatures, a gory blending of blood and water.

'Do you know the Flemish legend of Brabo?' asks Miles, slowing as they pass the fountain.

'Sounds familiar. Remind me of the details.'

'The giant Antigoon cut off the hand of anyone who refused to pay a toll when crossing the river Scheldt. The soldier Brabo killed the giant, cut off his hand and threw it in the river, which gave rise to the city's name.'

She takes in the life-size bronze soldier, the dead titan slumped at his feet. 'The prefix *ant* comes from the Old Dutch *hant*, which changed over the centuries to mean *hand* –'

'– and *werpen* means *to throw*,' he finishes.

'To throw a hand.' She laughs, surprised at how cheerful she sounds.

'What's so funny?'

'Reminds me of something my mother used to say.'

They turn into Sint-Jacobstraat, passing the façade of the Gothic church, only metres away from Rubens' crypt. She's more determined than ever that no one – not Sterck or anyone else – will assign the research of Antonia's letter and the map folio to someone else. Uncovering the mysteries of a newly discovered primary source about Rubens could catapult her career from middling scholar to world-renowned academic superstar. No one will take this opportunity from her.

She recalls how the conversation with her mother had finished.

'Only show your hand to those you can trust,' said Rachael. 'And remember, you've entered a highly competitive, male-dominated field. So be careful who you trust.'

16

On the afternoon of the visit, I danced from one foot to the other while Janneke tied my hair with the grey velvet ribbon. I rushed to keep pace with Papa's strides, my hand lost within his. Turning left from the Meir, we followed the Herentalse Vaart, where a freshwater canal was dug the previous spring. We stopped before a three-storeyed brick mansion, its upper row of lead-paned windows topped with crow-stepped gables.

A manservant ushered us into a spacious courtyard and lo, I felt I had wondrously stepped into a page from my Vasari. Before us stood a triple-arched portico, complete with Classical pediment, columns and statues. High on the façade were stone figures appearing to melt into the wall, dressed in robes clinging to their curves.

'They are caryatids,' said Papa, following my gaze, 'popular in ancient Greece and fashionable once more in Europe.'

I followed Papa into a dimly lit vestibule, empty except for a bench and a large storage chest. As we opened the door to the studio, I heard a voice speaking measured lines of Latin. Peeking from behind the folds of Papa's cloak, I spied a young gentleman standing beneath a window, reading from a lectern. Light from high windows flooded the cavernous room.

Papa motioned for me to follow. We dodged around people drawing, painting, and preparing paints and canvases. We stepped around a table with a collection of terracotta pots and glass bottles. A young man with dark curly hair, who was blending a blue paste, winked at me.

Papa gestured for me to sit on a stool next to his worktable. From this vantage point, I observed the studio. We maintained a whispered conversation. 'Describe what you see,' he said.

'A large panel leaning against the wall has a peculiar viewpoint ... stone archways around the border, clouds in the centre, and people flying like birds in the sky.'

'It will hang from the ceiling of the Jesuits' church near Grote Markt. When people look up to the heavens, it will inspire them in their worship.' Papa held a burin and made tiny scratches on a copper plate while he glanced at a drawing on the table. 'What else?'

'Another ceiling panel with swirling clouds, but not for a church, as it has many naked people.'

'An important commission from King James. The mythological story of Psyche ascending to Jupiter's throne. It will decorate the ceiling of the Banqueting House in London.'

I reserved the most terrifying painting until last. Four yards wide and three yards high, the canvas rested on wooden blocks and showed four horses rearing, their riders thrusting spears at snarling lions. The painting captured the moment a rider had fallen from his horse, his inverted body tumbling to the ground, a lion sinking its teeth into his thigh. The man's face was a grey mask of death.

'*The Lion Hunt*,' said Papa. 'The Master has asked me to begin an engraving.'

'Is that the Master over there?' I pointed to a figure with his back to us, facing *The Lion Hunt*. He wore a dark green smock over his clothes, and atop his head was a soft felt cap the colour of cinnamon. In one hand was a paintbrush, in the other, a *maalstok*, one of those long rods with a bulbous leather end that artists rest their hand upon while painting. Although of moderate height and slim build, his demeanour was imposing. Even with his back to me, I sensed he would dominate any room he entered.

'It is impolite to point, Antonia.'

I lowered my hand.

'Yes, it is the Master, Meneer Peter Paul Rubens.'

'What's he like?'

'Master Rubens will turn forty-four this summer. He spent a decade studying in Italy before returning home. He and his wife, Isabella, have two sons; Albert is seven and Nicolaas is three. His firstborn – a daughter, Clara – is a year younger than you. You will have seen him and his household regularly attend Sint-Jacobskerk, for they are devoted to the Catholic faith, like us.'

'But what is he like?'

Papa was silent for several minutes. 'He is the most learned and intelligent man I have ever known, with an extraordinary amount of energy, known for his sharp wit and gracious manner.'

On the other side of the room, the Master raised his hand and glanced in the direction of the man reading Latin. 'Enough.' His voice was quiet yet confident.

The Master stepped to the Jesuits' painting and gazed at it. Without looking from the canvas, he handed the paintbrush and *maalstok* to a hovering assistant. I could see the Master's face now. Chestnut-coloured hair fell to his shoulders. His beard ended in a fashionable point and his moustache curved upwards. In profile, his face was long with a high forehead, his nose ending in a droop. A pink glow flushed his cheeks, his lips rosy-red.

I liked him instantly. He looked to be the sort of man who would play with his children and smile at his wife. I pictured him tossing little Nicolaas in the air and enjoying his delighted squeals. He would rest his arm around Albert's shoulders as they sat abreast at a table, studying a book. I imagined Clara to be his favourite, sharing laughter and conversation as they strolled in the garden.

The Master swivelled on his heels and scanned the room, his eyes resting on me. I shrank in my seat. He stepped closer, stopping a yard from where I sat. 'May I introduce myself? I am Peter Paul Rubens.' He smiled and bowed.

Papa laid down his burin and rose to his feet.

'I understand, *meisje*,' said the Master, 'that you are the eldest child of my good friend, Lucas Vorsterman. Please accept my congratulations. I understand your papa and mama have welcomed a new son, named Lucas for his father.' The Master rested his hand on my father's shoulder. 'The arrival of a babe is indeed the happiest of occasions.' He squeezed Papa's shoulder, a smile passed between them, then he turned and walked away.

Thus, I met Master Rubens for the first time.

17

Sensor lights flicker to life as Charlotte and Miles walk along the deserted basement corridor, their footsteps echoing off the concrete floors. Mobile shelving units stretch into the distance, swallowed by darkness, an occasional one gaping open like a monster's maw. At the front of each shelving unit, a handwheel sits ready to move shelves to the left or right along tracks in the floor. Charlotte shivers with distaste, recalling her time in the archive compactors at Dartmouth, the groaning sound of metal on metal, the students' macabre jokes about being crushed in between the moving walls.

After turning into another corridor, they stop at a metal door. Miles swipes a keycard along a security panel. 'Staff replaced the damaged panel quickly.' The panel beeps, a bolt shoots back, the door clicks open.

The conservation room is clinically tidy. Tubing for an extractor fan hangs from the ceiling in fat loops, like a boa constrictor. Shelves are arranged with containers of disposable gloves, magnification visors, steamers, brushes and metal implements for examining fragile documents. The bright overhead lights, stainless-steel equipment and aroma of solvents bring back memories of her year working in the Toronto conservation studio.

'Where's Theo?' Charlotte's eyes are drawn to a large table in the centre of the room, containing a V-shaped stand draped in a white cloth.

'Texted to say he went out for a few minutes. He'll be back soon.' Miles removes the cloth, revealing the opened map folio nestled in the supporting arms of the stand. 'He said the folio is in excellent condition, except for the broken spine and tear. How's it feel to know you damaged a rare De Wit?' His eyes are bright, smile crooked.

Charlotte sits heavily on a chair at the table, leaning forward until her forehead rests on her folded arms. Closes her eyes, hoping the darkness will ease the nausea.

'I'm joking.' Laughing, he rushes to her side. 'I'm sure Theo–'

'It's just a headache. Too much walking, I overdid it.' Excuses roll off her tongue, just not the real one: anxiety over the damage she caused the De Wit. Not just one map, but a folio of seven. It has survived in pristine condition for over three hundred years, only to be broken by her carelessness. She's mortified. Her stomach churns at the thought of facing the conservator and what will surely be his contempt.

'I was concussed on the rugby pitch years ago,' says Miles. 'Took me a week before I felt my head was facing in the right direction.' He opens and closes cupboards, searching. 'What you need is a cuppa.'

'The English person's answer to everything,' she whispers to the table.

She hears a tap being turned, then water trickling into a container. Seconds later, he places an aluminium bottle in front of her. 'No tea-making facilities in the conservation room, but I found a non-spillable water bottle.'

She can't help but smile at his kindness. She takes small sips of water. Her stomach begins to settle.

Miles distracts her with a monologue about the quirks of his post-grad students, reassures her Theo is calm and reasonable. She's still sipping water when the door opens and a man enters.

'Theodore Giroux,' he introduces himself. His accent has the mellow endings of French.

'I'm sorry to hear about the break-in,' she says, 'and I'm very sorry about the De Wit. The damage. An awful accident.'

Theo shrugs, taciturn and pragmatic. 'We've used several conservators in the past. There's one I have in mind who may be able to repair the De Wit.'

Her anxiety eases. 'I'm relieved to hear that.'

'As for the break-in,' continues Theo, 'the lock and keypad were damaged when they tried to jemmy the door. Security quickly replaced everything and ordered an upgraded fingerprint keypad system, which will be installed next week.

'Wasn't there a theft from Utrecht's conservation room several years ago?' asks Miles.

'Yes, and Brussels University had a seventeenth-century document stolen last year,' says Theo. 'It was found two weeks later in a storage locker at Bruxelles-Midi station, thankfully unharmed.'

Charlotte scans his face, looking for any latent annoyance about the prized De Wit, but he is composed and professional.

Theo rolls a floor-mounted microscope to the table, adjusts its pivoting arm. 'I placed the folio in a drop-cradle to support the broken spine. Willem showed me the Rubens Crest and the seven letters you identified starting with D-N. Yesterday, I noticed something else unusual.' Passing out nitrile gloves, Theo pulls on his own. He points to a place name on the first map, then gestures for Charlotte to look through the microscope's eyepiece.

Adjusting the lens, the word *Antwerpen* comes into focus, followed by a tiny Roman numeral.

'Nine cities have a larger dot which is dark blue rather than black,' says Theo, 'as well as a Roman numeral after the name.' He slides a sheet of paper across the table. 'I've written them down.'

Antwerpen i
Venetia ii
Mantua iii
Florentia iv
Roma v
Madrid vi
Genoa vii
Paris viii
Londinium ix

'What's their significance?' asks Miles, looking through the eyepiece.

Lowering her head to study the map from a sharper angle, to Charlotte, the nine dots stand out like a constellation in the night sky. 'They're the cities where Rubens lived and travelled as an adult,' she explains. 'He was born in Siegen, Germany, but left when he was twelve. He was well travelled, but Antwerp was his home.'

'Was the folio made during his lifetime?' asks Miles.

'Forty-six years after his death—'

'We're not certain who commissioned it,' interrupts Theo. 'The cartouche names De Wit as the maker. The Rubens Crest suggests it was made for someone called Antonia Vorsterman.'

Miles peers at the map. 'Strange crest, hidden letters, nine cities … Sounds mysterious.'

'Something else puzzles me,' says Theo. 'Like most maps, it includes lines and border markings to show geographical coordinates, known today as longitude and latitude. Longitude wasn't accurately determined until the 1770s, so De Wit's longitude lines aren't accurate. Neither were his latitude lines, but that's not the point. His geographical markings are bizarre.' He motions for Miles to look at the upper border. 'Can you see them?'

'Yeah. Cross-hatched pattern and every few centimetres, a Roman number.' Miles moves aside for Charlotte to look through the eyepiece.

'There are tiny numbers disguised within the cross-hatching, numbers from one to ten along the east–west axis, same for north–south.' She leans away from the microscope. 'Don't most maps have numbers along the axes?'

'Geographical degrees are usually written in Arabic numerals from zero to 180 by increments of five or ten, with zero positioned on Greenwich. But this map uses Roman numerals, beginning on the lower left border, increasing by one.'

Miles rubs his chin. 'But as you say, Theo, maps didn't have accurate coordinates until the 1770s, so De Wit's map is typical of its day and simply incorrect.'

'But it's not typical of its day,' says Theo.

Charlotte leans back in her chair. 'De Wit was a prolific mapmaker, right?'

'Most successful in the Dutch Republic,' says Theo.

'What were his other maps like? Do they have borders marked with degrees, or with Roman numerals one to ten?'

'Always degrees,' says Theo. 'I've never seen a European map, De Wit or any other, marked with consecutive, low-digit Roman numerals beginning in the lower left corner.'

Charlotte wraps the lapels of her cardigan across her chest, nestling into the folds. She recalls Antonia's words from her letter: *each map conceals words, verses and directions in foreign languages to guide your path.*

Theo turns the pages to reveal a jagged tear. The pastedown of the inside front cover is made of marbled paper in crimson, mustard and blue, swirled like an oil slick. The paper is torn from top to bottom, forming a gaping pouch, exposing the thin wooden board of the inside cover.

Charlotte peers in for a closer look. Her tumble down the stairs had happened so quickly that her recollection of grabbing Antonia's letter is hazy. Seeing the jagged tear for the first time comes as a shock. Glancing up, she notices Theo watching her. He quickly looks away. Did someone see her holding Antonia's letter as she lay slumped at the bottom of the stairs? Is Theo waiting for her to admit to swiping something from inside the folio?

'I'll finish my assessment, decide how it'll be repaired and let Sister Anna know when it can be returned.' Theo drapes the cloth over the folio.

Charlotte sits up straight. 'Returned?'

Theo pulls off his gloves. 'Yes. To the Begijnhof.'

'At the history departmental meeting yesterday,' Miles explains, 'Sterck said Sister Anna is happy for the Begijnhof's documents to be placed in the university's permanent collection, except for the map folio. Apparently it belongs to one of the *begijnen* and she wants it returned.'

Charlotte's throat tightens as her panic grows. She looks from Miles to Theo, hoping this is a mistake, realising her opportunity to study the map folio is slipping away. 'But I need to study it.'

Theo rolls the floor-mounted microscope into the corner, tucks away the pivoting arm, oblivious to her fears.

'What did Sister Anna say about the damage to the map folio?' Charlotte's voice is pitched higher than usual.

'She doesn't know about it yet,' says Miles. 'Sterck decided to wait until it's been assessed.'

Charlotte eases back in her chair. So, she's not the only one keeping secrets.

'I may do the repairs myself,' says Theo, 'or send it to an external conservator, depending on the extent of the damage and how quickly it needs to be returned to the Begijnhof.' Pulling on his coat, he turns to Charlotte. 'If you learn anything to explain the geographical markings, please let me know.' Then he addresses Miles. 'Can you please make sure the door is locked when you go?' After hasty goodbyes, he leaves.

Miles leans against the bench. 'What now?'

'I'll read up on Grand Tours. See if there's one related to Rubens.'

'And what about Antonia Vorsterman? Who was she?'

'She was the daughter of Lucas Vorsterman, who worked as Rubens' engraver.'

'Are there many primary sources on this engraver?'

'Not many. He's mentioned in records of the Saint Lucas Guild, some letters by Rubens. Several historians mention him.'

'Anything on Antonia?'

'I'll do some research.' Charlotte tweaks the cloth. She longs to lift it aside, to study each map for clues, discover if anything is concealed within the pastedown's back cover. Perhaps another document to corroborate the existence of the treasures Antonia mentioned.

She needs to work quickly. The folio could be returned to its owner within weeks. She must complete her own investigation, formulate a plan, present her findings. If Sterck hears what she's working on, he may insist on bringing in a more prominent specialist to manage the project. There are Baroque art specialists from other European universities with more experience, more connections. How can she compete with them? A Canadian minnow trying to make a name for herself in teeming European waters.

Miles collects their discarded nitrile gloves, turning away to tidy the counter.

His backpack lies on the table, unzipped, items spilling out. Notebooks, pens and chargers, displaced when he'd rummaged for his phone.

Charlotte wriggles into her coat, eyeing the keycard poking from beneath a notebook.

He empties the water bottle, closes cupboards, returns to the table, and sweeps his belongings into the backpack. 'There's a bar nearby that makes great burgers. Let's get something to eat.'

18

Her hand trembles, and the keycard drops to the floor. Her second attempt is successful: the control panel beeps, the bolt shoots back, the door clicks open. She turns on the light and hesitates in the doorway, half-expecting an alarm to sound or a disembodied voice to call out.

But there's silence.

'Take a quick look,' she tells herself loudly, 'and see if there's anything else inside the map folio, then leave.' She keeps her voice calm, as if chatting about an everyday activity, even though she knows her actions are anything but everyday.

She slides the keycard into her pocket. Imagines arriving in the office on Monday morning, slipping it into Miles' backpack when he isn't looking, where it will be lost among the jumble of pens, paper scraps and chargers. He won't have noticed it was missing. He's too disorganised. Besides, she couldn't ask for his keycard without revealing her discovery of Antonia's letter. Work will begin on repairing the folio in the next few days, then it will be returned to the Begijnhof. This is the only time she'll have easy access to it. *It's better this way*, she tells herself.

'I'm only keeping the letter secret for a short time,' she says, her voice resonating in the empty room. Revealing too much too soon, and to the wrong people, will turn it into a bureaucratic nightmare – red-tape and endless discussions, higher-ups bickering for control. If this turns out to be the remarkable discovery she hopes it is, she'll be best positioned to lead the project. An extraordinary way to launch her academic career in Europe.

She glances at the wall clock: five am. The institutional face stares back at her, somehow stern and accusatory. *Thirty minutes*, she tells herself, *no more*. She sets an alarm on her phone.

It's early Sunday morning. The whole of Antwerp is either asleep or drowsy, especially security staff coming to the end of their shift. A friend in Toronto who worked as a security guard once told her that keycard records were rarely examined, and only if there was a major incident. This isn't going to turn into a major incident.

She takes calming breaths, wriggles into gloves. With her fingers tingling with excitement, she lifts aside the protective cloth. She opens the folio to the inside front cover, then uses a metal spatula to gently prise apart the torn paper, like a surgeon probing the innards of a patient. There's nothing else in the cavity.

Pushing aside the disappointment, she turns the pages until she reaches the inside back cover. It appears slightly puffed in the centre, springy to touch. Unusual. Normally, the entire sheet of paper is pasted to the inside cover. But this one appears to be adhered only around the edges, just like the front cover. Once again, her excitement surges. She selects a fine scalpel, then hesitates, the sharp blade hovering over the pastedown.

A glance at the clock shows she has twenty-five minutes left. She's unfamiliar with Theo's work habits. What if he's a workaholic who enjoys coming in early on Sunday mornings?

Her hands shake, palms sticky. Mouth dry.

God, what is she doing? If she's caught, there's no way she can justify her actions. Using Miles' filched keycard is putting his reputation on the line, and it will spell the end of their budding friendship if she's caught. Of course, that will be the least of her problems. She'll be fired, disgraced, her career over. Worse, she may be accused of involvement in the previous day's break-in. She could face charges. A criminal record.

The marbled endpaper swims before her eyes. With trembling hands, she lays the scalpel on the table. Her behaviour is unethical, illegal, unequivocally wrong. Nothing is worth this risk. Her insides are screaming for her to close the map folio, return the room to its former state, and leave. Now.

But then a tiny worm of a voice begins in her ear. *You'll never get ahead if you're not willing to take risks.* It hisses and mutters, buzzing with derision, warning of lost opportunities. *The best way to achieve greatness*, it says, *is to be remarkable. Be assertive. Take chances.*

She doubles over, struggling to catch her breath. Holds her hands over her ears, desperate to block it out. In the muffled silence, she recalls a colleague from Toronto University, Henri Quercus, who regularly distorted his research results in order to secure further grants. Henri's behaviour had continued for years before his deceptions were confirmed and his career finished. Charlotte knows of other colleagues who, while not corrupt like Henri, were known to be overly assertive in pushing their own agenda to achieve their goals. Many would have never succeeded unless they showed themselves to be go-getters.

She's hard-working and ambitious. Willing to take risks if it could lead to something exceptional. Determined not to let anything stand in her way. That's a far cry from Henri's duplicitous behaviour.

Resolutely, she picks up the scalpel. Slowly, carefully, she slides the blade under the edge of the marbled paper, every movement decisive.

Twenty minutes left.

Millimetre by millimetre, she eases paper from glued edge. The skills from her time in the Toronto conservation studio come back to her. In some places, the glue is brittle and separates easily. In others, it's more secure. Halfway along the lower side, the paper refuses to lift. It's stuck fast.

Using the spatula, she eases apart the gap she's created – gingerly, lest the paper tear – and shines the light from her mobile phone into the cavity.

There's something inside. She's so shocked, she nearly drops the phone.

A single sheet of paper is nestled within, tantalisingly close to her fingertips, but too wide to pull through the narrow opening. She needs to separate the remaining glue from the edge.

The minute hand jerks forward. Fifteen minutes.

She rushes across the room, grabs a dry steamer from the bench. Within seconds, it's powered up and dialled to the lowest setting. Her hands shake as she directs heat onto the glue seam, waiting for it to become soft and tacky. Cautiously, she separates the remaining edge of the pastedown. A few more inches and the gap is wide enough for her to slide in tweezers and draw the paper out.

A vellum page, yellowed and worn like Antonia's letter, covered in familiar handwriting. She slips the vellum into a protective archive sleeve, then slides it carefully into her satchel. Her breath comes in shallow gasps.

Her phone alarm pings, echoing around the room. *Hurry. Get out. Don't get caught.*

Heart hammering. Palms sweaty. She directs steam along the lower edge of the pastedown, warming the glue, pressing it back together. She tidies away tools, closes the folio, drapes the cloth back over it. Shoving the disposable gloves into her pocket, she grabs her satchel. Edging out the door, she checks the room for any evidence of her presence. Nothing.

19

'Don't ever pull a stunt like that again,' she mutters, furious at her own unscrupulous behaviour. 'Stupid. Stupid. Stupid.'

She continues berating herself as she crosses the university courtyard. Unprofessional conduct, stealing from Miles, plundering the map folio, risking everything to get ahead. *Stupid.*

But the tiny worm in her ear is annoyingly persistent. Any wrongdoing can be easily fixed, it soothes. Return the keycard, study the new document, present a research plan. Everything will be fine.

Charlotte unbuttons the top of her coat, savouring the cool air on her flushed neck. A chill prickles her spine as she exits the courtyard. Street lights cast eerie shadows, transforming shrubs into alarming shapes. The only signs of life are the aroma of freshly baked bread wafting from a nearby bakery, and a lone cyclist pedalling along a cross street ahead, bicycle lights glowing in the pre-dawn gloom.

She hears footsteps behind her, evenly paced, purposeful. Is someone following her? She slides the strap of her satchel across her body, securing it in case she has to run or is attacked. She'll protect the precious document, no matter what. She's risked too much to lose it now.

She speeds up. The footsteps behind also pick up pace.

'Idiot,' she mutters to herself. *Avoid deserted streets and always walk with friends after dark*, the safety posters declared. She'd discarded her pepper spray before leaving for Belgium; it's a prohibited weapon in much of Europe. She mentally assesses the items in her satchel. Notebook, pens, purse – all useless as improvised weapons – but she could grasp her keys in between her knuckles. Running and screaming may be the best option.

She turns into a side street, putting some distance between herself and the shadow behind. She strains to make out any sounds following her, but all she can hear are her own footsteps and raspy breaths.

Arriving in Grote Markt, she's relieved to no longer be hemmed in by alleyways. The bronze figure of Brabo stands at the apex of the fountain, his powerful pose strangely comforting. As she draws away from the Old Town, the roads widen, more street lights appear. She checks the time on her phone. Another ten minutes and she'll be safely in her apartment.

Her mother smiles at her from the screensaver: together on Pocologan Beach, heads touching, matching dark curly hair and pointed chins. 'Don't look at me like that,' remonstrates Charlotte. 'You would have done the same.'

Truthfully, she doubts her mother would have stolen a colleague's keycard to access a restricted area, used a scalpel to cut into a historic folio, purloined a hidden document. The question of guilt rankles. She knows what she's done is wrong. Unethical, deceitful – however labelled, it is wrong. Yet the pesky little voice that has wormed its way inside her head continues to insist that her actions were sensible. Pursuing an alternative course through official channels would take weeks, the voice wheedles, resulting in a bureaucratic impasse. She's simply sped up the process. Two documents possibly written by the same person can now be studied as a whole, better enabling her to decide if there is merit to investigating the notion of stolen treasures belonging to the Rubens family.

Justifying her actions brings momentary relief, but deep inside, she knows her behaviour is reprehensible. She is a thief.

Turning along Haverstraat, she's heedless of the fine drizzle beginning to fall, aware only of the unknown figure advancing from behind and the debate going on in her head. Tightening her hands into fists, she wants to shout her fear and frustration into the early morning air, desperate to reach the safety of her apartment, determined to unravel Antonia's clues, terrified she risks everything if she continues along this path. What are the treasures Antonia mentions? Are they still hidden, awaiting discovery? According to Antonia, the treasures were concealed within a roll of waxed cloth and carried home beneath a cloak. Paintings or drawings are the most obvious items to be rolled within waxed cloth. Are they paintings or drawings created by Rubens himself?

Stopping at an intersection, she hears the same measured footsteps again. She glances back down the street. About forty yards behind her is the figure of a man, wearing a dark jacket, hands thrust in pockets, head lowered against the drizzle.

She crosses the road and cuts to the right, then takes a left, hurrying past silent apartment buildings and shopfronts. In the next block, as she looks behind her, she sees the figure cut across the street and head towards her, his pace increasing. Thirty yards away now, closing fast.

The entrance to her apartment building is half a block away. She breaks into a jog, fumbles for her keys. Reaching the main door, she rams the key home, takes the stairs two at a time. Her breath is ragged by the time she's inside her apartment. Keeping the lights off, she steps to the window, peers outside.

The man strides past her apartment building, glances up as if he knows he is being watched, then continues along the street, his face in shadow.

20

May 11, 1621

With each visit to the Rubens studio, I was permitted more freedom. Papa sometimes sent me to collect copper plates from the cupboard, or ink and acid to test the depth of his incisions. As the weeks passed, I stepped like a cat around the room, exploring and observing. Assistants stretched canvases over wooden frames, priming them with gesso and linseed oil. Apprentices drew anatomical studies of twisting torsos, splayed limbs, and faces with dramatic expressions of dismay, surprise, euphoria or rage.

Some days we arrived to find the Master working alongside other eminent painters. The animal painter Meneer Frans Snyders often collaborated. His creatures were so lifelike, his reptiles looked to be slithering across the canvas, shiny scales frightening in their reality. Bears and wild boars snarled, saliva glistening on their teeth. Tables overflowed with slippery fish, slack-necked fowl and overripe fruit.

On other occasions, the Master painted bewinged *putti* with angelic faces, surrounding Our Lady holding the Christ child. The floral artist Meneer Jan Brueghel arrived to paint wreaths of roses, carnations, lilium and ranunculus for the plump little angels to float amongst, and also painted beetles and butterflies hiding in the foliage.

My favourite corner of the studio was the mixing table, where apprentices blended a rainbow of glossy paints. I loved the coolness of the terracotta pot nestled in my palm, the tangy scent of linseed oil. Santo Barzetti, the eldest of the mixers, was from Genoa and regaled me with stories in his lilting Italian accent.

'I was nine when I arrived in Antwerpen with Master Rubens in 1609–' said Santo.

'The same year as my birth,' I murmured.

Santo raised his eyebrows. 'You are only twelve? But you look and speak as if you are at least fourteen or fifteen.'

I blushed, uncertain whether I was pleased such a handsome man of twenty-one had noticed my maturity, or embarrassed that my developing curves may have caught his attention.

'I was an apprentice to begin with,' he continued as we stood side-by-side, blending a deep red paste. 'Apprentices usually begin from the age of twelve with grinding powders and mixing paints. They are forbidden to touch a pencil until they are sixteen. I showed such promise that I began mixing at age nine.'

I was quick with the sums. 'But that was twelve years ago. Why are you still mixing? Why aren't you drawing?'

Santo flicked his curly hair from his eyes with benign tolerance. 'I have shown such exceptional talent at mixing paints, the Master has made me his senior mixer. These' – he waved his hand at the youths sitting along the table – 'are my apprentices until I tell the Master they are ready for additional duties.'

It sounded to me as though Santo could well do with a lesson in humility. Still, I enjoyed his company, and delighted in his attentions.

I held a small flask with an elongated spout. With a nod from Santo, I tipped a stream of oil onto a mixing block of porphyry stone, where it sat in globules amongst crimson dust.

Santo rested both hands atop a pyramid-shaped stone, gliding it in figures of eight, blending the powder and oil. He tilted the stone and used a palette knife to scrape away the paste. 'Too thick. Needs more oil.'

Using a pipette, he dripped four beads of oil onto the surface and continued blending. Using the palette knife once more, he patted the paste into spikes, which held their shape.

'Perfect,' he declared, scraping the paint into a leather pouch and tightening the gut cord. 'The Master is working on *The Lion Hunt* tomorrow. The pouch will stop the paint from drying.'

Whenever work eased, Santo taught me about pigments and tested my knowledge.

'This one?' He indicated a powder the colour of egg yolk.

'Lead-tin yellow, made from grinding lead-tin oxide, used for highlighting jewellery, candlelight, sun rays.'

'What's the difference between these two?' He pointed at pots containing blue powders, one a deep navy similar to Delftware, the other a richer shade, like the stone in Mama's brooch.

'The first is smalt, made from grinding cobalt glass. The other is ultramarine, made from lapis lazuli.' I couldn't help but lift my chin a little, eager to impress Santo with my quick mind and to demonstrate that, despite my tender years and gender, I was worthy of his teaching. Santo indulged me in my swaggering, allowing me to match his own. What a pair we made, puffed with self-importance.

When Santo wasn't supervising assistants or mixing paint, he scrawled in a booklet covered in ochre leather with his initials stamped in the corner. While his paint-mixing skills were exceptional, his writing was deplorable. He wrote clumsily, more blots than words.

'What are you writing?' I glanced at his words, always curious.

'A list of the Master's works.'

'All his works?' I was amazed, for Meneer Rubens was prodigious.

'Whenever works are completed, whether they be drawing or painting, I record the details in this booklet.' He indicated a pile of drawings lying on the table showing a young woman with intricately braided hair. 'I am currently transcribing a description of the Master's *Pandora* drawings from a recent letter he wrote to his friend Meneer Snyders.'

I leaned in to study the beautiful *Pandora*, wondering if one day my hair would be as thick and lustrous, able to be twisted into a Classical hairstyle.

Santo's tutorship and the encouragement I received from the other apprentices filled me with a gratifying sense of acceptance, totally opposite to Meneer Terhoeven's constant reminders that I did not belong in the classroom. The Rubenshuis was a place I belonged.

Imagine my delight when the Master approached Papa's workbench one day and engaged me in conversation. Papa curtailed his burin scratching while Meneer Rubens offered me one of the bows I had seen him bestow on court envoys. His blue eyes reminded me of the little pot of ultramarine I had recently studied.

'I notice you have spent time with my Genoese assistant, Santo Barzetti. You may indeed believe everything he tells you about pigments, for he is a master at mixing' – Master Rubens flashed a smile in Santo's direction – 'but do not believe anything else he tells you. When he's not working in my studio, he is the greatest of rascals.'

Santo's grunt of indignation could be heard from across the room, eliciting much laughter from the apprentices.

Meneer Rubens turned his attention back to me. 'Having mastered pigment mixing, are you now ready to begin painting?'

'Sadly, sir, I have yet to develop any talent with the brush or burin,' I replied.

'Perhaps you are a musician? You play the virginals, *spinetten* or lute?'

'Alas, although I practise the *spinetten* regularly, I have yet to produce a pleasing tone from that murderous instrument.'

The Master chuckled. 'Murderous for whom?'

'Murderous for those who must listen to my playing and murderous for me, too, sir, who must continue practising despite having no talent.'

The Master's mouth twitched. 'So, what skills have you, Meisje Vorsterman?'

'I am learning Latin, French, Spanish and geography. I am studying the history of the Low Countries and the royal houses of Spain and France. I am quick with numbers and enjoy writing.' Heat rose to my cheeks. My recent boastful conversation with Santo had caused me to think too highly of myself. I heard Papa tut-tutting under his breath. 'There is so much I wish ... I could learn.' I stumbled over my words. Unable to maintain eye contact with Meneer Rubens, I stared at the black marble tiles, wishing they would heave apart and devour me whole, just as the Red Sea swallowed Pharaoh's army and the giant fish gulped Jonah.

The Master stepped closer. His shoes were brown leather, squared about the toes, pewter buckles tied with mustard grosgrain. His finger gently lifted my chin. My gaze travelled along his burgundy-stockinged calves and up over his green smock, until I looked into his face.

'It is admirable to seek knowledge at such a young age. Learn as much as you can. In the meantime' – he let go of my chin and smiled – 'please join my children in the kitchen for a meal. Learning requires nourishment.' He waved his hand towards the door. 'Across the courtyard, first door on the right.'

I was never more glad to hide my burning cheeks as I fled through the vestibule, to be swallowed into the warmth of the kitchen. Sitting with the Rubens youngsters, we guzzled bowls of steaming vegetable soup and freshly baked *roggebrood*.

Clara and I exchanged smiles. Within minutes of meeting, we exchanged birthdates and realised we were only ten months apart. Shyness was soon forgotten as we chattered about our love of kittens, playing outdoors, our shared enjoyment of Goose Game, which we agreed younger brothers should be forbidden from playing because of their penchant for cheating.

Later that night, tucked in bed, I considered the Master's words, wondering whether my self-pride would ever diminish. Such serious reflections, however, were quickly discarded as I recalled the happy moments shared with Clara. I was more determined than ever to do well in my studies so Papa would reward me with additional visits to the Rubenshuis.

21

Charlotte places the newly discovered document beside Antonia's letter, scanning from one to the other. The same vellum parchment, yellowed and worn. The same cursive handwriting, the descenders sloping to the left with distinctive rounded tails. But this new document has no salutation or signature. Technically, it could have been written by anyone. She looks through a magnifying glass, comparing the writing, searching for similarities and differences. She may not be a graphologist, but she's certain the documents were written by the same person: Antonia Vorsterman.

Extract from booklet, written by Santo Barzetti, originally of Genoa, while in the employ of Meneer Peter Paul Rubens in the city of Antwerpen, June 1621:

Seven preparatory drawings, pen and brown ink on paper, one by one-half Flemish ell, on subject of ancient Greek legend known as Pandora. Created in March 1621 by PPR in Antwerpen. Intended recipient Felipe IV of Palacio Real Madrid. PPR described female subject to FS as 'elegant, but difficult to render with the appropriate emotion, she being a young beauty who proffers gifts to all. The combination of surprise and confidence on her face is a challenge, a mixture of innocence and delight, guile and misapprehension, a sense of yearning and yet a hint of indifference, even disdain on her pretty features. This lady is indeed as fickle as they come.' Seven Pandora drawings lost, June 1621.

The initials *PPR* must refer to Peter Paul Rubens, while *FS* is possibly Frans Snyders, one of Rubens' closest friends and collaborators. The description sounds familiar. Charlotte opens her computer and scrolls through files, searching for a detail in one of the Master's letters to Frans Snyders. She has read this part of the letter dozens of times over the years, but never understood it.

Until now.

After locating the file, she paraphrases as she reads: '18 March 1621, My dear Frans ... My latest subject ... young beauty who proffers gifts to all ... mixture of innocence and delight, guile and misapprehension ... hint of indifference ... as fickle as they come ...'

Rubens hadn't named the female subject in his letter. Charlotte always assumed it was a noblewoman who came to the Master's studio to sit for a portrait. She's certain now it was Pandora. She holds in her hands a seventeenth-century primary source confirming that Rubens created a series of preparatory drawings of the Pandora legend, and within three months, the drawings were lost. Missing. Stolen. Whatever. No longer in the possession of their creator.

She re-reads Barzetti's extract. *Pandora*. Twice it appears. *Pandora*. After all this time.

Staring out the window, she mentally scrolls through the list – memorised after a decade of intense study – of every known artwork by Rubens. His extraordinary oeuvre is one of the many reasons he enjoyed such an exceptional following during his lifetime, and why he is venerated today. His ability to portray the emotions of his characters always captures her imagination. One look at his portrayal of Bathsheba and the bathing beauty's self-confidence is palpable. His interpretation of Samson's downfall focuses on Delilah's wariness. His Solomon highlights the king's calm determination in the midst of strife. Judith's resolve to slay Holofernes, Daniel's desperation for freedom, Thomas' disbelief of his Lord's omnipotence, every emotion depicted with subtlety and skill.

The extent of the Master's repertoire is unrivalled. Biblical stories, allegories, historical scenes, portraits and landscapes, he mastered them all. He painted Venus and Adonis, Perseus and Andromeda, Icarus and Europa, Prometheus and Phaëthon, nearly every myth of ancient Greece and Rome, but the story of Pandora never appeared in his repertoire. Three centuries of scholars have examined his life in painstaking detail, and there has never once been a mention of Rubens painting Pandora. Never presented to a patron, sold at auction, copied by a student or hung on a wall. Rubens' *Pandora* does not exist.

Until now.

She paces the room. The extract says they were lost in June 1621. Does *lost* mean *stolen*? In the letter to her nephew Gerard, Antonia writes that she *learnt how the treasures were removed, concealed within a roll of waxed cloth, carried home beneath a cloak, remaining hidden for at least sixty-five years.* There's no evidence the drawings have ever been discovered. No mention of them in historical documents, diaries, letters or art collections. If someone discovered them – whether thirty or three-hundred years ago, no matter their condition – there would be a hint of their existence. A scholar would have described them in a letter, a student made copies, an art collector listed them in a catalogue. But there are no descriptions, copies or catalogues. Nothing.

Until now.

Searching for Pandora online, Charlotte paraphrases aloud: 'Pandora. Greek mythology. First human woman created by the gods. Each god endowing her with gifts. She opened jar of gifts and released evils on humanity. Gift of hope remained inside after she closed jar. Greek poet Hesiod named her Pandora.'

Charlotte's frown transforms into a smile as she comprehends the magnitude of her discovery. Barzetti's extract, a new primary source, is of unparalleled value. It corroborates another primary source, the letter written by Rubens to Snyders in the same year, confirming Rubens drew the Pandora legend. Antonia's letter is directly linked to Barzetti's extract, confirming her knowledge of certain treasures being hidden, exhorting her nephew to find them. Seven drawings by the most celebrated artist of the Baroque era, hidden away like Tutankhamun's treasure, lost for four centuries, awaiting discovery.

'Incredible! Seven drawings by Rubens. Never acknowledged until now.' Her voice rings out to a deaf audience of floors and walls as she paces around the apartment, desperate to release pent-up energy. Her head is lighter, heart racing, insides vibrating.

Everything around her seems brighter: the shimmering green of the glass frog, raindrops sparkling off the window, even the fat grey snake of the Scheldt gleaming as it winds its way out to sea.

She grabs a notebook and pen, and begins writing, recognising the need to plan carefully: authenticate the letter and Barzetti's extract, cross-reference with other sources, study the map folio for more clues, visit the Begijnhof, speak to Sister Anna. All the while, she must be careful, otherwise the project could be lost to someone else. More importantly, every art dealer, treasure hunter, art academic and journalist will descend on Antwerp if they learn she is pursuing the artistic discovery of the century. The drawings would be worth millions. Unscrupulous people would do anything – cheat, steal, kill – to get their hands on such treasures.

Look for us, the seven *Pandoras* seem to whisper. *Rescue us from our dark existence. Admire our sultry eyes and baffling smiles. Find us.*

'Pan-do-ra,' Charlotte sounds out each syllable. 'Have you crumbled to dust? Or are you still in Vorsterman's secret hiding place?'

22

Charlotte pushes the office door open with her foot, and slides a tray of takeaway coffees onto a shelf.

Miles looks up, his expression unreadable. 'I wasn't expecting you to come in today.'

She hangs up her jacket. 'It's Monday, start of a new week.' She offers him a coffee.

'Thanks.' His voice is subdued. 'You spent Friday in hospital, and you looked exhausted when I saw you on Saturday.'

'I had a lie-in on Sunday.'

His eyebrows twitch. A look of surprise.

She turns on her laptop, eyes the folders stacked on her desk. They're askew, several papers protruding. Has someone been rummaging? Not that she can talk.

Taking a sip of coffee, she glances over the cup and realises Miles is watching her. His eyes flick down, too quickly, to stare at an open book. A stillness envelops the room, thick and heavy. He often blathers one hundred miles an hour, talking about anything and everything. Usually, he's in a constant state of motion – if he isn't pacing, he sits in his chair, twitching his feet, bouncing his knees, tapping a pen on the desk, a book, his chin. But this morning, he is still and silent.

'I have three lectures to prepare and four tutorials,' Charlotte says, 'and I need to look into Arnold's proposal for a joint lecture series.' She presses her lips together. Who's blathering now?

Miles drains his coffee, lobs the empty cup into the bin. 'When I arrived home on Saturday night, I realised my keycard was missing. Thought I left it in the conservation room.'

She picks up a folder. Her palms are sweaty.

He begins jiggling his knee, fingers tapping the edge of the desk. 'I remembered my backpack was on the table. Thinking back, I don't remember seeing the keycard when I shoved everything back into my bag. But then we had dinner and I forgot about it.' He pauses, staring at her. 'Until Theo called me this morning.'

Her cheeks burn. She swallows, her throat dry. *Oh god, he knows.* She wants to backtrack to Saturday and change everything. Not steal the keycard. Not lie and mislead and twist the truth. She should've handled it differently. Should've spoken to Miles and asked his advice. Been upfront about Antonia's letter. Trusted him.

Miles folds his arms across his chest. 'Theo asked why I visited the conservation room at five o'clock on Sunday morning.'

She's light-headed. Her chest tightens. She wants to leave, walk out the door, avoid those fierce blue eyes, but she stays. She knows what's coming. Sick with shame, she must admit what she did, face his anger, accept the consequences.

She opens her mouth to speak, but he keeps talking, his voice tight with fury. 'If you wanted to visit the conservation room again, Charlotte, you could've asked.'

Slipping a hand into her pocket, she draws out the card. Struggles to look at his face.

'Miles.' The word comes out a croak. She coughs, tries again. 'I wasn't thinking straight. I was stupid. I saw the keycard on the table and I thought ...' She stops. No explanation or excuse will be adequate. Nothing can justify what she did.

She slides the keycard across her desk and over to his. 'I'm sorry, Miles. You're completely right, I should've asked. I'm so sorry. Please forgive me.' She holds his gaze for a moment, then looks away, unable to meet his glare. Her stomach twists. She glances at files, folders and marmalade pots, anything but those angry eyes, flashing ice blue. No sign of their warmth now.

He snatches up the keycard. 'You've put me in a difficult position with Theo,' he says, his voice climbing. 'What could be so important–'

'I found a seventeenth-century letter,' she blurts, 'inside the map folio. I wanted to search the rest of the folio to see if there was another–'

'Whoa!' He holds up his hands. 'Slow down.'

She describes finding the letter by accident, then returning to the conservation room and discovering Barzetti's extract. Revealing cursory details about Antonia, the engraver and Rubens, she doesn't mention the stolen drawings. At this stage, the drawings are a fantasy. They may not even exist.

'Antonia Vorsterman? From the map folio?'

'It's an incredible source. There's so little primary source material about Lucas Vorsterman. It's invaluable.' She studies his face: brow furrowed, rubbing his chin. His anger seems to have played out. But what now? Will he forgive her? Will he understand she was being stupidly obsessive, that she didn't think of the consequences until it was too late?

She wants to make it right, to heal the rift between them. She appreciates his humour and his laid-back approach to university life, his enthusiasm for teaching history and debating its theories, his analysis of journal articles, his unruffled attitude towards deadlines and policies and other bureaucratic requirements, his hilarious mimicry of teachers and students, his ability to revive her afternoon fatigue with a cappuccino and sweet *boterwafels* from the café.

She's ruined it all.

'I got carried away with wanting to learn about Rubens. I should've asked about the keycard. I'm very sorry, Miles. And I'm sorry about making things difficult for you with Theo.'

'You're pretty obsessive when it comes to your work.'

She flinches and sinks back in her chair. She can't argue with that. 'What did you tell Theo?'

'I guessed it was you. After we left the conservation room, in the pub, you were distracted. At the time, I assumed it was your concussion, but when Theo called, it made sense.'

Miles picks up a ball made from hundreds of rubber bands stretched over one another and tosses it from hand to hand. Flipping it in a lazy arc, he catches it then fires it back into the opposite hand where it slaps against his palm, resounding like a baseball in a catcher's mitt. Tossing and passing, around and around, and all the while, watching her. 'I told Theo I left my scarf behind and went back to get it on Sunday.'

'Oh.' Her voice is small. 'Thank you.'

He tosses the ball in the air and catches it. 'Let me get this right ... You cut into a priceless seventeenth-century map folio with a scalpel?'

'Not exactly. I used the scalpel to ease the paper away from the cover. Glue in those days was made from animal fat. Depending on its condition, it either becomes brittle and separates, or becomes tacky when heated and lifts easily.'

'Sounds as though you've done this before.'

'I worked in a conservation studio for a year before I started my doctorate.'

'Is there any chance Theo's going to look at the folio and notice something is different?'

'I made sure the paper didn't tear. When the glue wouldn't separate, I used a dry steamer. Afterwards, I warmed the glue again and pressed it back together.'

'Let's hope it worked. I'd prefer not to explain this to him.' He flips the ball between his hands. 'Why didn't you tell us you wanted to see if anything else was inside the map folio? Theo would've understood.'

'Really? You think he would have let me cut into his precious De Wit without a formal proposal in triplicate? I've worked in academia long enough to know I would've had to develop a proposal, wait for it to be considered by a sub-committee–'

'Do you always break the rules?'

She tilts her head. 'Sometimes rules need to be ... reassessed.'

He misses the catch. The ball thuds to the floor and rolls under the desk. He ignores it. 'What is so exceptional about these documents that justifies breaking the rules?'

'It's an invaluable primary source–'

'You've already said that. I'm an historian, too, remember? I get the importance of primary sources. Is there information in these documents that makes them remarkable or unique?'

She reaches for her coffee. An unappetising sheen covers the milky surface. She takes a sip and pretends to savour it while considering her reply. 'I need more time to check the translation. It has some interesting information about Rubens–'

'Why was it hidden inside the map folio? Does it have something defamatory about Rubens? Was he a bigamist or murderer, plagiarist or fraud?'

'It contains ordinary day-to-day stuff … but valuable for a Rubens scholar,' she quickly adds.

'What's Sterck said about it?'

She stares at her desk.

'You haven't told him?'

'I will, but …' She gnaws on her lip. The quivering sensation beneath her ribcage is back, a tiny creature trying to escape. Fluttering. Incessant. She recognises it from yesterday morning, when she sat in the conservation room and held the scalpel. It wriggled within her again when she read Barzetti's extract and recognised the significance of her find, and it returned as she waited for the coffees this morning, knowing she had to return the keycard to Miles' backpack.

'But what?' he asks.

'I'd rather not reveal the existence of the documents to Sterck … yet.'

'Why?'

'I need' – she struggles for the right words – 'more time to … study it and … establish why it was hidden. Imagine if word gets out about the discovery of an incredible new primary source of Rubens. Scholars will descend on Antwerp, demanding–'

'I'm confused. One minute you're calling it ordinary and now you're calling it incredible. Which is it?'

'Both. I don't know. Once I've had more time, I can put together a proposal, discuss it with … Sterck …'

'Is it wise to keep him in the dark? He's your supervisor. Just explain the importance of telling no one until you're ready. He'll understand.'

'No.' She shakes her head. 'It's complicated.'

'If this backfires,' says Miles, 'you'll lose your job. Wouldn't it be safer to let him know?'

Charlotte smooths her palms over the desk, choosing her words carefully. 'Someone close to me had a research idea stolen once, and a co-worker developed it as their own. Years later, when I began working in academia, she warned me to be cautious, not to reveal too much before I had all the facts. Her experience has made me wary.'

His voice mellows. 'It's fine to be careful, but you can't work in a vacuum, Charlotte. Academic theft happens in all institutions.'

'Is it a problem in Antwerp?'

'I wouldn't say it's a *major* problem—'

'But it happens?'

He frowns. 'What's your next step?'

'I'm ... uh ... still putting together a plan.'

'Are you going to visit the Begijnhof?'

'It's on my list.'

'Need some help?'

His offer is so unexpected she's lost for words. 'Thank you. I ... I'll be fine. I'm going to ... to ... study the documents and then ... yes ... I'll visit ...'

'It may be helpful to have someone with you when you discuss the map folio with Sister Anna.'

'I've already caused problems for you, Miles. Made the situation with Theo difficult—'

'Why don't you let me be the judge of that?' he interrupts. 'Theo and I have been mates for years. We're okay.'

The tightness in her shoulders eases. Miles begins tapping a pen on the edge of a book, his energy returning. He may not have forgotten her horrid behaviour, but maybe he's willing to move past it.

'Have you already organised a visit?' she asks.

'Friday at nine.'

She lifts her eyebrows.

He reads her questioning look. 'Sterck is at a conference this week and asked me to meet with Sister Anna to discuss—' He stops. 'Why do you look so surprised? I'm one of his senior lecturers. He often asks for my assistance. I'm not incompetent, you know.'

'I didn't mean ... I just thought ...'

'Yes?' He waits, scowling.

'I assumed you didn't get on with Sterck.' She stumbles over her words, her face reddening. 'I overheard ... the day we met ... the two of you talking about somebody ... knowing your involvement about ... something ...'

'Which is none of your bloody business.' His eyes flash. 'I'll add eavesdropping to your misdemeanours, shall I, along with stealing and breaking rules. Bloody hell, Charlotte, you're difficult. You know that, don't you? And who the hell says you have to like your boss to work with them? Just because *you* have a weird hang-up about him ...'

She stares at the knots in the timber floor, the rubber band ball resting against a table leg. The lightness she'd felt moments ago has disappeared. Once again, she's been intrusive, thoughtless, impulsive.

He drops his hands on the desk. When he speaks, his voice is weary. 'Sterck wants me to ask Sister Anna if there are other historic documents they'd like to donate, and to reassure her the items can be placed in the temporary collection and returned at any time. You want to learn more about the map folio, so you can come with me on Friday. It'll give you a chance to ask questions.'

She wants to say *yes*, to jump at the chance, but hesitates. She's cautious about involving others. 'I'm grateful for your offer, Miles, but ...' She's uncertain how to continue.

He releases a long sigh. 'Can you see this from Sister Anna's perspective? If a lecturer is invited to the Begijnhof through Professor Sterck, who she knows, and another lecturer comes along ... no questions will be raised. She's a former historian herself, worked as a researcher for Brussels City Museum before joining the Begijnhof, so she's interested in history. But if a lone lecturer from the fine arts department contacts her out of the blue, she may be cautious, especially right now. They're all on edge following the recent accident at the Begijnhof and the ongoing investigation.'

Charlotte lowers her gaze to the lapel of his jacket. A thread hangs loose. She resists the urge to reach over and snap it off.

'Are you coming on Friday or not?' he asks.

'Thank you. Yes.' She slumps in her chair.

He reaches for the rubber band ball. 'I've never met a mother superior. I'm picturing a mix of Maria von Trapp and the sharp-tongued nun from *The Blues Brothers*.'

'I may be able to help.'

'How?'

'Six years in a Catholic girls' school. I knew the mother superior quite well.'

'How did you get noticed? Skip class? Smoke behind the sports hall? Climb over the fence to visit the boys' school?'

'Mother superiors don't only notice the students who are misbehaving.'

'Aaaah, of course.' He slaps palm to forehead in mock realisation. 'You were Miss Goody-Two-Shoes. Head prefect? Never put a foot out of place and, if you did, you were never caught, right?'

Charlotte offers a half-smile. 'Something like that.'

With a blink, she's back at Loretto College in Toronto's inner west. Seventeen years old, filled with pride to be selected as a prefect in her final year, a position of honour. But halfway into the first term, she'd been called into the headmistress' office, gently reminded that positive leadership required her to show empathy and encouragement, focus on the needs of the team, be outwardly and not inwardly focused. 'Don't let your position go to your head, Charlotte,' the mother superior had warned.

23

Charlotte walks along De Wapper, the long square crowded with tourists. She increases her pace, enjoying the sensation of her muscles being stretched and autumn sunshine on her face. Somehow, she will find the extra time she needs to accomplish everything on her agenda. What would she give for an extra hour in each day?

She replays her recent visit to nearby Grand Café Horta, where she'd squeezed in a hasty meeting with Arnold to discuss their proposed lecture series.

'Three lectures will cover the essential themes,' said Arnold, talking quickly, full of energy. 'I can focus on the diplomatic links between the courts of Western Europe during the Eighty Years' War, then you can introduce Rubens as one of the key players.'

She'd found Arnold to be an attentive listener as she outlined her ideas about Rubens' diplomatic work in the royal courts of Spain, France and England. As they discussed theories and jotted down a framework for each lecture, her enthusiasm soared.

Charlotte outpaces a tour group, relieved to be breathing fresh air and having a break from being indoors. When she's not presenting lectures or attending tutorials or meetings, she spends every spare moment researching the Vorsterman family in the Rubenianum Institute.

The institute's librarian had recognised her that morning, for her third visit in three days, welcoming her with a wave.

'We'll need to issue you with a staff card,' said the librarian with a laugh, 'if you keep visiting this often.'

Beginning with seventeenth-century sources, Charlotte had studied passages by Flemish sculptor Quellinus in which he mentioned his friend Lucas Vorsterman. She scrutinised Hymans' monograph on the engraver's work, Levin's nineteenth-century work on Flemish artists, an array of modern articles by Wijngaert, Sandrart, Oppenheimer, Luijten, Depauw and Van Hout. She studied passages in Dutch and French until her eyes confused the Dutch *de* with the French *le*.

Every article she read focused on the engraver's work. There was scant information about his private life. A small passage mentioned his inability to work in his later years due to his failing eyesight, how he was cared for by a daughter who was a Zwartezussen nun. Quellinus acknowledged the engraver had several sons and daughters, but gave few details about them. Was Antonia the nun mentioned? Did Vorsterman have more than one daughter? Damn it, why did these historians relegate the women to mere footnotes?

Halfway along De Wapper, she stops to admire the façade of the Rubenshuis. Banners flap in the wind, announcing a temporary exhibition. Without hesitation, she purchases a ticket. What better place to contemplate a Rubens mystery than his former home and studio? What better time to mull over recent events, hoping with her whole heart that Miles will forgive and forget her horrid behaviour?

Ticket in hand, she enters the vestibule. She tries to imagine a servant from yesteryear is standing in the doorway, greeting guests, collecting cloaks and hats, offering pewter goblets of ale, ushering visitors into the presence of the Master of Antwerp.

Her imagination is no match for reality. Hordes of tourists and a group of excited school children wander from one room to the next, heads craning, elbows bumping, mouths gabbling, a murmuring Tower of Babel.

Inserting earphones and turning on Vaughan Williams' 'Lark Ascending', Charlotte blocks out the clamour. She recalls the first art museum she'd enjoyed as a teen. The profusion of Madonnas in Ontario's art museum garnered little interest from her, but the treasures in the courtyard rooms captured her imagination: boxwood miniatures, ivory netsuke, snuff bottles, paintings of Dutch skaters, posters by Toulouse-Lautrec. As she visited more museums, the audio guides became more irksome than inspiring, so she replaced them with music. Over the years, Backstreet Boys and

Foo Fighters gave way to Gardot, Gershwin and Vaughan Williams. With music filling her head, she could switch off from the world, listen to her heart.

As she skirts around the school children, her mother's advice rings in her ears: 'Don't think about whether the artwork or exhibit appeals ... think about the emotion it stirs within you.' Focusing on her emotional response is uppermost in her mind as she enters the Rubenshuis kitchen.

Avondeten met Rubens, declares the exhibition sign. The English translation describes a typical supper with Rubens entertaining his friends Frans Snyders and Jan Brueghel. On the table, arranged like a still-life painting, a brace of partridge sits next to a platter of oysters. A basket overflows with artichokes, quinces and plums. A split melon displays glistening seeds.

'We've chosen a busy time to visit.' A voice hovers from behind, muted by her earphones, but still discernible.

A prickling sensation runs along her neck as she turns, then her breath catches in her throat. Sterck stands a metre away.

He nods in greeting and indicates the children swarming the kitchen.

She offers a half-smile, removes her earphones, tucks them into her pocket.

'Thought I'd pop in for a brief visit,' he says, 'but I forgot how busy it can be midweek.'

'Me too.' She tries to think of something else to say, but her mind is blank.

They study the display on the kitchen table.

'The food is so lifelike,' she says, staring at the plastic plums.

'My brain is expecting an aroma of melon.' He tilts his head back, sniffing at imaginary smells.

'Mmm ... yes.' After a moment, she edges towards the next room, wondering if he'll remain close. Other visitors drift alongside. A school of fish, moving as one.

He stands on her right, closer now. She leans in to examine a display of table linen, patterns in the white damask showing the four seasons, but his nearness is distracting. Did he see her enter the museum and follow her?

Don't be paranoid, she tells herself. They're colleagues with a shared interest in history. Bumping into one another at the city's most popular museum is understandable, inevitable, even.

They stand before a linen press, the thick wooden screw partially unwound, the separated boards displaying folded linen. The intricately carved press is decorated with tiny lions, their mouths agape, and *putti* hiding among foliage.

'Table linen was a significant part of a woman's trousseau in the seventeenth century.' His words come out stilted. 'Of course ... you already know that.'

It dawns on her that he's also self-conscious. Maybe he's racking his brain, like her, to think of conversation topics.

'I wonder if Isabella Brant or Hélène Fourment worked this linen press?' she asks, naming Rubens' wives.

They walk into the dining room together. The long table is set with a starched damask cloth and folded napkins, pewter plates and forks, bone-handled knives, green glass goblets with thick knobbly stems. Vases down the centre of the table contain a rainbow of flowers. Purple asters, orange marigolds, pink rosebuds, yellow freesias.

'My goodness, the flowers are real.' She breathes in deeply, the scent of freesias recalling her mother's garden in early autumn.

'I didn't think freesias were in Europe in the seventeenth century,' says Sterck.

She's only half-listening, picturing a pathway edged with clumps of freesias, her mother sitting beneath a silver birch, a book discarded in her lap, head tilted to the sky. Charlotte swallows hard. Her eyes sting.

Sterck folds his arms across his chest, shakes his head. 'Weren't freesias originally from South Africa and introduced to Europe in the nineteenth century? They wouldn't have been here in Rubens' time ...'

Charlotte is thankful for his chatter about flower cultivation, similar to the way Miles prattles on about various topics, distracting her when she's overwhelmed. Her earlier apprehension is fading. She's suddenly lighter inside.

Walking side-by-side, they stroll through the sculpture room with its domed ceiling, the hallways and bedrooms of the upper floor, the corridor to the Italianate wing, which houses the studio. They exchange comments about the Master's fluency in five languages, the family connections between his wives, the poignancy of the portrait of his firstborn Clara, her rosy cheeks similar to her father's, her pointed chin identical to her mother's. By the time they reach the garden and stand beneath the spreading arms of an ancient oak, their conversation has eased into silence.

He straightens his tie. 'How have you settled into Antwerp?'

'Very well, thank you.'

He tweaks his cufflinks. 'We haven't had much of a chance to talk since you arrived.'

She'd noticed the straightening and tweaking on the day they met. Is it a habit brought on when he's nervous? Is he nervous of her?

'It's been a busy few weeks,' she says, knowing it's a poor excuse for what is actually her avoidance of him.

'I knew your mother a long time ago.' His words are rushed. 'We met when we both lectured at Brussels University. We'd catch the train to Antwerp, browse through the flea market on Sint-Jansvliet, wander through the Rubenshuis, visit another museum after lunch, the Plantin-Moretus or Mayer van den Bergh, before returning to Brussels. A perfect Sunday.'

For a split second, her breathing stops. She is speechless; a lump forms in her throat. For the second time that afternoon, her eyes sting.

Her mother had only spoken about Brussels in relation to her work at the university, never friends, certainly never ex-lovers. Sterck's recollection of their perfect Sunday is personal, almost intimate. She wishes her mother had shared such stories with her, instead of only mentioning the rift that tore them apart. Perhaps in the early days, Sébastien and Rachael enjoyed a relationship filled with contentment and laughter. Are his reminiscences a sign of regret? Sorrow over lost love?

He reaches up to adjust his ruler-straight tie, then stops and lowers his hand to his side. 'I was very sad to hear of her passing. She was a gifted teacher and writer, an outstanding researcher. A special person. Enthusiastic about her work, so lively and witty. I'm very sorry for your loss, Charlotte. It must be difficult for you to not share these experiences with her.' His hand sweeps over the gardens.

'Thank you.' She swallows, her mouth dry.

'You look like her. Same shaped face, same hair. She always wore hers out. Curls everywhere.' He looks down, offers a wistful half-smile to the path.

Charlotte stares up at the branches of the oak, blinking away tears, grappling with the intense emotions that stir within. At the forefront are her mother's revelations about how Sterck betrayed her, stole her idea, presented it to his supervisor. *We were better off without him.* Yet, when Charlotte hears him share his memories of Rachael, she is conflicted, struggling to match her mother's words with this man, who appears respectful and kind. Who is he really?

24

May 28, 1621

The Rubens' kitchen became nearly as familiar to me as my own. Clara, Albert and Nicolaas were uncomplicated and good-humoured, overlooking the barriers that sometimes arise between the families of employer and worker. They conversed with ease, throwing a myriad of questions at me, revealing themselves to be inquisitive.

'Why are your fingers speckled with paint?' This from Nicolaas, the youngest, who had his father's blue eyes and a crop of reddish-blond hair.

'Don't you find it awfully dull sitting in Papa's studio for so long?' asked Albert. 'If that was me, I would die from boredom.' Albert, five years my junior, had inherited his father's rosy lips and sense of curiosity, but had yet to develop the discretion for which his father was famed.

'Stop being impertinent, Albert,' said Clara.

He glared at her, yet his displeasure was soon forgotten when Cook offered us slices of apple dipped in cinnamon sugar.

Clara and I sometimes worked together in the kitchen, stamping butter biscuits or rolling out *speculoos* dough. She was a blonde contrast to my dark curls, her eyes a deep blue while mine were brown. She was plump, dimpled and short in stature, looking younger than her eleven years. By contrast, I was tall and thin with curves that made me look older. To have a sisterly companion brought us both immense delight. Our quick repartee left us constantly giggling, finishing one another's sentences, rarely a moment's silence falling in any room we inhabited.

Today, Cook reached the end of her patience and ordered us from the room. 'Get out, you two,' she said, 'I cannot hear meself think. You be like a couple of ol' hens, cluckin' away.' She flicked a damp dishcloth at us as we ran squealing from the kitchen.

'Clara! Antonia!' a voice called out as we rushed through the dining room.

Mevrouw Rubens appeared in the doorway. A handsome woman, her copper-coloured hair was pulled into a roll at the back of her neck, accentuating a high forehead, pointed chin and arched eyebrows, giving her a perpetual look of happy surprise. Her mouth was a blend of two expressions: her pursed lips suggesting displeasure at our rowdiness, yet the hint of a smile implying delight in our laughter. She was dressed in a black gown of stiff cloth, the high collar curved around her jaw, plain but for a single ruff of white lace. A brooch with a dangling pearl sat at her throat.

'I have a task for you girls.' She indicated a basket filled with crumpled linen.

We joined her at the table. I folded tablecloths and napkins as Mama had taught me. Pressing linen was normally my least favourite chore because Mama used the time to read aloud from a psalter. Her monotonous tone lulled me into a state of indifference towards the intricate textiles and towards the psalms, too. Although Mama reminded me of the importance of married woman having a cupboard filled with expensive cloth, which should be used to adorn the dining table to impress guests, I couldn't understand why possessions should be used in this way. 'Tis a waste of time to be obsessing over mere cloth, when time could be better spent in more interesting pursuits.

Pressing linen in the Rubens household, however, took on a new appeal when it was accompanied by engaging conversation.

'Antonia,' asked Mevrouw Rubens while unscrewing the linen press, 'which topics do you most enjoy in the classroom?'

'History is interesting,' I replied, 'especially King Henry's many wives, although I felt sorry for poor Anne of Cleves.'

When the folded linen was in place, Clara turned the handle, lowering the boards until they pressed downwards. I ran my hands over the outer frame of the press, poking my fingers into the tiny mouths of carved lions' heads, tracing the *putti* hiding in foliage. My family's press had the same function, yet fewer embellishments.

'My favourite topic is geography.' I continued chattering about my favourite maps by Hondius and Blaeu, relieved I didn't have to listen to my pious, albeit loving mama, intone the psalms.

Mevrouw Rubens turned to her daughter. 'Wouldn't you like to take lessons on geography and history, Clara?'

Clara continued turning the handle. 'My week is already so busy with music, embroidery, learning Spanish and French. Whatever would I want with maps and history books?'

Mevrouw Rubens caressed her daughter's cheek. 'Indeed.'

Clara stood back so I could take over turning the handle. My arms ached as I finished the turns.

Mevrouw Rubens hooked the empty basket through her arm. 'The sun is shining. Go find the boys and play outside.'

The Rubens' garden was spacious and many times larger than my family's simple courtyard. In the style of a French *parterre*, it comprised symmetrical beds with hedges and gravel pathways. A massive oak tree spread its branches over the northern corner.

Our favourite game was *verstoppertje*. We took turns to be the finder, while the others hid behind the garden pavilion, amongst the hedges, under piles of hay in the stables. Once, Nicolaas crouched in a giant terracotta urn and it took such a long time to find him I feared he was injured and lying senseless somewhere. The cheeky youngster finally popped out of his hiding place and gave me such a fright.

On days when the rain was heavy, we continued the game indoors. Her father's studio was off-limits, but the rest of the house was our playground. Clara showed me ingenious hiding places, some of which were large enough for us to crouch together to continue our whispered conversations.

Clara became the sister I had always longed for, understanding me like no other. Even Betja van Helst, my friend from Eikenstraat, looked at me disapprovingly last week when I shared with her my preference for studying history rather than stitching my sampler. Only Clara appreciated my eagerness for academic studies, my determination to prove I am as bright as any boy. She was the confidante to whom I whispered my dismay at a future limited to being a wife and mother. I longed to have the financial means to live independently, surrounded by scholarly pursuits rather than bawling infants and a demanding husband. Clara was the only friend who listened to my outpourings. We would always remain the best of friends, even if our families guided us along different paths.

25

The red-brick walls surrounding the Begijnhof stretch twelve feet high and enclose an entire block. Miles scans the sightseeing app on his phone, offering snippets to Charlotte as they walk the outer perimeter. 'Founder Archduchess Isabella decreed its gates be locked at sunset ...'

Charlotte tugs at the high neckline of her navy blouse. Her hair is pulled into its usual braided bun, every curl tucked away, sensible and business-like. Glancing down at her outfit, she wonders whether she's overdone it; she suspects she's more suitably dressed for an interview to join the Begijnhof as a novice. Wishes she'd worn one of her mother's bright scarves.

They stop in front of massive wooden doors, large enough for a truck to pass through, and read the tarnished nameplate fixed to the wall: *Begijnhof Sint-Catharina*. After passing a gatehouse, they emerge into a large courtyard. Brick buildings rise three storeys high on all sides, each façade decorated with crow-stepped gables, typical of sixteenth-century houses of the Low Countries. A cobblestone drive borders the square, with a garden in the centre. Rows of apple, pear and plum trees, scarlet with autumn foliage, stand next to raised vegetable beds. The courtyard is deserted.

Chalky statues of the Virgin and Child peer out from the semi-circular tympanum above a chapel door. Blue-and-white plastic tape stretches around the lower façade of the belfry, a warning for visitors to stay back.

Charlotte's eyes are drawn to the top of the belfry. 'Willem mentioned a piece of masonry came loose and injured a visitor.' She indicates a pile of broken bricks next to the wall. 'Looks like more than one piece of masonry.'

'I read about it in the local newspaper,' says Miles. 'Some bricks came loose, and a visitor fell while jumping out of the way. Minor injuries, nothing serious. But the Begijnhof is now under investigation by local authorities and the Diocese.' He indicates a building with an ornate façade. 'Let's try over there.'

As they cross the courtyard, a door opens and a woman appears. She rushes down the steps with such speed her short salt-and-pepper hair ruffles into a crest, her pleated skirt puffing around her as she strides away.

'Excuse me?' Charlotte calls out in Dutch.

The woman turns. 'Can I help you?' She wraps a bulky grey cardigan across her chest, and the voluminous collar engulfs her petite frame. She reminds Charlotte of a pigeon, dressed in grey, small earnest face, deep-set eyes.

'We have an appointment with the mother superior,' says Miles, also speaking Dutch. 'We're from the university.'

'I'll show you to her office.' The woman waves for them to join her. 'Is this your first visit to Sint-Catharina's?' Not waiting for a reply, she launches into a commentary as if giving a prescribed tour. 'There's a difference between a *beguinage* and *begijnhof*. The first is a house where lay religious women live together. But a *begijnhof* is bigger, with a courtyard, its own chapel and infirmary.' A shy glance. 'I could tell from your accents you're not local.'

Nearby, an old Citroën is parked against the wall, its bumper dented and sky-blue body streaked with rust. Autumn leaves sit in sodden clumps against the worn tyres. The woman points at the words engraved along sandstone lintels above the door to each building. Faded paint highlights the word *Ziekenhuis*. 'A century ago this was the only hospital in Antwerp for the poor. Back then, most of the sisters were nurses.' She indicates the next building. 'The school was closed at the outbreak of World War Two and never re-opened.'

Following her to the office, they climb stone steps worn into curves. The buildings have an air of decay. Shabby window frames, cracked panes of glass.

Inside, the woman indicates chairs against the wall. 'You can wait there while I let Sister Anna know you're here.'

Too restless to sit, Charlotte roams the cavernous foyer. The large black-and-white floor tiles remind her of a chessboard. Tucked in the corner is a familiar piece of furniture. Polished smooth and resting on squat legs, the box-like table is made from multiple planks stacked together. Rising from the top, a thick wooden screw extends over a metre high.

'It's a linen press,' says a voice behind her. 'Have you seen one before?'

'I saw one in the Rubenshuis yesterday,' replies Charlotte, 'but I've never seen one in operation.'

The woman's cheeks are pink with spider veins. 'Allow me.' As she turns the handles, the wood groans and the box rises an inch from its base, gaps appearing between the planks. 'After folded linen was inserted, the screw was wound back down,' – the woman turns the handles clockwise – 'left for hours, even days, and *voila*, linen with sharp creases. Rather ironic for such an item to be in a *begijnhof*, considering women enter our doors to seek a life away from the trappings of marriage and materialism.'

'Makes it all the more special it has a home in the Begijnhof,' says Charlotte, 'to remind everyone how far women have come over the centuries.'

'Indeed.' The grey-haired woman smiles, introduces herself as Sister Anna. 'You're the Rubens expert from Canada. I'm pleased to meet you; Sébastien has told me all about you. Your Dutch is excellent – I'm guessing your relatives are from Belgium. Hubert is a common name in Flanders. Is your father from here?'

Charlotte's eyes widen. 'Father? No … my name … my mother … her grandmother was from Namur, but my mother was Canadian. I have her name.'

Miles crosses the foyer, extends his hand. 'Thank you for seeing us, Sister.'

'Please call me Anna. Shall we have tea upstairs in my office?' As they climb the stairs, she talks about Sint-Catharina's. 'There aren't many *begijnhofs* in existence today. We don't take formal religious vows and can leave at any time, but most *begijnen* promise not to marry for as long as they stay. One of our longest serving *begijnen*, Sister Léa, left Sint-Catharina's three weeks ago to return to her family in Arlon.'

Charlotte follows behind, wondering what Sterck had told the mother superior about her.

After entering an office, Anna waves them to chairs. The *begijn* from the courtyard appears with a tea tray, slides it onto the desk and scurries off. 'Thank you, Edith.'

'Professor Sterck sends his apologies,' says Miles. 'He had to attend a conference.'

Anna pours tea, passes cups, offers a plate of almond biscuits. 'Sébastien and I met at a history symposium. I'm pleased the university has found the almanacs interesting.'

'Primary sources are always valuable,' says Miles. 'We'd be happy to receive more donations.'

'Our library catalogue hasn't been updated in decades.' Anna turns to Charlotte, who nibbles a biscuit. 'Sébastien told me all about your interest in Rubens and the map folio. He said it was dedicated to the artist. Is it for a Rubens-inspired Grand Tour?'

Biscuit crumbs catch in Charlotte's throat, starting a coughing fit. She tries to talk. 'Not ... sure ...'

Miles focuses his attention on Anna. 'The items you donated have been placed in our temporary collection. If you'd like them returned ...'

Charlotte tries a mouthful of scalding tea, but it makes the coughing worse.

'Let me get you a glass of water.' Anna hurries from the room.

'What' – *cough* – 'are you doing?'

'If I can reassure her–'

'But–' Another convulsion sends her doubling over.

'Trust me.' He pats her between the shoulder blades.

Anna returns, places a glass of water on the desk in front of Charlotte. Resuming her seat, she turns a benign gaze on Miles. 'We don't need the almanacs. They can be placed in your permanent collection. It was the map folio I wanted to discuss.'

Charlotte finishes the water, clears her throat.

Anna clasps her hands together. 'The folio belongs to Sister Petra. She's nearly eighty, sick with a chest infection, making a slow recovery.'

'I'm sorry to hear that,' says Charlotte. 'When she recovers, I'd very much like to speak with her about the map folio, its history ...'

Anna frowns. 'It was sent to the university by mistake.'

Charlotte softens her voice. 'I won't take up too much of her time.'

'The map folio has been in her family for generations. That's all she knows.' Anna turns to Miles. 'Petra would like it returned as soon as possible.'

'If it's okay, the university's conservator would like to check the spine, make sure it's stable, then we'd return it,' says Miles. 'We should only need it for about a week.' He offers his best smile.

'Mmm ... very well,' murmurs Anna. Crossing to a dented filing cabinet, she rummages through folders, pulls out a loose page. The paper is flimsy, typewritten words on both sides faded. 'Years ago, before my time, a number of items were delivered to the Begijnhof as part of a bequest from Petra's mother, who died in 1982. The linen press, some large pieces of furniture now scattered throughout our buildings, several smaller items. This' – she waves the letter – 'mentions a portfolio box containing a map folio and other documents.'

'Portfolio box?' Charlotte's eyebrows arch up.

Anna reads aloud: '*Shallow black portfolio box with lid, containing letters, diaries, documents and map folio.*'

Miles leans forward. 'Do you know where it is?'

Anna shakes her head. 'It may be in our library. I don't want to disturb Petra while she's resting. Sadly, our library is a Herculean pile of dust.'

Charlotte glances at Miles, who returns a weak smile.

Anna moves to the window, motioning for them to follow. 'You can talk to Edith. She's been working in the library, clearing it to make room for our new second-hand clothing shop. If the portfolio box is there, she may know where it is. If she finds it, I'll need to ask Petra if she's happy for others to see it.' Anna gestures in the direction of the chapel. 'The *bibliotheek* is next to the belfry. I hope you're not allergic to dust. Poor Edith's been sneezing for days.'

26

As they cross the courtyard, Charlotte replays the meeting in her head. Years spent overseeing buildings in a state of disrepair would try the patience of a saint, yet Sister Anna was composed, with a no-nonsense approach. The informal atmosphere of the office – begonias on the window ledge, jumble of walking sticks in the corner, basket of *petanque* boules – reminded her of the cosy disarray of her mother's study. The coughing attack couldn't have come at a worse time, but in the end, Miles had done well to let the university retain the map folio for another week.

They arrive at the library. The word *Bibliotheek* is highlighted in cursive letters along the sandstone lintel. Pushing open the door, they enter a gloomy foyer.

'Hello?' Miles calls out.

The foyer has the same black-and-white checkerboard tiles as the office building, but these are covered in a film of grime. Cardboard cartons are stacked around the room. On the right are two open doorways, one in darkness, the other spilling a rectangle of light across the floor. The silence is punctuated by a volley of high-pitched sneezes. *Esch-ooo! Esch-ooo!*

The woman who showed them to the office appears in the lit doorway, a handkerchief to her nose. 'Have you finished your meeting?'

'Sister Anna suggested we chat with you about the map folio,' says Miles.

The woman's brow creases.

'You are Sister Edith?'

'Yes, but the map folio belongs to Petra.' She beckons them into the room, crosses to a table, and picks up an armful of notebooks.

Charlotte pauses in the doorway. Dust coats every surface, thickened over the years to chalky powder. Cobwebs tremble from light fittings. Shelves are packed with a clutter of leather-covered books and ledgers, spines cracked, gilt lettering worn away, titles now indecipherable shadows. Interspersed among the leather relics are hardback books with torn jackets, folders aged a mustard yellow. Three huge tables are piled with tatty journals, several stacks having collapsed and tumbled to the floor, as if vomited up by a library-dwelling monster.

Miles stands behind her. Emits a gasp.

'Thought your office was bad,' she whispers. Stepping around the mess, she moves to the nearest table, which is filled with periodicals. '*Nouvelle Revue Théologique 1908*,' she reads.

Miles calls out, 'This material is amazing. Is the entire library like this?'

Edith sneezes and blots her nose with the handkerchief. 'The foyer is finished, but there's another room like this next door, plus two more upstairs. I'm making slow progress. How can I help you?'

Charlotte rubs her dusty fingertips together. 'Anna said a portfolio box arrived at the convent in 1982. It contained the map folio, along with some old documents. She thought it may be in the library.'

'I haven't seen any portfolio box. Would've arrived before my time. I cleared the foyer in August and sent several cartons to the university. The map folio was accidentally caught up with the almanacs. They look similar.'

'It's described as a shallow black box, large enough to hold the map folio.' Charlotte uses her hands to show the rough size.

'I haven't seen anything that big, but the library is filled with clutter. Would be easy to lose anything in here.'

'Has Sister Petra mentioned it to you?'

'You could ask her yourselves.' Edith's affable demeanour flickers with mild irritation.

Miles returns a yellowed newspaper to the table. 'We understand she's not well. Anna suggested we speak with you.'

Edith continues packing notebooks into a carton. 'Could be anywhere. The Begijnhof is filled with old items, some of it interesting, much of it broken, unusable ... should've been cleared out years ago. Petra's always been curious about old objects ... art, furniture, books, photographs. Enjoys anything with a unique history. We've visited many museums together. My favourites are the small ones, like the Mayer van den Bergh. Beautiful collection of Pieter Bruegels.'

She's lost in reflection, staring at the wall with such intensity that Charlotte turns, hoping the portfolio box has miraculously appeared on a shelf, conspicuous and alone. But the shelf holds only periodicals.

'We visited the Royal Library Museum last month,' says Edith, 'for an exhibition on seventeenth-century mapmakers. Petra told me that several of the maps were like her *moeke*'s.'

'Like her what?' asks Miles.

'*Moeke* is an old Flemish nickname for *Mum*. Not used much today,' says Charlotte. 'Did Petra explain what she meant?'

'She never shares much, but she was happy on the way home ... kept humming and smiling to herself.'

'Has Petra talked to you about the map folio?'

'No, but I'm sure she'll feel better soon, so you can ask her yourself.' Edith purses her lips. Placing an armload of notebooks into the carton, she picks up a tape gun, drags it across the lid. A screech fills the room, suggesting the discussion is over.

'If you find it,' says Miles, 'we'd be grateful if you'd let us know.'

Charlotte offers her a business card. 'Thank you for your time.'

Edith curls the card in her palm. Looking at the floor, she scrapes the toe of her shoe, making criss-cross patterns in the dust. Her mouth softens, furrowed brow smooths, her irritation dissolving as quickly as it arrived. 'Sorry I couldn't help.' Burrowing into the collar of her cardigan, the tip of her chin disappears, reminding Charlotte again of a pigeon, this time fluffing its feathers, trying to keep warm.

27

Albert stood in the courtyard, hands over his eyes, counting aloud. Clara and I skirted around the back of the studio, entered the vestibule and tiptoed the length of the room. A door to our right led into her father's studio, prohibited from our games of *verstoppertje*. Another door led to the courtyard where Albert was counting.

Clara pressed a finger to her lips. Smiling, she pointed towards a large storage chest against the wall.

'No,' I whispered. 'We'll be locked inside when the latch closes and have no way of escape.'

She shook her head. 'Maria emptied it yesterday. The latch is broken and the chest will be removed tomorrow for repair.' Clara grasped the heavy lid and heaved it open. Gathering her skirts, she climbed inside. 'Come on, Antonia. It's perfect.'

Albert's muffled voice rang out: '*Ik kom.*'

'He's coming. Hurry!'

I clambered inside, curled myself into a ball, and rested my head upon bent knees. Easing the lid down, we descended into darkness. All I could hear was our stifled breathing and the pounding of my heart.

A door opened, footsteps crossed the vestibule and stopped. A bench creaked. 'Please sit,' I heard Meneer Rubens say.

I squeezed my eyes shut so tightly shadows danced before my closed lids.

A second set of footsteps crossed the floor. The bench creaked again.

Meneer Rubens began talking. 'We have discussed this issue many times. There is nothing left to say. Yet, you persist in returning to it, which I find most annoying.' His voice was stern but controlled.

'A great deal of my time is spent assisting the Archduchess, especially since the failing health of the Archduke, on negotiations with the troublemakers to the north. I do not have the patience nor the inclination to re-open the matter which you insist on disputing. It is inconsequential compared to the troubles besieging our city with which I am encumbered.'

There was a muffled cough, a faint clearing of the throat. Was the recipient of the Master's reprimand about to speak?

Meneer Rubens continued: 'Let me remind you once more about my success in being granted operating privilege for all my works. The magistrates have agreed to give me the exclusive right to control the reproduction of any of my created works, including engravings. Publishers have reproduced engravings of my artwork in the past, as you have done, but the right to own those reproductions and decide how and when they are produced, printed and promulgated now rests with me alone.' His voice had risen. 'Controlling that privilege is critical to protecting my work and securing my livelihood.'

Another cough, more clearing of the throat and then the recipient of the Master's displeasure finally spoke. It was my father.

Reaching out in the dark, I found Clara's hands and squeezed tight.

'With utmost respect, Master Rubens, I am also eager to secure my livelihood.' My father spoke in his usual poised manner. 'Engravers are not simply copyists. Like painters and sculptors, they are recognised as artists by the guild. As guild members, engravers are entitled to the same rights as any artist which—'

'There is no need to lecture me, Lucas, on the rights of guild members. I am fully cognisant of those rights.'

The bench groaned. Footsteps crossed the floor. I heard the rustle of stiff fabric, leather soles turning on stone tiles.

Meneer Rubens continued: 'While I concede the engravings display a highly skilled style, they are copied from paintings and, therefore, the operating privilege must be retained by the painter as the creator, not the engraver.'

Despite the stuffiness of our coffin-like space, goosebumps prickled my arms. I closed my eyes once more, squeezing back the tears that threatened to flow. I tried not to imagine the consequences of being discovered. As the argument between our fathers escalated, Clara pressed her legs against mine, recognising our shared fear.

'I mean no disrespect, Master Rubens.' Papa's voice was calm. The bench emitted a faint groan as he stood. 'However, the skill of engravers is well known. The engravers' art form is different from painters and requires unique skills. You have admitted that wielding the burin is beyond your proficiency. For this reason, you have hired me—'

'Yes, Lucas, you are correct,' interrupted the Master. 'I pay you to make engraved copies of works created by me.' His voice rose to a crescendo. 'You seem to have forgotten that pertinent fact.'

I flinched. My fear of discovery diminished next to the consequences Papa would face if he continued angering Meneer Rubens in this way. Would he be dismissed from his employment? Would he be banned from the Rubenshuis? My visits would come to an end, my friendship with Clara reduced to distant sightings while attending mass or visiting Grote Markt. I silently urged Papa to hold his tongue, show humility, accept the Master's decision for the sake of his employment, our family, my happiness.

'Lucas.' Meneer Rubens softened his voice. 'We have enjoyed a prosperous relationship and collaborated on many projects. You are, without doubt, the finest engraver in Antwerpen. Do not abandon all you have worked so hard to achieve.'

A long pause. 'Yes, Master.'

'You have such talent, my friend.' The Master's voice was gentle. 'I hope you will stay in my service for many years, but I hope you can understand my unwillingness ... my inability ... to hand you the operating privilege of engravings based on my work. It cannot happen. The magistrates have deemed it so. Let us have no more talk of this.' Footsteps sounded across the tiled floor. 'I am eager to see the engraving of my *Lion Hunt*. I leave for the French court soon and the Marquis de Chaussin wants to commission a similar painting. I want to show him the engraving so he can decide if it is the type of hunt scene he desires.'

Footsteps retreated. A door opened.

Meneer Rubens continued. 'I also want to finish the preliminary drawings for King Felipe's commission of *Pandora*. Are you familiar with the ancient Greek legend ...' The voice faded as the door closed.

I breathed a sigh of relief that Papa had held his tongue and accepted the Master's decision as I had silently begged him to do.

'Let's go,' whispered Clara.

We eased the lid up and peered out, checking the vestibule was empty. Running into the garden, we took cover from the rain under the oak tree, clinging together, trembling.

Papa did not speak as we walked home. He spent the evening cloistered in his workroom, not appearing for our family meal. Mama carried a tray with his favourite pork stew to the study. The tray was removed at nightfall, the untouched pork sitting in congealed lumps upon the plate.

28

Charlotte arches her back, stretching until her shoulder blades nearly touch. She has been sitting, stooped, for far too long. Forty-eight hours confined to the conservation room, broken only by brief sojourns to the bathroom, breaks in the hallway to gobble sandwiches, and returning to her apartment at night to catch a few hours' sleep. This time, she muses with a droll smile, Theo and Miles know she's here.

Theo had ushered her into the conservation room on Friday evening, handing her a visitor's keycard. 'How long are you planning to stay?'

'Most of the weekend, if that's okay. I'll go home to sleep, but I'm keen to study the folio before it's returned to the Begijnhof on Monday.'

Theo removed the dust cloth and opened the map folio. 'The restoration specialist matched up the torn edges. The spine was re-stitched and re-glued. I've photographed every page so they can be studied once it's returned.'

She sensed Theo's dismay at having to return the rare De Wit to the Begijnhof, and shares his disappointment. This may be her last opportunity to study it in detail.

The wall clock clicks to eight pm. It will be dark outside, and she still needs to prepare for tomorrow's tutorial. Although pleased with her progress, Charlotte is overwhelmed with the amount of information she's gleaned. As she gathers her notes, there's the sound of a keycard being swiped. The door beeps, opens a crack and then stops, blocked by the tilted chair she'd placed under the handle.

'Charlotte?' Miles calls out.

She slides the chair away. Although the campus attacks haven't touched her personally, she recognises a growing tendency to check over her shoulder, scan for strangers following her, look for anyone acting suspicious.

Miles opens the door. 'What's with the barricade?'

'Just being cautious.'

'How did your research go? Find anything interesting?'

'Too much.' She squeezes her eyes shut for a few seconds, hoping the tiredness will ease.

'I'll be your sounding board.' He sits, smiling broadly.

'My brain is scrambled, Miles. Not sure I can string two thoughts together.' She picks up a page covered in scrawl.

'Bounce a few ideas off me. Start with that.' He indicates the page in her hand.

Charlotte hesitates. Sure, bounce a few ideas off Miles, but reveal her full hand? She's not ready. But he is gently persistent, his enthusiasm catching. She feels herself gravitating towards his openness, softened by his crooked smile and shining eyes.

'I found more of those dark blue letters. Seven letters on each of the country maps.' She opens her notebook, scans the list, each map highlighting the same letters: D-N-A-P-R-A-O.

Miles studies the page. 'Do they highlight places where Rubens visited?'

'No. He may have visited Nonio in Piedmont, but never Penryn in Cornwall or Dalchork in Scotland.' She remains tight-lipped about the word that is spelt when the letters are unscrambled. And there it is again – those underlying sensations that draw herself to him, urging her to ask his advice and share the excitement of her discovery. She can't resist.

She moves her chair so they sit side-by-side, adjusts the microscope until it's focused on the decorative border. Her limbs feel lighter, her energy growing. 'I found more references to Rubens. Each miniature cityscape pinpoints a specific place he lived, each ruler one of his patrons.' She holds her breath for a few seconds, waiting for his reaction, wondering if he will notice her excitement, feel the buzz of energy.

Miles peers through the microscope.

She indicates the figure wearing a triple crown. 'At first I thought it was a generic representation of the Pope, but in the background is St Peter's Basilica and two symbols—'

'Eagle and dragon?'

'The Borghese crest. Paul the Fifth, from the Borghese family, commissioned St Peter's façade and was his most influential patron when Rubens lived in Rome.' She points to another figure. 'Charles the First of England, with symbols of a rampant lion, fleur-de-lis and harp from his coat of arms, and shown wearing the distinctive hat from the trial leading to his execution. This figure is Marie de' Medici with Notre Dame ... Philip the Fourth at El Escorial. They're not generic rulers. Each one is a patron of Rubens, depicted alongside the cities where he lived. The page is a homage to Rubens.'

'Why would Antonia commission maps to honour Rubens? Wasn't her father dismissed by Rubens and his career damaged?'

'I didn't realise you knew so much about Vorsterman.'

'I browsed a few books on your shelf.'

She wonders whether he also browsed through her folders. Surely he wouldn't be so intrusive. But who is she to point the finger?

'What else have you found?' he asks.

Tiredness gone, she points at the title cartouche on the first map. 'Europa enthroned, wearing brightly coloured Classical robes, dignified, esteemed. Now look.' She turns to the map of the Low Countries. 'Another title cartouche, but different. A man wearing elegant seventeenth-century clothes, not seated on a throne, but a simple bench, not proud or dignified. Look at his hands and feet.'

Miles peers through the microscope. 'Manacles?'

'Yes!' Her voice is loud with excitement; impatient to share her findings, her earlier cautions are forgotten. She turns the page. 'Map of the Germanic States with another title cartouche and the same man. This time, no manacles, but he's missing an ear. The next one' – she flips to the *Italies* – 'man in a pillory' – map of Iberia – 'same man behind bars.'

'Manacles, severed ear, pillory, jail,' says Miles. 'They're all symbols of a common thief.'

'It's Lucas Vorsterman.' She blurts the words before she can stop herself.

'How do you know?'

She hesitates, but only briefly. Her inner voice says to trust him. 'In her letter, Antonia mentions that her father always wore a particular cap whenever he worked at home … a red felt cap with a tassel. She kept it after his death as a keepsake and bequeathed it to her nephew Gerard. Paintings from that era often depict men wearing hats, but large ones. Wide-brimmed, decorated with feathers, worn outdoors to show social status. Her father's felt cap was worn indoors to keep warm.'

Charlotte points at the map for *Anglia*. The title cartouche shows a man sitting on a bench, his hands tied with rope. He wears the clothes of a gentleman: lace collar, coat with slashed sleeves, beribboned hose. On his head is perched a cap with a tassel, tinted bright red.

'The cartouches show the same man. Identical pointed beard, shoulder-length wavy hair. The figure is too small to detect individual facial features, and most men of that era wore their hair in that way, so it's not enough to indicate the figure is Lucas Vorsterman. But the red cap? It's not in keeping with the outdoors dress of a gentleman. Antonia describes her father wearing it in the privacy of his home. Also, look at the colouring of the figures. In every title cartouche, the man's clothes are muted browns and greys, while the cap is bright red, to help it stand out.'

'Why would Lucas Vorsterman be depicted as a criminal?'

She's gone too far to backtrack now, caught up in the thrill of the mystery. 'When the letters D-N-A-P-R-A-O are unscrambled, they spell Pandora. Every page has seven highlighted letters, all spelling Pandora. Seven letters. Seven maps. Seven Pandoras.'

'As in the ancient Greek legend?' asks Miles.

'Barzetti's extract mentions that Rubens created drawings of the Pandora legend,' she says, 'but they were lost.'

'And you think …'

'I'm not exactly sure what I think.' She waves her hand at her pile of notes.

'No wonder your brain feels scrambled after forty-eight hours of this.'

She picks up a second page, unable to remain silent. Turning to the Low Countries map, she trains the lens along the border. 'With the naked eye, the border looks like a series of uneven, cross-hatched lines, angled to the right. But magnified, you can see tiny script inside the border.' She points to the top left corner, translating the first line. 'The verse begins here, with the words *volt deze woorden, pas op* ... follow these words, take heed ...'

He adjusts the lens. 'Difficult to make out.'

'Old Flemish. I haven't finished the translation yet. Each country map has a verse in a different language. This one's Flemish, the Germanic map has a German verse, the French map has French and so on. Each verse has six lines. Six verses. Six languages. Six country maps.'

He looks at her wide-eyed.

'The more mysteries I find, the more bewildering it gets.' She pushes the microscope aside.

He stands, paces around the table. 'What have you found out about Antonia Vorsterman?'

'I've studied everything they have on Lucas Vorsterman at the Rubenianum Institute. Not much is known about his family. Married Anne Franckx. Antonia is the only daughter mentioned by name. Not sure if there were any other daughters. Three sons are named. Lucas the Younger followed in his father's footsteps and became an engraver. No information on Niels, so maybe he died young. Hendrik worked in the law courts, married, had at least four children. Hendrik's eldest was Gerard, who became a merchant and is the nephew Antonia wrote to. That's it. Nothing more on Antonia.'

Miles stops pacing. 'You're going to speak to Sterck about this, aren't you? Charlotte, you can't keep this to yourself.'

'I'm not keeping it to myself. I've shared it with you.'

'He's your supervisor. He should know.' Miles jabs the air above the map folio. 'This is the property of–'

'Sister Petra,' she interrupts, 'and it's being returned to her tomorrow morning. But, if *begijnen* take vows of poverty and can't own property, then maybe it's owned by the Begijnhof–'

'Charlotte, come on. You're talking semantics. What about Antonia's letter? Who owns that? When the map folio is returned to the Begijnhof tomorrow, will you hand over Antonia's letter as well?'

She swallows, shifts her gaze from the map folio to her notes. *Her* discovery. *Her* theory about stolen Rubens drawings. *Her* opportunity to unearth the artistic masterpieces of the century.

'Does anyone else know about Antonia's documents?' he asks.

'I've briefed a document analyst, Oscar Duval, in Brussels, and I'm meeting him on Tuesday. He's going to assess them, determine their authenticity and age. But no one else knows ...'

Miles lets out a harsh laugh. 'You sure about that? On a busy campus, nothing remains hidden for long. Someone will have heard rumours. It's impossible to have secrets in this place.'

29

Charlotte stands in the doorway, mouth agape. Her satchel slips from her shoulder, drops to the floor. She leans back against the door, forcing it closed. The sharp *click* of the latch striking home echoes around the apartment.

The floor is littered with papers, folders and books. Cupboards hang open, drawers upended, contents scattered. A potted bromeliad tipped on its side, dirt strewn across the window ledge. The glass frog sits benignly on the coffee table, staring at her with sightless eyes.

Whoever searched the apartment has left behind an aura of hot, frustrated energy. This was not a careful methodical search, but a frenzied ransacking.

She studies the door frame, handle and twin locks. No damage. The door wasn't jemmied. Whoever entered the apartment had a key, and closed the door behind them when they left. *What if they're still here?* a voice in her head insists. Light-headed, she leans against the wall to steady herself, and listens carefully for the slightest sound. The apartment is silent.

Stepping around scattered books and papers, she walks into the bedroom. A whirlwind has struck. Bedding flung aside, drawers half-open, clothes strewn. She locates a zippered jewellery pouch inside the bedside cabinet. The few pieces of jewellery she brought to Antwerp – more sentimental than expensive – are still inside. Her passport sits in the drawer, untouched, alongside a dish of coins.

This isn't a crime of petty theft. The perpetrator was searching for a specific item.

Her chest grows tight with fear. She tugs open the closet, pushes aside clothes, gropes for a suitcase at the back. It hasn't moved from where she placed it last week. She drags it onto the bed, and her fingers fumble with the zip. Inside, nestled among the few summer clothes she brought from Toronto, is a thin bundle wrapped in a turquoise scarf. She unwraps the scarf and holds the two pages. Her hands tremble as relief floods through her. Antonia's letter and Barzetti's extract are safe. For now.

Moving through the apartment, she looks behind doors, in closets, overcome with the need to check every corner. She rights chairs, returns cushions to the sofa, hangs clothes, replaces books on shelves, all the while checking if anything is missing. As far as she can tell, nothing was taken.

Only once the apartment has been returned to its usual neat appearance does she stop. She stands in front of the window with her back to the view, hands on hips, jaw clenched. Glaring at the frog, she commands it to reveal its secrets. 'Talk, damn it. Tell me what you saw.'

The frog returns her stare. Impassive.

She's already dismissed the idea of calling the police. All she could tell them is that she locked the door when she left for work at eight o'clock this morning and it was locked when she arrived home this evening. With no sign of forced entry and nothing missing, the police may not even consider it a break-in. The perpetrator must have used a key.

She imagines explaining her suspicions to the police: someone tried to steal two valuable seventeenth-century documents, which were hidden in the apartment and are technically owned by a reclusive *begijn*, who may or may not know of their existence.

'How did you come by these documents, Ms Hubert?' the police officer would ask.

Misappropriated sounds milder than *stolen*, but it won't change her dishonesty. Forget calling the police. She's on her own.

She pinches the bridge of her nose. *Think, damn it.*

Wrapping her arms across her torso, Charlotte tries to calm her breathing. All she can think about is who has access to a key, who knows about Antonia's documents, who understands their significance. Names come to mind. Oscar Duval – she'd briefed him about the documents in preparation for having them analysed. Miles – she'd described their contents, but he hasn't seen them. Perhaps someone from the university? Someone from the Begijnhof?

Her thoughts keep circling back to Sterck, to last week, when they stood in the Rubenshuis garden. She remembers walking away with the realisation that she should push her anger and prejudice aside, give him a chance to prove himself. She shouldn't blindly accept her mother's version of events. Every story has multiple viewpoints.

But all that is gone now, her distrust and bitterness returned. Anna had confirmed Sterck knew about the map folio, its link to Rubens, even her own discussions with Theo and Willem about possible connections to a Rubens-inspired Grand Tour. Sterck is well known at the Begijnhof. Anna calls him by his first name, mentioned their various meetings. Sterck, as head of the history department, has strong connections throughout the university. Miles described him as having a phenomenal memory, writing a huge number of journal articles. Her mother had warned her of professors who took credit for authoring numerous articles, mostly written by students. Could Sterck be doing the same? The most damning evidence is her mother's declaration that years ago Sterck stole an important piece of her research.

He is the one person involved in all the seemingly divergent parts of the puzzle. Either obliquely or directly, somehow he is entangled in the ransacking of her apartment, she is sure of it. Compounding all her distrust is the bitterness and anger inherited from her mother against this man.

Charlotte stands up straight, scrambled thoughts merging. The moment is surreal, a crazy blending of confusion and clarity, like mist moving aside to reveal a distant scene. Suddenly, everything is clear.

She opens a cupboard, extracts a folder, flicks through papers: medical insurance, receipts, employment contract … here it is … the lease for the Antwerp apartment. She knows the building maintenance manager has a key to her apartment; he fixed a leaking tap while she was at work last week. But neighbours, work colleagues – no one else has a key.

Halfway down the page, her eyes widen. When she'd arrived in Antwerp, she'd been told the apartment was for the use of short-term academic staff. The lease identifies the tenant as Universiteit Antwerpen. No surprise there.

The lease states that the representative of the university also has a key. The person's name is printed on the lease, beneath a scrawled signature.

'*Miss Ulrika Beulen*,' reads Charlotte. She remembers the day she arrived at the university and the outer office, the woman smoothing her black pencil skirt, nameplate on the desk: *Miss Ulrika Beulen*. Professor Sterck's personal assistant.

30

June 28, 1621

'I am not made of gold!' Papa yelled, each word reverberating through the closed door.

I sat on the stairs and looked through the balustrade into the foyer below, wondering when the door would open and Mama would appear. The ensuing silence suggested she was speaking, but her voice was too low for me to hear.

'I may be the most popular engraver in this city,' he shouted, 'but I am not paid enough to maintain your spending habits.'

The door opened and Mama rushed out, her skirts rustling with agitation, her face tight with misery.

I crept upstairs, keen to remain invisible. Like everyone else, family and servants alike, I had taken to moving softly about the house, as if trying to step around broken glass. Papa's uncharacteristic petulance had grown into irritability as the days progressed. Yesterday, he roared at Hendrik and Niels for roughhousing in the foyer, startling them so they knocked over a side table, a dish shattered on the tiled floor, and baby Lucas awoke, crying. Last night, Papa complained the fish was overcooked, the cabbage bitter, the carrots too salty. Janneke's eyes were red-rimmed as she collected the dishes at the end of the meal.

No matter how hard we tried to appease him, nothing brought a smile to his face. Ludo was too slow in bringing his cloak, the front steps weren't scrubbed to his satisfaction, Sint-Jacobskerk's bells were too loud, the wind too strong, the sky too grey. Worse, Papa had not checked my workbooks for nine days, thus my next visit to the Rubenshuis remained uncertain.

Adhering to a routine helped me push aside the sense of foreboding that blanketed our household. After completing lessons each morning, I worked with Janneke in the kitchen, learning various household skills which were apparently necessary for my future role as wife and mother. I mastered the vagaries of braising tripe, worked the goffering iron to crimp white ruffs worn for best, endured an hour-long practice on the *spinetten*. Next, I sat with Mama and listened to her account of Sunday's sermon, while keeping my hands busy with needle and thread.

'The Book of Proverbs says that idle hands make one poor,' said Mama, 'but diligent hands bring riches.'

I stabbed my needle into the crewelwork primula, longing for a moment of idleness with Clara in her garden.

Perhaps Papa heard my silent plea: the door to Mama's room opened and he appeared.

'Get your hat, Antonia,' he said gruffly, 'and come with me.'

We hurried along the streets. Sensing Papa had no interest in conversation, I remained silent to the beauty of summer sunshine and warmth bathing the city. My momentary joy upon following Papa into the Rubenshuis disappeared when he informed me I was not there to dally with Clara.

Papa collected a blank copper plate from the corner cupboard and began work on a new engraving. I sat on a stool next to him, wondering why I was there.

The studio was quieter than normal, Meneer Rubens having left the previous day for diplomatic business in Brussels. His chief assistant roamed from one side of the room to the other, giving instructions as apprentices prepared canvases. Santo was absent, so I was unable to pull faces at him from across the room.

With a sigh, Papa discarded the burin. 'Fetch me another copper plate, Antonia.'

Pleased to be given a task, I crossed the room to the corner cupboard. The copper plates, each one wrapped in linen, were normally stacked on the middle shelf. In their place, however, was a collection of beautiful drawings in the Master's distinctive hand. Drawn on cream-coloured paper using pen and ink, he had used white and ochre lines to highlight details of a woman's face. The uppermost drawing showed the face in profile: high forehead, Roman nose, pointed chin, lips parted in a beguiling smile. Her hair was a glorious mass of coiled braids and curls, with delicate tendrils falling all about, reminiscent of a haloed saint. I recognised the hairstyle from a drawing I had seen last month on Santo's worktable, but struggled to recall the woman's name.

I peered at the next drawing, which showed the same woman in a full-length pose, her body swathed in clinging robes, sheer fabric falling from her shoulders, evoking the statues on the façade of the Rubenshuis portico. This woman was no saint, I decided, but a character from a Classical story. Andromeda perhaps, or maybe Artemis.

Curious to learn more, I reached for the third drawing. The woman rested her fingers on the side of an ancient jar, while her other hand lifted the lid. She leaned in, eyes closed, nose lifted as if smelling the wisps of smoke escaping from the jar. She was not Andromeda, who was normally chained to a rock awaiting rescue by Perseus. Nor was she Artemis, who usually held a spear and was surrounded by baying dogs. This unknown goddess, with her feminine curves and teasing smile, was all seduction and charm. She had a similar doe-eyed look to the maidservants at the market, fluttering their eyelashes at the fishmonger's apprentice, looking over their shoulders with a knowing smile at the baker's son. But this goddess appeared to have more than seduction on her mind.

With a start, I realised Papa was standing behind me, staring at the drawing in my hand. I returned it to the shelf and arranged the drawings in a neat pile.

'I sent you to fetch a copper plate,' he whispered fiercely, 'and I find you otherwise occupied.'

'I was–'

'Go back to the worktable.'

I knew better than to argue and shame-faced, returned to the table. Hunched on the stool, I wondered if this would be my last visit to the Rubenshuis. Would my misbehaviour lead me to lose this privilege? I wrapped my arms around myself, wishing I could shrink into a ball of wool and roll under the table, to lie forgotten amongst canvas scraps and charcoal stubs.

Papa returned to the worktable, hurriedly straightened his tools, wrapped a roll of papers in waxed cloth. He fastened his cloak about his neck, then tucked the waxed roll within the folds of his heavy cloak. 'We're leaving,' he muttered.

As we crossed the courtyard, I spied Clara standing at a window, her downcast face a mirror of my own. With barely time to exchange waves, I followed Papa along the street.

He was deaf to the friendly greeting offered by Meneer Smits from across the canal, oblivious to the summer sunshine, unaware his scowl remained as he barged past Ludo. Refusing the manservant's offer to hang up his cloak and hat, Papa wrapped the cloak tighter about his shoulders, opened the door of his workroom, announced that he was not to be disturbed and slammed the door.

31

'The renovation of Building A's top floor is behind schedule,' says Professor Sterck, 'which means those of you who are sharing office space will need to do so for a few more months. I'm sorry for the cramped conditions, and appreciate your patience.' His gaze sweeps across the thirty people crowded into the meeting room. A dozen staff members are seated around a large table, while others stand against the walls.

Charlotte glances at Sterck's assistant, who stands near the door. Miss Beulen's grey hair is pulled into a tight chignon. Her gaze is fixed on Sterck, a look of professional interest or besotted reverence, Charlotte can't tell. She can't imagine calling the woman by her first name: *Ulrika* sounds too personal, a moniker used by family and friends. To Charlotte, and all university staff, she is always *Miss Beulen*.

Unfamiliar with her background, other than that she's been Sterck's assistant for fifteen years, Charlotte wonders what would induce someone to work for the same person for so long. Is she so entrenched in her role that she's willing to do his bidding? Did she give the apartment key to someone else?

Sterck turns to the head of the linguistics department. 'Filippo, do you have anything to add?'

Filippo Donati smooths his silk cravat. 'I've placed some conversation points online, which I'd encourage you to use when discussing the issue of academic theft with your students. Please remind them of the fine line between inspiration and appropriation, the importance of giving suitable credit where it is due, encouraging collaborative efforts and knowledge-sharing, and providing one another with regular feedback.'

'Thank you, Filippo.' Sterck neatens the papers in front of

him. 'Lastly, the police investigation about the campus attacks is continuing, so please remind your students to be extra vigilant.'

Charlotte shivers, pressing herself against the wall, reassured by its stability. She can't help but wonder if the recent apartment break-in has anything to do with the campus attacks.

People shift restlessly, sensing the meeting is coming to a close.

Sterck tweaks his cufflinks. 'I hope you can stay for refreshments.' He nods at his assistant.

Miss Beulen exits the room, reappears minutes later pushing a trolley laden with rattling glasses and bottles of beer and wine. She deposits a platter of cheese, pâté and rye bread in the centre of the table.

Edging her way through the crowd, Charlotte keeps her gaze on the back of Miss Beulen's head. She's eager to draw her into a conversation, hoping to determine whether this poised woman knows anything about the raiding of her apartment. Perhaps she will be unable to meet Charlotte's gaze, appear nervous, hinting at guilt.

Caught behind a portly gentleman, Charlotte is unable to reach Miss Beulen before the assistant disappears down the hallway. Cursing to herself, she scans the room, wondering who she can talk to about Sterck's assistant.

Theo and Karl are in the corner, talking with a trainee conservator. Arnold chats with a red-headed senior lecturer, who clutches his arm and throws her head back, laughing hysterically. Miles stands near a window with a beer in his hand, leaning in to talk with Sterck, both grim-faced. Sterck glances over his shoulder, then turns back to Miles.

What had Miles said to her? *It's impossible to have secrets in this place.* Amid all the light-hearted chatter filling the room, how many of these people are sharing confidences, divulging secrets, betraying trust? Everyone appears friendly and solicitous, but can any of them be trusted?

Arnold is now having a sombre conversation in the corner with a young man from the history department. Miles joins Theo and Karl in front of the window, laughing together. His fringe keeps falling across his eyes; he needs a haircut. She doesn't know Miles that well, and yet a sensation within – perhaps impulsive and foolhardy – has made her relax in his company, share details about the map folio. *Tread carefully*, she tells herself. *Not everyone can be trusted.*

A lady steps backwards into Charlotte, swinging around with a glass of red wine in her hand. 'Oh dear, I'm so sorry,' she says, staring with dismay as the stain spreads like an open wound across the front of Charlotte's cream blouse.

Charlotte grimaces, looking around for a paper napkin to blot the mess.

'Can I help you?' Sterck appears, offering a neatly folded handkerchief.

'Thank you.' She accepts the handkerchief, dabs at the stain. Tongue-tied.

'I spoke to Anna this afternoon,' he says. 'She was pleased the map folio has been returned to Petra. Did you discover any more mysterious clues before it was returned?'

'Mysterious … clues …' She repeats his words slowly, knowing she sounds foolish, unable to stop herself.

'I understand the map folio has a Rubens Crest, hidden letters and strange geographical markings,' he says. 'Sounds cryptic, like a treasure map.'

She abandons the stain, returns the handkerchief with her thanks. He appears to know everything about the map folio. Someone has revealed its secrets to him. Theo? Willem? Miles? *It's impossible to have secrets in this place.*

'Petra is still very sick with a nasty chest infection.' He shakes his head. 'Anna thinks she may have undiagnosed dementia. Still has rational moments, but over the past few months she's become disoriented. Let's hope you're successful in finding the portfolio box.'

'Yes.' She keeps her tone neutral, trying to compose a suitable response, but all she hears are his revelations.

'If I can help, please let me know.'

'Thank you,' she murmurs.

She's transfixed by his tie. Rows of stylised Inca suns with miniature faces. The tie is at odds with his tweed jacket. Quirky versus traditional. Which is he? She struggles to picture her mother with this man. Rachael: bright and sassy, quick to laugh, generous with praise, gregarious and fiercely emotional, ostensibly muddle-headed yet with a lightning-fast memory for quotes. Charlotte remembers sneaking downstairs as a child to sit in the corner during her mother's soirees, admiring the way Rachael circulated about the room, refilling glasses, encouraging guests to mingle. As the evening progressed, Rachael would be singing pop tunes and dancing on the coffee table. And *this* man: punctilious and solemn, lukewarm in demeanour, thin lips often drawn in a frown. She's certain he's never danced on a table in his life.

Sterck's mouth is moving, but she struggles to hear him. The noise in the room has escalated, everyone chattering.

'... best keep circulating,' he says, offering a quick smile before merging into the crowd.

Charlotte snatches up her coat, rushes from the room. Along the corridor and down the stairs, out into the courtyard. It's deserted, swathed in early evening shadows. Muted laughter floats from the room above.

She leans against the wall, relishing the crisp air, searching for answers about this man who is her father, who leaves her confused and tongue-tied every time they speak. One moment her heart is telling her to set aside her anger, to give him a chance. The next, it's saying be wary, feel only contempt. She doesn't know what to do.

32

Charlotte hears footsteps approach from the stairwell. The courtyard is empty. Suddenly feeling vulnerable, she backs into a wall recess, trying to melt into the shadows.

'Charlotte?' a familiar voice calls out.

She steps out of the gloom.

Miles stands in the light of the stairwell, buttoning his coat. 'Saw you escape. Thought I'd join you. Best part of the monthly meeting is the free beer at the end, but the meeting itself ... death by boredom. Would've needed my heart restarted if it went much longer.'

She smiles. He has a way with words.

He pulls on a beanie. 'I saw you got cornered by Sterck. You didn't look pleased. Everything okay?'

'Was it that obvious?'

Miles wriggles on a pair of gloves. 'You become tense whenever he's around.'

'I try not to.'

'Was he hassling you about something?'

'He's spoken with Anna. Knows about the portfolio box, about Petra. Probably knows about our chat with Edith.'

The sounds of footsteps and laughter drift from the stairwell. He moves into the shadows, lowers his voice. 'Theo said something to me tonight ...'

Despite the cold air, an uncomfortable heat spreads across her face.

Arnold and the red-haired woman descend the stairs, talking loudly. Waiting for them to cross the courtyard, Miles indicates a bench. They walk towards it.

'Theo reminded me that security was beefed up earlier this term because of safety concerns on campus. New outdoor lighting was added, as well as extra guards. Everyone's nervous. The police still don't have any suspects for the attacks.' Miles pauses, before adding: 'Security inside buildings was also increased, including the library.'

She slows her pace. 'What sort of security?'

'More CCTV cameras.'

'In the conservation room?'

'Possibly.'

When they reach the bench, she sits heavily, her insides coiled tight. Video footage may exist of her entering the conservation room, tampering with the map folio, stowing a document in her satchel.

Miles sits next to her. 'You okay?'

'Not really.' She tries to swallow the sour taste in her mouth.

'There's CCTV outside all major buildings,' says Miles, 'but I haven't noticed cameras inside the conservation room. Mind you … they can be well hidden.'

A fierce heat spreads from her face to her neck. She loosens her scarf, unzips her coat, the icy air doing little to calm her. 'What have I done?' she whispers.

Miles places a hand on her back. 'I'm sure it'll be fine.'

'Who would have access to CCTV footage?' she thinks aloud. 'The library manager and Theo, maybe the dean, heads of relevant departments. Shit! This isn't good.' She clasps her hands together tightly, kneading the knuckles.

'If someone saw you on camera cutting into the map folio,' says Miles, 'why would they wait to confront you?'

'What if they haven't looked at the footage yet? Maybe they only check it every few weeks.'

'Or maybe CCTV hasn't been installed in the conservation room and there's no footage to worry about. Besides, if there's compromising footage of you, Theo will mention it to me.'

She swivels to face him. 'I'm sorry for getting you involved.'

'What's done is done. No point in worrying.'

She momentarily closes her eyes, wishing she could brush off her anxiety as easily as Miles does.

Standing, he slaps his gloved hands together to warm them. 'I've got an early start tomorrow for hockey practice. Let me walk you home.'

'It's okay, Miles. I want to get my satchel from upstairs …' The tightness in her chest has changed to hollowness, the unpleasant warmth in her body turning to chills.

'Don't walk home by yourself, Charlotte. It's dark, and getting late.'

'It's okay. Karl lives in the next street, I'll walk with him. Or Professor Donati.'

'Perfect. He'll be able to dazzle any would-be attacker with his fancy cravat.'

She offers a half-hearted smile. 'If Theo says anything …'

'I'll let you know.' He strides across the courtyard, shoulders hunched against the cold.

Charlotte wraps her arms around herself, watching him disappear around the corner, wishing she'd accepted his suggestion to walk home together. Whenever he's offered work-related advice, it's always couched in positive terms, lifting her spirits, pushing aside her anxieties. Right now, she doesn't want to be alone. Less than a month in Antwerp and she's close to losing her dream job, for what? A long shot that seven art treasures, stolen centuries ago, have survived and are awaiting discovery.

She's distracted from her thoughts by the sound of muted footsteps, then silence.

The courtyard is empty, corners thick with shadows.

She hurries to the stairwell, taking the stairs two at a time, rushing around the corner of the landing. She slams into a figure, stumbles backwards, grabs the banister to stop from falling.

They call out *Sorry* at the same time.

'Are you okay?' asks Sterck.

'Yes, and you?'

'Fine, thank you. Well … err … have a pleasant weekend.' He continues down the stairs, disappears into darkness.

She climbs the stairs, replaying the collision in her mind: she'd rushed up the stairs, holding the banister to swing around the corner. He was standing there as she crashed into him. Both his feet were on one step – not treading between steps as if descending, but together on one step. Standing motionless in the stairwell. Listening.

33

July 3, 1621

'Gossip has no place in our household,' Mama said to Janneke and me as we donned our cloaks. 'When you visit the market today, remember to obey the Psalm which says to keep your tongue from evil.'

'Yes, Mevrouw.' Janneke bobbed a curtsy.

As we hurried along the street, dodging rain puddles and mounds of manure, I reflected on Mama's words. Assisting Janneke at the market was part of my education – not only the correct counting of coinage, but cajoling the *slager* into giving us the choicest cuts of pork, and checking the *eierverkoper* had not included a cracked egg in our bundle. The market was where I appreciated the nature of my privileged upbringing. My house was not as grand as Clara's, but my life was one of indulgence compared to those who struggled every day to fill their bellies and stay warm at night. The market was often filled with merriment, but also contained grim reminders of the brutality of our existence. Life could be harsh, and punishments awaited those who failed to follow the laws laid down by the *burgemeesters*.

I saw the boy as soon as we reached the square. He stood locked in the pillory, his head and hands poking through holes in the wooden stand. I couldn't see his face from where I stood, only his crown of greasy curls. I followed Janneke as she walked from one stall to the next, prodding a fish, hefting a cabbage. Every few seconds, my eyes were drawn to the boy.

He was too short for the pillory, forced to stand on tiptoe. His stockings had slipped, revealing muddy knees and calf muscles stretched tight.

Janneke noticed my gawping. ''Tis the Martens boy. Caught in thievery. He was lucky they didn't chop off his ear.'

'What will happen to him?'

'They'll let him out tomorrow. He'll crawl home and cop a right ol' clip about the head from his Pa.'

'For stealing?'

She snorted. 'Knowin' Meneer Martens, it'll be for gettin' caught.'

'What did he steal?'

'Does it matter?' She hoisted the basket on her hip. 'Thievery's thievery, whether it be pilferin' bread or shirkin' work.'

I couldn't help but stare at the poor creature. He was no more than Hendrik's age. Too young to be forced to stand all night without water, food or use of the privy. But old enough to know the difference between right and wrong. It was a cruel punishment, with a beating still to come.

'Wait here with the basket while I see if Pieter has a hock for supper.' Janneke eased the heavy basket to the ground.

The harshness of the boy's punishment troubled me, especially the beating he would receive from his father after already suffering a night in the pillory. Would he delay going home to avoid the thrashing?

Janneke stood at a nearby stall, holding a paper-wrapped parcel in her arms and conversing with a maid from the Van Helst household. They looked to be gossiping, despite Mama's warnings. I found a makeshift seat on the shaft of the turnip-seller's cart and settled down to wait.

A huddle of maidservants rummaged through the turnips, chatting together.

'She be too large for seven months. I wage the babe be born afore All Saints' Day.'

'She'll be announcin' it arrived early.'

'Dearie me, how did that happen?' They crowed with laughter, then became indignant as their conversation turned to a maid on Kelderstraat who was left broken-hearted when her sweetheart ran off with another.

'If my Wilbert so much as looks—'

'He best keep those butcher's knives of 'is locked away.' Giggling, they continued sorting through the turnips.

'Did yer hear a knife was drawn by one of the apprentices at the Rubenshuis last week? Against the Master, no less?'

'No!'

'None was hurt.'

'Don't matter. The apprentice will be chased outta town.'

''Twasn't an apprentice, but someone senior.'

They paid for their turnips and moved away. Observing the boy in the pillory, I considered how the crime of theft compared with threatening your master with a knife. I tried to imagine Ludo, our manservant, stealing from our pantry or threatening Papa with a blade. It was inconceivable. A good master would provide fair working conditions so a worker would never feel the need to threaten or steal.

Janneke and I were silent for most of the way home, carrying the basket between us. As we turned into Eikenstraat, she motioned for us to rest the basket on the cobbles.

'Everyone be talkin' about a story at the market, Miss Antonia.'

'Mama warned us against listening to gossip.' I tried to push aside the idle chatter of the turnip maids.

'There be talk of yer pa ... they be sayin' he pulled a knife on Meneer Rubens—'

'That's not true!' I admonished her. 'It was an apprentice who pulled the knife.'

'So, you heard it too?'

'It's idle gossip.'

'But yer pa—'

'How dare you speak of my father in such a hateful way. He is your master, provides well for you and deserves your loyalty.' My body was rigid, every muscle filled with fury.

'Miss Antonia, I fear there be truth in the rumours. Yesterday, your father told Ludo to prepare the household for a long journey. Most of the servants are being let go, but Ludo and I have been asked to accompany—'

'You're lying.' How could she listen to gossip and spin such horrible lies? Certainly, Papa had been irritable of late, but whatever had caused his unhappiness would pass.

Janneke reached out a tentative hand, but I stepped back.

'Miss Antonia, we be departin'—'

I turned and ran, ignoring her calls to help with the basket. I ignored Ludo's welcome, too, as he opened the front door, and his puzzled expression as I pushed past him and ran upstairs. I curled up in the attic, my ears ringing with the news that the folk of our city considered my father a criminal, and worse, that we were leaving Antwerpen. It was a mistake.

Papa's recent surliness – insisting on wearing his long winter cloak in the heat of summer, talking rudely to the servants, cloistering himself away in his workroom, ignoring me and the boys – is easily explained by a fever or toothache. Mama tells me I am often cross when unwell. 'Tis the same for Papa.

By the time Mama found me, I was in a tearful state. She led me to my bedchamber and tucked the eiderdown around my shivering body. 'You're ill, *mijn liefje*.'

'I don't want to leave Antwerpen,' I cried into the pillow.

'I had planned to tell you myself this evening,' she murmured, 'but it appears the servants have been talking.'

My sobs rose as I realised Janneke had spoken the truth.

Mama brushed the hair back from my forehead. 'We leave for England in ten days.'

I buried my face in the pillow. Leaving Antwerpen to live elsewhere was inconceivable.

'I don't want to leave our house, the oak trees and skating on the canals. They won't have our favourite cheese or Seville oranges. The English despise anyone who professes faith with the Pope; we'll be called Papists and shunned. I'm so muddled with learning Latin, French and Spanish, and now I'll have to learn English, too. I don't want to go on a boat across the sea as we'll surely drown. I don't want to say goodbye to our neighbours, my friends ... Clara.' The last word came out as a sob.

Mama whispered comforting words until I fell asleep. When I awoke in the morning, I thought it all a bad dream. But as I came downstairs, I spied wooden crates stacked against the wall. All our household possessions would accompany us across the Noordzee, far away from everything I had ever known.

34

Standing on a chair, Charlotte fastens a large sheet of paper to the living-room wall: three rows of six pages, each taped to the next. In the centre, the word *Pandora* is written inside a large circle. Lines meander in all directions, like the crooked legs of a spider, each leg finishing with more circles, lines and words. A big spider merging into little ones.

She climbs off the chair, stands back to survey her work. A mind map, charting her ideas and flashes of inspiration. Many will lead to dead ends, but all she needs is one idea to lead her to the missing Rubens drawings.

On Monday morning, before she goes to work, she'll pull the mind map off the wall, fold it and slip it inside her satchel, where it will sit alongside her notebook filled with her research. Neither will leave her side. Antonia's pages are safely with the document analyst, Oscar Duval. If someone turns her apartment upside down again, the notes and documents can't be stolen.

She eyes the new lock she had installed the day after the ransacking. Although the lease dictates that locks can't be replaced without notifying the landlord, Charlotte has no intention of informing Miss Beulen. She feels safer knowing no one else has a key to her apartment. If there are consequences to the new lock, she'll deal with them later.

The doorbell rings. She's surprised to find Miles in the hallway.

He smiles. 'Glad you're home.' His hair has been trimmed, his usual scuffed lace-ups replaced with neat loafers. Shirt tucked in.

She eyes the bottle of wine in his hand. 'Are we celebrating?'

Another lopsided smile. 'Why not?' Hints of woodsmoke aftershave and leather jacket waft past as she ushers him inside.

'I'll be back in a minute.' She edges towards the bedroom, remembering her sweatpants have a hole in the back seam.

'Hope you don't mind me dropping by unannounced,' he calls out from the living room.

'I stayed in today,' she replies from the bedroom, tying her hair into a ponytail, 'busy with work.' She wriggles into jeans; the zip refuses to glide closed. *Damn it.* He's out there, probably reading the mind map, which is meant only for her eyes.

He's facing the window by the time she returns. 'I miss this view. When I first arrived in Antwerp, the faculty put me in this apartment while I was looking for my own rental. Always enjoyed looking out on the Old Town.' Gabled rooftops and evening lights stretch towards the black ribbon of the Scheldt.

She's taken aback, catches herself wondering if he'd kept his key. Surely not.

He offers her the wine. 'Happy birthday.'

Lightness spreads through her body. She accepts the bottle with a smile, pushes aside her earlier twinge of apprehension. 'Thank you. How did you know?'

'Staff birthday list in the admin office.'

She removes glasses from a cabinet, opens the wine. Breathes in merlot.

'I was going to bring flowers' – he clinks his glass against hers – 'but decided on wine instead.'

'Good choice.' She takes a long sip, and a relaxing warmth spreads along her limbs.

'I like what you've done to the place. New artwork?' His tone is playful as he nods at the wall.

'I work best with visual prompts. I'm trying to come up with ideas to solve … the map folio … the …'

'The Great Rubens Mystery,' he finishes with a grin. 'Talk me through it. Two brains are better than one.' He nestles into the sofa.

She swallows wine, stares at the wall. The spider stares back, daring her to explain its convoluted pathways. She recalls Miles and Sterck, huddled together after the departmental meeting, grim-faced and secretive. She shakes off her suspicion.

Tilting his head, he reads along a spider leg. '*Seven preparatory drawings for Philip the Fourth commission – Stolen*. What's that about?'

'Barzetti's extract mentioned that Rubens created drawings of Pandora, but they were lost.'

'Lost as in stolen?'

'Possibly.' She wears a mask of nonchalance.

He points to another spider with scribbles about the engraver. 'What about the relationship between Rubens and Vorsterman?'

She sips wine, pleased to avoid discussing the *Pandoras* when so much remains unknown. She's happy to talk about Rubens and Vorsterman: employer and employee, comrades and rivals, long-time friends and one-time foes. A relationship of contradictions.

'Their connection was complex,' she says. 'Vorsterman began working for Rubens in 1618. Rubens was already established as a successful artist, court diplomat, master of his own studio. He wrote about Vorsterman to a friend in 1618, saying the engraver was an excellent copyist, hard-working and lacked the egotism of others. Their relationship was fruitful … in the beginning.'

'What happened?'

'Several historians believe Vorsterman became resentful about being treated as a copyist. By 1621, he worked exclusively for Rubens and began to sign engravings with his own monogram. Critics believe Vorsterman was putting his own style into the works.'

'Was that a problem?'

'Rubens paid Vorsterman to make engravings of his most famous works so they could be easily duplicated and used as a marketing tool to promote his work and secure new commissions. The engravings were supposed to highlight *his* style, not the style of his engraver. In 1621, Rubens wrote that the engraver had declared it was his own name that gave the engravings value.'

'What did Vorsterman do?'

'They argued. Rubens wrote to another friend, describing his engraver as having a mental disorder. Vorsterman reportedly attacked Rubens in June 1621, but the details are sketchy. Possibly a knife was involved, but nobody's certain.'

'Did Rubens write about the attack?'

'Only mentioned it vaguely. Before the attack, Rubens had obtained a unique triple privilege – what we'd call copyright today – of all engravings made of his artworks in the Spanish Netherlands, France and United Dutch Provinces. The law was on his side.'

Miles tops up their wine. 'What happened to Vorsterman?'

'Took his family with him to England, secured patronages from various nobles, enjoyed moderate success.'

'Sounds as though his success was trivial compared to that of Rubens. Must have annoyed Vorsterman, seeing accolades piled at Rubens' feet, while he received little recognition.'

'Absolutely! He would've been furious. By winning this privilege, Rubens reduced Vorsterman's earning potential. Even though the guild recognised engravers as artists in their own right, he was considered a copyist, less important than a painter.'

'Do you feel sorry for Vorsterman? Did he get a raw deal?'

She perches on the edge of the sofa, swirling the wine in her glass. 'I can see it from both perspectives. During his lifetime, Rubens was lauded across Europe as a hugely successful painter, international diplomat and intellectual. He used engravings of his artworks to promote himself as the leading painter of his time, advance the reputation of his studio of highly skilled apprentices, and gain lucrative commissions. By the age of thirty-three he was so prosperous, he redesigned a palatial house on De Wapper, which became his family home and studio. He bought Castle Het Steen as his country escape. He was knighted by Philip the Fourth of Spain and Charles the First of England.'

Miles leans forward, captivated.

'Vorsterman was a gifted engraver, employed by Rubens, but he wanted more recognition than he felt he was given. He wanted–'

'More money,' Miles interrupts.

'Undoubtedly.' Charlotte laughs. 'But more than anything, he wanted appreciation and respect. He wanted acknowledgement for the critical role he played in his employer's success. He wanted Rubens to stand before the grand Pooh-Bahs of Antwerp, pat him on the back and loudly declare, *I couldn't have my success without you, Lucas.*'

She finishes her wine, slides the empty glass onto the table, her throat parched from talking.

'Same issues today,' says Miles. 'Giving credit where credit is due. Ensuring senior managers ... or Pooh-Bahs ... don't take all the acclaim.'

She remembers her mother's cautionary tale of the professor taking credit for his students' research. It's similar to Rubens' practice of employing numerous assistants to produce abundant artworks, all signed by his hand, despite many of the minor components – distant vistas, foliage, animals, cherubs, secondary characters – being completed by apprentices. Several of Rubens' apprentices went on to distinguished careers of their own, but most were relegated to the status of assistant or underling.

Miles tips the last of the wine into their glasses. 'Have you always put Rubens on a pedestal?' His voice is gentle, no hint of mockery.

She pauses before answering. The last two months have taught her that grief has the capacity to clear away the inconsequential stuff of life and allow new insights. Her artistic hero Rubens is still high on a pedestal, as is her darling mama, adored and respected. But everyone has flaws.

She's grateful he doesn't rush her to answer. 'He's still my artistic hero ...'

Miles raises his eyebrows.

'He was full of his own importance ... not as aware as he could have been about the people who helped him achieve his success.' Pausing, she adds: 'Not perfect, but human.'

'Aren't we all,' says Miles quietly. He sips his wine.

They sit in silence. She stares at the mind map. Lines, circles and words blur together. She's light-headed. Too much wine on an empty stomach.

'What's next?' His voice calls her back to the present.

Stomach growling and keen for a distraction, she's overcome with an urge to be flippant. She tips her head back against the sofa, grinning. 'Order pizza.'

Miles pulls out his phone. 'I know a place that delivers.'

Charlotte rummages in the kitchen and finds a bottle of syrah. 'Sod the hangover,' she mutters, wrenching out the cork. *Sod healthy food,* she decides, emptying a bag of crisps into a bowl. *Sod work deadlines, security cameras and fathers returning from the grave. Sod 'em all.* And she smiles, feeling happier and more relaxed than she has for a long time.

She downs another glass of wine as they debate the merits of Italian versus French cuisine. They devour the pizza, sitting side-by-side on the sofa. In between doughy mouthfuls, their conversation turns to travel experiences, Miles regaling her with his adventures in Vietnam, she reminiscing over hiking in Peru. Having finished the second bottle of wine and opened a third, their voices become more jovial, bantering with ease. When only greasy crumbs remain, they slump against the sofa cushions.

'Great birthday,' she says. 'Thank you.'

'You're welcome. What's the time difference between Antwerp and Toronto?'

'Six hours.'

'Guess you've already had birthday phone calls from home?'

She swirls the wine, takes a sip. There's a harshness to its aftertaste she hadn't detected before. 'My family's small ... an aunt, some cousins, my mother ... She ...' Her voice cracks. Specks of sediment sit in the bottom of the glass. She stares at the blur of burgundy, the glass snugged in her palm. 'My mother died ... nine weeks ago.'

Her ribcage aches, as if a weight sits upon it, squeezing the air from her lungs. One breath. Two. The tightness eases, but a sense of hollowness remains, as if the cavity holds only air. She's hit with a flashback of a cloudless day in high summer, so luminous the sky is bleached white. The day of her mother's funeral. The weather was more suitable for strolling along the shores of Lake Ontario, listening to sails flapping in the wind. Not standing before an open curtain, watching her mother's coffin glide backwards. Bone and sinew obliterated. Only ashes remain.

'I'm so sorry,' says Miles slowly. 'I had no idea.'

She hears the sadness in his voice, his words of condolence expressed in the same tone as those who attended Rachael's funeral, who arrived at the door bearing casseroles, cards and clichés. Each word spoken gently, as if the bereaved are so brittle they will shatter if someone speaks to them too quickly or too loudly.

'I've heard of her work, but didn't know she'd passed away so recently. She taught at Brussels years ago, didn't she? Then moved back to Canada?'

All Charlotte can do is nod. She swallows the pain in the back of her throat; doesn't trust herself to speak.

'It feels trite to say I'm sorry for your loss, but I am. My parents are still alive, so I don't know what you're feeling. How are you coping?'

The pain in her throat moves to her sternum. She wants to mask her despair with bluster. Pretend she's okay, brave, coping. 'We had time to prepare.'

'Did she know about your plans to move to Antwerp?'

'She was very supportive.'

'Is your dad also an academic?'

She studies a distressed hole in her jeans. Wraps a loose thread around her finger. Twist. Snap. 'He wasn't around. My mother raised me.'

Outside, a police siren wails.

'I'm sorry. Must be tough …'

'You don't miss what you've never had.' She knows it's a lie, but says it anyway.

The siren tapers to a moan.

'Nice ring,' he says. 'Is it from someone special?'

She follows his gaze, aware that he's staring at her hands. The turquoise catches the light. Deep sea-green, veins of copper, teardrop-shaped, bezel-set in silver. She's been absently twisting it around her finger, still unaccustomed to wearing it after all these weeks.

'Belonged to my mother.' Charlotte's mouth is chalk dry.

The first wave of a headache is flowering at the base of her skull. Excusing herself, she goes to the bathroom, leans against the sink, stares at her reflection. Why couldn't she have inherited her mother's eyes, or her grandmother's or anyone else's other than her father's? Even the same gold flecks among the green. Forever a reminder.

She gulps water with two paracetamol. Alcohol has loosened her tongue, her inhibitions. What was she thinking?

35

Charlotte walks along Kloosterstraat, joining shoppers at the weekend market. She savours the last sip of her second coffee, a pick-me-up after last night's red wine, then drops the cardboard cup in a bin.

The pavements are filled with trestle tables crammed with crystal and china, copper pots, soup tureens and vinyl records. Crates with hinges, doorknobs and locks sit next to battered military helmets and porcelain dolls. Chandeliers hang from clothing racks alongside moth-eaten fur coats.

At a stall displaying antique frames, she squints into a foxed mirror, surprised by her reflection: face pale, eyes shadowed, hair windblown.

Miles appears in the reflection, hand raised in greeting, smiling. 'Sorry I'm late.'

'It's okay. I've been busy.' She opens her shopping bag to reveal a bottle of Côtes du Rhône, a block of Herve cheese and some tissue-wrapped parcels. An old marquetry box was an impulse buy, along with a set of vintage linen napkins. Mementoes of her time in Antwerp.

They rummage among the vintage wares at a nearby stall.

'Check this out,' he says, holding an amethyst-coloured glass frog. 'Matches the one on your coffee table.'

The comical frog sits on its haunches, ready to shoot out a sticky tongue. Charlotte turns it over to read an etched signature on the underside – *Daum France* – before returning it to his palm.

'Not tempted?' asks Miles.

She's surprised he noticed the little object alongside the books and notepads scattered over the table last night. 'Mine belonged to my mother. She collected glass in different shades of green. I wouldn't feel right having one in a different colour.'

She pictures the crystal in her mother's house, displayed on shelves in the sunroom. A shimmering mirage of transparent green objects by Lalique, Daum, Gallé and Tiffany, in shades of apple, emerald, olive and pine. Now, they sit in darkness, packed inside a storage unit.

Hoping for something to ease her gloom, she begins flipping through a box of sepia photographs on a nearby table, and pauses at a photograph of corseted ladies and bow-tied gentlemen from yesteryear. Seated on picnic rugs, they stare sombrely into the lens, except for a couple at the back who turn to one another, soft smiles, hands touching. Did her parents share these looks in the beginning? How long did it take for looks of love to be replaced with recrimination?

Flipping through the photographs quickly, they become a blurred slideshow of people in various stages of their lives. Newlyweds, couples clasping their first child, siblings grouped around parents, comrades in uniform, friends in tennis whites, families at the beach.

Her mother denied her a father because of the lies she'd spun throughout Charlotte's life. Revealing on her deathbed that he was alive and living in Antwerp was a horrible betrayal. Whatever bitterness had passed between them, nothing could justify lying to her daughter for all these years.

Charlotte continues flipping through the photos, faster and faster, oblivious to the images. Tension builds in her chest, her jaw clenches. She could have had a father if not for Rachael's lies. Perhaps he would have been kept at a distance, but at least she would have had a *real* father, not a stranger who she knew only through her mother's prejudiced opinions. Someone she could have developed a relationship with, and spent time getting to know.

'Charlotte?' A soft voice at her side and a light touch on her arm stills her flailing fingers.

Releasing the photos, she steps back, muscles quivering.

'You were in another world,' says Miles.

She takes a shuddering breath.

'I've found some old maps you may like to see.' He guides her to another stall.

She's thankful for his awareness of her vulnerability, knowing not to bombard her with personal questions. He allows her to simply be.

They stand side-by-side, flicking through old maps. This time, her hands move calmly. She pauses at a faded map of an island surrounded by spiny-backed sea monsters with blowholes, webbed feet and curled tusks. The title cartouche names it *Islandia*, the monsters giving it a mythical feel. It takes a moment before she recognises it as Iceland.

'Is that by Ortelius?' asks Miles, leaning over to examine the cartouche.

'Yes, a later print from the original.' She recognises the work of sixteenth-century local mapmaker Abraham Ortelius.

'Maybe they have a Frederik de Wit. Not a first state, of course.' He laughs. 'Imagine discovering a first state De Wit in a market.' Still laughing to himself, he goes in search of the stall owner and returns minutes later. 'No maps by Frederik de Wit, but several by his apprentices.'

The owner spreads three maps across the table, talking in rapid Dutch about the provenance, pointing out the makers' marks, explaining how to tell the difference between a map created by De Wit and one by an apprentice.

'I assumed the mapmaker would always be named in the title cartouche,' says Charlotte, 'even if they were an apprentice.'

The owner shakes his head. 'The rules of the Saint Lucas Guild were strict. If the apprentice hadn't completed his apprenticeship, he was obliged to use the name of his master. But apprentices often placed symbols, like secret signatures, in the title cartouche to indicate their involvement.' He indicates a tiny symbol on a map of Drenthe. 'The initials JS inside the outline of a ship were the secret signature of Johannes Schipman.'

They wander away from the stall. 'Maybe a secret signature exists on De Wit's map folio,' says Miles. 'Perhaps it was made by one of his apprentices.'

'If it was, it may explain why it's a one-off … why no prints have been made.'

'We can search for a secret signature on the photographs Theo took,' says Miles.

Charlotte bristles at his use of the word *we*, suggesting this is their joint project, not hers alone. 'Sounds as though apprentices back then struggled for recognition as much as we do now,' she says.

'At least nowadays,' he says, 'we have laws protecting authors from intellectual theft–'

'Laws aren't always successful in protecting the innocent,' she interrupts.

'All the more reason for trusted colleagues to work together.'

She tilts her head, offering neither agreement nor opposition.

Stopping in the middle of the pavement, he turns to face her. 'Are you still determined not to speak with Sterck about the map folio?'

'The time isn't right, Miles. I have too many questions, not enough answers and right now, I need a break from thinking about the Rubens mystery. I've come to the market to clear my head.'

'Maybe the best way to clear your head is to let someone else look at the documents and offer a new perspective.' His eagerness is clear.

She doesn't reply. Bewildered by the charm of his crooked smile and blue eyes, she wishes her trust in him was unshakeable.

'Antonia's letter and Barzetti's extract,' he continues. 'If I'm going to understand what this is about, you need to let me see them.'

36

July 11, 1621

Despair filled my waking hours and disturbed my sleep, and no amount of consolation from Mama brought me peace. Niels' and Hendrik's animated chatter about sailing speed and cargo space could not distract me from my low mood. They strutted about the house playing at sea captains and deck hands, hollering out commands to adjust sails and climb rigging, but my misery remained. I cared not whether our vessel was a two-masted caravel or a square-rigged fluyt; either was capable of sailing me away from the home I loved.

Our house was no longer a calm haven. For days, we endured disruption and noise as our possessions were packed into wooden crates, with Mama calling out instructions and the servants rushing about with armfuls of linen, books, plates and glassware. The breakables were nestled within mounds of wood shavings. The floors were littered with the stuff, its sweet smell permeating every room, reminding me our departure was imminent and assured.

Beds were disassembled, linen bundled into crates. Mattresses were dragged into the courtyard and the stuffing discarded, the covers cleaned and readied for new stuffing on arrival in London. The dining table and chairs, cabinets, side tables, even Papa's huge workroom cabinet and the *spinetten*, were lashed to wagons and deposited at the dock for transfer to a ship. I stood on the stoop and watched the wagons head to the dock, trying to reassure myself that even though our furniture was accompanying us to England, there was no reason to think our relocation was permanent.

Mama and I were glum as we wrapped the family Bible in a blanket, along with psalters, prayer books and the crucifix that hung on her bedroom wall.

'Where in London shall we attend mass?' I asked.

'We'll decide once we've settled into our new home.' Her voice cracked.

I watched her face for tears, but she remained stoic.

Throughout the preparations, Papa remained in his workroom, leaving the house only once, accompanied by Ludo, to visit the docks and arrange our passage.

'We depart early morning at high tide, four days hence,' said Ludo, standing in the kitchen with the servants gathered about, 'and expect to land at Margate the following afternoon, all going well.'

'What do ya mean ... all goin' well?' asked Janneke, hands on hips.

I sat in the corner, listening to their discussion, bouncing baby Lucas on my knee.

'A sea voyage has many challenges,' said Ludo, his eyes mischievous. 'We may be shipwrecked or attacked by pirates.'

Janneke's eyebrows arched upwards.

'Or Protestant soldiers to the north may regain control of Zeeland,' continued Ludo, 'and take over our ship before we reach the open waters of the Noordzee.'

'All nonsense,' I called from the corner, irritated with Ludo's attempt to trifle with the ignorance of the servants. 'The Zeeland coast is at peace since Marquess Spinola marched his troops to the Rhineland, so there is no need to fear northern soldiers attacking our ship.'

'Such a clever little miss,' said Ludo, grinning. 'All we must contend with is possible shipwreck, marauding pirates and sea monsters.'

Janneke flicked a damp dishcloth at his backside, scolding him for his trickery. 'Outta me kitchen, you rascal, and no more silly talk lest ya be scarin' the youngsters.'

Hendrik and Niels cavorted through the doorway, wielding sticks and playing at sword fights, looking anything but scared.

I cuddled baby Lucas and slipped out of the kitchen. Filled with a muddle of emotions, I wanted my fears eased by the one adult I had always trusted. My faltering steps led me to the door of Papa's workroom.

Standing at the closed door, I buried my nose into the baby's downy hair and breathed deeply his sweet scent. The baby nuzzled my neck, his fingers pulling at my curls.

'Dearest Lucas,' I whispered into his hair as tears filled my eyes. 'What is to become of us?'

He cooed happily, oblivious to my distress.

On the other side of the door, Papa sat in solitude, planning his household's future with little regard for our feelings. We existed to do his bidding, accept his decisions, trusting we would be safe, wherever in the world he sent us. At his whim, my life was directed, my future planned, my friends selected or rejected. The decisions he made for his own life had calamitous effects on my own. Papa had discarded my future in Antwerpen, my friendship with Clara and my happiness as easily as the worn mattress stuffing in the courtyard.

I had attended mass since I was a youngster and heard the warnings in Deuteronomy of being cursed for dishonouring my parents. Whether or not I accepted Papa's decisions was of little consequence. I had no choice but to comply. I was forbidden from entering his workroom, forbidden from speaking unfavourably of our impending departure, forbidden from visiting the Rubenshuis to farewell Clara. At least Janneke and Ludo had the choice of whether they would accompany us to England. I was not so fortunate. Like the linen press or a crate of goblets, I was to be bundled up and shipped to a new destination, my cries of frustration ignored. I was a chattel, to be stuffed in a crate and muffled with wood shavings.

37

Standing before the lead-paned window, Charlotte scans the square outside. Raindrops splatter the glass. There's still no sign of her. Perhaps she's changed her mind.

She reflects on the past week. She's managed to cram every spare hour, in between lectures and tutorials, with research into the engraver, his daughter, his relationship with Rubens, the map folio. After spending countless hours squinting at Theo's high-resolution images of De Wit's folio, all she sees now are map markings and miniature cityscapes when she closes her eyes at night.

Charlotte recalls her recent telephone conversation with Sister Anna. Having confirmed the map folio had arrived safely back at the Begijnhof, she'd asked after Petra, hoping the *begijn*'s health had improved and she would be able to answer Charlotte's questions. Anna's tone was conciliatory yet brusque: 'Petra needs to rest.' Hanging up the phone, Charlotte had flicked through her notebook, re-reading her notes about Edith, Petra's friend, an art enthusiast and museum lover. Perhaps Edith knows more than she realises. Maybe Edith would like to join her for a museum visit. Another phone call. An invitation.

The door to the museum opens and a grey-dressed figure enters. Edith shakes raindrops from her umbrella.

'Thank you for the invitation.' Edith offers a hesitant smile. 'I've been here before … several times.'

'We could go to a different museum if you prefer,' says Charlotte.

'The Plantin-Moretus is one of my favourites.' A wider smile this time, shy but pleased.

Tickets in hand, they enter the first room. The oak-beamed

ceiling is black with age. Gold embossing faded from the leather wallpaper. A scent of beeswax and cedar polish.

Charlotte gestures at a framed painting, the nameplate declaring it to be *Balthasar Moretus*. The gentleman looks off to the side, wistful and guarded.

'Balthasar was several years older than Rubens,' says Charlotte. 'They met as students. He took over running the printing company in 1610 after his father died. He commissioned Rubens to make illustrations, title pages and family portraits.'

'He looks sad,' says Edith. 'As if someone close to him has died.'

Charlotte considers Balthasar, noticing the mournful look in his eyes for the first time.

They enter the heart of the sixteenth-century printing house. Grey light slips through thick windows, highlighting the sheen on the timber floors and walls. Six age-blackened printing presses are arranged down the length of the room. Opposite each press is a desk with a slanted tabletop comprising wooden trays, each divided into small compartments filled with miniature metal punches. Thousands of reversed letters and numerals, stained black with ink.

They wander into the next room and study the objects inside a glass cabinet. Leather covers speckled with gilt. Illuminated manuscripts festooned with curlicues of blue and yellow.

Edith beckons her to another cabinet, pointing to a massive tome opened at Genesis. 'The *Polyglot Bijbel*,' she says excitedly, 'in five languages, by Christophe Plantin. When Petra and I visited the museum earlier this year, we discussed the people who made this treasure. It was a spiritual endeavour for them, a way of acknowledging God's greatness. Petra said it wasn't wrong to admire beautiful objects or artworks, so long as it doesn't distract from our devotion to God. Look but don't covet, give all glory to Him. Amen.' Her hand flutters the sign of the cross, lips moving in Latin mime: *In nomine Patris et Filii et Spiritus Sancti*.

Recognising the Latin phrase reminds Charlotte of her school days. Daily exposure to Catholic practices had left an impression on her. Although tolerant to the beliefs of others, she is baffled that a person would voluntarily choose to cloister themselves away, pledge obedience to an earthly leader and higher power, forego the pleasures of personal freedom, sex, financial security and more. Placing complete faith in a divine being is an extreme level of devotion, one she struggles to comprehend. But more frightening to her is the idea of having total faith in another human.

Edith rubs her sleeve at the fingerprints on the cabinet. 'So peaceful here.'

'Not like the larger museums,' says Charlotte.

They enter the library and browse exhibits on bookbinding and illuminated manuscripts. White plaster busts stare down from the shelves. The room is deserted except for a couple listening to audio guides.

Edith calls her over to a cabinet. 'Here's a portrait of Lucas Vorsterman by Anthony van Dyck.'

Inside the cabinet is a buff-coloured sheet of paper. Charlotte peers down at the face of Antonia's father. She's delighted his portrait is on display, a lovely surprise to come face-to-face with him. Seeing the engraver rendered in ink on paper is more agreeable than studying his digital face on a screen, as she has done so many times.

'He looks worried, don't you think?' says Edith.

Charlotte takes in the graceful lines, crosshatching and shading. The engraver's features are handsome. A broad forehead, long nose, hair in curls, swept to the side. Lips pursed between a curled moustache and pointed beard. His furrowed brow and sideways glance suggest anxiety.

'Yes, he does look concerned,' says Charlotte.

Edith taps the glass cabinet above Vorsterman's portrait. 'Petra has a copy of this engraving in her bedroom, tacked on the wall next to copies of other engravings. Galle's *St Francis*, Bolswert's *Peacocks* and a portrait by Pontius ... the one with a man wearing a starched ruff the size of a millstone. Looks like a torture device. Do you know it?'

'Yes.' Charlotte smiles, enjoying the comical description, impressed with Edith's knowledge of Baroque art. 'Sounds as though Petra appreciates art as much as you. She's interested in Flemish engravers, is she?'

Edith peers closely at the image of Vorsterman. 'I'd be interested, too, if I was related to one.'

Charlotte's face is suddenly warm. 'Related to an engraver?'

'Yes. Petra is a descendant of Lucas Vorsterman. We stood on this spot a few months ago and she began reminiscing about her family. Apparently her genealogy traces back to Lucas Vorsterman. Over the centuries, their family name changed through marriage to Van Vliet. Her full name is Pietronella van Vliet, but we know her as Petra.'

Charlotte stands still, gaping. 'Petra is related to Lucas Vorsterman?' She tries to keep her voice steady, but knows it is shaking. It's impossible to remain calm upon hearing such astonishing news.

Edith remains composed, unaware of the impact of her revelation.

'What else did Petra say about her family?' asks Charlotte, her heart racing, desperate for details.

'Not much. She said he was an engraver for the Plantin-Moretus and later worked for Rubens, then Van Dyck.'

'What about Petra's family? Her parents? Were they from Antwerp? Does she have siblings? The portfolio box?' She stops, realising she's gabbling. Dozens of questions flood her mind, too quickly for her to make sense of them. Voiced aloud, they are jumbled pieces of a puzzle.

Edith strolls to the next cabinet, oblivious to Charlotte's excitement. 'Petra doesn't talk much about her family.'

Charlotte presses her lips together, hoping Edith will continue reminiscing, drop another fragment. They wander to the end of the room where a large globe, polished to perfection, sits on a carved base.

'When we last visited here, Petra was cross with me.' Edith is pensive, concentrating on the globe.

Charlotte holds her breath, careful not to break the spell.

Edith frowns. 'It was a silly misunderstanding. I thought it was exciting to be related to a famous artist. If it was *me* with a distinguished engraver in my family, I'd want to see their original work. I grew up in an orphanage and never knew my family. After the orphanage, I went from one foster home to the next, one job to another, until the Begijnhof became my family. I suggested we ask the curator if they could show us Vorsterman's original engraving plates. The Plantin–Moretus was a major publishing house for three hundred years and has a large archive.'

'What did the curator say?'

'We never found out. Petra said we shouldn't trouble them. When I suggested it again, she became cross. Told me she didn't need to hunt down her ancestors, covet their possessions, obsess over their treasures.' Edith's voice grows loud. 'Said we should spend our time appreciating the present and preparing for the future, not digging up the past.'

Charlotte murmurs softly, trying to soothe Edith's agitation. Understandable that she's frustrated. Petra's words are at odds with her behaviour. She insists her family's map folio is returned, and she displays copies of her favourite Flemish engravings on her bedroom wall – including a portrait of her ancestor Lucas Vorsterman – suggesting she cherishes their kinship. Yet, she admonishes Edith for showing interest in the engraver and his creations. Which is it? Is Petra proud of her ancestry? Or does she believe such pride distracts from devotion to God and should be suppressed?

Edith glides her hand along the balustrade, her buoyant manner gone. She addresses the taciturn faces of Christophe Plantin, Jan Moretus and their plaster descendants. 'Humans are complex creatures. Saying one thing yet doing another. Filled with faith yet doubting. Trusting one minute, suspicious the next.' Her voice has a brittle edge to it. She leans on the balustrade, head bowed, shoulders quivering.

Charlotte hesitates, unsure if a comforting touch would be welcome. They barely know one another. But Edith's distress is palpable. She places a reassuring hand on the woman's back.

38

'My Old Flemish isn't as good as yours, but I got the gist of it.' Miles passes the document wallet across the table to her.

Charlotte hugs it to her chest, relieved to have Antonia's letter and Barzetti's extract back in her possession. Handing over the documents to the analyst, Oscar Duval, had been difficult, especially given the wrecking of her apartment, the attempted break-in at the conservation room, and talk of academic theft floating around campus like an invisible cloud of poisonous gas. Passing them to Miles had been equally difficult; she's still unsure of his loyalties.

'What did you think?' She slides the documents into her satchel. Having handed them to him after their visit to the outdoor market last weekend, she's keen for his opinion.

'Rubens' *Pandora* drawings were stolen, weren't they? And you think they're still hidden and you plan to find them?' He is confident, elated.

She nods in agreement, her feelings bizarrely mixed. Satisfaction, knowing he has reached the same conclusion as her. Dismay, it is no longer her secret alone. Relief, having shared the burden.

'Antonia was clear in her letter to Gerard about what she wanted him to do and Barzetti's extract was unequivocal about which of Rubens' drawings went missing, but it will be like searching for a needle – or seven needles – in a haystack. I can understand why you're reluctant to reveal what you found to Sterck,' says Miles, 'or anyone else.'

She curves her hands around a coffee cup. It seems that Miles has instantly calculated the risks, understood her rationale, silently labelled her shrewd and suspicious. She shrugs inwardly, refusing to feel irritated by such labels. After all, they are the truth. But, curiously, his comment about not revealing her findings to Sterck suggests that Miles may also have doubts over whether Sterck can be trusted.

'Let's order more coffee and you can tell me about Duval's tests.' He beckons to a waiter, orders drinks.

Early evening and the café's customers are sipping cappuccinos and hot chocolates. The mechanical symphony of a coffee machine churns in the background. The barista works like a conductor, tapping out dregs, refilling the brew basket, guiding the hissing wand into milk.

Miles and Charlotte sit at a table in the far corner, wedged between window and wall, looking out on the massive fountain in the dusky shadows of Grote Markt. The Roman soldier remains eternally poised to throw the giant's hand across the square.

Charlotte recalls her mother's advice about not showing her full hand: *only reveal it when you're ready*. So much for waiting. Nearly everything's exposed now.

Miles leans in to be heard above the coffee machine. 'What did Duval's analysis reveal?'

Despite her misgivings about sharing the findings, it's also a relief to finally discuss them with a fellow historian who understands the importance of authenticating primary sources. 'Antonia's letter is dated the fifth of November 1686. The vellum and ink analyses confirmed it's from between 1675 and 1695, plus or minus seven years.'

'And Barzetti's extract?'

'Tests confirmed the same age. Handwriting analysis verified the penmanship is by the same author as Antonia's letter.'

The waiter arrives with fresh cappuccinos. On the side of each saucer is a small biscuit in the shape of a hand. Charlotte enjoys the local custom of a small treat being served with hot beverages at cafés. The treats are usually wafers or *speculoos*, but this is the first time she's been served an *Antwerpse Handje*, a speciality of the city. She tightens her lips to stop from smiling at the crazy idea her mother is sending her a message from beyond: *time to reveal your hand*.

Miles doesn't appear to notice. 'What do you know about Santo Barzetti?'

'Rubens mentions him in letters, first as his apprentice from Genoa, then his senior paint mixer, later his personal assistant.'

'Do any sources mention Barzetti's booklet?' Miles blows on his coffee, takes a sip.

'Only the extract from the map folio.'

'What about Rubens' *Pandora*?'

'The only other mention is in Rubens' letter to his friend Frans Snyders.'

Miles stares at the tabletop as if mesmerised by the pattern of coffee rings. Charlotte waits for his next question, sensing it is close, enjoying the to and fro, the two of them batting a dilemma across an invisible net.

'Why didn't Antonia simply tell Gerard where the drawings were hidden?' he asks.

'In her letter, Antonia says she promised her father she would never speak of his secret while she lived.' Charlotte nibbles the fingertips off the *Handje* biscuit.

'If she didn't want to speak about it,' says Miles, 'she could've written a letter for Gerard to read following her death. Technically, she would still have kept her promise and not divulged anything while she lived. Would've saved making cryptic clues and commissioning maps.'

'We're playing a guessing game now.'

'Doesn't hurt to imagine Antonia's motives. May point us in the right direction.'

Charlotte glances at him from over the rim of her cup, mildly irked by his use of the pronoun *us*. He's already coupled himself to her discovery. 'What was happening in 1686 when the map folio and Antonia's letter were created?' she asks, shaking off her concerns.

'Europe was in chaos. Spanish Hapsburg power was waning while France, under Louis the Fourteenth, was becoming stronger. Antwerp was threatened by the French in the south and the Dutch Republic in the north.'

'Antonia mentioned the same unrest in her letter. The Scheldt closed for trade, soldiers heading off to fight the French in Namur. It explains her motives. She couldn't risk writing down the location of the *Pandora* drawings and the information falling into the wrong hands–'

'So, she used cryptic clues only a family member could understand.' Miles finishes the sentence, eyes alight.

They fall silent, glancing around the café. Three young women sit together, laughing as they study a mobile phone. In the far corner, Arnold and a bearded man are deep in conversation, referring to a pile of papers spread across their table.

Charlotte pictures the mind map and her list of tasks – meet with Petra, learn about Petra's family connection to Vorsterman, research the geographical markings, finish translating the six verses inside the maps' borders – all while continuing her lectures and tutorials. As for the attempted looting of her apartment, she's realised her skills don't extend to investigating modern-day crimes. She has to accept that the perpetrator may remain unknown.

His voice floats nearby. 'Do you need some help?'

She snaps back to the present. 'I'm sorry. What did you say?'

'Would you like some help translating the verses?'

She fiddles with a disused sugar sachet. 'I've already done some of it.'

'I know you're fluent in Old Flemish and French, but how's your Italian?'

'I'll use a translation app.' She keeps her voice light, keen to maintain a firm grip on her research. It's great to bounce ideas off Miles, but she doesn't need to share everything. No need to admit the verse on the *Italies* map is in fact not Italian, but a dialect her translation app doesn't recognise and that she has yet to identify.

'The nuance of the language may be lost,' says Miles, 'and besides, it's not even Italian.'

'What?' She's surprised he'd studied the tiny script around the *Italies* map.

'It's Genoese, a dialect of Liguria. I could do the translation for you.'

'Genoese?' Her eyebrows shoot up. 'You understand Genoese?'

'I'm full of surprises.'

'Blond hair and blue eyes … you hardly look Italian … and your name …'

'Ligurians are often blond-haired and blue-eyed. My maternal grandparents emigrated to England from La Spezia after the war. My nonna taught me Italian and Genoese. After school, in her kitchen–'

'Let me guess, she taught you how to make spaghetti?' Charlotte smiles, enjoying the image of Miles wearing an apron, honing his pasta-making skills with a grey-haired nonna.

'Not spaghetti, but *strangolapreti*, a type of spinach gnocchi. We also made *smacafam*, which–'

'*Smacafam*? Seriously?' She laughs. 'You're making that up.'

He manages to laugh and look indignant at the same time. 'It's a type of polenta with sausage. You're getting off topic. We were talking about the verses. Let me do the Genoese translation.'

'I … I'm fine, it's only six lines–'

'Do you *ever* accept help from anyone?' His eyes narrow, tone sharp.

She opens and closes her mouth, tightens her jaw.

'Haven't you realised by now I'm on your side?' His eyes flash. 'For god's sake, Charlotte, I covered up for you with Theo,' he lowers his voice to a hiss, 'I haven't pushed you to speak with Sterck, and I introduced you to Sister Anna.' He gestures in frustration, his annoyance clear.

They stare at one another before she breaks the silence. 'Just then, you looked very Italian. All that hand waving …' Her voice trails off. Of course he's on her side.

He offers a faint smile.

She rummages in her satchel, pulls out a page, passes it to him. In her scrawl are the six verses, each one a different language. The space next to the Genoese verse is blank. 'Thank you, Miles … for everything. I'd be grateful if you helped with the translation.'

He accepts the page. Pulls a notebook and pen from his backpack.

She stacks cups and saucers – 'I'll get these out of the way' – and carries them to the counter.

'More coffee?' asks the barista.

'No, thank you.' She leans against the counter, watching Miles from the other side of the café, his head bent over the paper. Normally light-hearted, his bluntness and scathing tone have rattled her. He was right. She didn't want anyone's help. Never had. Fiercely independent, even as a young child. It had been a source of pride for her mother to have a daughter so self-sufficient. 'You marched off to school,' Rachael told her, 'and never looked back.'

Independence is one thing, she muses, but her constant suspicion and distrust of others is exhausting.

She stares out the window. The stone figure of Brabo is alight in a jaundiced glow. Antonia would have walked across this very spot, but in the seventeenth century the darkened square would have been filled with the calls of nightwatchmen, the ripe odour of rotting vegetables from the market, the Brabo fountain a prescient ghost. Antonia would have trudged over cobblestones, unaware that three centuries later, someone would look out on this same scene and think about her, trying to understand what happened so long ago between a painter and engraver, a father and daughter, crippling guilt and blind promises.

The café is emptying. Arnold waves at her from the door as he and his coffee companion depart. The barista cleans the steam valve and the coffee machine gives a final hiss.

Miles holds his phone above the piece of paper, keeping his hand steady. *Click. Click.*

She hurries back to the table. 'Have you finished?'

'I need to check a few words when I get home. I think the author wasn't fluent in Genoese.' He rests the phone on the table. 'Translation is a bit clunky, but the key points are there. The first few lines are about Rubens, then it refers to Vorsterman.'

Moving her chair so they sit side-by-side, they read silently together, beginning with the first verse.

(Old Flemish)
> *Follow these words, take heed and bide you well:*
> *When I have passed and sink into the ground,*
> *Then turn your eyes to find a certain prize,*
> *Entrust to you these words, you will succeed;*
> *'Tis only you who search, your lips be bound,*
> *Avowed to search alone 'til you prevail.*

(German)
    Many would seek this prize for their own gain,
    'Tis not a crown nor for reward nor sale;
    Its glory rests in seven ladies fair,
    Their rounded curves and grace bring joy to all;
    Yet they belong to one who was maligned
    And to his name they must now be returned.

(Genoese)
    Success, renown and glory was this man's.
    Acclaimed by kings and queens, his fame well known;
    With pride and arrogance he did succumb
    Such that he brought another man to fall;
    Consumed by jealousy, the other did
    Commit a crime and hide his shame for years.

(Spanish)
    Now that I will soon pass from this world
    'Tis time for secrets all to be revealed,
    Laid bare for those to hear, my promise made
    While I live my lips will not confess,
    The crime and anger, jealousy and rage,
    He wronged us all when sin took hold of him.

The phone beeps. Before Miles swipes the screen, Charlotte glimpses a flash of a white text box with three words: *Happy to help*.

'We're closing now, folks,' says the barista, appearing behind them.

Miles twists in his seat. 'Okay. We'll finish up.'

Charlotte stares at the phone in his hand. Two white initials identify the recent sender as *SS*. Her stomach drops. She looks back to the verses, but they've transformed into meaningless scribbles. May as well be Sanskrit.

(French)
    Recall the games and puzzles of your youth
    Whene'er another birthday passed you by,

Such larks and merry sprees we did enjoy
To look at ordinary objects anew;
All twist and turn, then will it be revealed
Cartography and foreign tongues the key.

(English)
Make right this wrong, return the ladies fair
To those who live beyond the once great man:
His progeny in Londerzeel reside.
At last the ghosts can slumber peacefully,
Enjoy sweet dreams, forgiveness will take flight
The shame all gone and everyone set free.

Miles is talking, but she hears nothing. There's a heaviness in her chest. Suspicion returns.

39

'We shouldn't be here, Miss Antonia,' said Janneke, eyeing the imposing façade. 'Your mother said to make haste at the market and speed home as there be aplenty to do 'fore we depart.'

'This will only take a moment.' I pushed open the door and entered the courtyard, relieved the manservant recognised me with a friendly wave.

Janneke huffed and puffed behind me, trying to keep up as I hurried over the cobblestones towards the door in the corner.

As I entered the kitchen, Clara looked up. Bewilderment, then delight, filled her face, and with a cry, she rushed into my arms. 'Is it true? You're moving to England? Say it isn't so.'

It was too much to bear. I muffled my sobs against her shoulder. Within days I was to be separated from my sisterly companion, the only person in the world who so easily discerned my moods, understood my dreams, could boost my spirits with a game of knucklebones or a jest about annoying brothers.

The rustle of silk and the touch of a comforting arm prompted me to look into the kindly face of Mevrouw Rubens.

'I hear your family is preparing to depart our city, Antonia.'

I released my hold on Clara. Standing tall, I adjusted my skirts, wiped tears from my face and gazed into her eyes. 'I have worked hard these past years to learn how best to run a household. I know how to care for linen, pewter and glass, barter for goods, deal with tradesmen who come to the door. Many people declare that my behaviour, knowledge and skills are that of someone who is at least fourteen or fifteen.'

Janneke stepped from the corner of the kitchen. 'Miss Antonia, you must not–'

'Hush, Janneke. Let me finish.' I nudged her aside. 'I've learnt how to plan meals, manage servants, organise the laundry. I'm tall enough to work the linen press on my own. My musical skills on the *spinetten* may be lacking, but I continue to practise. Surely my ability to work hard and complete chores can make up for any deficiency I have with music.'

The room was silent except for the crackle of the fireplace. A maidservant stirred broth in a pot, while Cook rolled pastry on the table, both working with exaggerated care, staring at their tasks, not daring to look up.

'I would be a credit to your household, Mevrouw Rubens, and if it pleases you, I could also assist Albert and Nicolaas with their studies. I have studied alongside my brothers with a tutor ... Latin, French, Spanish, mathematics, geography and history ...'

Janneke tugged on my arm, leaning in to whisper. 'Please, Miss Antonia, we must leave.'

I shrugged her off and held Mevrouw Rubens' gaze. 'Let me stay here and work for my board and keep. You'll be pleased with my work.'

The Mistress touched the pearl brooch at her throat. She tucked her skirts beneath her and sat down, then clasped my hands between her own, her fingers soft and cool. A polished garnet set within a gold band glittered on her middle finger. 'Antonia, you are an accomplished young lady. I would be proud to have such a kind-hearted, diligent person join our household.'

I held my breath.

'But your mama and papa would miss you dreadfully and I couldn't take from them their only daughter.'

I shook my head. 'They shan't miss me at all. They have three other children, all boys, and—'

Mevrouw Rubens pressed her finger to my lips, cupped my face between her palms, smoothing away my tears with her thumbs. 'You're a dear child, Antonia, and everyone in this household will miss you, especially my Clara, but we will exchange letters.'

Tears rolled down my cheeks.

Clara wrapped her arms around her mother. 'Please, Mama ...'

Mevrouw Rubens embraced us, remaining silent, allowing us a few moments to accept that my plan to remain in Antwerpen was futile.

I leaned against Clara, my sister in all but name, and committed to memory the sound of her voice. Closing my eyes, I breathed in the chamomile scent of her hair, and tried to remember the last time we had worked in the kitchen together. Was it to make spiced bread or butter cookies? The kitchen had always been my favourite place in the Rubenshuis, always filled with the hubbub of servants talking, children laughing, pots being clanged, vegetables chopped. Now the room was silent, but for the logs crackling in the fire.

Footsteps approached from the other side of the kitchen door. A distinctive tread, deliberate and slow, bringing to mind the day Clara and I huddled in the storage chest.

Mevrouw Rubens straightened quickly. She lowered her voice. 'Hurry, Antonia. Say your farewells and return to your family. It's where you belong.'

Clara wrapped her arms around me, holding me tight. 'I promise to write.'

Mevrouw Rubens eased us apart. 'Enough, Clara. Let her go.'

The kitchen door swung open and the figure of Meneer Rubens stood in the doorway. He was silent, motionless, frowning.

Mevrouw Rubens hurried Janneke and me into the courtyard. I glanced over my shoulder for one final look at Clara and met the stern gaze of the Master. I had never seen such a steely look.

40

Charlotte walks along the street as if on automatic pilot, skirting around dawdling shoppers. She imagines the mind map spider, stretched across the wall of her living room, its legs twisting in all directions. Every evening when she arrives home from work, she returns it to the wall, studies it, fixates over it, adds another leg here, a scribble there. And every morning before she leaves, she folds it up and tucks it into her satchel. She's begun referring to it as a creature. Living and breathing, cunning but mute, scowling at her, defying her to make sense of its copious mutant legs. *Get me down from here*, it mewls in her dreams.

Refreshed from a long sleep, she'd woken that morning and set off with a vague idea of dropping by the Begijnhof to say hello to Edith. Perhaps she would be interested in visiting another museum next weekend? Charlotte had enjoyed their recent visit to the Plantin-Moretus – not just because of the startling revelation about Petra's family connection, but also the pleasure of sharing an afternoon with someone else who loved art and history.

She turns into the familiar square of Ossenmarkt, pauses at the massive wooden doors, and recalls her telephone conversation with Anna from two weeks ago. Petra's chest infection had developed into pneumonia, resulting in a hospital stay. The elderly *begijn*'s condition sounded dire, so Charlotte had been relieved to hear from Edith, during their visit to the Plantin-Moretus, that Petra's health had improved and she had returned to the Begijnhof to continue her recuperation. 'When I saw her,' Edith said, 'she was looking much better, sitting up in bed leafing through one of her art books.'

Although eager to talk with Petra about the map folio and

portfolio box, Charlotte realises she needs to wait for at least another week before she can make such a request. The elderly *begijn* is still recovering. Charlotte must be patient.

After passing the gatehouse, she enters the courtyard. Sparse autumn leaves cling to the branches of the fruit trees. The rusty blue Citroën is parked against the wall of the Ziekenhuis, in the same position as her previous visit. Charlotte has seen quite a few vintage Citroëns puttering around the streets of Antwerp, painted in the popular sky-blue, but she doubts the Begijnhof's car is in regular use. Like the Begijnhof buildings, the car is in dire need of an overhaul.

She spots a familiar figure in the garden. With her back to Charlotte, Edith wields a rake, scraping leaves into piles. Her movements appear half-hearted. She leans on the rake, head bent, shoulders shaking. Even from this distance, Charlotte can tell she is crying.

Charlotte walks towards the garden, rests her hand on the metal gate. She hesitates. Does she know Edith well enough to offer comfort for whatever is troubling her? Should she slip away unnoticed?

Edith squares her shoulders, wipes a hand over her face. Enough crying, her body language says. Time to get back to work. She resumes raking.

Charlotte pushes open the gate. The hinges screech, loud and offensive.

Edith turns with a look of surprise.

'I was passing by and wanted to thank you for an enjoyable visit to the Plantin-Moretus earlier this week,' says Charlotte.

'Thank you for inviting me.' Edith's tone is subdued.

Charlotte shifts her gaze to the pumpkin vine running rampant in the garden bed, not wanting to stare at Edith's tear-stained face. 'What a beautiful garden. You must have a green thumb.'

'Petra's the gardener, not me.' Her voice fades.

'I'm sorry for interrupting your work.'

'I could do with a break,' says Edith, moving to a stone bench.

Charlotte follows, pausing as Edith picks up a small notebook from the bench. They sit.

'What's your secret?' Charlotte indicates the vegetables. 'It's like a Garden of Eden.'

Edith holds up the notebook. Pocket-sized, bound in red cardboard, the cover splotched with dirty fingerprints. She fans the pages and stops in the middle, holding open a page filled with numbers and squiggles. 'Petra's garden journal.'

'I'm not much of a gardener.' Charlotte glances at the pages. Columns are filled with planting dates and weather conditions, pest eradication and crop yields. Symbols pepper the margins, abbreviations underscored in different colours. It makes little sense. A Rosetta Stone of horticultural riddles.

'I've tried to keep up with the garden since Petra became ill, but it's more work than I realised. And now ...' Edith's hands drop to her lap. The book closes.

'It's a large garden,' Charlotte reassures her.

Edith sits with shoulders slumped. Bare branches tap together in the breeze.

'I was the one who found her,' whispers Edith.

'Found her?'

'The bell rang for morning prayers.' Edith squeezes her hands together, knuckles waxy. 'I went to her room. She looked so peaceful. First time I've seen her with her hair out, spread across the pillow, long silver strands. Never seen her without a veil. Most of us stopped wearing them years ago, but Petra was a traditionalist. S'pose five decades in the same place will do that to a person.'

More silence, longer this time.

Edith swivels around to face Charlotte, her eyes red-rimmed. 'You *do* know, don't you?'

'I'm not sure ...'

'Petra died last night.'

PART TWO

'You must trust and believe in people or life becomes impossible.'

– Anton Chekhov

41

Dear Clara,

Six weeks have passed since we said farewell, yet so much has happened my mind is all ajumble with the sights, sounds and smells of this city. I apologise that I have had to wait so many weeks before writing to you, but Mama refuses to pay for my letters to travel via the courier service to Antwerpen, insisting they be conveyed free of charge by acquaintances. I am relieved she is willing to send my letters. I cannot approach Papa with such a request, as his mood is often grim.

Papa has not mentioned how long we will remain in London. Every time I see him looking glum, I hope he will give up this foolhardy plan and announce we are returning to Antwerpen.

He was a recluse for most of the journey, stomping about the deck, with ne'er a look in our direction, gazing across the Noordzee. I left him to his gloomy disposition and explored the ship with Hendrik and Niels. They played at pirates and sea captains, using oars from the jolly boat as makeshift weapons. Our fears of sea monsters and shipwrecks were forgotten as we slid across the deck in time to the pitch and roll of the waves, enjoying the sting of salt spray, smell of tarred rope, sound of sails cracking in the wind. We were free from the usual restraints of Mama and Janneke, who remained below deck, taking it in turns to heave into buckets and calm the fretful baby. Thankfully my constitution is so robust I experienced no ill effects from being tossed upon the Noordzee.

At Margate, our possessions were lifted ashore for the onward journey to London. Despite my silent prayers that the *spinetten* slip from the hoist and plummet to a watery grave, it survived. We jolted our way over potholed roads and moved into a house at Blackfriars.

With a reception room on the ground floor to entertain clients, and a light-filled workroom on the first floor, Papa is free to continue his work.

London is cluttered with half-timber houses leaning together, eaves nearly touching by the third storey, turning streets into tunnels. The main thoroughfares are cobblestoned, but the alleyways are rammed earth, which become oozing mud whenever it rains, which it does frequently. My pattens are of little use in keeping out of the muck. When it rains, shopkeepers set out boardwalks in front of their establishments, which become slippery, crowded and hazardous. Yesterday, I saw a gentlewoman tumble headfirst into the mire and had to stifle my laughter at the absurdity of her squealing in the mud like a piglet.

Papa spent most of our early weeks in London away from home, meeting with men to discuss potential commissions. One moment he was filled with enthusiasm, declaring he was close to obtaining work as an engraver, that he would soon be lauded as the finest in London. The next, he grumbled that your father has a foot in every royal court of Europe, including that of King James, that he would never be free from the shadow of the Master of Antwerpen.

Dear Clara, I mention this as I know you share my frustration over our fathers' conflict, which has torn us apart. I wish they had never argued about the wretched privilege. I wish they had never grown so ambitious they were blinded to the needs of others. I wish rumours had never spread about a fight between them, for I still cannot believe there is any truth in it. I wish my father had never insisted we leave Antwerpen. I wish I had never set foot in the sodden city of London. My heartsick wishes could fill this and all my future letters, but I will try to find more positive thoughts to share with you, otherwise you will tire of my complaints.

My father must have impressed several noblemen, because by the fourth week following our arrival a steady stream of visitors to the Blackfriars house reignited his congeniality. The walls of our home now echo with lively debate and the clink of wine glasses as guests enjoy refreshments. Visitors with plumed hats and brocade tunics are ushered into the foyer, where art is displayed and commissions secured.

Papa becomes puffed with pride each time he secures a new commission, announcing at the dinner table that he is an engraver in his own right and not a simple copyist. If I ever speak of my accomplishments I am accused of pride, while Papa's pronouncements of his success are acceptable. Perhaps when I reach adulthood, a little boastfulness will be tolerated.

Last week, the household was all aflutter with the arrival of a distinguished guest. Mama bustled along the corridor and found me lurking on the stairs. 'Private Secretary to Thomas Howard, Earl of Arundel is here to discuss a commission.'

The following day, William Braye's appearance caused Mama to flap about the kitchen, hissing instructions to Janneke while I sat unnoticed in the corner.

'For goodness' sake, girl, use the green glass goblets and stamped pewter. Viscount Braye is a confidant of George Villiers, Duke of Buckingham. We don't want him thinking we're paupers.'

I followed Janneke to the door of the reception room, peering around her girth, curious to glimpse our esteemed visitor. He looked unremarkable in his all-black attire and scruffy ginger beard.

Janneke smirked as she re-entered the kitchen, having delivered the tray of refreshments. 'I seen finer beards on billy goats.'

Billy goat or not, such commissions keep haunches of venison on our table, our beds soft with feathers, the pantry stocked with sugarloaf, peppercorns and cinnamon. By the second month of our arrival, Mama rustled about in new silk skirts of cerulean blue, and I received a rabbit-fur muff.

This morning, Papa reminded us of the importance of mastering English. 'The best way to learn a new language is full immersion.'

'Like drowning?' I asked.

His moustache twitched. 'Precisely. Except this you will survive.'

I have missed our lively repartee and am relieved the closeness Papa and I once shared is showing signs of returning. Existing on distant terms with him has been unbearable.

Next Monday, we begin working with our new English tutor. I pray he has a more likeable disposition than the odious Meneer Terhoeven. I am thankful Papa is allowing me to continue studying alongside Hendrik and Niels; life would be tedious if my days were filled with only chores, embroidery and playing the *spinetten*. I overheard Papa talking with our new tutor earlier this week and was pleased to hear him describe me as 'a gifted linguist, who looks and acts older than her twelve years'.

Do write soon. I eagerly await your reply.

Your loving friend,

Antonia

42

'He wants to see me now?' Charlotte glances at her notes. 'I'm preparing a tutorial. Could it wait until this afternoon?' She tries to ignore her scratchy eyes. She's working brutal hours to squeeze in her research about the stolen drawings among her university commitments. Ever the perfectionist, she refuses to let the quality of her lectures and tutorials suffer.

Miss Beulen is insistent. She is required immediately, won't take long.

By the time Charlotte walks along the corridor and enters the office, she's seething. With a faint smile, she acknowledges Miss Beulen sitting behind the desk.

'He'll be with you shortly,' says the assistant.

Charlotte frowns at the nameplate: *Miss Ulrika Beulen*. The name is an irritating reminder of her failure to discover who was responsible for ransacking her apartment. She'll stick with investigating seventeenth-century crimes.

A faint *ping* from the computer. 'You can go in now, Dr Hubert.'

Charlotte enters the inner office. Professor Sterck sits behind the enormous desk, a phone held to his ear. He gestures for her to sit in a chrome armchair while he finishes his phone conversation. '… little progress since the latest incident … thank you … goodbye.'

Sterck hangs up. 'Thank you for coming to see me.' He shuffles a handful of papers together. 'I understand you discovered something unusual about the map folio.' There are no rambling pleasantries, he gets straight to the point.

Her heart hammers. 'I'm not sure …'

Sterck fixes her with a cool green gaze. 'I'm well informed of everything happening in the department, especially any unusual discoveries. I believe the map folio had something inside the cover.'

Fighting the urge to clench her hands, Charlotte leaves them draped over the armrests with deliberate nonchalance. Her palms begin to sweat. He knows about Antonia's letter. Has Miles blabbed? An image flashes in her mind from the evening in the café last week: the shock of seeing the initials *SS* on his phone.

She silently wills Sterck to reveal his hand. What else does he know about the map folio?

'When the folio was damaged, the inside cover was torn. It contained an historic document, which you sent off for analysis.' His eyebrows lift. 'Invoices from Oscar Duval' – Sterck brandishes the pages in his hand – 'radiocarbon, chemical analysis, gas chromatography, mass spectrometry, graphology.'

So that's it. No one to blame but herself. She'd asked Oscar Duval to send the invoices directly to her, but perhaps they were bundled up by mistake with some others. She should've been more careful, should have insisted on receiving the invoices in person when she collected the historic documents from Duval's office.

Sterck pins her with his gaze. 'Having worked at other universities, I expect you understand the necessity of discussing your progress with your supervisor before sending material to an external specialist. Requests for off-site work need prior approval. I didn't sign any requests. You've earned this department excessive–'

'I'll pay them myself.'

He doesn't seem to hear. '–invoices for what exactly? A seventeenth-century letter? I'm sure it's interesting, but as for its historical significance, that should have been discussed–'

'I understand.' She tightens her jaw, fuming at being spoken to in such a belittling manner, but also furious with herself for not being more careful, and anxious whether he knows about her search for the *Pandora* drawings. Has he seen Antonia's documents? Does he know about the *Pandoras*? She's not ready to reveal her theories.

They stare at one another. Her hands grip the armrests, all attempts at nonchalance now forgotten. His fingers are interlaced, knuckles blanched.

About to launch into a terse justification, Charlotte stops herself. He's fixated on invoices and departmental budgets. He doesn't know about the details of Antonia's documents. She begins to calm.

Sterck leans back, face softening, looking contrite. 'Charlotte, I'm sorry. That came out much harsher than I intended. I've come from a meeting with a student accused of plagiarism and I've brought my irritation with me. I apologise.'

She offers a faint smile. 'How can we fix this?'

'I'll send the invoices to accounts for payment.' Waving his hand in a dismissive gesture, his tone is mellow now. 'I trust the information you gleaned from these tests was helpful. The letter is about Rubens?'

'Yes,' she replies, realising he sounds curious, almost friendly, rather than intrusive.

'Does it reveal anything unique?'

'It's too early to tell.' She smooths her hands over her trousers, wiping away the clamminess.

He shuffles pages together. 'Our budget for external consultancy will cover the costs.'

'Thank you.'

'I hear you've been delivering excellent lectures.'

She offers a soft smile. 'That's encouraging to hear. Thank you.'

'Are your tutorials going well?'

'Yes. My students are very enthusiastic.'

'Good ... good,' he murmurs, fiddling with the signet ring on his little finger. He clears his throat. A long pause. When he finally speaks, the words tumble out. 'I need to go away for a few days, and I want to speak to you about something before I leave. I'm not sure how to begin ...'

With a tiny flinch, she realises she's holding her breath. Awareness unfolds: his confidence has dissolved, replaced with nervousness. Is he about to share the real reason he called her into his office? Were the invoices an excuse?

'I should have spoken to you about this when we first met' – his voice is hoarse – 'but I wanted to find the best moment, and there never seemed to be the right time.'

She swallows. Throat dry.

'My father died recently and … I should have spoken to you sooner … about …' He falters. Licks his lips. 'I hadn't seen him in years. Unresolved issues, which I should've dealt with long ago. I always thought we'd talk about it one day, but we never did and now it's too late.' His voice slows. 'I've learnt that if you wait for the right moment, it may be too late. I don't want to make the same mistake with you.'

She folds her arms across her chest, intuitively making herself smaller. Is he trying to tell her that he knows about her?

His voice is low and measured, as if he has practised this speech, selected each word with care. 'I realise you never knew my father, but I don't want to have any more regrets about the past, or any blame to come between us. We've had too many regrets already, even though they've remained unspoken. If you would like to come to his funeral, you would be welcome. If you don't want to attend, I understand. But I want you to have the choice. It's your decision. After all, he was your grandfather.'

Her arms, heavy and limp, unfold into her lap. She replays his words, trying to understand them. *Your grandfather.*

He knows. He knows about her. But Mama said he never knew she was expecting. It's not possible. He knows, has known from the start. About her.

She blinks rapidly, focusing on the blue Murano bowl on his desk. Nothing makes sense. She wants to be far away from him, his words, this admission or confession or whatever it is. He wants to make it right, get it out in the open, no more secrets or blame or regrets. He knows about her.

Sterck places a white card on the desk in front of her, murmurs something about funeral details. 'I'm sorry I told you like this, Charlotte. I was waiting for the right time, but … I wanted you to hear it from me. I wanted to tell you … I've always known about you.'

He sits still, face pinched, watching and waiting.

A minute passes. Two.

She stares at his face, knows his mouth is no longer moving, but wonders if somehow he is still talking and she is unable to hear him over the muffled roar in her ears. She can't listen. Can't talk. Numbness and pain merge.

He leans forward. 'This must be a shock for you. When you're ready, please, we should talk. I'm sure you have questions.'

Charlotte gets slowly to her feet. 'I need some time to myself, to think.'

He opens the door for her. 'I understand. We can talk later, whenever you're ready.'

She nods, acknowledging she's heard him, but in reality, she's dazed and leaden. Her feet propel her back to the shared office. Miles is out. Slumping into a chair, she tries to make sense of what Sterck has just told her.

The silence is a dull howl, filling her ears, fogging her mind. *He's always known he is my father. Always known I am his daughter. Always known I exist, that I am his.*

She tries to recall the details of their first meeting, in the auditorium. There had been no hint of him knowing her true identity. When they'd met at the Rubenshuis, he'd offered his condolences for Rachael's passing, but made no mention of their romance. Their true relationship remains unspoken. Even now, with the past revealed, he still hasn't acknowledged his connection to her mother, their relationship implied only through a grandfather. *My* grandfather. Dead.

She doubles over, pain coursing from toes to skull, intersecting somewhere deep in her chest cavity, battering against her ribcage. Her breaths come in shallow bursts at the realisation that her mother lied to her for all these years.

He's always known. It was Mama who didn't want him, banished him from our lives, said he was dead, said he never knew of my existence. Mama lied.

Her lips part in a low moan. More virulent than her anguish and misery is a fierce anger. How could Mama betray her trust in this way, weaving an entire history of falsehoods? *He never knew I was pregnant. He doesn't know he's your father. He died years ago. We were better off without him.* Lies built upon lies, each one wrapped up in prejudice and misinformation, twisted around a core of bitterness.

43

September 29, 1621

Dearest Clara,

It was wonderful to receive your letter. I laughed when I read of Albert and Nicolaas hiding in the cupboard and jumping out to scare Cook.

I apologise for my comments about your father in my previous letter. I hope you did not take offence, as none was intended. Naturally he is the Master of Antwerpen, for his skills are unmatched by any other, and he is well known in every royal court for his diplomatic expertise. He was always courteous and kind to me, except on the day I said farewell in your kitchen and his stern gaze filled me with concern. I sincerely hope his anger with my father does not extend to me. As for the appalling gossip about my father physically attacking yours, I am relieved you have heard nothing further. Please let me know if new information emerges. Just because our fathers' relationship has come undone, the same need not happen to us.

My mastery of the English language is progressing, albeit through unapproved methods. Much can be learnt while loitering in corridors, listening in on conversations. Visitors' talk is so much more interesting than the idle chatter of servants. I would prefer to listen to discussions of the Spanish Match between Prince Charles and the Infanta than remain in the kitchen to hear Janneke's endless complaints of grey skies, filthy streets and over-salted cheese.

Our new tutor, Mister Constantijn Cuypers, is youthful, soft-spoken and Catholic. Born in London, he resides in Blackfriars with his parents, who are originally from Brussels. Although he speaks perfect Flemish, he uses only English with us. Whenever Janneke enters the room, he flushes beetroot red. It is obvious to everyone he is sweet on her, but she tells me she has no interest in skinny men who prefer England to our homeland.

Twice a week, Mister Cuypers takes us on excursions to practise our English. Janneke joined us last week, on a day when mist hung like gossamer over the Thames. We squeezed into a wherry, with Janneke jiggling baby Lucas on her knee, and made a round trip between Blackfriars and London Bridge, scooting past dozens of boats plying their trade on the river. It was a delightful jaunt apart from spying half a dozen heads impaled on spikes on the bridge's gatehouse, their empty eye sockets plucked clean by the crows.

'Are those Catholics who refused to take the Oath of Allegiance?' I asked.

Mister Cuypers would not respond, instead trying to distract us with an explanation of how the arches support the many shops built upon the span.

Lively discussions about politics and religion have surrounded me for years, so I went to Papa with my questions about tensions in the court of King James. Thankfully, Papa's glum mood is lifting more regularly, so he sometimes allows me to sit with him in his workroom. Except for the smaller windows and darker floorboards, I could be in his Antwerpen workroom. Against the wall is the familiar oak cabinet with the heavy doors carved with foliage and fruit, and the year 1608 chiselled into the moulding.

'Why does the Protestant king want his son to marry the Catholic princess from Spain?' I asked.

'Royal marriage negotiations are complex,' he replied. 'By linking two royal houses in marriage, there is hope peace will be maintained and the high cost of war avoided.'

'Mister Cuypers said the English Commons prepared a petition to seek war with Spain, for the Prince of Wales to marry a Protestant princess, and for stronger anti-Catholic laws to be enforced in England. If these laws occur, will we return to Antwerpen?'

Papa looked at me from beneath his furrowed brows. 'Did Mister Cuypers also tell you King James dissolved Parliament upon hearing the petition? The King is no fool. He knows the discord between Catholics and Protestants has bloodied his country since Henry the Eighth broke from Rome in 1534. He has no desire to return to those days. There is no need to fear. We are as safe in London as in Antwerpen. My work allows me to dance on both sides of the fence. I shall use this to my advantage to secure work and keep us safe.'

Papa focused on a book propped on a stand, the pages open at a nobleman's portrait. His eyes flitted between the portrait and a copper plate in which he was scratching the man's likeness.

I pointed at the book. 'Your engraving is the same as the portrait—'

'Is it?' he interrupted. 'Look closely at the part of the man's face I have finished engraving, and tell me whether it is the same as the picture in the book.'

Studying the two images, I realised Papa had given the man less hair atop his head and trimmed the curls around his ears. 'His hair is different.'

'I have also increased the number of lines around his eyes and across his forehead. The Earl of Arundel's private secretary commissioned an engraving to accurately show the Earl's current age.'

'Is your engraving still considered a copy?'

'It is an original work, created by my own hand and therefore not a copy.'

'Can you print from the engraving and sell the copies?'

'Indeed, that is how I earn my living.'

'Do you own the original engraving plate? Can you do with it as you wish?'

Papa placed the burin on the table. 'Why all these questions?'

'Sometimes I hear you called an engraver and other times a copyist. I am curious to know which is correct.'

'Which do you think I am?' The kindness in his eyes showed he was not annoyed by my questions, although his expression remained serious.

'You are' – I watched his face, waiting for the slightest change – 'an engraver.'

A soft smile appeared beneath his moustache. 'Years ago, when I first began duplicating images onto copper, I was a copyist. But nowadays, because I create my own works, I am an engraver, an artist in my own right.'

'You dance on both sides of the fence,' I said.

He chuckled, picked up the burin and began humming a Flemish folk song.

'Do you miss Antwerpen?' I asked.

'I miss the cheese of our homeland, but we have one another and that is all that matters.'

'But you like Somerset cheese now.'

'I enjoy sharp, crumbly Cheddar just as I enjoy the intense flavour of Herve from our homeland. But there is no reason to yearn for something out of reach. The markets here do not sell Herve, so I have a new favourite.'

'I hope you won't replace me with a new favourite as easily as you have your cheese.'

He smiled as he tweaked my chin, leaving a smudge of charcoal.

It is wonderful to see Papa's happiness emerge after months of gloominess. Although I will never concede London is superior to Antwerpen, my family lives here satisfactorily. Hopefully only for a short time.

Your loving friend,

Antonia

44

Charlotte slams the notebook closed, walks to the window, slumps onto the sill. Doubling over, she releases a growl of pent-up frustration.

She remains hunched over, her eyes closed, concentrating on the tightness in her shoulders and back. *Relax, let the tension go*. But it's no use. Ever since Sterck's disclosure two days ago, she has seethed with resentment over the double betrayal. Sterck's revelation, coupled with her mother's lies, have left her doubting her ability to ever trust anybody again. Rehashing conversations, both recent and from long ago, she tries to recall precise words, an expression, a nuance, anything to make it feel different, to diminish the wrong, lessen the hurt. But the wound remains, like a deadweight in her chest, painful and raw. The lies and betrayals will always exist. It's too late for them to disappear. Too late for her mother to ask Charlotte's forgiveness, for trust to be restored. Her heartbreak and grief has turned to fury. How dare they? How dare they lie as if lies don't matter? As if someone's life, *her* life, *her* feelings don't matter.

Her choice to not attend the funeral had been made quickly, without qualms. Why should she attend the funeral of a complete stranger? Even Sterck had admitted being estranged from him.

She straightens up, turns towards the window, and stares at her reflection. Her breath fogs the glass, her image fading. She's still sitting at the window when the door opens.

Miles drops an armful of folders on the desk, sits in the chair. 'I've just come from a meeting. Sterck said Petra died on the weekend.'

'I meant to tell you,' says Charlotte. 'Edith told me when I visited the Begijnhof on Saturday.'

She leans her head against the window. Did Anna telephone Sterck with the news or did he hear it from another source? Is there any information, however remotely connected to the university, to which Sterck is not privy?

'I visited again this morning,' she says, 'to check on Edith, see how she's doing.'

She recalls her visit to Anna's office earlier in the morning. She'd offered her condolences, hoping they didn't sound like the platitudes she'd received when her mother died. Petra had been nearly eighty years old, a *begijn* for five decades, Anna said. Charlotte felt humbled to hear of Petra's years of dedicated service and faith.

She had found Edith sitting alone in the chapel. After expressing her sympathy again and asking if there was anything she could do, Edith asked Charlotte to sit quietly by her side, keep her company. Together, they gazed up at the stained-glass window. A two-dimensional fragmented Saint Catherine, robed in deep purple and gold, gazed back at them, impassive and serene. Charlotte remembered the times after her mother's funeral when her aunt had visited and sat quietly at her side, and how comforted she'd felt by her silent presence.

'Petra and Edith were close,' says Charlotte to Miles. 'Sint-Catharina's is small. About twenty *begijnen* live there. Some, like Petra, have been there for decades.'

'Must be difficult for them.'

'She died in her sleep.'

'Peaceful way to go.'

'It's a strange feeling.' Charlotte twists the turquoise ring around her finger. 'I never met her, but I feel as though I knew her.' She moves across to her desk, stares down at the notebook with her *Pandora* research. Her mouth softens as she recalls opening the notebook last week and discovering Miles had scrawled the words *Great Rubens Mystery* across the inside cover, along with a jagged diagonal line simulating a rip.

'What's this? Defacing private property?' she had quipped, mildly irritated but also amused.

'Like you haven't damaged private property before,' he replied with a teasing grin.

'I've never–'

'In the conservation room, with the scalpel, a priceless De Wit, Miss Scarlet!'

'I didn't vandalise it,' she retorted.

She opens the notebook, idly flicks through pages, the writing swimming before her eyes. Her hopes of talking to Petra, her strongest lead yet, have come to a dead end. Literally. She shuts the notebook. Closes her eyes. Rests her head in her hands.

'What's next?' asks Miles.

'What do you mean?' she murmurs, head still propped in her hands, eyes closed.

'Your research ... to find the *Pandoras*?'

She sits back and stares at him. 'Miles ...' She shakes her head, unable to complete the thought.

'You're resourceful. You'll find another lead.'

She emits a soft harumph.

'You're a professional researcher, Charlotte. You do this for a living. You're good at it.'

'You warned me it would be like searching for a needle in a haystack.'

He begins pacing around the room, arms gesturing. 'Study the photographs Theo took of the maps. There may be something you missed. Examine land and house ownership records of the Vorsterman family. Trace their genealogy.'

Staring at the wooden floorboards, she lets his words float over her. He doesn't understand the complexity of the search, how implausible it would be for such delicate drawings to have survived, hidden away, for nearly four hundred years. Perhaps they were found centuries ago, tossed in the corner of an attic, and have long since succumbed to mould and damp.

Charlotte recalls an exhibition at The Met she attended years ago, catching the bus south from Dartmouth to view over one hundred of the Master's finest drawings. Simply titled *Peter Paul Rubens: The Drawings*, she had explored the exhibition and studied each masterpiece in silent awe. Drawn on paper and executed in pen and brown ink, Rubens used ink wash to indicate light and shade. A touch of white to highlight the tip of a nose, sheen on a cheek, glimmer in the eyes. Smudges of grey to indicate shadows along the jaw, under the neck, a dimpled chin.

Each drawing was created by Rubens on heavy cream-coloured paper, now speckled with age-spots and stains, creased and worn. Every line and dab, rendered in pen and ink, at risk of being obliterated by paper-loving insects, smeared and abraded by careless handling, deteriorating due to excessive temperature, moisture or light. Four-hundred-year-old drawings on paper are incredibly delicate compared to oil on canvas. Miles has no idea.

'Have you thought of contacting the Antwerpen Historische Genealogie Society?' he asks. 'They may have information on the Vorsterman family. They're a volunteer organisation–'

'I know of them,' she mutters.

'Their records are extensive. Sterck is their president, so you could speak to him–'

She leaps up, voice loud. 'The last person I want to involve is Sterck.'

Miles stares at her, mouth agape. 'He has valuable contacts. Why are you so reluctant to ask for his help?'

'He'll slow me down with his bureaucratic style, establish sub-committees, consider everything at a snail's pace.'

Now she's the one pacing, waving her arms. It has nothing to do with being his daughter, she tells herself; it's his precise, exacting style. She doesn't want to be dictated to on her own project. She's willing to hear suggestions, but not be bulldozed. Happy to have a mentor, but not an autocrat. She knows enough about Sterck's character to predict where he would stand on the issue of the *Pandoras*.

'All the work I've done ...'

'You don't want to lose control,' says Miles.

They fall silent. A gust of wind rattles the windows.

'I understand your reluctance to ask for help,' says Miles. 'Budget constraints have made everyone tense. You've heard of others being underhanded about securing support for projects, swiping ideas, taking recognition when it's not due. Makes it difficult to trust. But not everyone's like that, Charlotte. Don't judge everyone by the same mould.'

'Yeah. Okay.' She offers a cursory nod. Crossing to her desk, she tidies a stack of folders. Her mind flashes back to Miles and Sterck exchanging whispered words, muttering together, furtive looks, text messages. Can Miles be trusted? Her suspicions won't vanish.

'You can't work in isolation,' he continues. 'When you work on a project, if it's going to be successful, you need to be a team player, accept suggestions from others, recognise there are others with experience and skills who can help.'

She's tempted to fire off a scathing retort, but tightens her jaw and says nothing.

His hands jab at air. 'You keep so much to yourself; not only this research, but your thoughts, who you are. You're so closed off.'

'There's nothing wrong with being private.' Her cheeks flush.

'True' – he frowns – 'but it's an exhausting way to live.'

His psychoanalysis is irritating. She wants it to stop, but throwing acerbic remarks at him may damage their relationship. She may have questioned his trustworthiness at times, but she also cares about him, doesn't want to hurt him.

Miles pulls a sheet of paper from a folder on his desk, thrusts it at her, irritable. 'Meant to give you this.'

She scans his messy handwriting, recognises the third verse from the *Italies* map. The Genoese verse is written alongside his English translation.

'I checked a few Genoese words with my nonna.' His tone is gruff. 'It's all correct.'

'Thank you.' She scans the doodles Miles had scribbled on the page, pausing at the initials *SS*. He has embellished them with thick twisted curves, speckled with dots, reminiscent of pretzels. She has to ask him. Has to know if they refer to Sébastien Sterck. Did he text Sterck with details of the verse while in the café? Has he been feeding information to Sterck?

'I'm curious,' she hesitates, wanting to know, but fearful. She points at the initials. 'These doodles. What are they?'

He smiles. 'When I speak to my nonna on the phone, I often doodle her initials. Her name is Silvana Salatina.'

'Salatina,' she repeats. Confused.

'It means pretzel in Italian.'

'Silvana Salatina is your grandmother?'

'Sì,' he replies in Italian.

Charlotte closes her eyes for a moment, then opens them and smiles warmly. 'Thanks for your help, Miles. I appreciate it.'

45

Charlotte slips unseen through the side door of Sint-Jacobskerk as members of the set-up crew disappear into the cavernous interior. She walks down the deserted south aisle, inhaling the chalky odour of ancient dust. Stone columns soar up and up, meeting at the roof in a spangle of ribbed vaults. A towering expanse, eerie with echoes and shadows.

The concert is due to begin in an hour. She had purchased the ticket from Karl two weeks ago but remained indecisive about attending, unsure whether she wanted to be alone or with people. The past week had left her mentally fatigued, her mind replaying the conversation with Sterck on a loop: *I've always known about you. I've always known about you.* On a whim, she'd picked up the ticket and headed to the church.

The strange echoes around Sint-Jacobskerk set her teeth on edge. The screech of chairs being dragged across the floor. Voices of the set-up crew calling out. She flinches at the slightest noise.

Hurrying along the aisle, she follows its curve around the choir until she reaches the easternmost point of the church. She enters a side chapel. Marble statues gleam in the half-light, ghostly and surreal.

It's too dark to make out the painting above the altar, or read the inscription on the marble slab in the floor, but she knows them well. 'Petrus Paulus Rubenius.' She whispers the Latin. Leaning against the low balustrade separating visitor from entombed, she waits for the sense of peace to envelop her, as it always does.

But tonight, she's too jittery. It was reckless to slip into a dark corner by herself, she realises. Especially with this morning's shocking news that a fourth person has been attacked.

Miles had burst into the office before nine, gesturing with alarm, his hands devoid of the usual takeaway coffees and cinnamon scrolls. She stared stupidly at his empty hands, thinking he must have forgotten it was *his* day. He always got the coffees on Thursdays.

'It happened last night, after ten. History student. Female. Second-year Master's program. She was unlocking her bike and a man crept up on her. He was wearing a balaclava, pushed her over, grabbed her laptop bag.'

'My god, that's awful. Was she hurt?'

'Minor bruises. Happened so quickly she had no time to react.'

Charlotte sat in a daze as Miles reeled off facts. Four attacks in eight months. Three females, one male. All post-grads from the Arts Faculty. Campus police still investigating. Security measures to be increased: more night guards, police patrols, CCTV, outdoor lighting.

Will it be enough? she wonders. Will the latest victim quit the university and leave Antwerp, overwhelmed with fear?

She gazes up at the altar painting and shivers. The discordant sound of a cello fills the air, notes wavering as the instrument is tuned. A violin joins in, then a flute, the notes jarring at first, then gliding into harmony. She swivels towards the music, nose in the air as if smelling the chords.

The music stops. Ringing silence.

A sound comes from the apse, far removed from the concert preparations. The faint tread of footsteps approaching the tomb, leather soles placed carefully upon flagstones. Someone is close by.

She turns and runs, fleeing the chapel and eerie footsteps, slowing only once she glimpses the audience, hears the buzz of conversation.

Flashing her ticket, she walks down the main aisle, looking for a seat. Catches sight of people she knows. Willem, easily recognised by his height, who waves and smiles at her. Arnold, talking to a cluster of people from the history department.

'Charlotte!' Karl beckons her over.

After shuffling along the row, she sits down, makes small talk, relieved to sit among familiar people. Safe.

She closes her eyes when the first mellow notes of the cello begin Pachelbel's 'Canon'. The harpsichord provides the steadying chords of the underlying heartbeat, holding the elements of the composition together. The violins float with the melody, drawing in then moving out, urging the descant to rise into the vaulted ceiling. The pressure nudging against her temples begins to ease. The skin around her eyes relaxes. For a moment, she soars with the music.

At the closing notes of Telemann's final 'Paris Quartet', she lets out a protracted sigh. Joining in the applause, she agrees with Karl when he comments on the amazing acoustics.

'I know one of tonight's organisers,' says Karl. 'He'll take our group up the tower. It's normally closed to the public.'

A flurry of people begin moving down the aisle. Karl herds a group to one side, introducing his friend who will guide them up the tower. Charlotte is caught in the throng, ushered through a narrow door and up a curved stairwell, which they climb in semi-darkness. They troop one behind another, searching for steps in the gloom.

'One hundred and sixty-three feet to the top,' the guide calls out. Laughter and talk dwindle as all but the fittest begin to puff.

Charlotte stumbles on an uneven step, bumps against the person ahead. Hears heavy breathing from the person behind. She's hemmed in. Panic surges. She's assailed by a flashback of the stranger following her as she walked along deserted streets. Wild imaginings of being followed by a stranger wearing a balaclava, snatching her satchel with its precious contents, becoming the attacker's next victim. In every dark stairwell, on every shadowy corner lurks a variation of this stranger. Even tonight, standing before Rubens' tomb, her mood is diminished, fearful someone is watching her.

This constant suspicion has affected every aspect of her life since arriving in Antwerp. Yesterday's heated discussion with Miles comes rippling back. His accusations of her being judgemental, refusing to accept help, keeping her thoughts to herself, being closed off. All completely true. He spoke the truth, and it stings.

She's tired of being distrustful and alone. Miles is right: it's an exhausting way to live. He's on her side. She needs to let him in, to demonstrate her trust. And she's so damn weary of being alone.

By the time she reaches the outside deck, her breath is ragged. The inky sky is dotted with stars. Immense and spectacular, stretching to oblivion.

The small observation deck is crowded, people crushed together, joking about the cold. Shivering, Charlotte wraps her arms around herself, wishes she'd worn a thicker coat. Pushed up against the stone parapet, she's buffeted by the wind. People squeeze past. A figure stands behind her.

'You look freezing,' says Miles, leaning over her shoulder.

She nods, lips too cold to form words, but suddenly warm.

He stretches out his arms, resting his hands on the stone half-wall, curving his body around her as a windbreak. He points out the city's features: 'Stadhuis ... Sint-Pauluskerk ...'

She closes her eyes and leans back, his chest warm against her, his breath soft on her neck.

46

November 7, 1621

Dearest Clara,

The English have strange customs I will never understand, no matter how long I live in this grey, damp land. Two nights ago, the evening peace was shattered with sudden cheers. As we peered from the window, crowds surged along the street in the direction of Ludgate Hill. In the middle of the mob, four men pushed a cart which carried a life-sized puppet of a man wearing breeches, waistcoat and a towering black hat. Papa and the menservants rushed outside and were soon lost in the laughing throng. I was forbidden to follow and had to satisfy my curiosity with my nose pressed to the glass. Life can be dull for girls. The men returned hours later, filled with laughter. The event commemorated a Catholic Englishman called Fawkes who unsuccessfully attempted to blow up Parliament sixteen years ago, and is remembered each year with a burning effigy. The English are indeed eccentric people.

Nearly four months have passed since we arrived in London. Our mastery of English improves and local influences have slowly crept into our household. Hearty Flemish stews, meatballs and fennel-seed bread are often replaced with such local dishes as goose stuffed with apples, game pie oozing with gravy and buttered samphire. Although Janneke complains at having to use unfamiliar ingredients, I've seen the pleasure with which she licks venison gravy from the plate.

Mama, who at first was a staunch adherent to all things Flemish, has weakened her resolve and allowed certain English customs into our home. When a neighbour suggested one way our family could better integrate would be to adopt a more local style of dress, Mama finally acquiesced.

'Perhaps I should try these soft lace collars,' she said as we eyed the limp lace in the windows of the haberdashers on Hatfields Lane.

The next day, she ordered Janneke to pack away the goffering iron for stiffening the ruffs. None was more pleased than Janneke to store the irons in an oak chest, knowing blistered fingers would be a suffering of the past.

Although some local influences are accepted in our household, one practice we avoid is Protestantism. We are required by the *Act of Uniformity*, made law in 1558, to attend the local Protestant church and worship from the Book of Common Prayer, but that doesn't stop Papa from leading us in Catholic prayers morning and night.

'What happens behind the closed doors of my home,' said Papa, after prayers one evening, 'is the business of God and me. No one else.'

Papa was quick to point out that English laws are lenient enough to allow Catholics to live and work in England.

'Take me, for instance.' He thumped his chest. 'I am Catholic and have numerous patrons and am considered one of the most successful engravers in London. Anthony van Dyck, who is Catholic, worked in London earlier this year and was well received by the Protestant court.'

'Meneer Rubens is also Catholic,' said Hendrik. 'Has he also worked for King James?'

I held my breath, wondering how Papa would respond. But he busied himself cutting a lump of Cheddar and appeared not to have heard Hendrik.

Mama regularly declares her aversion to all things Protestant, insisting the use of Protestant books of liturgy and following non-Catholic rituals are betrayals of the True Faith. She attends church at St Mary-le-Bow with a grimace upon her face, moving her lips but not speaking aloud the words from the Protestant prayer book. Her Catholic prayer book is hidden in her upstairs chamber.

Yesterday, on our return from church, Mama directed me upstairs.

'I saw you in church today reciting the Protestant Prayer of Confession. You must follow the Catholic form.' Mama indicated I was to kneel at the prayer stool in her chamber.

'What if someone notices me reciting the Catholic *Confiteor?*'

'There is no need to speak the *Confiteor* aloud while in church, but say the True Words silently in your heart, remembering God hears all prayers.'

I remained on my knees for the next hour, repeating the *Confiteor* until she was satisfied it was perfect. When I next attend church, I will appear Protestant on the outside, but my Catholic heart will silently repeat the prayers of the True Faith.

This must be what Papa means when he talks about dancing on both sides of the fence.

Your loving friend,

Antonia

47

A gust of wind sets the windows rattling. Crossing the room, Charlotte hovers her palm over the gaps, the icy air reminding her of last night's freezing wind atop Sint-Jacobskerk tower. 'Is there anything we can do about this draught?'

Miles tears a page of discarded newspaper, rolls it into a thin wad and shoves it into the gap. 'I've done this the past two winters.'

They work together, shoving newspaper into all the gaps, pausing occasionally to look outside.

Naked branches are silhouetted against a silvery sky. People scuttle across the courtyard, scarves and coats flapping. Everyone moves quickly, except a small figure in grey. The woman walks to a door, scrutinises the sign, then moves to the next door. Continues along the façade: walking, pausing, reading. She looks familiar.

Charlotte peers into the courtyard. 'My goodness ... is that Edith?'

Miles wipes condensation from the glass. 'Could be.'

'She looks lost.' Scrabbling under the desk for her boots, Charlotte tugs them on, then pulls on her coat. Hurrying through the doorway, she calls over her shoulder: 'Back soon.'

A minute later, she arrives in the courtyard, puffing out clouds. Edith has retreated to a bench, holding a card in her purple-gloved fingers. The bright purple stands out against the grey of her outfit.

Charlotte slows her pace. Two yards from the bench, she stops. 'Edith? Hello.'

The *begijn* looks up, eyes wide. She holds up the card. 'Your business card doesn't say which entrance. I was going to call first, but changed my mind and decided to walk over. Sometimes it's easier talking face-to-face.'

'Why don't you come inside? I'll make some tea.'

Fifteen minutes later, with her hands wrapped around a steaming mug, Edith remains uneasy, flitting from one topic to the next: the Royal Museum's latest exhibition, bottling autumn fruit, selecting hymns for Petra's funeral.

'It's a difficult time. So many decisions to make.' Charlotte remembers the tasks facing her in the days after her mother's death.

Sliding the empty mug onto the desk, Edith studies the dirt under her fingernails. 'I worked in the garden this morning, then read Petra's journal. The planting schedule, getting rid of leaf spot.' She scrapes under a nail, dislodges a tiny clump of earth. Talks to her fingers. 'The last few pages are confusing. It's Petra's handwriting, but the words are different from the rest of the journal. Not about gardening, but poetry, Bible verses, personal thoughts. She mentioned the portfolio box.'

Charlotte's pulse quickens. She looks across at Miles, who returns her wide-eyed gaze.

Edith pulls the red-covered journal from the pocket of her cardigan. Opening it to a page near the back, she offers the journal to Charlotte. 'Petra wrote out a poem by Keats, then crossed it out.'

Charlotte tries to make out the words beneath heavy slashes of ink. The paper is torn in several sections where the pen pushed too heavily.

A thing of beauty is a joy for ever;
Its loveliness increases; it will never
Pass into nothingness; but still will keep
A bower quiet for us, and a sleep
Full of sweet dreams, and health, and quiet breathing.
                    John Keats, Endymion, 1818

Edith's words tumble out. 'I don't know much about poetry, but it sounds to me like this poem is all about beautiful objects and how much happiness they bring. Petra enjoyed going to art museums and looking at beautiful objects. She loved paintings, sculptures, old maps, engravings. Why would she write out this poem and then cross it out? And at the last minute, just before she became ill, she cancelled, for no reason, a museum visit we had planned together. Simply told me she wasn't going to visit any more museums. Said she'd had enough ... obsessing ... over ...' Edith's face crumples. Her fingers work the pleats of her skirt, scrunching the fabric.

Charlotte rests her hand on Edith's forearm, gives her a reassuring squeeze.

Hadn't Anna mentioned Petra may have been suffering from undiagnosed dementia? Such an indiscriminate disease with complex symptoms: confusion, forgetfulness, personality changes. Charlotte reminds herself to simply offer comfort, not solutions. Soothing words and an encouraging presence are what helped her during the early days of her own grief.

'Petra was nearly eighty,' she says, patting Edith's arm. 'A remarkable age. So devoted.'

Edith pulls a handkerchief from her pocket, dabs her eyes.

'Were these Petra's favourite verses?' Charlotte points to the writing under the poem.

Turn my eyes away from worthless things;
Preserve my life according to your word.

Psalm 119:37

Watch and pray that you may not enter into temptation.
The spirit indeed is willing, but the flesh is weak.

Matthew 26:41

'No. Petra's favourite verse was from Isaiah chapter forty.' Edith turns to the last page, which is filled with crabbed writing. 'This is what I wanted to show you. The Bible verses relate to it. Petra wrote about temptation, her ancestors and the portfolio box.'

The same handwriting fills the final pages of the journal, but here, it is faltering. Several words, so wobbly, are almost indecipherable. Others are scribbled out, leaving redacted rectangles. Charlotte reads Petra's scrawl aloud.

Please forgive me for the times I have fallen into temptation, when
I listened to the uncharitable thoughts filling my mind and ignored

the needs of my sisters. I have tried to focus on God, but I have
proven myself to be weak and unworthy of this life of servitude.
I beg forgiveness for obeying my heart and being lured by the sins
of Envy and Greed. Again and again, my head is turned by
Materialism and Man-Made Beauty. No matter how many times I
tell myself physical objects are trivial and worthless, I still surrender
to their lure and they constantly pull me away from the life of duty
I committed to decades ago—

'Petra was a private person,' interrupts Edith, twisting the handkerchief around her fingers. 'Didn't talk much about herself. She was hard-working, devout, solitary. We talked about paintings and visited museums together …'

Charlotte exchanges a look with Miles, mutely conveying her hope that Edith continues reminiscing.

'I remember the first exhibition we saw together,' says Edith. '*Nature and Fantasy* at the Royal Museum in Brussels. First time I ever saw paintings by Arcimboldo … apples for cheeks, pear for a nose. What was the moustache? Asparagus? And the portrait of a lady made of flowers. So beautiful …'

Charlotte glances at the open journal on the desk. The writing is unsteady, the touch light. Yet every so often, the pen had pushed with greater force, engraving the paper with an imprint, the pen held with a fierce emotion, frustration or anger, perhaps?

'The Brueghel exhibition was one of our favourites …' Edith continues talking.

Charlotte scans Petra's writing. A tirade of guilt, focusing on deficiencies and attempts to overcome them. *Materialism and Man-Made Beauty … physical objects are trivial and worthless.*

Edith's reminiscing shifts to Petra. '… often found her alone in the chapel, kneeling in prayer. I didn't understand until later she was filled with guilt. Torn between her duty as a *begijn* and loyalty to her family. Then the accident with the bricks falling from the belfry, the investigation. We had to stop giving public tours. Everything at the Begijnhof is in such a bad state. Every day is a struggle. Then Petra's death.' Tears trickle alongside her nose. She blots at them with the handkerchief.

Charlotte gently touches Edith's shoulder.

Edith's recollections move to Petra's final weeks. 'When the map folio arrived back at the Begijnhof, I carried it to her bedroom. I felt awful about sending it to the university with the almanacs. She was quite cross when we realised what had happened, and was relieved to have it back. She put it inside a large box, placed it inside her cupboard.'

Another five minutes of tearful reminiscing pass before Edith stows her scrunched handkerchief in her pocket and picks up the journal. She reads aloud the final paragraph of Petra's writing.

There is nothing left for me but to deny myself even the trivialities of my ancestors. Cast them aside. As Matthew instructs, if my right eye causes me to stumble, gouge it out and throw it away. I have done this. Not thrown away exactly, but set aside, far from temptation. Yet guilt remains. I promised Moeke I would look after the treasures in the portfolio box and ensure they lasted for the next generation. But it is too much. Please forgive me, Moeke. I am weak and unworthy. I pray the right person is guided to Moeke's belongings, where those Beauties, which are both a source of joy but also an anguish to me, are set aside. I hope whoever comes after me will look at these Beauties and find peace.

48

December 5, 1621

Dearest Clara,

Enclosed with this letter is a sampler, which I have been labouring for three months. I hope you enjoy rearranging the letters to discover a hidden message of sisterly affection.

Thank you for your Christmas well wishes. It was wonderful to read of your family's activities as you prepare for advent celebrations at Sint-Jacobskerk.

I was saddened to hear your father still feels animosity towards my papa. I had hoped their enmity would ease over time and would be limited to themselves, but it appears your father's anger may also extend to me, given I am a Vorsterman. Does your father know we exchange letters? Will he forbid you to write? Who in your household organises the sending and receiving of our letters?

Oh, Clara, we are blameless of our fathers' disagreement and yet we suffer. I will try not to worry about these concerns and, instead, share with you our Christmastide celebrations.

Tomorrow, we celebrate the Feast of Sint Nicolaas. Baby Lucas, now ten months old, is wide-eyed with awe. Niels chatters with excitement, reminding his older brother to be on his best behaviour lest Sint Nicolaas punish his naughtiness by leaving a piece of coal in his shoe. Hendrik is filled with bravado, confident his virtues will outweigh his misbehaviours. As for me, I try to complete my studies and chores diligently, but it is difficult to remain cheerful, knowing this is our first Christmastide in London's bleakness.

The past week has been busy. Three fat geese were plucked and I collected the downy feathers floating like snowflakes around the courtyard. Chestnuts were roasted, *worst* smoked, *speculoos* baked. Ludo supervised the delivery of wine into our cellar from the

Farringdon wine merchant, and a delicious aroma filled the kitchen when Janneke heated red wine with cinnamon, cloves and orange peel.

On the day of our Christmastide gathering, Hendrik and Niels were scrubbed as much as the geese and warned to remain quiet, a near impossible task for lively young boys. Poor Lucas was strapped into an embroidered bonnet and resembled a trussed goose.

Mama presented me with a new lace collar. 'Made in Brussels,' she said, arranging the delicate tatting around my shoulders. 'Keep an eye on your brothers, Antonia, and keep them from mischief.'

Being the eldest can be tiresome.

We smiled obediently to each guest who arrived, but soon grew tired of standing like tin soldiers in the foyer, speaking only when spoken to by the adults. I lingered near groups, listening to talk of the King's wish for greater religious tolerance, their outrage over Spain's insistence the English Prince convert to Catholicism if he marries the Spanish Infanta. There is clearly no end to the unrest between Protestant and Catholic in this country. While dissension remains in the Commons it will heighten anxiety in every Catholic household in England, including ours.

Hendrik and Niels quickly became restless. Mama raised her eyebrows at me from across the room and I turned to see Hendrik gingerly place a snail into a bowl of roasted chestnuts. Thankfully, I rescued the snail before our tutor's mother, Mevrouw Cuypers, plucked what she believed to be a tasty morsel from the bowl.

I spied a stooped gentleman entering the foyer. 'Mister Hawthorn has arrived,' I announced. Hendrik and Niels happily followed me, eager to greet our favourite guest.

Mister William Hawthorn first visited our house in October when Mama was introduced to him by one of our Catholic neighbours. Formerly a parish priest in Hatfield, Mister Hawthorn has forsaken his open Catholic practice and became one of those furtive laymen who serves as confessor to hundreds of Catholics practising the True Faith in the secrecy of their homes.

I was unaware of Mister Hawthorn's true calling when he first visited. It emerged gradually over the ensuing weeks. To my brothers and me, he is a charming visitor who converses in clumsy Flemish, and pulls sweets from his pocket with a flourish. Mama becomes serene whenever Mister Hawthorn appears on our doorstep, her complaints of London easing. Papa enjoys Mister Hawthorn's willingness to debate and criticise (in private) the King and Commons, and also appreciates the opportunity for confession from the comfort of cushioned armchairs with snifters of *brandewijn*. I sometimes come upon Mister Hawthorn in the morning, his slumbering form draped in a cloak, his feet stretched out upon the settee.

Mister Hawthorn has a calming influence over Papa. One night last week, I overheard Papa becoming furious about being unfairly treated.

'... because he is a favourite diplomat of the royal court in Brussels, he has the magistrates in the palm of his hand and they agree to whatever he wants,' said Papa, his voice climbing, easily heard through the closed door.

Mister Hawthorn's tone was too soft to hear his reply.

Papa continued, his voice louder: 'They agreed to award full operating privilege to him, and my own rights were completely ignored. He used his power as a prominent diplomat and successful artist to take advantage—'

He stopped mid-sentence and I heard the muffled voice of Mister Hawthorn calming him.

You of all people will appreciate how relieved I was that Mister Hawthorn was able to soothe away Papa's anger. I hope he spoke to Papa about the importance of compassion, forgiveness and not allowing one's anger to take hold, which is what Mama often speaks to me about.

Blessings to you this Christmastide.

From your loving friend,

Antonia

49

'You seem convinced the portfolio box is critical to your research on Rubens.' Anna peers over the frame of her glasses at Charlotte. 'Wasn't Petra related to Vorsterman, not to Rubens?'

Charlotte returns Anna's unflinching stare. 'Vorsterman worked for Rubens.'

'And you believe these family papers will reveal something important about Rubens?'

'Possibly.'

'All this because of what Petra wrote in her garden journal?' Anna taps the red-covered notebook on her desk, shifts her gaze to Miles. 'Are you of the same opinion? I don't want our Begijnhof turned upside-down for no reason.'

He leans forward. 'Research is often like this, analysing documents, hunting for the next clue. We'll be very careful when searching the Begijnhof.'

'You'll let me know if you find anything?'

'Of course.'

Anna picks up a flimsy piece of paper, typewritten on both sides. 'This is the list of furniture and other items delivered to Petra when her mother died in 1982. Maybe the portfolio box is among the furniture.'

Charlotte stares at a bowl of shiny persimmons on the windowsill. She concentrates on maintaining the composure she has forced upon herself for the past three weeks while waiting for an appropriate time to visit the Begijnhof following Petra's death. It would have been disrespectful and intrusive to visit too soon after her passing, asking to search for the portfolio box. Having waited patiently for three weeks, she now sits in Anna's office, reciting a silent plea: *say yes, say yes.*

Anna waves the paper, frowning. 'I doubt there's anything of interest here, but you may look around if you wish.'

'Thank you,' Miles and Charlotte say in unison.

Anna straightens, stiff and businesslike. 'Please refrain from wandering around the buildings on your own. Edith will accompany you. Although ours is not a closed order, many of our *begijnen* choose to work in a quiet atmosphere. They are not to be disturbed.' Her eyes flicker over Miles. 'Men are notably absent from our grounds, so please remain with Charlotte and Edith at all times.'

'Of course.' Miles nods in agreement.

'And please don't enter the belfry. You've probably read in the newspaper about the falling masonry. Thankfully the visitor wasn't seriously injured. The local council have inspected the belfry, and some minor work has been carried out to make it safe while we investigate a long-term solution. In the meantime' – she frowns – 'we've had to suspend our guided tours.'

'I'm sorry to hear that,' says Charlotte. 'Edith said she enjoyed giving them.'

'Yes, indeed,' says Anna. 'It was a small income stream, but welcome nonetheless.'

She hands the typewritten page to Charlotte. 'Edith knows the buildings better than anyone. I'm sure she'll be able to help you locate the items. I imagine they're scattered everywhere. It will be like looking for needles in a haystack.'

Charlotte remembers Miles' words and resists the urge to smile.

'You'll find Edith in the vestry.'

As they leave the office, Anna calls out: 'You're not the only ones interested in the map folio. I had a call last week from someone asking to see it.'

'Who?' asks Charlotte, frowning.

'He said he was a cartography scholar, working for one of the international map libraries. Can't recall which one. Started with a B, I think.'

'Bayerische?' asks Miles.

'Brussels?' asks Charlotte.

'I don't recall. Not that it matters because I declined the request.' Anna makes a soft tutting sound. 'I wasn't about to agree to a complete stranger examining Petra's personal belongings. Wouldn't be right.'

Having said their goodbyes, Miles and Charlotte descend the stairs in silence.

As soon as they reach the deserted courtyard, Miles releases a barrage of questions. 'How has someone heard about the map folio owned by a reclusive dead *begijn* from Antwerp? Who else has seen it besides a few *begijnen*, you, myself, Willem, Theo, Sterck and the conservator who repaired it? Who else knows about Antonia's letter and Barzetti's extract besides you, myself and Oscar Duval? How has a cartography scholar–'

'Supposed cartography scholar,' interrupts Charlotte.

'What?'

'Just because the person *said* he was a cartography scholar doesn't mean he actually is one. It could be someone snooping around for the map folio, trying to find Antonia's letter or the *Pandora* drawings.'

'You're sounding paranoid.' Miles offers a soft laugh, although his expression remains worried.

50

Miles holds open the chapel's oak door, waiting for Charlotte to enter ahead of him. Stepping into darkness, they blink, wait for their eyes to adjust. Patterns emerge from shadows: a central aisle of herringbone tiles, squat twisted columns, alcoves with chalky statues. At the far end, the stained-glass window of Saint Catherine, a wheel tucked under her arm as a grim reminder of her martyrdom. The chapel appears deserted, the pious saint the only occupant. As they draw closer, Saint Catherine's details come into focus: serene, solemn, eyes rolling heavenwards. *More deranged than divine*, thinks Charlotte.

They find Edith in a small room next to the altar. She stands at a table littered with white dahlias and lilies, and in the centre, an enormous vase overflowing with greenery. She pokes a lily into the arrangement, listening as they explain the reason for their visit.

'Was Anna annoyed because I showed you Petra's journal?' Edith is partly obscured by the foliage. 'I should have spoken to her first, but she's been busy preparing budgets and renovation quotes for the Diocese. I didn't want to trouble her with something so trivial.'

'She seemed fine,' says Miles, 'but asked we stay with you the whole time.'

'We could start in Petra's bedroom,' says Charlotte.

Edith snips a flower stalk. 'I cleaned out her room two weeks ago. She didn't have many possessions. Some art books in a cupboard. A box under the bed filled with pictures of paintings, exhibition catalogues and ticket stubs going back forty years.' She pokes a dahlia into the vase. 'No need to visit her bedroom. The portfolio box wasn't there. Neither was the map folio.'

'The folio's missing?' Miles asks, exchanging a worried look with Charlotte.

'When it arrived back from the university, I brought it to her bedroom,' says Edith.

'And it wasn't there later?' asks Charlotte.

'Haven't seen it since.' Gripping the vase, she begins to lift it.

'Let me help.' Miles lifts the vase. 'Where will I put it?'

'There's a stand next to the altar,' says Edith as Miles follows her through the vestry door.

Charlotte watches them disappear, grimaces at the thought of the map folio shoved into the back of a cupboard, damaged, forgotten. Did Petra place the map folio inside the portfolio box before setting it aside somewhere in the Begijnhof?

As soon as Miles and Edith return, Charlotte places the typewritten page on the table. 'The seventeenth-century heirlooms were delivered to Petra at the Begijnhof in 1982.' She slides the paper across the table to Edith. 'Cabinets, wardrobes, desks, beds and other antiques.'

Edith glides her hand down the list. '*Kast, eiken, Vlaamse, zwarte ebbenhout inlegwerk.* Cupboard, oak, Flemish, black ebony marquetry. Let's start with this one. It's here.' She indicates an elaborate two-door armoire against the wall.

Charlotte swings open the doors and an odour of mothballs wafts into the room. Hanging inside are dozens of white surplices and grey habits.

Edith runs her fingers over the musty garments. 'We stopped wearing these in the nineties.'

They rummage through the clothes. There's nothing else inside.

Edith touches inlaid ebony and mother-of-pearl on the doors. 'Such a beautiful item belongs in a museum, not this dusty corner.'

Miles grunts as he pushes the cupboard from the wall to check the back, which reveals spiders mummified in cobweb tombs.

They fall into a pattern. Edith reads from the list, escorting them to the relevant building. Charlotte and Miles inspect the item, then cross it off the list. They examine the underside of a massive oak table in the dining room, searching for a place a flat box could be concealed. A study holds a leather-topped desk, side tables, a

Baroque cabinet. Bedrooms contain ornate wardrobes and single beds more suited to a chateau. The portfolio box is nowhere.

Edith peers at the list. '*Linnenpers, walnoot, Vlaamse, zeventiende eeuw.* The foyer.'

They inspect the linen press, turn the wooden screw, check all the planks, look beneath the thick table, finding no hiding places. Having swept their hands over every surface and tapped the thickest parts of each piece of furniture, hoping to find a hollow space, they have found nothing. No hidden compartments large enough to hold a box.

Charlotte rubs dusty hands along her trousers, her pessimism growing as each item of furniture is inspected. Anna's words are at the forefront of her mind. If the cartography scholar is genuine, how did he find out about the map folio? Whether he's a treasure hunter or an art thief, his presence signals that competition is close by.

'What's next?' she asks.

'*Gesneden huwelijk bed*,' replies Edith.

'Where would a *begijnhof* place a carved marriage bed?' asks Miles.

'The attic, of course,' says Edith.

They traipse across the courtyard to the *bibliotheek*. Up the stairs, across a landing, up another flight of stairs. Edith directs them to a narrow door in the corner of the second-floor landing.

The door sticks as Charlotte wrenches it open, the rush of air causing cobwebs in the stairwell to flutter. She feels along the inside wall. No light switch. After turning on the torch on her phone, she ascends slowly, holding the phone behind her to illuminate the stairs for Edith and Miles.

They huddle together in the confined space, heads tilted to avoid brushing against the cobwebs above. Afternoon light spills through a dormer window. As their eyes adjust to the gloom, the chimerical silhouettes gain definition, lose their ghostly character, becoming a mundane collection of broken chairs, lopsided hat stands, cracked mirrors.

'Where does that lead?' asks Charlotte, pointing to a narrow door in the far wall.

'The belfry,' replies Edith. 'Usually the tower is entered from the ground, but this was put in decades ago for the bell ringer to access the belfry via the *bibliotheek*. It's been kept locked since the brickwork came loose.'

Charlotte edges between a dented tin trunk and a stack of crates. Something leaning against the wall has caught her attention. She shines the light along the shape. Intricate carvings emerge from the gloom: cherubs entwined with ribbons, roses, carnations and myrtle. Symbols of love and marriage, hidden from celibate eyes. 'Found the marriage bed,' she calls out.

Miles grasps the footboard of the disassembled bed, easing it away from the headboard. An object slides down and hits the floor with a thud.

Charlotte drops to her knees, groping in the shadows. Thick dust. Cardboard corners. 'It's stuck. Can you move the bed?'

Miles wriggles the massive footboard until it rests against his thighs. Charlotte leans over and lifts a box from its hiding place. She carries it to a table near the window. It's large and flat, made of worn black cardboard, its corners scuffed and dented.

At last, at last, she chants to herself. Her fingers tremble, easing off the lid.

Inside is an object wrapped in black cloth. Miles folds back the fabric. A familiar dark green cover, cracked leather, flaked gilt.

'The map folio.' She smiles with relief. Petra must have returned it to the portfolio box before placing the box in the attic.

Miles lifts the map folio from the box and lays it to one side. Underneath is a collection of yellowed papers, leather-bound booklets and tattered envelopes.

Charlotte's hand hovers above a letter. Paper threadbare, ink feathered and faded, familiar handwriting.

June 30, 1686 – Mijn liefste neef Gerard …

'My dearest nephew Gerard,' translates Charlotte, exchanging a smile with Miles.

She yearns to hold the letter to the feeble light and read Antonia's words, search the box, touch every item, discover the *Pandoras* nestled inside. No longer a secret kept by one family for centuries. *Those Beauties, which are both a source of joy but also an anguish*, wrote Petra. Hidden, but now discovered for all the world to enjoy.

Charlotte knows she has to wait. Protective gloves, good light, a clean surface. Handled incorrectly, the delicate papers could crack and crumble, irreparably damaged.

She peers into the gloom. The back of her neck prickles. 'Edith?'

Edith cowers in the shadows next to the dormer window, staring through the glass into the courtyard below. Eyes wide, hand covering her mouth.

'What is it?' Charlotte moves to her side, Miles close behind.

Edith points out the window.

They look out into the courtyard. Anna stands in the middle of the cobblestoned driveway, in front of the *bibliotheek*, deep in conversation with Sterck. Anna motions towards the building. Sterck glances up, scans the façade and dormer window. Then they walk towards the door of the *bibliotheek*.

51

March 24, 1622

Dearest Clara,

Every time I receive another letter from you, I am relieved to know you have not been forbidden to write to me. Your mother is kind-hearted to deliver my letters directly into your hands and send yours by courier to London.

I hope our fathers remain unaware of our letter exchange. I am pleased you have not overheard further angry words from your father about mine. Let us hope their animosity towards one another is waning.

Thank you for your birthday wishes. I can hardly believe I am thirteen. In answer to your questions, yes, I continue to grow tall and am thinner than ever. Hendrik called me Stork Legs last week and received a clip over the ears from Papa.

Papa was so pleased with my studies he allowed me to join him and Mama on a visit to the family home of our tutor, whose parents were celebrating their thirtieth wedding anniversary. Mama wore a new gown of jet silk with slashed sleeves and a soft lace collar. I wore a new dress of ochre-coloured worsted yarn with puffed sleeves and a blue silk sash. I felt grown up walking to the Cuypers home, holding my long skirts out of the muck.

The Cuypers family live in a townhouse on Canwicke Street and are well established in London's Flemish community. Papa admires Meneer Cuypers for his lucrative trading business, which includes a flotilla of square-rigged fluyts plying the waters of the Noordzee. 'Meneer Cuypers knows the art of diplomacy,' said Papa. 'Every port along the Noordzee has ever-changing trade restrictions, yet he manages to appease the officials, whether they be English, Dutch, Flemish, Spanish, Catholic or Protestant.'

Papa admires anyone who is successful at juggling multiple allegiances.

Mama praises Mevrouw Cuypers for organising secret Catholic meetings, led by Mister Hawthorn, in her upstairs parlour twice a week. Mama also admires her for raising six sons, all of whom have thrived, evading the usual childhood illnesses that send so many to an early grave.

Imagine the horror of six boys in one family. Our tutor, Constantijn, is the third son. The eldest, all swagger and smirk, is twenty-six. The youngest is aged thirteen, a freckle-faced boy with a penchant for keeping frogs in his pocket.

Papa steered me to a table which held the largest book I had ever seen, the double-page spread measuring five by three hands. 'Meneer Cuypers has recently returned from Antwerpen, where he purchased an exceptional map folio,' said Papa. 'It was created by Abraham Ortelius, a cartographer from Antwerpen, who was a member of the same Sint-Lucas Guild as I. He died more than twenty years ago and this folio is his most famous creation.'

'*Theatrum Orbis Terrarum*.' I read aloud the Latin title and translated it into English: 'Theatre of the World's Orb.'

Papa turned the page to a map named *Islandia*, showing an isle with spiny-backed sea monsters cavorting in the ocean. Another map displayed the Americas with ships around the coastline, while a map of the plains around the Caspian Sea depicted hump-backed animals. Each page was vibrantly coloured, with oceans tinted ultramarine, land shaded in malachite. It reminded me of the mixing table in your father's studio, Clara, where Santo blends pigments. I am so used to the grey shades of my father's engravings, and the drab skies of London; to see such vivid colours made my eyes ache with pleasure.

When I next sit with Papa in his workroom to practise drawing, I will ask whether I can use coloured pigments rather than black ink. I am determined to try my hand at creating my own map, inspired by an Ortelius map. My first map will show the streets of Blackfriars and, if Papa gives me coloured pigments, I will use them to distinguish between shops, houses and churches. Like Ortelius, I want to include tiny pictures within the map: a spool of lace to show the Hatfields Lane haberdashers, a bunch of yellow carrots for the market, a red cap to show where Papa purchased his hat. I will create a personal symbol, perhaps my initials surrounded by an oak leaf to represent the oak trees along my street. I may include other symbols with secret messages as well. My imagination is awhirl with ideas. Perhaps one day I will be a cartographer like Ortelius.

I have not heard of any female cartographers, which makes me more determined than ever to be the first. The painter Mevrouw Clara Peeters no doubt felt the same determination to prove her artistic skills. Despite not having permission to register in the Sint-Lucas Guild, she is still renowned for her beautiful still-life tableaus. I recall your father has a painting by Mevrouw Peeters hanging in his foyer, the one displaying a pie, orange and olives, her name painted like an engraving along the knife handle. I will experiment with ingenious ways to sign my creations.

Mister Cuypers sometimes brings map folios to our geography lessons. I will ask for permission to copy a country map to practise drawing boundaries, mountains and waterways. Then a city map, to learn about drawing cities from a bird's view. Then I will create my first map. At first, I will be a copyist. One day, if I am talented enough, I may be a cartographer in my own right.

Your loving friend,

Antonia

Post scriptum: Mama is expecting again. It would be wonderful to have a baby sister this time, otherwise we may end up like the Cuypers family.

52

Edith shrinks back from the window, muttering. 'He made Petra so angry.'

'*Who* made Petra angry?' asks Miles.

'He did!' Edith points to the advancing figure of Sterck.

'Did Petra know Professor Sterck?' asks Charlotte.

Edith's brow creases. 'Who?'

'That man is Professor Sterck, from Antwerp University. Did he—'

'He mustn't have it,' interrupts Edith. Stepping to the table, she places the map folio back in the box, jams on the lid, thrusts the box into Charlotte's arms. 'It belonged to Petra. He can't have it.'

There comes the distant sound of a door banging shut.

'Let's go.' Miles steers Edith down the attic stairs, Charlotte close behind. Across the landing, down another flight, treading softly.

By the time they reach the first-floor landing, Charlotte's mind is tumbling. The size of the box makes it awkward to carry, impossible to slip into her satchel. The fragile papers are being jostled, could easily be damaged.

Miles peers through the balcony railing to the ground floor. Voices float up from below. His face is grim. 'We need to make a decision.'

'We could put the box in one of these rooms and later—' Charlotte stops, staring at Edith.

With a finger raised to her lips, the *begijn* gestures for them to follow her into the nearest room. Edith points to the far wall where a narrow door, painted the same olive-green as the wall, butts alongside a bookshelf.

'It leads to the next building, which is the old school,' says Edith. 'Follow the passageway to some stairs. Go down and you'll be in the school. There's a door leading onto the street. It was used by the children years ago, to enter the Begijnhof for their lessons. The door will lock behind you. Perhaps it would be best if Charlotte stays with me, and if you …' She touches the box Charlotte holds, then turns to Miles. Edith's eyes are wide, this time not with fear, but determination. 'The man with Anna mustn't have it. Petra wouldn't have wanted that.'

Charlotte tightens her grip on the box. 'What's Anna going to say—'

Stairs creak. Footsteps come closer.

'I'll take it,' whispers Miles. 'You stay here. Join me when you can.'

Edith opens the door, revealing a narrow passageway.

Charlotte places the box in his arms. 'I'll meet you in our office.'

Miles steps into the passageway, swallowed by darkness. Edith closes the door, easing the latch home with a faint click.

'Hello?' Anna calls out.

'We're in here.' Charlotte walks out to the landing.

Anna arrives at the top of the stairs, puffing, chest heaving, Sterck behind her.

'Professor Sterck, I wasn't expecting to see you.' Charlotte's tone is higher and brighter than normal.

He offers a greeting as he wanders into the room. Pausing at the nearest shelf, he tilts his head to read the book spines.

'Have you found anything of interest?' asks Anna.

'Dust!' Charlotte smiles at her own joke. 'I've never seen so much dust. You did warn us.'

Anna looks around the room. 'Where's Dr Thornton?'

'He had to leave,' says Charlotte. 'We were about to come downstairs.' She steps over to Edith, who concentrates on the list in her hands. 'We've ticked every item off the list, haven't we? Cabinets, linen press, wardrobes …'

Edith hands the page to Charlotte, walks to the landing, eyes on the floor.

Sterck opens a book resting on the table, uses his thumb to flutter through the pages, releasing the odour of displaced dust. 'Your library has some fascinating documents, Anna.'

Charlotte folds the page and slips it into her pocket, distracted by Sterck, who is two paces away. This is the first time they have stood in the same room since his revelation that he's always known she is his daughter. His father's funeral has come and gone, Charlotte receiving no message from Sterck, urging her to reconsider. However, he has repeated his suggestion that they meet to talk. She hasn't replied, shoving his offer aside, relegating it to the back of her mind, alongside all the other memories she's too angry to face.

Edith calls out from the landing: 'I'm going to show Dr Hubert out.'

'Yes, of course.' Anna paces the length of the room, pausing to look at the overflowing shelves and tables. 'Such a mess. It's overwhelming. Sorry we weren't able to help.'

'Thank you for lending me Edith,' says Charlotte. 'She's an excellent guide. The Begijnhof is a beautiful place.'

Anna smiles. 'It's a special place to many people.'

Charlotte follows Edith down the stairs, Anna's words ringing in her ears: *A special place.* The Begijnhof is important to people in different ways: a place to rest from the demands of serving others, a haven away from the clamour of the modern world, a retreat for the dispossessed and troubled. Begijnhof Sint-Catharina is for humanitarians, the benevolent, the selfless. Not for people who hyper-focus on their own goals, or make underhanded decisions as she has just done. Despite Edith's insistence the portfolio box not be handed over, regardless of the fact that Miles and Edith encouraged the subterfuge, Charlotte cannot condone her actions.

53

Edith and Charlotte pause at the front door of the *bibliotheek*, pulling on hats and scarves. Stepping outside, they fumble with overcoat buttons and gloves, fingers stiff with cold. Dead leaves swirl in flurries as they cross the courtyard. Daylight is fading. Edith pulls the shawl collar of her coat around her neck, sets off towards the main entrance.

'Edith! Wait.' Charlotte half-runs to keep up. 'What's this all about? How did Petra know Professor Sterck?'

Edith slows. 'I've seen him twice before. Once here. Another time at a museum. Both times, he spoke to Petra and she became upset.'

'About what?'

Edith hunches her shoulders into the wind, continues walking.

'What were they talking about?' Charlotte persists.

Arriving at the main entrance, they huddle against the shallow porch of the gatehouse, which offers some protection from the wind.

Edith burrows her hands into her pockets. 'I first saw him earlier this year. I came downstairs and they were in the foyer. Couldn't hear what he was saying, but when she walked past me to go upstairs, she looked annoyed.'

'And the other time?'

'Petra and I were at a museum last summer to see an exhibition. We borrowed Anna's car. Petra was teaching me to drive her old blue Citroën.' A tiny smile flickers across Edith's face. 'At the end of the exhibition, Petra waited in the foyer while I went to the museum shop. When I came out, I saw the same man talking to Petra. She stood up and walked away from him, looking angry.'

'Did she say anything about it afterwards?'

'Petra kept her feelings to herself. I didn't pry.'

Charlotte softens her tone. 'Why shouldn't Professor Sterck see Petra's portfolio box?'

Edith's eyes are fierce. 'I don't know him, but I saw how upset he made her. When I read her journal, it was so sad. The family papers in the portfolio box, whatever they are, gave her happiness at an earlier time in her life. Maybe later in life, they filled her with sadness, but I doubt the professor cares about that … or Petra.' She crosses her arms over her chest. 'Will you find out what's so special about the box?'

'I'll do my best.'

'Does it have something to do with the engraver?'

'Maybe.' Charlotte is unable to look the *begijn* in the eye. She imagines Edith possessing an omnipotent third eye, capable of reading her mind and detecting falsehoods in a flash. Too many years at school, she muses, surrounded by catechisms, rosaries and shrewd Loretto Sisters who instilled an everlasting ethos of guilt.

The chapel bell echoes around the courtyard, indicating the half-hour.

Edith looks at the ground, slides the edge of her shoe back and forth between the cobblestones. 'Look after Petra's portfolio box,' she says. 'Please bring it back when you're finished.'

Charlotte nods, opens her mouth to speak, then stops. What can she possibly say? Thank you for your trust? It would sound trite. She towers over Edith, yet feels insignificant. Her own assertiveness and manipulation are crass next to Edith's kindness. This unassuming *begijn*, with her bird-like features and gentle demeanour, has such humility and hope. Those traits are deserving of admiration, too.

54

June 16, 1622

Dearest Clara,

Thank you for your latest letter with all the news from home. I am sure your mother will be pleased with the embroidered needlecase you are making for her birthday. I wish I could be there to help with the linen press and other chores as you prepare for her special celebration. Please pass on my fondest wishes to her.

I am grateful she continues to send and receive our letters and, yes, I agree her manner appears to have become secretive of late. It is a little strange she now insists you pass your completed letters to her when she is alone in her bedchamber. Do you suppose she is concerned your father will discover our letter-writing and put a stop to it? Let us hope this is not the case.

Thank you for your encouraging words about my interest in becoming a cartographer. While Papa encourages me to attend lessons, and Mister Cuypers allows me to study his map folios, I will strive for my dream to come true, no matter how difficult it may be to achieve.

I had hoped to finish my Blackfriars map and send it to you with this letter, but our household has been filled with concerns over our local community.

Two nights ago, Papa arrived home with a grave look upon his face. Minutes later, Mister Hawthorn was ushered into the front parlour where he joined Papa. I sat in the shadows, listening to Papa reveal a terrible tale.

The second son of Meneer Cuypers has betrayed his family in the most dreadful way. At the age of twenty-four, he has deserted his father, the family business and the True Faith, escaping to the home of a staunch Protestant who is a trading rival of the Cuypers family.

'The Cuypers' son told his father,' Papa said to Mister Hawthorn, 'that his conscience no longer permits him to continue practising the blasphemies of the Popish faith and he has converted to Protestantism. The son has done worse than betray his family and faith. He has gone to the clergyman at St Mary-le-Bow and reported of secret Catholic meetings held in his mother's parlour at Canwicke Street.'

Fear rose in me, knowing these are the meetings Mama attends twice a week. While Catholic people are permitted to live in England, meeting together to observe the liturgies of the Catholic faith is outlawed. Our family is now at risk. Mama could be arrested. As the head of the household, Papa is responsible for the actions of his family and may be accused of breaking the law.

Mister Hawthorn sounded unconcerned. 'There is no proof our meetings are Catholic. No Catholic prayer books are present. I wear no vestments. We use no chalice or ciborium—'

'You are a bigger fool than I realised,' interrupted Papa, 'if you believe the absence of such items will stop you from being arrested and questioned in the harshest possible way.'

'I will pray those persecuted for their belief will be protected.'

'My wife has attended your meetings at the Cuypers home, which puts my family at risk.' Papa's voice trembled.

'Lucas, please,' said Mister Hawthorn. A chair scraped the floor and I imagined him moving closer to rest a reassuring hand on Papa's shoulder. 'Let us pray for protection ...'

Their voices became so hushed I heard nothing more. I returned to my bedchamber, wondering whether it was religious fervour alone that caused the Cuypers' son to desert his family and faith. Perhaps he had tired of living in the shadow of his eldest brother, who will one day manage the family's trading business, and decided to work for a competitor? Or had he fallen in love with a Protestant girl and decided to convert to her faith? Does our tutor, Mister Constantijn Cuypers, share his elder brother's wayward beliefs? Can we trust him to remain loyal to our family?

Whatever his reason, the second son of Meneer Cuypers has deceived more than his family. The Flemish community in Blackfriars, fellow Catholics, neighbours, friends – we are all at risk because of his disloyalty. Such betrayal comes at a price. Loyalty and trust once shared is gone forever.

With great sadness and a heavy heart, I remain your loving friend, Antonia

55

The floor of the office is littered with papers, folders and books.

'Damn it!' Charlotte stands in the doorway, hands curling into fists. 'Not again.'

Miles is under the desk, gathering papers from the floor, a stunned expression on his face. 'The door was locked when I arrived, but ...' Lost for words, he climbs to his feet and deposits an armful of papers on the desk, next to the portfolio box.

Charlotte places her satchel on a chair, relieved Antonia's letter and Barzetti's extract are carefully wrapped within it, safe from thieving hands, alongside her notebook and mind map. But the replica mind map she had made for Miles, for him to consult if he needed to check a key point while she was at a lecture or tutorial ...

She hurries to the filing cabinet and sees the lock has been jemmied. At the back of the cabinet, an art pad protrudes, pages ripped. She closes her eyes, realising someone now has key information about their search for the missing *Pandora* drawings. Maybe not every piece of the puzzle, but crucial details all the same.

'The replica mind map is gone.' She examines the torn edges of the art pad, seething with fury.

'What did you mean when you said *not again*?' asks Miles.

She hesitates, anticipating his reaction. 'Four weeks ago, I arrived home to a similar mess. No sign of forced entry, door locked, apartment wrecked.'

'Was anything missing? Money or jewellery?'

'No.' She predicts his next question, knowing she can't escape it.

'What did the police say?'

She lifts her eyebrows.

'You didn't go to the police.' He closes his eyes, his exasperation clear.

Studying the lines between his brows, blond hair falling across his forehead, she recognises his concern for its true nature: genuine, without hidden agenda. He has always been encouraging and helpful, taken risks for her, expecting nothing in return. His behaviour is reminiscent of the trust and kindness Edith has shown.

Alongside Charlotte's frustration is a tiny flicker of excitement. Two ransackings indicate someone is aware she's on the trail of something remarkable. She is on the brink of an exceptional discovery, and it will disappear if she doesn't keep a firm hold. Composure and rational thinking are needed, not emotive reactions.

She steadies her voice. 'We don't need the police. Help me put everything back in its place. While we're clearing up, we can check if anything else is missing.'

'We need to call the police.'

'We don't, Miles. I doubt anything else was stolen. Whoever did this didn't find what they were looking for' – she indicates her satchel containing the precious documents – 'and I don't want to explain to the police how I came by these documents.'

'The only others who have keys to our office are maintenance staff. Anyone could have filched the keys from their office. I'm more concerned about you. Who has keys to your apartment?'

'It's okay, Miles. I've had the lock changed and kept all copies of the keys myself.' She rights a chair, picks up books from the floor.

'Who had keys to your apartment?' He repeats the question. 'Stop cleaning. Sit down for a minute.'

Sitting in a chair, she jams her hands between her knees. 'The building maintenance man had keys. He visited a few times for minor repairs.'

'What about neighbours or work colleagues? Did you give any of them a spare key?'

She shakes her head. 'The only other person who had a key is listed on the lease.'

'The apartment is leased by the Arts Faculty,' he says, 'for short-term academic staff, so someone from admin would be listed on the lease.'

She waits for him to make the connection.

'I stayed in the same apartment when I arrived in Antwerp and Miss Beulen organised the lease.' He slumps onto a chair. 'Surely, you don't think ...'

56

'I can't believe it,' says Charlotte, pulling off the nitrile gloves with a snap. 'I was certain they'd be here.'

She scans the contents of the portfolio box, laid out in chronological order on a long table. Paces around the dining room, restless with frustration, navigating a pile of hockey sticks against a wall, hiking equipment in a corner, a guitar covered in dust. Miles keeps his apartment just as messy as the office.

They had decamped to his apartment, armed with archive sheets and portable equipment for inspecting fragile documents. Neither felt safe working in the office or in Charlotte's apartment. 'My building has keypad security,' Miles said, 'and there are double locks on my apartment.'

She turns to the window and stares at her reflection in the inky sky. Behind her, reflected in the same window, Miles sits at the table, examining a document.

'In her journal,' says Charlotte, 'Petra wrote *those Beauties*, capital B, *are set aside.*'

'You've said that twice,' says Miles, peering through a magnifying glass at a booklet. It is pocket-sized and tatty, covered in mustard-coloured leather, initials *SB* stamped on the front.

'What else could she be referring to?' asks Charlotte.

Miles grunts.

'She called them *treasures*.'

Another grunt.

'The stolen drawings, passed down from generation to generation.'

He puts down the magnifying glass. 'We've emptied the box, Charlotte.'

Having prodded each surface of the empty box, they had discovered no telltale bulges to suggest an object hidden within. Miles even peeled back a corner of the box's lining, inspected the cavity, confirmed it was empty.

Charlotte walks around the table, surveying the letters, inventories, genealogy charts, booklets and map folio. Next to each item is an index card where they have written a summary: date, author, description. Each item has been scrutinised with a magnifying glass, catalogued, slipped into a clear archive sleeve. Fifteen documents retrieved from the portfolio box. No drawings.

Miles stretches his arms above his head, stifles a yawn. 'It's nearly midnight. We've been at this for hours. Let's call it quits. Tomorrow is Saturday; we've got the entire weekend—'

'Maybe Petra wasn't referring to the *Pandoras* when she wrote about the treasures in the portfolio box.'

'You're obsessing again,' he mutters. 'I need sleep.'

'Maybe these' – she spreads her arms wide, indicating the documents on the table – 'are the treasures. Documents dating back to the 1600s, Barzetti's booklet, personal letters, De Wit's map folio. Perhaps *these* are the treasures Petra and her ancestors have been keeping safe from one generation to the next.'

'When Antonia mentions the word *treasures* in her letter to her nephew Gerard,' asks Miles, 'is she simply referring to the map folio and Barzetti's booklet?'

Charlotte shakes her head. 'I don't think so. In her letter to Gerard, Antonia states he will receive the map folio on her death. She never refers to it as a treasure. She encourages him to use the map folio, with its hidden verses and puzzles, to unravel the secrets and discover the treasures. As far as Antonia is concerned, the treasures are the *Pandoras*, which she wants Gerard to locate and return to the Rubens family.'

'And Petra?'

'Maybe Petra, her parents, grandparents, great-grandparents, et cetera, never knew anything about the *Pandoras*. Maybe *they* thought of the portfolio box, map folio and documents as treasures, cared for from one generation to the next. Maybe they never read Antonia's letter. Maybe Gerard never found it. Maybe they regarded the linen press, marriage bed and other heirloom furniture as their family's treasures.'

'That's a lot of maybes.'

She pulls out a chair and sits. Her eyes are scratchy from lack of sleep, but her mind spins with ideas.

'What's so special about this one?' He gestures to the pocket-sized booklet in tatty leather he's been studying.

'*That* one is incredible.' Picking up the corresponding index card, Charlotte flaps it in the air, her enthusiasm for all things Rubens never far away. She reads aloud her handwritten summary.

Leather-covered booklet. Dated 1609–1640. Author Santo Barzetti of Genoa. List of paintings, drawings and sketches completed by Rubens until his death in 1640. Written in chronological order, including description, intended recipient, city of creation. Includes following entry: 'Pandora. Created March 1621. Seven preparatory drawings, pen and brown ink on paper, one by one-half Flemish ell [70 x 35 cm]. Intended for Felipe IV, Madrid. Lost June 1621.'

Her disappointment at not finding the drawings is tempered by realising the value of Barzetti's booklet. 'This booklet confirms the existence of the *Pandora* drawings. It also establishes the provenance of other artworks which have baffled historians for decades. For example, historians have debated whether *Daughters of Leucippus* in Oslo's National Gallery was created by Rubens or one of his followers. Barzetti's booklet may confirm whether or not the Oslo work is by Rubens. This booklet is priceless.'

Miles leans back in his chair, reaching for a half-finished bottle of beer from a side table. Nearby are the remnants of a Thai takeaway meal.

She picks up another two index cards. 'Antonia's letter to Gerard makes her intentions clear. We weren't far off with the idea of a Grand Tour.'

Letter dated June 30, 1686 from Tante [Aunt] Antonia, addressed to 'Mijn liefste neef Gerard' [my dearest nephew Gerard]. She

compliments him on his success as a lawyer, implores him 'to
take every opportunity to travel and study the Great Masters ...
wait until unrest with the French is resolved before venturing from
Antwerpen ... I shall provide you with a folio with all necessary
maps to complete your tour ... study each corner of the folio as it
contains everything required for your forthcoming travels and any
journey to follow.'

List of items headed 'Artikelen Voor Reis 1693' [Items For
Journey], listing items for an extended journey including writing
case, foreign dictionaries, Aunt Antonia's map folio.

'The cryptic verse from the British map instructs Gerard to find the
drawings and return them to *his progeny in Londerzeel*,' says Miles.
'Why Londerzeel?'

'Albert was Rubens' eldest son. He settled in Londerzeel, a town
south of Antwerp, after his father's death in 1640. When the map
folio was created in 1686, Albert's adult children were living in
Londerzeel. They were the closest living relatives.'

Miles indicates the documents in the middle row on the table. 'The
ancestry of the Vorsterman family ... extracts of guild membership,
household inventories, letters, diaries, genealogy charts.'

'They demonstrate the link from Lucas Vorsterman to Petra.'
Charlotte picks up a handful of index cards, paraphrases aloud:

Three genealogy charts, various handwriting, first dated 1595–
1708, second 1711–1842, third 1819–1941.

Inventory of family heirlooms, dated April 1741. List of trousseau
of Katrijn Vorsterman, including carved marriage bed, wardrobe,
linen press, dining table, chairs, armoury, silverware, porcelain,
books, 'Groottante' [Great Aunt] Antonia's map folio.

Diary, 'Journaal van Katrijn Vorsterman-Wouters 1741–1779'.
Journal describes family's interest in travelling, studying Great
Masters, importance of 'protecting family legacy' and 'keeping safe
the family's treasures'.

Diary by Pieter Wouters II, written 1815–1825. Diary outlines family's interest in Flemish art, his desire to upgrade family home to a mansion on Antwerp's prestigious Meir, insistence family preserves their 'esteemed name' and 'family treasures'.

Inventory of household goods, dated 1865, describes furniture bequeathed to Cornelis Wouters, eldest living child of Pieter Wouters II. List includes same items mentioned in earlier inventory [1741], including 'leather map folio'.

Letter, dated September 14, 1910, from Gerhard Wouters to his bride, Elena. Letter outlines his intention to maintain 'palatial family home in Antwerpen' and 'newly built country property in Gistel'.

Letter, dated March 15, 1940, from Elena Wouters to her daughter IG van Vliet. Letter describes imminent German invasion, their intention to relocate to family's country property in Gistel for duration of war, bringing all heirlooms and valuables. She urges daughter, son-in-law and their child Pietronella to join them.

Newspaper clipping, dated September 18, 1944, with black-and-white photograph of two women and child before grand house. Caption: 'Mevrouw Elena Wouters and family in front of Villa Wouters, following German army's retreat from Flanders, September 1944.'

Letter, dated June 30, 1982 from IG van Vliet to her daughter Pietronella, asking her to keep safe the family's possessions for future generations, remembering 'beauty needs to be preserved for posterity'.

Charlotte waves the cards. 'A common theme–'

'More like an obsession,' interrupts Miles.

'Okay, let's go with obsession – with preserving their good name, keeping their treasures safe, making sure the heirlooms are preserved from one generation to the next. Even Petra wrote about it in her journal, apologising to her mother for not keeping her promise to look after the treasures and ensure they were preserved for future generations.'

Charlotte returns each index card to the relevant item. Her hand hesitates above the newspaper clipping. She peers at the grainy photo. The child looks to be five or six, hair in braids, dressed in a smock and pinafore. Petra would have been five when Belgium was liberated in 1944. Is this a young Petra with her mother and grandmother?

Charlotte eyes a yellowed page on the table. Splotched with dirty marks, edges frayed, it contains no words, only five columns of Roman numerals. Picking up the page inside its clear protective plastic, she passes it to Miles. 'This one's baffling.'

I	vii	v	vi	iv
II	vi	iv	vii	iii
III	ii	v	ii	iii
IV	vii	vii	iv	vi
V	vi	vii	vi	ii
VI	v	iii	vii	iv
VII	iv	iii	viii	iv
VIII	iv	ix	v	ix
IX	vii	ii	vi	ii
X	v	v	vi	vi
XI	vi	ix	viii	i
XII	vii	vii	v	viii
XIII	iv	viii	vii	iv
XIV	iii	viii	ii	ix

'No date, but clearly old.' He peers closely at the surface. 'Looks like vellum. The numerals are similar to Antonia's handwriting. Same up-stroke on the lower-case numerals, same slant, serifs identical. We'll need to get it analysed by a document specialist.'

She mentally adds another item to her to-do list, but remains cautious about approaching Oscar Duval or any other specialist. Unclear of who is responsible for the two ransackings, wondering if there will be further attempts, she is reluctant to reveal these latest historic documents to anyone. Or let them out of her sight.

'If the drawings are found,' asks Miles, 'what would they be worth?'

'Depends on condition, quality, whether they're signed. If all seven are found together in optimum condition, they could fetch as much as twenty million euros at auction. Maybe more.'

Miles lets out a low whistle. 'Unscrupulous people would be willing to do anything to get their hands on them.'

'*Now* do you understand why I've been reluctant to reveal the details to others? Why I've been nervous of talk on campus about stealing ideas? A thief wouldn't think twice, given the opportunity, to steal artistic treasures worth millions.'

'Stealing artworks by an Old Master is a massive escalation from stealing research ideas from a work colleague.'

'Only in monetary value,' she says.

The silence accentuates the clicking of the nearby radiator. Miles runs a hand through his hair, rubs his chin, twitches his foot, unable to remain still.

She keeps her voice offhand. 'Soon after I arrived on campus, you mentioned academic theft happens in all institutions, including Antwerp.'

His foot stills.

'Is there someone in particular you need to warn me about?'

'Only vague rumours.' His brow furrows.

'If you suspect someone–'

'I'll let you know if I hear anything concrete.' There's an edge to his voice.

'Sterck already knows about Antonia's letter–'

'It's not Sterck I was thinking about. You're jumping to conclusions. Sterck may be a prickly fellow, but he's not bad. You should try trusting–'

'Okay. Okay. You've made your point.'

His tone turns reflective. 'In the past week, he seems to have mellowed. Did you hear his father died recently?'

She opens her mouth to speak, then quickly closes it. There is nothing she feels ready to share.

57

July 17, 1622

Dearest Clara,

I cannot wait for your letter in reply, but must write immediately with the saddest news. My heart is so heavy I can barely write.

The betrayal of the Cuypers' son set in motion a series of events which has torn apart the happiness of our family forever. The day after that treachery, a clergyman from St Mary-le-Bow visited our home and spoke to Papa and Mama. The discussion took place behind closed doors, and I was unable to hear anything. But I knew the circumstances were dire when Mama reappeared, stifling sobs and clutching her large belly as she climbed the stairs.

'A few days of rest is all she be needin',' said Janneke as she carried a tray of food to Mama's bedchamber.

I slipped into Mama's room the next day and was dismayed to see her pallid cheeks, shadowed eyes, a despondent look upon her face.

'Tell me what I can do, Mama,' I said, holding her listless hand.

She stared at the wall, muttering to herself. 'All were admonished with the harshest words and warned about the peril if we continue flouting the law. We have done no wrong in God's eyes, yet are declared guilty. We stitch our embroidery while softly chanting the *Pater noster* and the *Gloria Patri*. We bow our heads when it comes to the confession. *Confiteor Deo et beatae Mariae*. Be obedient to Our Lord, trust the True Faith ...'

Mama refused to be drawn into further conversation. Only the smallest morsels of food passed her lips, even sweet apricots remaining untouched upon her plate. Day after day, Janneke came downstairs and delivered Mama's message to Papa as we sat at the breakfast table: 'She says she still be too poorly to attend church today and she be needin' rest for her confinement.'

Papa could have railed at her, pulled her down the stairs, insisted she attend church as a show to the St Mary-le-Bow clergyman that she had heeded their warnings. But Papa could no more force his wife down the stairs than beat his child, mistreat a servant or raise a knife in anger.

Mister Hawthorn visited often, sitting with Papa in the front parlour, talking for hours. With the door firmly closed and their voices hushed, it was impossible to hear their conversations. I was desperate for news of our future, an indication we were free from danger, that Mama would not be arrested.

Her pains began within eight days of taking to her bed.

Janneke came clattering down the stairs, calling to Ludo to fetch the midwife, all the while muttering: 'More than a month early. 'Tis not good.'

I wasn't permitted to see Mama during her confinement, but I stayed close by, watching the maids bustle in and out, carrying linen, dried herbs, bowls of water. Her anguished cries could be heard through the house, followed by hours of silence, during which Janneke tried to reassure me that Mama was resting and all was well. But her cries would return, shrill at first then diminishing to moans. By the second day, the physician arrived to draw blood. This time, the stench of wet metal wafted past as the maids carried bowls of blood from the bedchamber.

The babe was finally delivered. A boy, blue-lipped and bald, making mewing sounds like a near-drowned kitten. The household stood in a circle in the front parlour. Papa, my brothers, myself and the servants, all staring at the floor. Mama remained upstairs, too ill to move. Mister Hawthorn held the swaddled creature in the crook of his arm, murmured prayers, made the sign of the cross with holy oil on his tiny wrinkled forehead. By nightfall, the babe breathed its last, his soul departing like a gentle puff of air.

'Come sit with your mama,' said Janneke, guiding me into the bedchamber.

Mama was beyond grief, lost in a fevered dream, her eyes remaining closed, lips moving with deranged murmurings. Her restless hands plucked at the blankets covering her stomach, searching in vain for the creature she had carried within. She lingered in this state for two days, becoming quieter, then finally grey and silent.

Mama is gone. All sense of reason is gone. My heart is broken.

Antonia

58

Someone grips her shoulder, shakes it. 'Charlotte, wake up. I've had a brainwave.'

She opens her eyes. Hockey sticks lean against the wall. Hiking boots on the floor. A guitar.

'Wake up.' The voice is persistent.

Recognition unfolds. She slept on his sofa last night, too fearful of the attacker and too exhausted to walk the fifteen minutes to her own apartment. Miles had insisted she spend the night. 'Sleep in my bed. I'll have the sofa,' he said. She politely declined, uncomfortable with evicting him from his bed.

'I've had a brainwave,' he repeats.

She wraps the blanket around her shoulders and stares at him. He is fresh-faced and bright-eyed with a pleasing cedar aroma about him, suggesting rest and rejuvenation. She, on the other hand, is sluggish and fuzzy-brained, her eyes scratchy from her late-night study of Barzetti's booklet.

He thrusts a towel at her. 'Have a shower. It'll wake you up. I'll make coffee.'

Ten minutes later, she emerges from the bathroom with wet hair and follows the smell of coffee into the kitchen.

Miles bounds around the table, returning the documents to the portfolio box. 'Remember those strange geographical coordinates on the first map? This morning, while you were asleep, I went to work and made enlargements, using the photographs Theo took before the folio was returned to the Begijnhof.' He's talking so fast she has trouble understanding him.

'Help me clear the table,' he says.

Too confused to argue, she adds the genealogy charts to the portfolio box.

He unrolls four A2-size sheets of paper, matching the edges to form a super-sized map. The pictures of cityscapes and rulers, stunning as colourful miniatures, are unremarkable as grey enlargements. Lush blue, green and crimson now colourless.

'This is the first map enlarged,' he says. 'The geographical coordinates use lower case Roman numerals, numbered one to ten, around the border. The vellum list also has lower case Roman numerals, one to ten. I thought ... maybe there's a connection.'

'Go on.' Her curiosity grows.

'I know we haven't had the vellum list analysed to confirm its age, but comparing it to the map folio and Antonia's documents, it could easily be the same age.'

'Okay.'

'What if the vellum list is a key for the map?'

She remembers the cryptic verse from the French map – *recall the games and puzzles of your youth* – and nods for him to continue.

His words come out rapid-fire. 'The vellum list could be a series of map coordinates. Cryptic clues using map-reading skills may be the type of challenge Antonia created for Gerard to solve. In her letter to him, she said *remember the puzzles of your youth.*'

Charlotte's pulse begins to race. 'The fifth verse says something similar. And the last line is *cartography and foreign tongues the key.*'

The room is quiet.

They move in sync. He grabs rulers, pencils and magnifying glasses, while she twists the flexible arm of a floor lamp until it illuminates the table. He pulls over two chairs. She reaches for the vellum list. They sit side-by-side, huddled over the enlarged map of Europe.

'Do you know anything about geography?' she asks.

'Studied it for two years at university before changing to history. You?'

'Very rusty.' In fact, her map-reading skills are akin to a ninth grader's, having dropped the subject at the earliest opportunity.

He indicates the east–west axis of the map. 'Geographical coordinates use degrees, minutes and seconds on two axes to pinpoint an exact spot on a map. Grid numbers on the east–west axis are called Eastings. North–south axis are Northings. Eastings are written before Northings. Mind you, that was for a system invented in the nineteenth century. No idea what method was used for this map.'

She's about to make a suggestion, then stops. Eastings and Northings? She's out of her depth.

He picks up the vellum list in its archive sleeve. 'The five columns aren't evenly spaced. The first column is numbered one to fourteen. The next two columns are bunched together, then there's another gap, then the final two columns. Let's assume the first two lowercase columns are Eastings and the next two are Northings. This gives us fourteen four-digit grid references to locate.' He begins drawing equidistant lines along the east–west axis. 'We don't have degrees, minutes and seconds as in modern-day coordinates, but we have ten-by-ten grids already marked on the map. Each of these can be subdivided to help pinpoint the fourteen coordinates.'

I	vii	v	vi	iv
II	vi	iv	vii	iii
III	ii	v	ii	iii
IV	vii	vii	iv	vi
V	vi	vii	vi	ii
VI	v	iii	vii	iv
VII	iv	iii	viii	iv
VIII	iv	ix	v	ix
IX	vii	ii	vi	ii
X	v	v	vi	vi
XI	vi	ix	viii	i
XII	vii	vii	v	viii
XIII	iv	viii	vii	iv
XIV	iii	viii	ii	ix

'How do you know to divide each large grid into smaller ten-by-ten grids?'

He continues drawing lines. 'Each axis is numbered one to ten, so subdividing further by tens will make it easier to pinpoint each coordinate.'

'You're only guessing.'

He continues drawing. 'Do you have any better ideas?'

She swallows away any objections. His suggestion is a stab in the dark, but it's more concrete than her own vague ideas. She picks up a ruler and pencil, and begins drawing lines along the north–south axis.

When all the lines are drawn, they match up the pages.

'What's the first coordinate?' he asks.

She hovers her finger along the first row of the vellum list. 'Eastings seven five, Northings six four.'

Miles aligns a ruler on the *vii* of the horizontal axis and slides it in an easterly direction by five smaller grids. With a second ruler, he locates the *vi* on the vertical axis, then moves the ruler to a further four lines in a southerly direction. They examine the intersection: a pinprick on the map, indicating a town in the Austrian Alps.

'Kitzbuhel,' says Miles. 'Isn't that a ski resort?'

'It is now, but I doubt it was famous for skiing back then. And I doubt Rubens or Vorsterman ever visited there.'

'Let's keep going to see if a pattern emerges.'

With Miles working the rulers and marking locations on the map, Charlotte writes the fourteen locations in the notebook.

'Ipswich in England? Koper in Slovenia?' she says. 'Doesn't make sense.'

They stare at the fourteen marks on the map. Haphazard dots, forming no recognisable pattern, their significance a mystery.

'Let's try something else.' Miles picks up the rulers. 'We've assumed the first references are Eastings and the second Northings. Let's swap them around.'

'But you said Eastings come first.'

'Yes, for a system devised in the nineteenth century. This map was made in 1686.'

Repeating the process with the numbers swapped, they locate fourteen alternative locations. As each one is found, Miles marks it on the map with red pen while Charlotte writes it in the notebook.

'It still doesn't make sense.' She rubs her temple, struggling to concentrate on the place names.

I	Koblenz (Germany)
II	Innsbruck (Austria)
III	Jerez (Spain)
IV	Kortrijk (Belgium)
V	Basel (Switzerland)
VI	Imola (Italy)
VII	Naples (Italy)
VIII	Nice (France)
IX	Echternach (Luxembourg)
X	Novara (Italy)
XI	Kassel (Germany)
XII	Aachen (Germany)
XIII	Siena (Italy)
XIV	Toledo (Spain)

He snatches up a blank sheet of paper and scribbles fourteen letters across the page. 'Forget the towns. They don't matter.' Eyes wide, he jabs a pencil on the paper, shouting with excitement. 'The first letter of each place name. Look what it spells.'

'K-I-J-K-B-I ...' Her brow furrows.

'Separate it into three words: *kijk binnen kast*.' He waves his hands, triumphant.

'*Look within cabinet*,' she translates. Jumping to her feet, she paces around the table. '*Kast* means cabinet, closet or cupboard.'

'We'll go back to the Begijnhof and look at Petra's furniture again,' says Miles.

'We've already inspected every item.'

'We'll look more carefully. Antonia's clue was specific − *kijk binnen kast* − look within cabinet.'

Charlotte shakes her head. 'We've already looked at each *kast*. If we ask to search again, Anna will become suspicious. Edith may tell her about the portfolio box, and Anna will insist we return it.' The prospect of returning the portfolio box fills her with alarm. Isn't *she* the best person to decide how its contents should be examined? Isn't *she* the one who best appreciates its value to the world of academia, especially Barzetti's booklet? She needs time to develop a plan, to ensure the portfolio box won't disappear into the dusty rooms of the Begijnhof's Bibliotheek, to live among cobwebs and ossified spiders as a memorial to Petra and her long-dead ancestors.

'We've found Antonia's clue,' says Miles. 'Why do we need the portfolio box?'

'We can worry about the portfolio box later.' She's quick to deflect the issue. 'We need to find out if there's other furniture Petra inherited, perhaps in another building, a different location.'

'Why don't we—'

She lets out a gasp, remembers Edith handing her the lawyer's letter that itemised the possessions delivered to the Begijnhof in 1982. It's in the pocket of her jacket.

She grabs the jacket from the back of a chair, and retrieves the flimsy paper. Cringes, realising the historic letter is typed on thin paper, could easily have been damaged when she shoved it in her pocket.

On one side is the list of furniture and possessions. She turns over the page to read the lawyer's instructions.

The words are lawyer-speak. Precise directives for managing the bequest of Mevrouw IG van Vliet, the endowment to her sole beneficiary, a daughter Pietronella, now Sister Petra, a *begijn* at Begijnhof Sint-Catharina. Modern household goods to be donated to local charities as nominated by the beneficiary. Antique items to be delivered to the beneficiary at the aforementioned Begijnhof. The family's country property to be prepared for long-term rental.

The family's country property.

Charlotte turns to the portfolio box, draws out the letter written by Petra's grandmother. She paraphrases the letter Elena Wouters wrote to her daughter, prior to the German takeover of Belgium in 1940: 'German invasion is imminent ... we shall relocate to the family's Gistel estate ... bringing all valuables ...'

'Gistel!' she shouts. 'There's a family estate in Gistel!'

Miles reaches for the faded newspaper clipping. They scan the grainy image of two women and a girl before a palatial house. Steps lead up a grand entrance portico, bay windows, an octagonal tower on the left wing of the house, spreading branches of ancient oaks.

Miles reads aloud the caption: 'Mevrouw Elena Wouters and family in front of Villa Wouters, following German army's retreat from Flanders, September 1944.'

Villa Wouters.

'We're going to Gistel,' says Charlotte, eyes alight.

59

September 13, 1622

Dearest Clara,

Thank you for your comforting words following Mama's passing. Whenever I enter her bedchamber, I expect to see her sitting at her desk. Then I remember, she is no longer with us.

I agree with the concerns you expressed in your letter about who could send my letters to Antwerpen now that Mama has died. Papa is filled with sadness and so busy with work that I felt unable to ask him for help. In truth, our relationship has become distant once more, and I am nervous he would forbid me to write to you lest our fathers' animosity return.

Fortunately, Mister Hawthorn mentioned to me his regular correspondence with a cousin in Antwerpen, and has kindly offered to send my letters alongside his own.

Mama's passing has brought about much change in our family. My day-to-day life has been tipped on its head and I have little time to draw maps. Much of my time is now spent on managing the servants, supervising the boys and balancing the household ledgers, with my focus on ensuring the smooth running of the household so Papa can complete commissions. I am unable to attend many lessons with Mister Cuypers, sometimes managing only one lesson a day.

Janneke reassured me I am capable of taking on this new role, despite being only thirteen. 'Your mama did teach you well,' said Janneke, 'but now you be runnin' the household, you'll have little time for scribblin' maps and other frivolities.'

I try my best to demonstrate a spirit of compassion towards Papa, knowing how he suffers from Mama's loss. But there are moments when I am overcome with tears.

When stitching the monogram on Papa's kerchief, which Mama had left unfinished in her sewing basket, I suddenly felt as though she was sitting beside me, offering silent words of encouragement.

Papa is as dedicated as ever to his work, committed to providing for his family, but he is filled with sorrow.

He found me in the dining room as I was stacking pressed linen in the cabinet.

'Antonia, can you please arrange for Ludo to deliver the engravings and invoice on my desk to the Duke's private secretary. I also need someone to collect the copper plates I ordered from Brasher's in Ludgate and paper from Tate's in Bow Lane. Mister Hawthorn is arriving at the ninth hour, so please have Janneke serve supper in the front parlour.' His tone was courteous but leaden. He turned away, as if to leave, then stopped.

I hoped he was on the verge of offering a few words of appreciation for the way I had stepped into Mama's role. Perhaps he might acknowledge how I, too, felt sadness over her loss, and offer me reassurance and compassion.

'The candles in my workroom,' he said, 'have an unpleasant odour. Please tell Ludo to replace the tallow with beeswax.' He left the room before he saw my tears.

Our family made a pathetic sight last Sunday as we trudged along Bow Lane, returning from church. Papa strode in front while we tried our best to keep up. Lucas wriggled in my arms, hollering to be put down so he could clamber in the mud. Hendrik walked behind Niels, firing spitballs of sodden paper at the back of his head, ignoring my pleas for him to cease. Once home, Hendrik pinched Lucas, kicked Niels, yanked my hair. Papa was oblivious to the discord, tossing aside his cloak and withdrawing to the workroom.

The boys are grieving over Mama in their own ways. Hendrik continues to play pranks, but there is a nastiness to his antics, as if venting his anger over Mama's loss. Niels has become timid and tongue-tied, given to crawling into my bed at night to curl up like a kitten. As for Lucas, the first few weeks after Mama's passing were heartbreaking, watching him scamper from one room to the next, calling for her in his sweet voice, unable to comprehend he will never see her again.

I can only assume Papa's inability to show us any tenderness is due to the severity of his own grief. An invisible band of iron has tightened about his heart, all his compassion squeezed dry. Two months have passed since her death, and still we wait for him to emerge from his stupor.

I recall Mama in my every action. Her dark eyes stare back at me from the looking glass every morning.

Your heartbroken friend,

Antonia

60

Charlotte stares through the car's window at the unchanging countryside. The terrain looks as if a prehistoric giant smoothed a palm across every rise to create a billiard table of West Flanders. Despite the lack of hills, the car struggles to reach the speed limit.

'Karl spent the last year restoring his Citroën. She's an old girl, but doing well.' Miles pats the worn dashboard.

Remembering Karl's towering frame in the low-ceilinged staff kitchen, she wonders how he folds his legs into the cramped car. 'How old is ... she?' Charlotte takes in the faded blue paintwork, the clunky knobs and small rear-view mirror mounted low on the dashboard.

'About 1966.' Miles gives her a quizzical smile. 'First time in a vintage car?'

She's about to reply, but her phone buzzes. It's Edith, calling to ask about the portfolio box. 'We need to study it further,' replies Charlotte, 'but we're heading to Gistel now, chasing a lead.'

After finishing the call, she stares glumly at the road ahead. 'We'll have to return the portfolio box to the Begijnhof eventually. Don't want Edith getting in trouble.'

'Edith's a history and art enthusiast. Anna's a former historian. If we explain everything, they'll understand the importance of the documents being properly preserved and available for historians to study.'

'True, but the final decision will be up to the beneficiary of Petra's estate.'

'Wouldn't that be the Begijnhof?'

'Not necessarily,' she replies. '*Begijnen* don't take vows like nuns. They can leave the order at any time. Anna mentioned that one of the *begijnen*, Sister Léa, left Sint-Catharina's a month ago after more than three decades. *Begijnen* are also allowed to own possessions and property. Their possessions don't automatically become the property of their *begijnhof* on their passing.'

'So whoever inherits Petra's estate, will receive the portfolio box ...'

Charlotte pictures the box with the valuable documents, now inside a gym bag and locked in the boot of Karl's clapped-out Citroën. They had debated where to leave it, eventually deciding the safest option was to bring it with them, unwilling to risk a break-in at Miles' apartment. She grimaces at every jarring bounce as the Citroën's archaic suspension endures Belgium's notoriously bumpy roads. Frowning at the grey clouds moving in from the west, she hopes the car's boot is leak-proof. A sudden prickle of fear runs along her spine, knowing how easy it would be for someone to break into the flimsy boot. Shudders at the thought of the documents being damaged or stolen.

'... and they'll also inherit Villa Wouters, assuming it's still standing,' Miles continues.

'And anything inside the villa, including valuable drawings.'

Miles lets out a low whistle. 'Imagine the fight over ownership of drawings by Rubens.'

'Let's not get ahead of ourselves. We have to find them first.'

Miles nurses the whining Citroën around the outskirts of Ghent then Bruges, before turning towards Gistel. Driving along the town's main street, they pass a real estate agency, hardware store, small supermarket, several cafés and clothing shops.

Miles eases the car into a parking space. 'Looks as though Gistel only has one agency.'

'Is our story straight?' She peers into the rear-view mirror and smooths flyaway hairs, trying to look less dishevelled.

'All good.' He straightens the collar of his jacket. 'How do I look?'

She smiles, filled with gratitude that he agreed to her scheme. 'Like a respectable fellow looking for a house to buy.'

They begin walking along Gistel's main street. 'May as well play the part,' he says, reaching for her hand.

Her body is suddenly warm, her insides buoyant, calmed by his closeness. She's not merely pleased to be swapping ideas and solving cryptic clues with a fellow historian, but genuinely happy that Miles is by her side, and they are sharing this adventure.

Sizing up the lone agent as they walk into the office, they quickly settle into their planned spiel. Miles is full of smiles, convinces the agent they are interested buyers, asks for a print-out of listings in the Gistel area.

'I've included properties for sale in and around Gistel,' says the agent, pulling a bundle of pages from the printer and handing them to Miles. 'Sorry I can't take you around myself. No one else in the office today, so I need to mind the fort. Why don't you drive around, look at the houses from the outside? If you want to see inside any, I can organise appointments. What size house did you say you're looking for?'

'At least five bedrooms, three storeys with a mature garden.' Miles repeats the criteria they had discussed, based on the grandeur of the house pictured in the newspaper clipping.

Charlotte recalls the imposing entrance portico and large bay windows in the faded photograph. Historic houses of this scale would have heritage orders prohibiting their demolition, regulating future renovations. The upkeep of a grand house would be costly. The beneficiary of Petra's estate, whoever it is, would surely be eager to divest themselves of any asset likely to be a financial drain. Given the struggling economy, few people would have the cash to maintain a large country estate, or to rent such a property. She imagines the once-impressive house is run-down and neglected, perhaps unoccupied.

'We read about historic houses in the area,' continues Miles. 'Would you happen to be familiar with one called Villa Wouters?'

The agent shakes her head. 'Doesn't sound familiar.' She offers a toothy smile, wishes them luck.

Miles leafs through the house listings as they walk along the pavement. 'Any idea where Villa Wouters is located?'

'I searched online for historic homes in Gistel,' she replies, 'but found nothing. The earliest mention of the family's Gistel house is 1910, so we'll start by eliminating houses built after that date.'

'Not many of the listings include year of construction. Most only have an address.'

'We'll do the best we can. Also, we don't know if it's vacant. The lawyer's letter said it was to be rented out, but that was back in 1982 and–'

She comes to an abrupt stop. Stares in disbelief as a familiar figure emerges from a red-brick townhouse across the street. Her insides turn cold. She's light-headed and breathless. *Hide!* she silently screams. *Don't let him see us*.

The figure pauses in the doorway, begins to turn in their direction.

She grabs Miles by the elbow, drags him into the nearest shop. Floral displays fill the front window, buckets of flowers and greenery against the walls, the heady scent of lily and rose. Standing behind a palm, she peers through the window. 'Did you see him? He came out of the townhouse across the street.'

'Who?'

'Sterck!'

'Are you sure?'

'Yes!' She leans over a tub of gerberas to scan outside. Sterck, wearing his distinctive tweed jacket, is walking along the pavement, away from the florist.

A faint cough. A shop assistant stands behind them, smiling. '*Kan ik u helpen?*'

'I'll have a bunch of those, please,' says Charlotte, gesturing at a container of yellow roses.

'Would you like them gift wrapped?'

'Yes, please.' Charlotte turns back to the window. 'What's he doing in Gistel?'

'Wish I knew.'

'Who else knows Petra has a family house in Gistel?' she asks.

'I don't know.'

The shop assistant reappears, holding a paper-wrapped bouquet.

'Could you help us, please?' Miles points to the townhouse. 'The building across the street ... is that a business?'

'The *advocaten*? It's a law firm, run by Meneer Gossens.'

Charlotte mumbles her thanks, pays for the flowers, scrunching the yellow roses to her chest as if in a trance. She opens the door and steps out without looking, nearly colliding with a lady pulling a shopping cart. Charlotte mutters an apology. Pieces of the puzzle slide together. Doubts clarified. Disbelief turning to fury.

'Are you okay? You look pale.' Miles is at her side, hand under her elbow. He takes the flowers.

She pulls the lawyer's letter from her pocket, passes it to him. 'Gossens is the name of the lawyer who handled the estate of Petra's mother in 1982. Sterck knew Petra. He just visited her family lawyer. He knows something.'

61

February 4, 1623

Dearest Clara,

Nearly four months have passed since I last received a letter from you, and I fear the worst. Has your father discovered our correspondence and forbidden you to write? I hope I am mistaken and perhaps your letters have gone astray, lost by a careless courier. Please write to me, if you can. I miss hearing from you.

I will continue writing in the hope you will receive my letters and write in return. Let me share with you our latest news, some of which is entertaining and will cause you to smile.

Nearly seven months have passed since Mama died, and Papa is showing signs of considering marriage again. I understand there are benefits to having a wife to manage the household – and I would be grateful to no longer supervise the servants or balance the household ledgers – but for Papa to consider marriage to either of the widows who are openly pursuing him is madness.

One of the suitors is the widowed sister of Mevrouw Cuypers. Introduced to him last Christmastide, she tracks Papa down whenever we attend church and looks at him with the eagerness of a beagle.

'She be droolin' soon,' whispered Janneke as we stood on the other side of the nave and watched Papa offer the widow a gracious bow.

'Perhaps she'll play fetch.' I smirked.

Janneke sniggered before elbowing me in the ribs. 'The other one has arrived.'

A tiny woman with a large ostrich plume in her hat sidled up to Widow Beagle and, with a matching look of docility, gazed up at Papa. The ensuing conversation between the three of them was so animated the ostrich plume tickled Papa's nose.

Rather than show irritation at the fawning, Papa appeared to enjoy it. He puffed out his chest and smiled at Widow Beagle and Widow Ostrich in turn.

Widow Ostrich is English, with two young boys by her late husband, which would increase the number of boys in our family to five – imagine the horror – if she successfully woos Papa.

Janneke and I exchanged snide comments about the widows as we began walking home, but then she turned the conversation in a surprising direction. 'Yer papa is still young. 'Tis expected he will take a new wife afore long.'

'Barely seven months have passed since Mama died.'

'The mourning period is over, Miss Antonia, and it is clear yer father be ready for a new wife. With someone else to oversee the household and children, you could enjoy more time with your studies.'

'Mama was agreeable to my interest in academics and mapmaking, but a new wife may not be so accommodating. She may forbid me to study, expect me to care for the youngest children, practise the *spinetten*, do needlework.'

'There be worse occupations.'

'Both widows would prefer to stay in London, so there is little hope we will ever return to Antwerpen–'

Janneke pulled me to a stop. 'Who says a new wife will have a voice in where you live? There be no point in frettin' over a future outta yer control.'

I fumed all the way home, knowing Janneke was right, and feeling embittered at the realisation that as a girl I had no control. Whoever Papa chooses as his new wife may influence him in small ways, but important decisions will always rest with him. I had seen my own mother compelled to make a new life for herself and her family in a foreign country with a religion opposed to her own.

Women who successfully follow their own path in the world, and overcome the obstacles placed in their way, are rare indeed. I know of only two women who have succeeded as artists. Mevrouw Clara Peeters has become a successful painter, with her still-lifes as beautiful as those by Meneer Snyders and Meneer Adriaenssen. Across the Alps in Lombardy, Signora Anguissola has developed a reputation as a skilled portraitist and has been compared favourably to Herr Holbein, Signore Bronzino and Meneer van Dyck.

I will look to these women as my inspiration to achieve independence and success, and focus on the memory of dear Mama, recalling the lessons she taught me to be diligent, trustworthy and honest.

Please write to me. I remain your loving and loyal friend,
Antonia

62

Miles slows the car to a crawl, pauses in front of a two-storey house. Contemporary entrance, sleek windows, manicured lawn. 'Too modern?'

'Definitely.' Charlotte discards a page from the listings onto the back seat, where it joins other cast-off pages and a bunch of wilted yellow roses. Thirteen houses crossed off the list so far: some too small to be considered villas, others from the wrong era, most without the grand entrance portico and bay windows from the 1944 newspaper image.

'What's next?' asks Miles.

She enlarges the map on her mobile phone. 'Head along Moerestraat. Take the second right.'

They head away from town, leaving behind street lights and suburban houses. Shadows lengthen as daylight stretches to the horizon. Drizzle mists the windscreen. The wiper blades screech, smearing rather than clearing.

A house comes into view at the end of the lane. It is larger and older than the previous buildings. Waist-high weeds cover the front yard, grass grows across the gravel drive. Neglected and weary.

'Looks promising.' Miles coasts to a stop.

The three-storey façade is made of red brick. Beneath a wide portico, columns flank the front door. An octagonal tower, crowned with a steeple, abuts the left wing. Ancient trees crowd the yard.

'It looks smaller and not as grand as the house in the newspaper,' she says. 'What do you think?'

'Let's take a closer look.' Miles rummages in the glove box and pulls out a torch.

As they walk up the front path, the neglect becomes unmistakable. Paint flaking from door frames, windows with cracked glass, piles of dead leaves on the porch.

'Would've been amazing in its heyday,' he says.

Charlotte's phone buzzes as they reach the first step. 'You go ahead,' she tells him. 'I'll catch up.'

She shelters under a gnarled pine. The screen glows in the dim light: *unknown caller.*

'Hello?'

'Charlotte? This is Sébastien.' His voice sounds milder over the phone, almost friendly.

She presses the phone close to her ear. Palm sweaty. Tongue-tied.

'Charlotte? Are you there? It's Sébas—'

'Yes … yes … I'm here.'

'We haven't had a chance to speak, not since … when I told you …' His voice, normally confident, is hesitant.

'Yes.' She can't think of anything else to say.

'Charlotte, I understand you didn't want to attend the funeral, but we should still talk.'

There's a long pause.

'I've been very busy.' It's true, but she also recognises it for the excuse it is.

'It's often hectic this time of year. Perhaps after final lectures we could meet?'

A disconnected slide show flashes in her mind. Sterck in the auditorium, office, hospital, Rubenshuis, meeting room, Begijnhof. The sharpest image is from today, in Gistel's main street. She can't shake her suspicions. Festering emotions remain coiled within.

'Now isn't a good time.' Her tone is brittle.

'Can I call you next week to arrange a time?'

'Yes … no … I'll message you.' Her hands are shaking. 'I'll call you … next week. I have to go now.' She ends the call, puts the phone on mute. She wants to focus on the *Pandora* drawings, not deal with her father, her mother, their past. She can't face this now. Closing her eyes, she imagines sweeping the history of lies into a steel trunk, locking it away.

Regaining her focus, she opens her eyes. Grey clouds drift across the sky, and fat raindrops begin to fall as she runs up the steps to the entrance portico. Miles is nowhere in sight. She takes a few minutes to collect herself. Breathes deeply, exhales slowly.

'Miles?' she calls out.

A rattling sound comes from around the corner of the verandah.

Miles stands against a sash window, using both hands to wiggle it upwards, grunting with effort.

'Looks as though you're trying to break in.' A deserted house, growing darkness, Sterck's phone call, and suddenly she's skittish.

'It's not breaking in if a door or window happens to be open.' Moving to the next window, he jiggles it. Stuck fast. He tries another.

She walks to the opposite end of the verandah, running her hand along a balustrade. Paint flakes against her palm. A broken swing tilts to the floor. Attached to the wall, she spies a flat box with a small door. She tugs it open. Inside are rows of switches, dusty and cobwebbed. An electricity meter, the numbers frozen. A handwritten card stuck to the inside of the door shows the names of rooms next to corresponding electrical circuits. She squints at the faded script: *Elektriciteit geïnstalleerd 1921. Villa Wouters, Kievitstraat, Gistel.*

'Miles, it's definitely Villa Wouters,' she calls out, triumphant. She reads the worn card for a second time, and then a third, struggling to believe that it's true. After all this time, all their efforts, deciphering cryptic clues and searching for houses, they've found it. They're one step closer to finding the *Pandoras*.

Footsteps run along the verandah.

'Look.' She points to the card, her hands shaking with excitement.

Miles peers inside the meter box then turns to her, grinning. 'Bloody fantastic!' He grabs her waist, lifts her, spins her around.

She laughs and throws her arms around his shoulders. Walls and windows blur together as they twirl and whirl along the verandah.

She's floating; the stress of the past week has disappeared. Breathless, her heart racing, she relaxes into his embrace, thankful he's been a part of the journey leading to this moment. She

wouldn't be at Villa Wouters if not for his encouragement, loyalty
and wry humour, boosting her spirits when she felt like giving up.
That she kept the initial details of the search to herself is irrelevant.
This is *their* search now.

Without thinking, she reaches around his neck. Buries her head
against his shoulder, eyes closed, taking in his scent, his breath
warm on her neck.

They stand still. Strong arms hold her tight. His mouth brushes
along her jaw, her cheek, finding her lips. She returns his kisses, soft
and lingering. She draws him in closer, instinctively wanting the
space between them to disappear.

63

The only sound is rain pelting against the verandah roof.

'We're crazy,' she whispers, smiling. Slides her hands from around his neck until they rest against his chest. She leans back, placing a hair's breadth between them. The rational side of her brain tells her to slow down, wait, keep her life uncomplicated. But seconds later, she's telling herself to throw caution aside, trust her heart.

He draws her close, tightening his arm around her waist. Traces the line of her jaw with his finger. Another lingering kiss.

She nestles against him and shivers. Deepening shadows, eerie house, the thrill of his nearness. Content with silence, knowing she doesn't have to fill it, she reaches for his hand. She's reluctant to break the spell.

'Let's see if a back door is unlocked,' he finally says.

The path along the side of the house is shrouded in darkness. Towering oaks stretch their boughs to the house, sheltering them from the rain. The back garden is filled with overgrown box hedges, rose bushes dense with brambles, a dormant stone fountain thick with lichen. A flight of steps leads to a verandah with a back door.

A glass panel in the lower corner is smashed, jagged slivers protruding around the timber frame. The door is open. Miles gives it a gentle push and it squeals on rusty hinges.

'We may not be breaking in,' she says, 'but we're still entering unlawfully.' Her conscience gnaws at her. Sneaking the portfolio box from the Begijnhof and her illicit entry into the conservation room are too recent to ignore.

'We've come this far.' He pulls out his phone, stands back to get the entire door within shot. 'We can show a photo. Explain the door was already open.'

Her heart beats faster. She swallows, pushing aside her misgivings. 'Let's do this,' she says, trying to sound confident.

Miles pulls the torch from his pocket, sweeping its beam into the room, illuminating a cast iron cooker and a wall of kitchen cupboards.

They stand motionless in the doorway, ears straining for the slightest sound from inside the house. Stepping inside, their feet crunch on broken glass.

They follow a corridor to a grand foyer. Crowning the walls is a bas-relief frieze – miniature figures dressed in classical robes, hair curled in the fashion of ancient Greece – a gilded background, rubbed bare in patches, glowing with a burnished sheen. A wide staircase hugs the wall, ascending gracefully up and up, towards a domed skylight. On the half-landing, an arched window, the lower half boarded up. The upper half, made of stained glass, reveals a life-sized angel with golden hair and flowing saffron robes, arms spread wide, wings unfurled.

Their footsteps echo through the cavernous rooms. Once grand, now filled with cracked parquetry flooring, curtains askew, patches of mould spreading across walls and ceilings. In the dining room, wallpaper hangs in fat, curled ribbons. The rooms are empty: no large cabinets, closets, cupboards or sideboards. Nothing that could be described as a *kast*.

Miles swings the torch beam to a corner of the library, illuminating a stained mattress on the floor, candle stubs stuck to a shelf. 'Squatters. Explains the smashed door.'

By the time they climb to the first floor, the sun has melted to a puddle on the horizon. The stained-glass angel's dress, glorious yellow in daylight, has faded to a muddy bronze.

The house is creepy. She wants to search and leave quickly. 'Why don't I look in these rooms, while you check those?' She indicates a series of doors opening onto the landing.

Shadowy ghosts play tricks on her, leering from doorways and through balustrades. Reflections from a mirror on the back of a bedroom door make her jump, bringing on bouts of nervous laughter. Wandering into a bedroom, she turns on her phone's light and shines it over windows and walls. She checks inside a built-in robe, startled when a humanoid shape looms out of the shadows, relieved it's only a tattered dressing gown on a coat hanger.

'Have a look at this.' His voice rings out.

She finds him in a large bedroom at the front of the house, scanning the light over the intricate surface of a colossal four-poster bed. Each post is topped with an ornate finial resembling a pineapple. The headboard and baseboard are covered with pairs of lovebirds and rosebuds.

'The family had more than one antique marriage bed.' She sinks onto the lumpy mattress.

'Not suitable for a *begijnhof*,' says Miles.

'Too wieldy to manoeuvre down the stairs.' She pats the mattress, immediately regretting it as plumes of dust escape into the air.

He scans the light along the walls, slowing the beam when it illuminates a massive, age-blackened cabinet, recessed within an alcove. Two metres high and three metres long, nine doors, three in each row, with each panel intricately decorated with foliage and fruit. Carved in the centre of the top moulding, in sinuous loops: *1608*.

'We found it,' she whispers, sliding off the bed. She stands motionless. After two months of searching, she is remarkably calm.

Although Antonia never entered these rooms, having died centuries before her descendants took possession of the Gistel mansion, her ghostly presence is everywhere. Charlotte pictures Antonia as a child crouching in a stairwell, eavesdropping on conversations. Antonia, her arms wrapped around a bed post, talking to her mother. Antonia, running her hands over the cabinet's carved foliage, observing her father at work. Antonia: inquisitive and watchful, brooding about whispered secrets, burdened by duty, loyal to the end.

Stepping towards the cabinet, Charlotte's foot kicks a solid object. It skids across the floor, coming to rest with a metallic clang against a radiator.

Miles picks it up: it's an old tyre iron. He discards it against the wall.

The doors of the cabinet are ajar, displaying empty shelves. Each door and shelf is peppered with gashes and gouges.

Charlotte runs her hands over the shelves. Wood chips scatter the surfaces. She detects the aroma of cut timber. 'The wood chips are fresh.'

'The tyre iron ...' He moves the light beam to the floor in front of the cabinet. It is littered with fragments of splintered wood. He drops to his knees, twisting to look at the underside of the central door. Hollowed out. Narrow, forty centimetres deep. A secret compartment.

She kneels and cranes her head up, shining the light into the cavity.

Empty.

Convinced her eyes are mistaken, she slides her arm inside. Stretches her fingers as far as possible, skin scraping against rough timber.

It's no good. The cavity is too narrow for her to reach any further. She eases her arm out, skin chafed, then shines the light once more into the space to convince herself it is empty.

'The far corner! Something's caught.' She scrabbles across the floor, grabs the tyre iron. 'Hold the light steady.' Poking the metal bar into the cavity, she gently prods the inner corner. A piece of paper comes loose, freed from the timber joint. She catches it in her hand.

Triangular in shape, about the size of her palm. The paper is thick, cream-coloured, speckled with age-spots and stains, reminiscent of the paper she has seen on numerous visits to museums. One side is blank. The other side bears brown and ochre smudges, thin lines of dark brown ink, a few lines of white. Possibly depicting a heel, the bony protrusion of an ankle; it's difficult to tell.

She rests the scrap carefully in her hand. Shines her phone's light from every angle. The paper is delicate and old, the markings similar to the copious drawings she has studied over the last decade. This could very well be the work of the Master. She slips the scrap in between archive plastic, which Miles has pulled from his backpack.

She's unable to talk. Her mind paralysed. Every part of her numb.

They sit side-by-side on the floor, their backs against the cabinet. The scrap, covered in protective plastic, rests on her knees.

Taking her hand, he holds it between his palms, caressing her fingers. 'I'm sorry.'

Someone has beaten them to it.

64

April 25, 1623

Dearest Clara,

I am pleased to send you the Blackfriars map with this letter. I hope you enjoy searching for the words and pictures hidden amongst the streets, and deciphering the secret message. Concealed within the page is my secret signature. A clue: look for a certain nut.

I have missed receiving your letters. If your father has discovered our letter-writing and forbids it to continue, I hope we can somehow maintain our friendship. Please try to write. In the meantime, I will continue writing to you as if we are still the closest of friends.

My fourteenth birthday last month was celebrated with a note from Papa that required me to decipher a series of cryptic clues. I received a set of three pigments, lead-tin yellow, smalt and vermilion, which I used in your Blackfriars map.

Papa, having received new commissions, has employed a new maidservant and manservant, so I enjoy a little more time to myself to draw maps. His success in London has surpassed his own expectations. Although I am pleased to see him happy, I fear his achievements in London mean we may never return to Antwerpen.

While Papa remains silent on the possibility of taking a new wife, the two widows keep us entertained whenever we attend church. Janneke reports back to me whenever she overhears a snippet of their conversation. Widow Beagle asserts she is a more suitable match for Papa, given she is also from Flanders. Widow Ostrich contends she is able to add to Papa's offspring, given she has produced two healthy boys by her late husband.

The widows are not alone in measuring their personal success by their ability to care for a man and bear his children. Janneke speaks longingly of acquiring a husband, in the same way she wants a pet parrot from Batavia and silk petticoats from Paris. The Van Helst girls, my neighbourhood friends from Antwerpen, talked constantly of improving their needlework, musicianship and other mundane skills in the hope of catching a distinguished husband. How tiresome to be fixated on gratifying a man.

Whether housemaid or queen, women are trained in a life of subservience and obedience to men. If a woman chooses to turn away from this life and take the veil, her subservience to a man is replaced by obedience to God.

Thoughts of my own possible marriage are far in the future. You alone, Clara, know my feelings about matrimony and my preference to create an independent life for myself as a mapmaker. Imagine my dismay when Papa cornered me in the upstairs parlour this week, where I sat mending a collar, and began talking about the prospect of my own marriage.

'It won't be long, Antonia, before we start considering matrimony for you,' said Papa.

'My days are too busy with household duties.' I indicated the sewing in my lap, the household ledger on the table.

'Have the new maidservant do the sewing and ...' He was unable to name the specific tasks occupying my time.

Papa, as with many men, remains oblivious to the monotonous duties of women. Dirty clothes are discarded and within days reappear in the wardrobe, cleaned, mended, ready to be worn. Breakfast appears on the table at the appointed hour. Late-night suppers are ordered, presented on gleaming pewter, the remnants cleared away when guests depart. Boots are polished, floors swept, windows cleaned, all these tasks completed invisibly.

'Thank you, Papa. It will allow me to return to my lessons–'

'Only three lessons a week, and they must focus on French and English. Mastering foreign languages is important if you are to find a well-educated husband. Perhaps a diplomat or merchant ...'

Leaving Papa to his daydreams of procuring a distinguished son-in-law, I looked at the table, where a corner of my latest map poked out from beneath the household ledger.

Papa followed my glance. He pulled out the unfinished map, peered at the title cartouche. I hoped he would praise my drawing of the mythical Roman soldier whose brave deeds are said to have named the city Antwerpen.

'You've been neglecting your embroidery and the *spinetten*. Those skills need more of your attention than scribbling maps.' He discarded it on the table.

My Utopian childhood seems to have come to an end. The future I have longed for is moving out of reach.

Once more, I urge you to write if possible.

Your loving friend,

Antonia

65

Miles offers his hand to the lawyer. 'Thank you for seeing us without an appointment.'

'You're lucky you caught me,' says Jasper Gossens. 'I just returned to collect some papers.'

Charlotte introduces herself, studies the lawyer's face, wondering how someone who works in an office has acquired such a golden tan. He looks to be in his late fifties. Too young to be the Meneer Gossens who authored the letter from 1982.

Their decision to visit the lawyer had been spontaneous. They'd been subdued as they left Villa Wouters, unclear of their next move. Driving through Gistel's main street, Miles suddenly veered to the side of the road and parked in front of the lawyer's office. 'His lights are on. Maybe he's in the office. Worth a try.'

While Miles and Jasper Gossens talk about house-hunting, Charlotte stands in the middle of the office, disconnected from the conversation.

She wanders to a corner to examine some old photographs on the wall. A sepia image of fishermen mending nets. A shop-lined street with early automobiles and horse-drawn carts. A man and two teenage boys beside the tiller of a boat, its mainsail ballooned with wind.

'My father and I on the first sloop we built,' says Jasper.

'With your brother?' asks Charlotte.

'My cousin.' Jasper points to the sweeping lines of the boat. 'Smooth ride. Twelve knots on a good day. Do you sail?'

'No, I don't.'

'Thoroughly recommend it. Whenever I get the chance, I'm out on the water.'

'Have you always lived in Gistel?'

'Born and bred. We're a third-generation law firm, founded by my opa in 1920.' He ushers them to leather armchairs. 'So, you need some advice on a property purchase?'

Charlotte looks at Miles, tilting her head, wordlessly urging him to do the talking. She's struggling to focus on the present. All she can think about is the battered *kast*, the fragment of drawing. How close they came.

The leather armchair creaks as Miles shifts in his seat. 'We're interested in a Gistel property.'

'Which one do you have in mind?'

Miles folds his hands, squeezes his knuckles, looking uneasy. 'It's located east of the N33 motorway – isolated place, historic building with character, needs work. The agent said it was due to come on the market soon. We'd like to know if the property has any liens or restrictive covenants.'

'We're history buffs,' adds Charlotte, 'so we're keen to know the property's history, when it was built, previous owners.'

Jasper taps his fingers on the armrests. 'Normally I'd suggest you visit the Rating and Valuation Department, their nearest office is in Bruges, and ask for a land title search, but I know how slow they can be in providing details. I'll check if I have any information on this one.' He moves to a desk, sits behind a computer. 'What's the address?'

'Villa Wouters on Kievitstraat–'

The lawyer waves for him to stop. 'I know it. Our firm has represented the family for several generations. There are no liens or covenants except a heritage order dictating that renovations require planning approval. It's stunning inside. Beautiful stained-glass window and neoclassical frieze in the foyer.'

'Sounds as though you know the house well,' says Charlotte.

'I visited often as a child.' Jasper's tone becomes wistful. 'It was my aunt's house. My uncle married her several years before I was born. They had one son. She often invited us over for family gatherings. Didn't mind my brothers and I running like banshees through the house. She appreciated us coming over to spend time with her boy.'

'Did your cousin inherit the property on your aunt's death?' asks Miles.

'No. It was left to my aunt's child from an earlier marriage. Her first husband died during the war.'

'What happened to your aunt's first child?' asks Charlotte.

'She left home after my aunt and uncle married. Lived in Antwerp. Died only recently.'

'Who did she leave the property to?'

Jasper laughs, looking embarrassed. 'Goodness, I'm revealing all the family skeletons.' He frowns. 'Actually, I'm not at liberty to say.'

'We don't mean to pry,' says Miles. 'We're both historians, so we're curious about the background of the house.'

'Are you freelance historians?'

'Academics,' says Miles.

'Where do you work?'

'The University of Antwerp.'

Jasper folds his hands over his stomach, chuckling. 'What a small world. You probably know my cousin, Sébastien Sterck. He works at the university, too. It was his half-sister who inherited the house years ago and died last month. You just missed him, actually. He was here a few hours ago.'

66

Charlotte stares through the Citroën's dirty windscreen, waiting for Miles to return with food and water for the journey back to Antwerp. Dazed, she stares at Gistel's main street, but sees nothing, overwhelmed by the information Jasper Gossens so blithely delivered.

Sébastien Sterck is Sister Petra's half-brother, which means Petra is, or was, Charlotte's half-aunt. Even more astonishing, this means Charlotte is a distant relative of the engraver.

Lucas Vorsterman, *her* ancestor, worked in the Rubenshuis, created engravings of the Master's artworks, discussed commissions with him. Maybe they shared meals and raised their glasses together. Her ancestor, Lucas Vorsterman, argued with Rubens and they had a spectacular falling out. Work colleagues and friends, later divided by bitterness and anger. *Her* ancestor had been part of this incredible yet divisive partnership.

She shakes her head. The first time she held Antonia's letter, she was reading the handwriting of a distant relative, about whom she still knows so little. What else can she glean about the life of Antonia from her letters to her nephew?

Caring for her family and being loyal to them were of paramount importance. Well educated, conversant in political affairs and geography, a gifted linguist, creator of cryptic clues. But what else? What of her siblings? Was she as devoted to her mother as she was to her father? Was their family time in London happy? Is that where she learnt the English written in the border of the British map? Did she learn Genoese from Santo Barzetti? Did Antonia inscribe the Genoese on the *Italies* map herself? Did she commission the map folio from De Wit and embellish it herself with cryptic clues?

Charlotte recalls the genealogy trees from the portfolio box, penned by various members of the Vorsterman, Wouters and Van Vliet families – *her* ancestors. Her father's ancestry is a near-perfect duplicate of Petra's. It's her lineage, too. Yet her half-aunt remains a distant figure, revealed only through Edith's occasional comments. It would have been a surreal experience to talk with Petra about their mutual fascination with art and history, discuss their shared ancestry.

Charlotte examines the bluish veins on her hands. Does she share any physical attributes with Petra? Maybe the same pale skin, or smattering of freckles or unruly hair? Is their love of art more than a nurtured passion? Is it a genetic trait?

What does this revelation mean for the search of the elusive *Pandoras*? How does it explain Sterck's presence in Gistel? As the eldest surviving relative, Sterck is a likely beneficiary. If he inherits Villa Wouters, he will own everything inside the property, including anything hidden inside the antique *kast*.

But *is* Sterck the beneficiary of the estate? She recalls Edith's observations of the fraught interactions between Petra and Sterck. Perhaps she left Villa Wouters to the Begijnhof.

Charlotte mutters aloud. 'This would give Sterck every reason to break into the villa and steal the drawings before the Begijnhof can lay claim to them.'

As soon as she voices the idea aloud, she realises how ludicrous her suspicion sounds. Yet every piece of the mystery points in some way to Sterck's involvement. She clenches her hands in frustration.

Miles slides into the driver's seat. Hands her a bottle of water and a bulging paper bag. 'Found a bakery still open and bought some cheese pastries. Let's head back to Antwerp and decide on our next step tomorrow.'

'Tomorrow? Why wait? Sterck's involved,' she says. 'I'm not exactly sure how, but he's involved.'

Miles fumbles the key, dropping it on the floor of the car. 'We don't know that for sure,' he says, his voice weary.

'On the same day we see him in Gistel, Villa Wouters is broken into. It's too much of a coincidence.'

Miles scrabbles under the seat. 'That could have been squatters months ago.'

'Sterck had the opportunity to speak with Anna, to learn about our interest in locating the antique furniture. He knew about Villa Wouters and the antiques. He was estranged from his half-sister, Petra. We can't sit here doing nothing.'

Miles locates the key. 'We're dealing with people's reputations, Charlotte. You can't go around accusing—'

'Sterck is annoyed he didn't inherit Villa Wouters,' she interrupts. 'He hears a valuable object is inside so he breaks—'

'Enough with the baseless accusations!' yells Miles.

They sit in silence.

Charlotte scratches at some loose skin near her thumbnail until it bleeds. She has no evidence, knows her accusations are emotive and flimsy. But, damn it, she can't let them go.

Miles fits the key in the ignition. Gripping the steering wheel, he turns to face her. When he speaks, his voice is calm. 'We've had a long day. It's late. I'm not suggesting we ignore what we've learnt, but it needs careful consideration.'

Charlotte is distracted, glancing into the rear-view mirror. Something has caught her eye: a figure standing under a street light, ten yards behind the Citroën. Twisting in her seat, she stares out the back window. The street light illuminates a woman wearing a beige coat, and holding an object to her ear, perhaps a phone. She takes a step towards the car, then stops.

'Miles, we should go.'

'What's wrong?' He turns, following her gaze.

Charlotte fumbles with her seatbelt. 'Let's go.'

The engine wheezes into life and he eases the car from the kerb. They sit in silence as the town peters out, replaced by fields.

'Why the sudden departure?' he asks.

'It was the real estate agent. She was staring at us. Didn't come over to ask about our house-hunting. Her behaviour wasn't normal.'

He laughs. 'And ours is?'

'I was worried she'd think we were the ones who broke the door at Villa Wouters.'

'We could have told her the truth.'

'I suppose, yes.' She gazes out the side window.

'Are you always this distrustful?' He stares at the road ahead.

She turns to look at him. The dashboard lights cast eerie green shadows across his face. She remembers the gentle touch of his lips, the tenderness of their embrace. They'd laughed easily while exploring the house, holding hands in the dark, jumping with fright at reflections in mirrors. He'd been kind and empathetic when they'd discovered the drawings were gone, understanding her need to sit in silence, to grasp the enormity of the destroyed cabinet, realising how close they had come. He'd read her emotions instinctively then, but doesn't understand her now.

'Please don't psychoanalyse me, Miles.'

A freeway sign looms out of the dark: *Antwerp 122 km.*

He turns onto the freeway. She curls up in her seat, huddles against the passenger door, closes her eyes. Oncoming headlights flare against her closed lids. The sound of tyres swooshing through water. Heater purring, benumbing her into a welcome cushion of oblivion.

She's gliding through a house. Moonlight streams through windows, illuminating a frieze of tiny people high on the wall. Each figure is talking, lips moving yet mute, robes fluttering in a non-existent breeze. Her mother floats around her, drifting higher, her Grecian robe a mass of undulating ripples. After reaching the stained-glass window, she reclines against its surface, arms outstretched, mimicking the angel behind. Smiles. The glass shatters in slow-motion, in silence. Sparkling shards float across the night-time sky, weightless, joining millions of stars. Mama is gone.

Charlotte jerks awake.

Hazard lights flashing, indicator clicking, the car motionless by the side of the road.

She peers through the windscreen. Headlights illuminate horizontal rain, trees bending in the wind.

Miles stands in front of the car, hunched against the rain, buffeted by gusts of wind. His phone is wedged between ear and shoulder, and he uses both hands to open the car's bonnet. Moments later, he closes the bonnet and returns to the driver's seat, wipes rain from his face. 'Not sure what's wrong. Karl's not answering, so

I've called roadside assistance.' He tugs a beanie over his ears. 'It's miserable out there.'

She's heedless to what he's saying. Dazed from sleep, the image of the shattered angel remains imprinted on her retinas.

'Roadside assistance will be at least an hour. The operator said it's a busy night.'

A car whooshes past, spraying water across their windscreen.

'Are you cold? I'll check if Karl has a picnic rug in the back.' Miles steps out of the car to rummage in the boot.

Charlotte checks her phone for messages, recalls putting the phone on silent hours ago. Three missed calls from Sterck in the last hour. What could be so urgent that he would call her three times? She slips the phone into her pocket.

'Found this old rug. It smells of motor oil, but it's better than nothing.' He slides across the bench seat until their legs touch. Unfolds the rug over their knees. Rests his arm along the back of the seat, drawing her close.

A lorry hurtles past, rocking the car. The hazard lights glow hypnotically. She curls into his warmth.

'I'm sorry about before,' he says.

'S'okay,' she mumbles. 'Been a disappointing day.'

He tucks a loose curl behind her ear. 'I want to help.'

'You've already been a huge help.'

'Not the drawings. Not work. *You.* I want to help you.'

'I need help, do I?' There's an edge to her voice.

'Something's troubling you. Help me understand.'

Her throat is scratchy, chest aching with heaviness. 'I'm fine.'

'You're filled with anger. From the day we met, you've been determined to find Sterck guilty. I don't know what the problem is, but you can tell me. I'm here for you.'

She wraps her arms across herself, instinctively protective.

'Talk to me, Charlotte.' His voice is gentle. 'You're a closed book.'

'I've shared more with you, Miles, than I've shared with anyone. Ever.'

She tries to control her breathing. She's blinked away tears so many times over the past few months, she can't do it anymore. They course down her cheeks and drip off her chin unchecked.

His hand strokes the back of her neck.

When she finally speaks, her voice is hollow. 'My parents broke up before I was born. I thought my father was dead, but apparently he's been alive all these years. I met him for the first time when I arrived in Antwerp two months ago. Miles—' She stops, tries to compose herself. When she speaks again, her voice is hoarse. 'Sébastien Sterck is my father. Their break-up filled my mother with so much anger and bitterness and I can't … I can't … let it go.' Her sobs arrive like the storm. She folds herself into his arms, releasing the pent-up emotions.

67

July 19, 1623

Dearest Clara,

Having received no letters from you for nearly ten months, I have concluded your father has forbidden you to write to me any longer. The alternative, that you have forsaken our friendship, is too upsetting to contemplate. For the sake of my sanity, I will pretend you still respond to my letters and so, I will share details of a mysterious happening in our Blackfriars house.

Mister Hawthorn continues to be a frequent caller. At least once a week, he arrives in the late afternoon when Hendrik and Niels have finished their lessons. We gather around the kitchen table and have delightfully disjointed conversations as he practises Flemish and we practise English.

After the evening meal, Papa and Mister Hawthorn adjourn to the front parlour, where their conversation continues into the evening. Snippets of their discussion float into the foyer as Ludo enters and exits the room. He is kept busy replenishing their wine and bringing plates of cheese and pickles to sustain them during their discussions regarding the Widows Beagle and Ostrich, the intrigues of the Duke of Buckingham, and religious unrest in the Commons. Of late, however, their conversation has become more personal.

A humid summer night last week made it difficult to sleep. I wandered from room to room, relishing the creaks of the sleeping house. I sat on the stairs, catching the meagre breeze from the stairwell's open window, my warm cheek against the cool plaster wall. I heard Papa and Mister Hawthorn's broken conversations about concealing past sins, begging forgiveness, making amends. I was suddenly wide awake to the unprecedented sound of Papa weeping.

'Lucas ... Lucas.' Mister Hawthorn spoke soothingly.

'You cannot understand,' said Papa. 'I must live with my wrongdoing. No matter how many times I seek forgiveness, it hangs over me.'

'No sin is so bad that Our Lord will not forgive you,' said Mister Hawthorn.

'I should have righted this wrong earlier, but it is too late. I was blinded by ambition, filled with anger and jealousy, losing all sense of reason, hiding my guilt. Now I must live with my wrongdoing for the remainder of my days. I have put my own ambition and pride above caring for my family. Nothing can justify my behaviour. Dishonour and hardship will befall my family.' His voice broke.

I heard no more of the exchange. Instead, I hurried to my bed, stepping carefully over creaky floorboards. Pulling a sheet over my head, like Papa, I hid my shame.

By the following week, my inquisitive nature resurfaced. Again, I found myself sitting on the stairs in the dark, enjoying the cooling breeze, filled with curiosity as to why a carpenter had been called to our house in the early morning and still worked late at night.

No one told me the scruffily dressed worker was a carpenter. I deduced this myself, having spied his tool bag and the sawdust on his clothes as he sat in the courtyard eating his midday meal. The sounds of tapping, grinding, cutting and hammering that came from Papa's workroom alerted me to some form of minor construction taking place. My attempts to ascertain what was happening were thwarted.

'Do not disturb him,' said Janneke when she saw me about to knock on the workroom door.

But now in the quiet of the night, with everyone else asleep except for Papa and his mysterious visitor, I sat with my ears straining, eager for my curiosity to be appeased.

The sound of muffled voices grew clearer as the workroom door opened. The heavy tread of workman's boots echoed in the night-time quiet of the house, then I heard a gruff voice with a strong London accent. 'Yessir, it be troublin' times with Parliament dissolved an' the future unsure for–'

Papa interrupted with whispered words. Coins clinked into a palm.

The gruff voice continued, 'That be right, sir. Need to help one another, us belongin' to the true—'

Papa whispered once more.

'Yer papers be well hidden,' the voice continued. 'Won't nobody find 'em.'

I scurried to bed. It didn't make sense that all that cutting and hammering was to make a hiding place for mere papers. Wouldn't it make better sense to have a secret place to conceal jewellery and coins? Or, if we could be incriminated for owning Catholic prayer books and psalters, wouldn't it be wise to hide them away?

Your loving friend,

Antonia

68

'Last one for tonight.' The stationmaster points to a train gliding out of the station. 'Next train to Antwerp is at six-fourteen tomorrow morning.'

'What about a bus?' asks Charlotte.

'Last one has left.'

'Taxi?'

The stationmaster raises his hand above his head to indicate the thunderous din of rain pelting onto the roof. 'To Antwerp, at this hour, in a storm? Unlikely. Come back in the morning.' He closes the ticket booth window.

Charlotte turns away. The station concourse is empty except for Miles sitting at a bench, holding his phone to his ear. Letters on the display board flicker in unison, revealing a list of trains departing the next day. She paces along the platform, coiled with impatience. She has to meet with Sterck, needs to see his expression as she asks him about Villa Wouters.

Miles pockets his phone and walks towards her. He carries the gym bag containing the portfolio box, retrieved from the Citroën. 'I told Karl roadside assistance couldn't get the Citroën started and it was towed to Oostende. When's the next train?'

'Tomorrow morning.'

'We're stranded in Oostende for the night?'

'No.' Pulling out her phone, she continues walking towards the exit. 'There may not be any trains or buses, but I'll find a taxi. Someone must be available to drive us to Antwerp.'

'On a Saturday evening, an hour and a half one-way in a storm? Seriously?' He laughs.

The doors slide open and they're almost knocked off their feet, buffeted by driving wind and rain. They retreat back inside, sheltering around the corner of the entrance.

She's cursing, but he's laughing as he shakes rain from his hair. 'Let it go, Charlotte. No one will be interested in making a two hundred and forty kilometre round trip in a gale. Let's find a cosy restaurant–'

'Let it go?' Her voice is tight, irritated by his laughter, annoyed he has dismissed her ideas so quickly.

He reaches out, tries to draw her into his arms. 'I didn't mean you should forget about the villa or the drawings.'

She turns away from his embrace. Scrolls her phone, trying to find the number of a local taxi.

'I just meant, let's have a break. You've been working hard, so many late nights. Have a rest. We'll enjoy a nice meal, a bottle of wine, have a good night's sleep, and in the morning, you'll feel refreshed and able to think more clearly, more rationally.'

She glares at him. 'Think. More. Rationally?'

'I meant after a good sleep, you'll be able–'

'Miles, all I've been doing is thinking rationally about this situation. All my investigations have focused on finding a logical solution.'

'Really?' His voice climbs. 'You're consumed with the idea Sterck is involved. You admitted you're not sure how he's involved, but you're still determined to find fault with him, based solely on his past with your mother. To me, that's not rational.' As soon as the words are out of his mouth, he starts apologising. 'I'm sorry–'

'Not rational? Is that so?' Her tone is icy. She scowls at him, then at her phone. Furious at him for thinking he has the slightest understanding of her personal situation, furious at being stuck in this godforsaken city in a storm, furious she can't locate a taxi to get home, furious at herself for explaining her actions to this neanderthal who has no idea what she's going through.

'Charlotte–'

'It appears no taxis are accepting bookings because of the storm.' She shoves her phone into her pocket. 'We can either sleep on a station bench or find a hotel.' She turns to the exit.

They leave the station, leaning into the wind, rain stinging their faces. They hurry past bars with music, people sheltering under umbrellas, and push open the door of the first hotel they see. A man behind the counter looks up.

Miles wipes rain from his face, places the gym bag on the floor. 'Do you have any rooms available?'

The hotel clerk advises them of room rates and check-out times. Places a registration form on the counter, along with a room key.

'Two rooms, please,' says Charlotte.

The check-in process complete, Charlotte and Miles stand in a lift that clunks its way to the third floor.

'I'm sorry, Charlotte. I shouldn't–'

'It's okay.' Her voice is gruff.

'Do you want to get something to eat?' He leans against the wall, his arm brushing hers.

'No, thanks. I'm not hungry.' She stares at the floor.

'Can we at least talk?'

She turns to face him, taking in his rain-soaked coat and dripping hair, the lines between his brows. Every minute of the past thirty-something hours has been filled with tension, like elastic slowly stretching, coming close to snapping. 'To be honest, Miles, I'm exhausted. I need some time to myself.'

He tilts his head a fraction, as if he's about to lean in and kiss her. But he remains still. Offers a thin smile. Wishes her a good night's sleep.

The lift door opens. She picks up the gym bag and walks along the hallway. All she can think about is finding her room, shutting herself away.

A dim overhead light bathes the room in greyness. The room smells of stale cigarettes. Rain drums against the window.

She turns on the television, flicks through channels, hears news of the storm, turns it off. She can't get comfortable. The armchair is scratchy, the bed lumpy. She paces from window to wall, reliving each moment. Words, looks, touches, his hand around her waist, drawing her close. The warmth of his arms, his lips. Laughing together as they explored the house. The way he held her while she sobbed. But then, harsh words. She wants to swallow them back. Press backspace, delete, reboot.

Sitting on the bed, she removes her shoes. Tells herself to climb into bed, close her eyes, let her body and mind rest. The search for the drawings has been turned on its head, but that doesn't mean it's over.

There's a faint knock on the door.

She's slow to stand, her stomach twisting. A part of her wants it to be him, yet she also wants more time to herself, time to settle her emotions.

Another knock, slightly louder.

Treading gingerly to the door, she peers through the peephole. He stands in the hallway, hands in his pockets, his expression downcast. He stares at the door, as if he can see through solid timber. They are separated by only four centimetres of wood, yet so much more.

Leaning her forehead against the door, she closes her eyes, sadness welling in her chest. She imagines talking to him. *I'm going back to Toronto in four months*, she'd say. *It can't lead anywhere*. Perhaps she could explain she needs more time. *I'm not saying no, I want to say yes, but I can't. Not yet.*

She remains silent. By the time she turns back to the peephole, the hallway is empty.

Curling up on the bed, she stares at a plastic telephone on the bedside table. Wishes she could pick up the handset and hear her mother's voice at the other end. Pour out her troubles in a cathartic purge. *Miss you*, Charlotte mouths into the pillow. Tonight, her mother's lies and betrayal are a distant memory, unimportant.

She begins drifting towards the shadows of sleep, several times nearly tipping into blackness, but jolting awake with vivid memories of feet crunching on broken glass, the cloying scent of roses, the blinding glare of headlights. She's unaware of how long she hovers in and out of consciousness, until a vague thought snags her memory.

She sits up quickly and fumbles for her phone. Five missed calls, all from Sterck. No voice messages. Damn! Her phone is still muted. The last call was twenty minutes ago. Something must be wrong for him to call five times.

Her hands are shaking as she calls his number; she nearly drops the phone when he picks up on the first ring. 'I'm sorry to call so late,' she says. 'My phone was on mute. Is something wrong?'

'I've been trying to reach you. The police called me.'

'Police?'

'Were you in a town called Gistel today?'

'Yes,' she whispers.

'The police want to question you and Miles. I've been trying to call him, too, but he's not answering. Do you know where he is?'

Charlotte's face prickles with heat. 'Why do the police want to question us?'

'A house in Gistel was broken into, the door smashed open.'

She wants to explain it wasn't them, but she says nothing. It's not Sterck she has to convince of their innocence. Pressing the phone hard against her ear, she tries to block out the howling wind, desperate to detect his tone. Is there a hint of blame or frustration beneath his composure? She can't tell.

'The police can discuss it with you.' His voice drops, hesitates. 'There's more.'

Her palms sweat.

'Anna called me this afternoon. It appears you may have in your possession an item from the Begijnhof. Apparently, it was taken yesterday, without Anna's permission.' He speaks the last three words so quietly they're barely audible.

Charlotte glances at the gym bag resting on the armchair. Edith had given them permission to remove the portfolio box from the Begijnhof, but it wasn't Edith's permission to give.

'And,' says Sterck, 'Dean Mulder told me a complaint has been lodged against you. Apparently, there's CCTV footage of you entering the conservation room without authorisation, and it happened close to the attempted break-in–'

'I had nothing to do with the break-in.' The words fly out of her mouth in a burst of fury.

Sterck remains calm. 'Mulder has asked to see you in his office, nine o'clock Monday morning. He's put you on suspension, pending further investigation.'

Charlotte swallows. Mouth dry.

'You should have someone else with you when you meet with him. A work colleague or someone from human resources. Or, if you like, I could–'

'I'm … I'm not sure. Let me think.' A dull roar fills her ears.

'If there's anything I can do, Charlotte.'

'Thank you. I'll let you know.'

She's already pacing the room as the call ends. A sudden coldness hits her insides. Her heart races. This can't be happening. She desperately wants to see Miles.

She dashes along the corridor and thumps on his door. *Wake up, wake up*, she silently cries.

No answer.

Thumps again.

Still no reply.

She rushes down the stairs. The clerk glances up from behind the desk.

'The man I arrived with–'

'He checked out. Left this for you.' The clerk slides an envelope across the counter.

69

Dearest Clara,

Although I still have received no response from you, I plan to send this letter to Antwerpen with the help of our Flemish neighbour who writes regularly to her sister. Mister Hawthorn, for reasons I explain below, is unable to send my letter. I live with the hope you are somehow able to receive this and learn of our troubling circumstances.

All anyone can talk about is the breakdown of the Spanish Match. For nine years the royal houses of Stuart and Hapsburg have squabbled over marriage negotiations between Protestant Prince Charles and Catholic Infanta Maria. Nine years of fierce debate have now come to an end with the betrothal dissolved. A massive outpouring of anti-Catholic sentiment has descended into the streets.

Troublemakers smashed the windows of the wine merchant's shop in Farringdon, simply because he is Catholic and imports his wine from Spain. Fights broke out between opposing factions in a tavern in Ludgate, resulting in three men stabbed and the civic guard called to drag the culprits to jail.

We have not heard from Mister Hawthorn for two weeks and I fear he has fallen foul of troublemakers who would harm a former Catholic priest. Two weeks ago, Papa was expecting him for supper and he did not arrive. There was no message. It is out of character for him to ignore an invitation, and we suspect the worst.

Papa has lost at least one major commission and may lose more. Yesterday, I entered his workroom in search of a new quill and, finding him absent, I am ashamed to admit that I read a letter on his desk from the personal assistant of the Earl of Arundel. The letter declared that the Earl can no longer associate with a Papist engraver, and several commissions were cancelled.

Worse, rumours abound that members of the Commons are so offended by the Spanish they are calling for war against the Spanish Hapsburg Empire.

Our countries could be at war against one another by wintertide, yet Papa appears to be the only Flemish Catholic in London who is indifferent to the dangers. He speaks about employing an assistant, gaining new commissions, restocking the cellar, when he should be booking our passage on the next fluyt.

It is not safe in England. We need to return to Antwerpen before harsher anti-Catholic laws are approved by the Commons.

I know I should display loyalty and obedience to Papa, but sometimes I doubt whether he understands the gravity of our situation. He has become adept at juggling multiple allegiances – rubbing shoulders with Protestant clients to earn their patronage while practising his Catholic faith in secret – but he fails to see the danger surrounding us.

Papa refuses to discuss the situation with me. He steers our conversation to such mundane topics as Widow Beagle's interest in lacemaking, my progress on the *spinetten* or Hendrik's misdemeanours.

I must maintain a semblance of normalcy within our home, despite the unrest. If the boys see my fear, they will become anxious. Niels is about to turn nine, so I will continue our family tradition of preparing a cryptic puzzle for his birthday. I will draw a map of our Blackfriars house, fill it with clues, and he will be so busy running from room to room looking for answers he will not have time to worry.

Your loving friend,
Antonia

70

Dazed, she walks to a corner of the deserted foyer. Slumps into an armchair. Opens the envelope.

Dear Charlotte,

Sorry to leave suddenly like this. I've gone back to Antwerp. Something has come up which needs attention tonight. You made it clear you want to be alone. The best thing I can do is give you some space.

I can't imagine what you've had to deal with over the past few months, even years. I imagine you're hurting. I want to be there for you, but if you don't want me, I can't force it. This needs to be your decision.

You may not want to hear this, but you're wrong about Sterck. He helped me out of a difficult situation last term. One of my post-grad students was angry about the low marks I'd given her. She accused me of being prejudiced against her, sabotaging her research. She threatened to go to the dean and have me charged with professional misconduct, saying everyone would believe her over me and I'd be dismissed. Even though I was innocent, I was worried her lies would spread and my name would be dragged through the mud. When enough mud is thrown, sometimes it sticks.

I went to Sterck and he helped clear it up. He encouraged her to abandon the bogus charges and smoothed it over without it getting on the grapevine. It could have ended in a mess, but he handled it with discretion. She ended up transferring from Antwerp.

Although I'm indebted to him, he's never made me feel I owe him anything. He may not be the easiest person to talk to, but he's not bad. Talk to him. Listen to him. Give him a chance.

> *You don't have to do this on your own. I'm here if you*
> *want me.*
>   *Miles*

Her eyes fill with tears. She drops the letter in her lap, sinks her head into her hands, presses her wrists to her eyes, trying to staunch the tears. She's been foolish in so many ways, ignoring Miles, who has only ever shown her loyalty and friendship. She's been blinded by prejudice and obsessed with seeing the worst in Sterck, filled with suspicion and distrust. She's been stupidly, irrationally suspicious of him, obsessing over Mama's bitterness, refusing to listen to his side of the story. And Miles. Bad enough to have ruined her own career, but not Miles'. He doesn't deserve this.

Stifling her sobs, she tries to get herself under control. *Just breathe.* Wipes her eyes with the palms of her hands. Stares at the hotel's maroon carpet.

A pair of scuffed brown shoes appear.

'Can I get you a cup of tea?' asks a Belgian voice. 'You look upset.'

She looks up into the sympathetic face of the hotel clerk.

Her shoulders twitch. It's not the clerk's kindness that surprises her, but how unexpectedly British it sounds. She's in rural Belgium and a local is offering to soothe her troubles away with a quintessential British panacea. She recalls the endless cups of tea Miles drinks every day, half-consumed cups left around the office, the numerous times he's made her tea as a pick-me-up. *This'll make you feel better*, he'd said.

'Thank you very much, but no.' Her voice is scratchy.

'Have you heard all trains from Oostende are cancelled?'

She stares at him blankly.

'The storm is worse,' he continues. 'Debris on the tracks. Local flooding. Trains won't be running until at least Monday evening, maybe Tuesday.'

'Thank you for letting me know.'

His shoes squeak as he retreats.

How is she going to get to her meeting with the dean? She pulls out her phone. She'll apologise, explain about Sterck, the accusations and suspension, being stuck in Oostende. Miles is calm, his suggestions sensible.

She calls his number.

No signal, the screen announces. She tries again, but receives the same obstinate message.

She approaches the clerk. 'Is there somewhere else in the hotel I can get a stronger signal?'

The clerk places a phone on the counter. 'Try the landline.'

This time the call goes through, but Miles doesn't answer. His voicemail invites her to leave a message, his tone cheerful, at odds with her distress. Her eyes well with tears again. Any minute, she'll be blubbering.

Back in her room, she uses the hotel phone to call his number. Once more, it goes to voicemail. 'Damn.' She wants Miles. No one else.

Her teeth begin chattering. She wraps herself in the duvet. Sitting on the edge of the bed, she hovers her hand above the hotel phone. She's been too suspicious for too long, hasn't given him a chance. Ever since she arrived in Antwerp, she's been blinkered and prejudiced, consumed by the past, unwilling to see, refusing to listen. *Give him a chance*, Miles had said.

Whenever her mother had spoken about Sterck, her words were filled with bitterness. *We never needed him. He was horrible.* No wonder Charlotte assumed the worst. She now wonders if Rachael's memories had blurred and distorted over the years. Had her emotions combined fact and fiction to create a different version of events? Whatever happened between her parents is their history, not hers. Charlotte needs to listen to his version, judge for herself.

She recalls all the times she has spoken with Sterck. He has never been disagreeable, always showing her professionalism, consideration and politeness. Any anecdote about his alleged improper behaviour is based entirely on Rachael's accusations. Charlotte has been foolish and narrow-minded.

She picks up the hotel phone and calls the number quickly, before she can change her mind. His drowsy voice answers on the second ring.

'Sébastien, I've made a terrible mess of everything.'

A faint clearing of his throat.

'Are you there?' Her voice is hesitant. Maybe this was a mistake, maybe he can't help, or doesn't want to. She's missed her chance.

'It's okay. I'm here.' His tone is reassuring.

'I'm sorry about everything, Sébastien. I should have spoken to you about my mother as soon as I arrived in Antwerp. Got everything out in the open. I want to talk to you, about her and you and me, but right now I'm in an awful mess. I'm stranded in Oostende. The car broke down. Trains and buses and taxis aren't running because of the storm and probably won't be running until Monday or even Tuesday. I'm at Hotel Bassin on Kaaistraat. I've got no way of getting back to Antwerp for my meeting on Monday with the dean. If your offer still stands, I'd be grateful if you'd come with me to the meeting? And,' her voice threatens to break, 'can you please come and get me in Oostende?'

'Of course, I'll get you.' She hears a wardrobe opening, coat hangers jangling.

She closes her eyes. He's coming.

'I don't know how long it will take me to drive there. The A10 from Ghent is closed with flooding, but I'll go via Bruges.'

'Thank you.'

'You sound exhausted. While you're waiting, try to get some sleep.'

'Okay.'

'We can sort this out.'

Her throat constricts. 'Thank you,' she repeats, barely able to get the words out.

After the call ends, she smooths out Miles' crumpled letter. *Need to make it right with you, too.*

She crawls under the duvet, draws it around her neck. Tries to replay the conversation in her head, but fatigue rolls in like a swift tide. Seconds before falling into a deep sleep, she has the sensation of tumbling. Hovering on an edge then drifting backwards, floating through air, hoping he will catch her as she descends.

71

September 27, 1623

Dearest Clara,

We are coming home. Papa booked our passage this morning. I will send this letter to you with the help of our Flemish neighbour, who is returning to Antwerpen ahead of us.

The Blackfriars house is filled with wooden crates and servants rushing about with armloads of glassware, pewter, books and linen. Furniture is being protected with blankets and prepared for transport. Wood shavings litter the floor. I am delirious with joy, picking up handfuls of the stuff and throwing it in the air, dancing in circles as it descends like snow.

Papa used vague terms to explain the reason for our swift departure.

'Your brothers have acquired too many English customs. It is time to return to our homeland before they become more English than Flemish,' said Papa.

I bit my lip to suppress a smile.

'Your mama's sister has written from Antwerpen with news of a suitor who would make you a favourable match. He is interested in meeting you on our return. Although the marriage would be several years away, a betrothal could be possible now.'

I didn't listen to whatever else Papa said about the nameless suitor. All I could think about was returning to my beloved Antwerpen and seeing you at last. Once we have settled into the Eikenstraat house, I will win back Papa's affections. He will realise I am too young to consider marriage, that my inquisitive mind has destined me for a different future.

Papa tweaked his moustache, with a look of concern on his face. 'I will contact Meneer van Dyck when we return to Antwerpen, as I believe he may require an engraver.'

Papa still refused to mention the true reason for our return.

I know we are departing England due to the harsh anti-Catholic laws soon to be sanctioned by the Commons, and because of Papa's increasing loss of commissions. Mister Hawthorn's continued absence, troubling indeed, is surely due to the growing contempt with which Catholics are regarded in this country. It saddens my heart that Papa and I once discussed such challenging topics with enthusiasm, but now our conversations are limited to the trivialities of household duties and prospective suitors. But I will win him back.

I look forward to hugging you in person, dear Clara, in a few short weeks.

Your loving sister and friend forever,

Antonia

72

Sébastien places a towel on the bathroom counter, along with a wrapped bar of oatmeal soap. He studies Charlotte's reflection in the mirror. 'I spoke to the dean and he's agreed to postpone your meeting until later in the week.'

'Thank you.'

He pauses at the door. 'Is there anything you don't eat?'

She shakes her head. He leaves, closing the door.

Looking around the bathroom, *his* bathroom, she tries to process everything that has happened in the past two hours. His offer for her to come back to his apartment – a shower, a home-cooked breakfast, the opportunity to talk, *really* talk – had felt right, and she'd found herself readily accepting. But now she's by herself, for the first time since being collected from Oostende, and she's filled with apprehension. What is he really like? How will they begin to talk about everything they need to share?

She steps into the shower, twists the massage jets to full force. Hair drenched, muscles pummelled, skin singing from a thousand needles. Revived.

Memories from the morning snap into focus. The first hour of the journey back to Antwerp had been spent in stilted conversation. Like a poker player revealing one card at a time, Charlotte had shared details of Vorsterman and Rubens, Antonia's documents, the cryptic clues, her theory about the seven *Pandoras*, the smashed door, looted cabinet, discarded tyre iron, the paper scrap. When describing the smashed cabinet, she examined his profile, looking for a nervous flinch or expression to indicate she had hit a nerve. But he remained calm, impenetrable. When she mentioned seeing him in Gistel and learning he is Petra's half-brother, he simply nodded in agreement, offering no additional information.

Charlotte dries and dresses. Opening cabinets in search of a hairdryer, she finds labelled boxes lined up on shelves. Overcome with curiosity, she slides out a box labelled *Motion Sickness*, and recalls her own travels, being lulled to sleep along winding roads by the sedating magic of Dramamine. What else has she inherited from him?

She wipes splashed water from the bench, folds the damp towel over the bath. As she lines up a tissue box with a flowering *Spathiphyllum*, she recognises another shared trait. All this tidying, arranging objects, organising items into labelled boxes and colour-coded folders, is a mutual quirk. She stares at her reflection. His green eyes stare back.

She checks her phone for missed messages. Nothing from Miles. Calling him again, she leaves a message. 'Miles, could you please call me? I'm with Sébastien. He collected me from Oostende. I've told him about the *Pandoras*, and something's happened at work. The Gistel police … it's too complicated to explain. I need to speak with you.' Her voice quavers and she ends the call.

Facing the bathroom door, the imp in her belly returns. She opens the door and walks resolutely along the hallway.

Sébastien stands at the kitchen counter slicing oranges. An Italian-style coffee percolator burbles on the cooker. Smell of frying bacon.

'Breakfast isn't quite ready yet.' He twists an orange half onto a juicer.

'Can I help?'

'No need. Why don't you relax?' He indicates a set of double doors.

She enters the sitting room. Leather sofas the colour of molasses, reading lamps on side tables, a maidenhair fern in a copper pot. Bookshelves cover an entire wall, a library ladder propped against the uppermost shelf. In the centre of the room is a large ottoman arranged with weighty tomes. She walks around it, scanning covers – *Mystical Giants of Easter Island*, *Views of the Andes*, *Aztec Figurines* – and recalls the ghoulish masks in his office. Studying a framed photograph on a side table, she recognises the same teenagers on the sailing boat: a young Sébastien at the tiller, his cousin Jasper Gossens at his side.

She wanders into a darkened alcove, flicks a switch and is startled by an abrupt blaze of light from the opposite wall. Floor-to-ceiling glass shelves, illuminated from behind, display a collection of crystal vases, sculptures and bowls in a myriad of greens and blues. Lalique's *Poissons* vase in electric blue sits alongside a school of frosted emerald fish. An olive vase by Gallé reveals a dragonfly hovering above water. A jade-green bowl, acid-etched in Art Deco patterns, sits beside a Fenton goblet in opaque apple green. Spheres of electric-blue Murano glass hold trapped air bubbles. Daum's *pâte de verre* sage frog with bulging eyes, a clone of her mother's frog, sits on a shelf eyeballing her. A dazzling wall of translucent blues and greens, refracted light, luminous and surreal.

'Do you collect?' asks Sterck, appearing at her side.

A lump forms in her throat. She shakes her head, not trusting herself to speak.

'Did your mother continue her collection?'

'Yes, but mainly in green.' Her voice wobbles. She stares at the frog.

He follows her gaze. Crossing to the shelf, he touches the frog. 'We each bought one at Les Puces de Saint-Ouen during our weekend in Paris. The seller said they were by Daum, the French crystal manufacturer. It was the beginning of my collection. And hers.'

A sensation of warmth unfurls in Charlotte's chest, spreading to her face. Stillness is all around her, in the shimmering blues and greens of the glass wall, the gentle burbling of the coffee pot in the background, the quiet presence of her father, standing close but giving her space.

The snippet about their Paris visit gives her a glimpse into a moment when their relationship was full of promise. She can't hope to understand the desire that pulled them together, the anger that tore them apart, but she's ready to think of them in a new way.

'Breakfast is ready,' says Sébastien.

They sit opposite one another at the kitchen table. He places before her a stack of fluffy pancakes, topped with Canadian bacon, maple syrup dripping down the sides. He pours orange juice, offers coffee.

Touched by his efforts, she finds it difficult to swallow, even though her stomach is growling.

'There's extra if you need it.' He indicates a bottle of *sirop d'érable pur*.

The real stuff from Canada, not imitation. She blinks away the prickling sensation in her eyes. This isn't the time for sentimentality.

She loads her fork with pancake, chews, swallows. 'It must be sad to see your family home in such a state of disrepair. Did you live there your entire childhood?'

'I left when I was sixteen and changed my surname. I was close with my paternal grandmother, so I took her maiden name. Didn't want to have the same name as my father. He was a bruise of a man, I wanted nothing to do with him until much later, when it was too late.' Sébastien sips his coffee. 'I took your mother to Gistel several times. She loved the stained-glass angel and the Grecian frieze. She met my mother.'

Charlotte sips her coffee. 'Were you close with Petra?'

'Not particularly. Our mother was eighteen when she had Pietronella with her first husband. I was born nineteen years later. Petra left home when I was two and joined the Begijnhof. The difference in our ages never eased as we grew older. We were always a generation apart, never understood one another, often clashed about the smallest things.' He rests his knife and fork on his plate. 'Your mother never met Petra, but I think they would've enjoyed one another's company. I regret not making more of an effort to introduce them.'

'I'm curious to know, when your mother died ...' Charlotte pauses, realising she's prying. 'Anna mentioned furniture from your mother's estate was delivered to the Begijnhof, to Petra ...'

He senses her question before she finishes it. 'After I left home, my mother and I drifted apart. Pietronella had always shown more interest in our family history, so it was natural for the heirlooms to be left in her care after our mother died.'

He nods towards her hands, which are on the table, restlessly moving. 'When I took your mother to Gistel for the first time, I gave her that ring.' He indicates the bezel-cut turquoise on Charlotte's finger, which she has been twisting absently.

She drops her hands to her lap, stares at the ring, too shocked to reply. For years she'd seen her mother wear the ring, with no mention of its history.

Sébastien talks about the first day her mother visited Gistel. 'The villa looked rather grand back then, with maids looking after the interior and gardeners caring for the plants and lawn. My mother, Irma, was a keen gardener–'

'Irma?' Charlotte is suddenly confused.

'My mother's name was Irma. It's a traditional name for Belgian girls.'

'Irma is my middle name,' says Charlotte softly.

The nature of her parents' liaison unfolds with heartbreaking clarity. Despite the end of their relationship, her mother had clutched on to fragments of the past, choosing to wear a ring and bestow her paternal grandmother's name on her newborn daughter.

Sébastien clears his throat. 'We should start at the beginning.'

All she can do is stare at him.

'In order for you to one day, hopefully, trust me, we need to start at the beginning. Just a moment, I need to get something.' He stands and walks into the sitting room.

Minutes later he's back, placing a lidded box on the table in front of her. He carries dishes to the kitchen, leaving her alone with the box.

Lifting the lid, she pulls out a thick bundle of envelopes, each one addressed to her childhood home: *Miss Charlotte Hubert, 9 Kenworthy Avenue, Scarborough, Toronto*. The stamps are marked *Belgique-Belgi*ë. The sender's name and address absent. The first letter is postmarked *October 1989*, a week before her second birthday. The postmarks on the subsequent letters continue until *1998*. The letters remain unopened.

Her hands tremble. The hammering in her chest rises to her throat.

He stands on the other side of the table.

She swallows, tries to regain control. When she is able to speak, her voice is low. 'You keep saying *the beginning*. What do you mean?' She's in denial, refusing to acknowledge the significance of the letters in her lap, evidence of his persistent attempts to forge a link with his daughter.

'The beginning of us,' he says.

73

October 16, 1623 – Antwerpen, Spanish Hapsburg Empire

I dispatched a note to Clara on the day we pulled into port. Meneer Rubens may have refused to send her letters to London, but now they need only travel a few streets. Clara can simply hand them to a manservant for delivery. I eagerly awaited her reply. I knew she would be pleased to hear we had returned to Antwerpen.

The servants emptied crates, stuffed mattresses and hung bed curtains. Windows were polished, tapers set in sconces, flagstones scrubbed. *We are home, we are home*, I sang to myself as I dashed from one room to the next, directing servants, calming the boys, soothing the tears of a new kitchenmaid. Our Eikenstraat house gradually transformed into a home. I did my best to make our home as comfortable as possible, despite Mama's absence.

Papa spent his days meeting with prospective clients and, upon arriving home each evening, tossed his cloak and hat at Ludo and stormed off to his workroom in a foul mood.

On one occasion, I heard him venting his frustrations at poor Ludo. 'I once created magnificent engravings for the Earl of Arundel and Duke of Buckingham, but now I'm reduced to making copies of Van Dyck's paintings.' He slammed the drawer of the cabinet. 'Van Dyck may paint well, but he's barely old enough to grow whiskers.'

Janneke and I visited the market and agreed nothing had changed in our two-year absence. I hoped to spy Clara at the market, but she was nowhere to be seen.

Visitors to the market were full of praise for Archduchess Isabella's reign as governor, following the death of her husband two summers past. Although the Scheldt remained closed to trade, rumours abounded of her plan to lay siege to Breda and annex it from the United Provinces.

I greeted Betja and Marta van Helst, my neighbours since childhood, and conversation moved to the Archduchess. 'She rules wisely,' I said, 'and shows educated women are capable of great accomplishments.'

Betja shrugged. 'She manages to rule, despite being a woman.'

'She hasn't been weakened by childbirth,' said her younger sister, Marta.

'Not true,' said Betja. 'She birthed three babes early in her marriage, but they died before they crawled.'

I clamped my mouth shut, knowing any attempt to steer the conversation to the business accomplishments of women would fall on deaf ears. Betja, two years my senior, talked only of securing a wealthy husband. Marta, the same age as me, was equally obsessed.

Betja regaled me with dull facts about marriage in Antwerpen. Although laws allowed girls as young as twelve to marry, they required the consent of their parents, and the practice is rare. Some girls marry as young as seventeen, but most wait until they are eighteen. Betrothals often last for several years, and negotiations usually begin years in advance.

I was pleased to bid farewell to Betja and Marta, and hear no more of marriage.

On Sunday, six days after our return to Antwerpen, our household was a merry sight as we walked to Sint-Jacobskerk. Even Papa gave a contented smile as he led us into church, greeting acquaintances while striding along the nave with his gaggle of children and servants behind. When we took our place in the south transept, a sense of calm washed over me. Our time in London will be a dim blight on my memory.

The Rubens household arrived, the Master at the fore, resplendent in a velvet doublet with slashed sleeves. Mevrouw Rubens wore a plum-coloured gown, white lace at her throat. Nicolaas, looking grown-up in breeches, had lost his baby plumpness. Albert, tall and lean with his mother's copper-coloured waves, wore the smugness of early youth. Two dozen apprentices and servants ranged around Meneer Rubens, all dressed in their best, hair slicked, faces scrubbed shiny.

I searched for Clara's blonde curls amongst the sea of chestnut and copper. My gaze wandered from face to face, eager to spot her dimpled cheeks, the pointed chin inherited from her mother.

She was absent. Six days since our return, and not a word from her, not a sight.

74

Sébastien scrapes pancake remnants into the bin. 'My goal was to become assistant professor by age thirty, associate professor by thirty-six. I worked long hours and was focused ... *too* focused ... too ambitious.' He slides plates into the dishwasher.

Charlotte folds place mats and remains silent, understanding he has waited more than three decades to unburden himself.

'I promised to go with her to Toronto for Thanksgiving, to meet her family, but changed my mind at the last minute. We argued, eventually agreed I would go at Christmas.' He washes the coffee pot, upends it on the drying rack. 'But as Christmas approached, I didn't want to leave. Several other senior lecturers were vying for the position of assistant professor and I was worried they'd get a step ahead of me. I made some lame excuse about not going. She was furious. We had another argument. Soon after, I became assistant professor at twenty-nine and she moved back to Canada.' He rests his hands on the bench, emits a long sigh. 'Making assistant professor at such a young age should have been one of the high points of my life, but it came at a terrible cost. All I can remember is feeling incredibly low.'

From her position by the sink, Charlotte is unable to see his face clearly or read his expression, but she can see his body is slumped with remorse.

'After she returned to Toronto, I learnt through a mutual friend she was pregnant. I called. I wrote. She didn't reply. I flew to Toronto, arrived on her doorstep. She closed the door in my face.'

'You came to Toronto?' Charlotte holds a wet saucepan, water dripping on the floor.

'She said she knew I wouldn't change my workaholic, egotistical ways and she didn't want a future like that for herself and her child. Said she was better off without me.' He scrubs at a greasy frying pan. 'I sent you birthday cards and letters. After ten years, I received a large envelope filled with them, all unopened, with a note from her, telling me to stop writing, saying she had told you I was dead.'

While he continues talking, he wipes the bench, keeping his hands busy, his emotions at bay. He shares the darkness of the relationship, the thrust and parry that led to the irreconcilable breakdown.

'In her final weeks' – Charlotte pauses, nervous about broaching the subject – 'she mentioned having a key idea in her research stolen, said before she had a chance to publish, her idea appeared in someone else's work. The person was more senior to her, and ended up gaining additional funding for new research while her project was sidelined.'

He dries his hands slowly, turns to face her. 'Rachael accused me of intellectual theft. She had shared a theory with me about Maarten van Rossum, who was a military tactician in the service of the Duke of Guelders and involved in the 1542 siege of Antwerp. We discussed it in detail. My work on the Guelders Wars put me in a unique position to be a sounding board for her specialisation in the border wars of the Low Countries. When Rachael and I became romantically involved, we decided to keep our personal and work spheres as separate as possible. We still bounced ideas off one another, but we didn't publish journal articles together or participate in joint lecture series. Having clearly demarcated lines between our work and private lives was important to us.' He thrusts his hands in his pockets.

The only sound is water dripping from the tap. She waits.

'I was careless,' he continues. 'One Friday after work, sitting around with colleagues and my supervisor, we started debating the outcome of the siege of Antwerp. Rachael wasn't there. I mentioned Maarten van Rossum. The discussion became boisterous. We were trying to outdo one another.' He stares at his feet then looks at her, a pained expression on his face.

'You revealed Rachael's theory,' says Charlotte softly.

He nods. 'It was only a passing comment, but the damage was done. My supervisor swooped on the idea and turned it into his own.'

'And she never forgave you.'

'It broke our relationship. My procrastination about meeting her family, obsessing over my work ... her idea being stolen was the final straw.'

Charlotte silently grieves the pride and misunderstandings that had overwhelmed her parents. She tastes her own bitter remorse. She had judged Sébastien harshly, blinded by her own prejudice, quick to see guilt in his every gesture and word. Her distrust affected her work at the university, her hunt for the *Pandoras*, even the development of her friendship with Miles. She has lived with suspicion for so long, but finally it is starting to dissolve. A callus, thick and unyielding, beginning to soften.

So much of the past remains to be shared, but they've reached their limit for now. She spies the bundle of birthday letters resting on the kitchen table. Correspondence sent over three decades ago from an unknown father to his unknown daughter. They will remain unopened until she's in the right headspace to read them. Another day, another week, they will talk again. There will be time in the future, when their minds are not teeming with urgent demands requiring their attention.

They edge into a conversation about her meeting with the dean, how to explain her unauthorised entry of the conservation room, returning the portfolio box to Anna. She's relieved Sébastien is in a position to play the role of mediator. They settle on a plan.

'Are you sure you're okay with this?' he asks.

'It's better this way.' She walks into the sitting room, pacing from shelves of crystal to shelves of books. Restless. Nervous. She leaves the doors open so she can hear the conversation.

He calls the number, presses *Speaker*, places the phone on the table.

A female voice answers on the third ring. '*Hallo. Dit is zuster Anna. Hoe kan ik u helpen?*'

'Hello, Anna. This is Sébastien.'

Charlotte listens to the exchange of pleasantries. Sébastien's tone is reassuring, balancing between concern and impartiality. He is a skilled negotiator, focuses on the key issues, acknowledges the wrongdoing, encourages consensus.

'I agree it wasn't handled in the best manner,' he says. 'I can assure you our staff do not make a habit of borrowing documents—'

'Borrowing?' Anna's tone is high-pitched. 'I would hardly call the removal of the portfolio box *borrowing* …'

Charlotte pauses in the doorway. *It's going to be all right*, he silently conveys with an encouraging smile as Anna's voice climbs. Her protest continues, with Sébastien offering soothing murmurs. Charlotte wonders if he will mitigate her appropriation of the portfolio box by explaining he is actually its owner, having been bequeathed it by Petra. But he remains silent. Does this mean Petra left everything to the Begijnhof?

Sébastien agrees the portfolio box will be returned at the earliest opportunity, that they will apologise in person.

In person, Charlotte muses. That will only be possible if she speaks with Miles, apologises for pushing him away. Why hasn't he called or texted?

Sébastien finishes the call. Charlotte slides into the chair opposite.

'She'll be fine once it's returned, and you and Miles speak with her.' He tilts his head. 'I've sent him several texts, but haven't heard from him. Has he contacted you?'

'I've left messages. I'm sure he'll call back. When he's ready.'

'Did you …' begins Sébastien. She can tell he's searching for the right word. '… have a misunderstanding?' he finally adds.

Her throat tightens. She nods, unable to speak.

'He'll call,' says Sébastien. 'He's not the sort of person to bear grudges.'

She winces, remembering Miles trying to ease the tension with laughter, her refusal to listen to reason. He'd challenged her about being prejudiced against Sébastien, and she'd pushed him away, stung by the truth.

Sébastien swiftly changes the topic. 'I suspect the Begijnhof is experiencing financial difficulties. After the incident with the masonry, the building inspector issued an order to fix the building before tours can recommence.'

'Anna mentioned the tours were a steady source of income,' says Charlotte, 'and they're hoping to open a second-hand clothing shop.'

'Budget restrictions are being imposed by the Diocese for all religious institutions. New income streams will help the Begijnhof become financially independent.'

'Don't religious institutions gain a significant part of their income through bequests from deceased members?'

He fiddles with the ring on his finger. 'I'm not sure whether bequests go directly to individual institutions or into the general coffers of the Diocese for dividing up.'

'Institutions *can* accept bequests from benefactors. Sint-Catharina's is filled with stunning, museum-quality antiques bequeathed to Petra from her mother–'

'*Our* mother.' His tone is brusque.

'Sorry, of course. Your mother.' She inwardly curses her clumsiness. 'Is Villa Wouters … does it … what I mean … wouldn't Petra's bequest of her estate to Sint-Catharina's put them in a less precarious financial position?'

'Indeed it would, *if* Petra had bequeathed her estate to the Begijnhof. However, Petra left all her assets, including Villa Wouters, to me. I'm the sole beneficiary of her estate.'

Charlotte opens her mouth to speak, then closes it. Less than twenty-four hours ago, she had sat in Karl's Citroën and tried to convince Miles that Sébastien was somehow involved in the break-in at Villa Wouters, assuming his anger and jealousy over being disinherited was the motive.

Her carefully constructed rationale for his alleged crimes shatters into a million fragments. Sébastien is not the modern-day thief. Why break into a house you own? Why steal objects belonging to yourself?

'You look surprised.' His eyebrows twitch. 'It's common for siblings to leave their estate to one another on their passing.'

His voice hints at mockery, while his features suggest banter. She isn't familiar enough with his expressions to interpret the nuances.

'The antiques at the Begijnhof include museum-quality pieces,' she repeats.

'If Anna wishes to sell the antiques to help with the maintenance of the Begijnhof, she's welcome to do so.'

'And Villa Wouters? You're going to sell it?' She suddenly realises she cares about the derelict property. More than a hiding place for priceless drawings, it holds poignant links to her past: to a time when her parents were a couple, a distant time when her ancestors purchased the property and relocated from Antwerp to Gistel.

'I haven't decided yet.' There's the glimpse of a smile. 'It's a unique property. Remote location, overrun garden, dilapidated house with a heritage order. What's not to like?'

She returns his smile.

75

Two weeks after our return to Antwerpen and still no word from Clara. Crowds filled the streets to celebrate Sint-Lucas Feast Day, but Clara was absent. My five hand-delivered notes remained unanswered. Something was wrong.

As Janneke and I walked to the market, I directed her to turn left along the Herentalse Vaart, ignoring her complaints about the circuitous route. Within minutes we stood before the grand façade.

Janneke frowned. 'Why are we here, Miss Antonia?'

'We will knock on the door and ask after Clara.'

The manservant stared at me blankly before his face transformed with recognition. 'You are taller, Miss Antonia, and more grown-up.'

'I am here to see Miss Clara.' Glimpsing past his shoulders, I spotted the empty courtyard beyond. 'May I come in?'

He took a step forward, his bulk barring my entrance. 'Sorry, Miss, but I cannot let you pass.'

'Why forever not?'

Hearing footsteps crossing the inner courtyard, the manservant stepped back and Mevrouw Rubens appeared. Her normally serene features were drawn with fatigue, her mouth thin. Dressed entirely in black, she had replaced her usual white lace collar with one of black voile, severe against the pallor of her skin. The pearl brooch which often adorned her throat was absent.

'Antonia, please wait. I have something for you.' She retraced her footsteps, entered the house and reappeared several minutes later holding a small cloth-wrapped bundle.

She looked into my eyes with such sorrow I knew what she was going to say before she spoke.

'Clara was sick for several weeks with a fever then rash; it became painful for her to swallow. The physician tried everything, but nothing could be done. Her end was peaceful. Three nights ago, she drifted away in her sleep and is now with the Lord.' Mevrouw Rubens closed her eyes, stemming the tears.

I stood motionless, unable to speak. My dear Clara was gone. For the past two weeks, as I impatiently awaited her response to my letters, she had lain in bed, mute with illness.

Mevrouw Rubens pressed the cloth-wrapped bundle into my hands, murmuring that the exchange of letters could not be allowed to continue, but her voice was a jumble of words and tears. Nothing made sense.

I don't recall my response. Janneke guided me home, where I sat in my bedchamber, once more cloaked in silence and grief.

As dusk fell, I unwrapped the bundle. The letters I had sent to Clara during the past two years tumbled from my lap to the floor. Some had been opened, wax seals broken, paper worn thin from being re-read and refolded. Others were unopened, the wax seals intact, their contents unread. My Blackfriars map was still sealed inside my letter from six months ago, never opened.

Someone had whisked my letters away from Clara before she had a chance to read them all. Someone filled with anger towards my father, my family and myself, blinded to the hurt they caused two innocent girls who only wanted to be friends.

The tenderness and sorrow Mevrouw Rubens had shown me appeared genuine. Her eyes had displayed no hint of anger. Her tears were real. She had tried to maintain the exchange of letters, not curtail it.

I felt certain the blame rested with Meneer Rubens. Filled with animosity towards my father, he had forbidden Clara from writing to me. Animosity at my father's arrogance in putting himself above the Master, for demanding the ownership of engravings based on his employer's work, continuing to argue with the Master, to ignore reason. And maybe, just maybe, there was a glimmer of truth in the awful rumours of the past two years. Maybe my father was guilty of threatening the Master with a knife.

It explained so much. Papa's insistence we suddenly move to London, his undisguised self-conceit in obtaining lucrative commissions and emerging from the shadow of his former Master, his reluctance to return to Antwerpen and resume work as a copyist.

How else will my life be marred by the pride of my father?

76

Sébastien's gaze moves around the room. Ever since ushering him into her apartment, she has sensed his curiosity. He surveys the room, trying to uncover the character of the daughter who has until so recently been a stranger. She had done the same upon entering his office for the first time, and when visiting his apartment that morning.

His expression is its usual mask. She's beginning to realise his cool eyes and calm demeanour hide a softness within. She recalls colleagues labelling him aloof and brusque, yet she has seen a kind-hearted side to him. Miles, too, has experienced this disparity, describing him as blunt and driven, yet admitting the professor had helped him out of a crisis, expecting nothing in return. Her father is a chameleon, presenting an unsentimental attitude to the world and revealing his softer side to only a few.

She follows his gaze to the Daum frog perched on the coffee table. 'I brought it from Toronto.' Her voice wobbles.

He turns to the window, focuses on the distant view, giving her time to recover. 'What a pleasant view,' he murmurs.

Excusing herself, she retreats to the bathroom. Climbing onto the counter, she stretches above a built-in cabinet, reaching for a large envelope on the top, hidden from view. Returning to the living room, she empties the envelope's contents, placing her research notebook and mind map on the table.

'I hid them away.' She indicates the gym bag containing the portfolio box next to the front door. 'I couldn't fit the portfolio box in the hiding place, so Miles and I took it to Gistel with us.'

Having shared everything about her search for the *Pandoras*, she wants him to see the convoluted pathways of her research, keen for his opinion.

They sit on the sofa, the notebook open on his lap while she talks excitedly about her theories. She reveals the cryptic clues, explains her reasoning, shows him the fragile scrap of paper. Recounts her fear when she walked into her apartment, then the office and found them upended. She confesses her reluctance to trust anyone, her dismay at Anna's revelation about the cartography scholar. When she finishes, a weight has lifted, her entire hand revealed.

Holding a photo depicting the title cartouche of the Low Countries, Sébastien peers closely at it. He turns it around until the manacled figure of Lucas Vorsterman is upside-down, then points at the decorative swirls around the cartouche, a tiny outline hidden among the curlicues. 'What's that?'

She squints at the page and spots a miniature acorn with the intertwined initials AV in the centre. She remembers the stall owner at the market explaining the practice of apprentices hiding their personal symbols. Her heart beats a little faster. 'It's possibly a secret signature to show Antonia enhanced the De Wit maps herself.'

Sébastien is wide-eyed. 'The map folio may not be a Frederik de Wit?'

'I'll leave that mystery up to the map scholars to solve.' She is light-headed from the adrenaline rush. Can't help but smile at the thought of Theo's face if he discovers the prized De Wit was either partly or completely created by a little-known female amateur.

Sébastien closes the notebook slowly. 'What made you change your mind about me?'

His question takes her by surprise. 'Miles told me I should give you a chance. He said you helped him when a student threatened him with trumped-up charges of misconduct.'

'The dean and I investigated the charges. They were fabricated. I spoke to the student. She ended up leaving because she felt unsafe on campus. She was one of the women who was attacked.'

'How awful.'

Sébastien smooths his beard, his expression stern. 'The situation is serious. Four students have now been attacked.'

'Any progress finding the attacker?'

'The dean has appointed me to liaise with the police, but they haven't revealed anything of their investigation to me. I'm in the dark, like everybody else.'

Charlotte's phone hums. She excuses herself, crosses to the bedroom, wanting privacy when she speaks to Miles. She leaves the door ajar and sits on the end of the bed. From this angle, she can see the sofa where Sébastien re-examines the notebook.

'Miles?'

'This is Oscar Duval,' says a voice, so muted it comes out as a soft growl.

'Oh,' she tries to hide her disappointment. 'How can I help you?'

'My office was broken into and the hard copies of your reports were stolen,' says Duval bluntly, without preamble. 'The paper and ink samples I collected for the analysis are also missing.'

Her mouth is suddenly dry. 'When?'

'About two weeks ago–'

'Two weeks ago?' Her voice is loud.

Sébastien walks to the bedroom, stands in the doorway. 'Miles?' he mouths.

She shakes her head.

When Duval speaks, his tone is tight with sarcasm. 'I have hundreds of clients. I keep my reports on the computer and hard copies in my filing system. Everything in my office was overturned' – he pauses for emphasis – 'the contents of cabinets dumped over the floor. It's taken me this long to sort through the mess and verify what was stolen.'

'I'm so sorry.' She cringes, realising her outburst was insensitive and rude.

'The police are still investigating, but the case is a low priority considering nobody was maimed or killed.' He lets out a growl of irritation.

She wonders whether this ransacking showed the same pattern as that of her apartment. Did the thief use a key then lock the door when leaving? Softening her tone, she tries to sound contrite. 'I'm so sorry to hear what's happened. It's awful. Was there any sign of forced entry?'

'The back window was smashed.'

'Were other reports stolen?'

'Yes.' His tone is blunt, unwilling to reveal further details. 'The police may contact you for questioning.'

'Thank you for calling and, again, I'm sorry for my reaction. I hope the police are able to find who's responsible.'

The conversation ends. God, what a mess.

'Charlotte?' Sébastien remains in the doorway. 'Are you okay?'

'That was Oscar Duval. His office was broken into and his reports on Antonia's documents stolen.'

Sébastien frowns.

'Do you know him personally?' she asks.

'I've commissioned work from him many times. He's analysed documents for Miles, Karl, Arnold Blauwmann, Jeanette Chevalier, Filippo Donati ...' He reels off several other names. 'He's mentored several of our post-grad students interested in document analysis.'

Her mind jumps to Miles. She calls him again, but this time the call ends, suggesting his phone is turned off, out of charge or set on *Do Not Disturb*. Her regret for the way she treated him, and her longing for him to call her is replaced with a growing unease. Something isn't right.

77

'Remain loyal to my family and stay true to myself,' I tell my reflection each morning as I peer into the looking glass while brushing my hair. Some days, the command rings hollow. Although my heartache over Clara's passing is great, I try to remind myself every day of the advantages of my birth.

Papa has allowed me to return to the classroom two mornings a week, studying alongside Hendrik and Niels under a new tutor. Meneer Driessen tolerates my presence, focusing most of his energies on teaching the boys, occasionally correcting my Latin.

I poured all of my sadness over Clara's passing into creating a new map. Having drawn the defensive walls, streets and squares of Antwerpen onto a large rectangle of parchment, I am now inscribing the place names. A decorative border surrounds the map, comprising miniature drawings of the city's most notable buildings: the Stadhuis, Cathedral of Our Lady, Sint-Michielskerk, Sint-Jacobskerk, the newly completed Sint-Augustinuskerk.

Papa condones my mapmaking as long as I complete my chores. Our conversations are limited to household expenditure, managing the servants, and Papa's requirements for entertaining clients. Although he attempts to talk to me about possible suitors, discussions on this topic are one-sided. I catch myself at times, staring at him, recalling his harmful decisions, and look away lest he sees the sadness in my eyes.

Papa joined me in the upstairs parlour one afternoon, watching as I mended a lace collar. 'A betrothal will soon be announced between the elder Van Helst girl and the nephew of Burgemeester Jan Happart.'

I murmured an acknowledgement and continued stitching, recalling how Betja had cornered me at church last Sunday to regale me with the details of her intended's fortune.

'The wedding will take place this spring,' said Papa, 'once she has turned seventeen.'

'Betja is pleased,' I replied. Silently, to myself, I railed at the foolishness of someone so young embarking on marriage. No doubt her mother has taught her the skills of managing a household – after all, I was nearly fifteen and had managed our household since Mama's passing more than eighteen months ago – but birthing babies and raising children? I couldn't imagine doing either at such a young age.

'Before long, we will be securing a match for you, Antonia. Given your good family name, there will be many suitors interested in your hand.'

'Indeed.' I focused on the stitches, mutely fuming at the way he spoke of me, as if I was a piglet being readied for slaughter. In less than a month I would turn fifteen. I wish Papa would focus on finding himself a new wife.

Undeterred by my disinterest, Papa launched into an endorsement of a possible suitor. 'You would do well to consider Edwin Kappel. He is a chief clerk at court, from a good family. Although the marriage could be delayed until you are older, it would be wise to secure his hand soon ...' Papa droned on about Meneer Kappel's annual income and connections with the royal court, many of whom would make lucrative patrons for Papa.

I continued stitching, refusing to look at him. Although I admired the Archduchess and her court, I had no desire to become the wife of one of the court's numerous lackeys, where my every action and word would be judged in wearisome detail. When Papa finished his monologue, I politely offered my thanks for his advice.

'It would be helpful,' said Papa curtly, 'if you showed more enthusiasm for your future.'

I placed the sewing into my basket. 'I am not convinced marriage at such a young age is the right path for me.'

Papa leapt from his chair, his face red. 'I will judge what is best for you, Antonia.' He swept out of the room, slamming the door behind him.

It saddened me to consider the change in our relationship. Once, Papa and I had laughed easily, debated politics, discussed local events. He encouraged my pursuit of academics, telling me I was as clever as my brothers, if not more so. I had trusted him, once. But all this has changed. He now sees me as someone who can secure the future and fortune of our family through an advantageous marriage.

I imagined Papa's reaction if I told him of my longing to become a mapmaker. Two years ago I would have trusted him with such a revelation, but not now. He would threaten to enter me as a novice in Archduchess Isabella's newly established Begijnhof Sint-Catharina, where I would be relegated to a life of prayer, poverty and serving the needy.

78

Charlotte holds the gym bag in the crook of her arm, trying to keep the contents from being jostled as she walks along the pavement with Sébastien at her side. Although not heavy, the broad, flat shape of the portfolio box makes it awkward to carry.

Sébastien had offered to carry it, but she politely declined. The discomfort is nothing compared to the remorse she feels for her underhanded behaviour, her frustration when she imagines the portfolio box, with Barzetti's priceless booklet, being returned to the Begijnhof and enveloped by dust.

She presses the pedestrian button and casts a sidelong glance at Sébastien.

'Have you had any thoughts,' she asks, 'about telling others we're related?'

They step onto the road as the pedestrian signal turns green.

'How would you like to handle it?' he replies.

She's slow to respond, considering the options. 'When I first arrived, I didn't want anyone assuming nepotism played a part in my appointment. Now I've been here two months, I don't mind others knowing I'm your ... you're my ...' She struggles to say the words *daughter* and *father*; they feel incongruous for their newly formed relationship.

But now that I'm suspended and under investigation,' she continues, 'perhaps it's not a good time.'

Will the university charge her with professional misconduct? Will she be asked to resign? Will she be acquitted? Whatever happens, she doesn't want people assuming her kinship with Sébastien played a role. If her name is to be dragged through the mud, she doesn't want Sébastien or Miles dragged with her.

Neither of them deserves such treatment. She's responsible for her actions.

'We could hold off telling anyone for the moment. After everything's settled down, we can decide then. How does that sound?'

'Fine.' She clears her throat. 'Miles already knows. I told him yesterday, while we were in Gistel.'

'He's discreet.'

She's relieved Sébastien feels the same way about the situation, satisfied Miles won't gossip.

'I had a feeling you two would get on,' says Sébastien. 'I was pleased when I noticed Miss Beulen had allocated you two to share an office.'

She smiles inwardly, thinking he sounds like a father puffed with pleasure at his own efforts. The fact that the office sharing had been organised well before Sébastien met her, before he could judge whether she and Miles would be compatible, remains unspoken.

She wonders if he volunteered to be her supervisor, seeing an opportunity to spend time with the daughter he had never known. She decides to simply ask, relieved to get the question out in the open.

'It's not the usual practice for the head of one department to supervise a senior lecturer from another,' he admits, 'but given we're from the same faculty and your appointment is short-term—'

'More short-term than I planned,' she says under her breath.

'—I assigned myself as your supervisor before anyone else had the chance to volunteer.'

Overcome with a sudden burst of energy, she increases her pace, legs stretching out to seize more pavement, free arm swinging higher. He knew about her for all these years and wanted to meet her. Wants to spend time together. Wants to know her.

Minutes later, entering the Begijnhof courtyard, her elation fizzles away as she remembers the reason for her visit: to apologise to Anna for her behaviour. Her anxiety over Miles' absence compounds her tension. Where is he?

They spot Edith in the garden and Anna descending the office steps.

'I'll say hello to Edith first,' says Charlotte, 'then join you and Anna.'

'Give me ten minutes with Anna first,' he says. 'I'll give you a wave to join us. Is that okay?'

She's beginning to recognise that his style is more consultative than authoritarian. Her mother's descriptions painted a picture of a different man, more dour and rigid. She wonders if his personality has softened over the years.

As she pushes open the gate into the garden, Edith greets her warmly, but is distracted by Sébastien's appearance. 'What's he doing here?' she asks, eyeing him on the far side of the courtyard with Anna.

'He wanted to speak to Anna about the portfolio box.' Charlotte has a clear view from the garden, yet remains partly obscured by the low-spreading branches of a plum tree. The professor and mother superior face off, he in a stance of acquiescence, arms loose at his sides, she edging towards confrontation with hands on hips.

Edith uses a rake to spread straw mulch over a garden bed. 'They're probably talking about how I helped you and Dr Thornton take it from the Begijnhof.'

'I suspect Anna is more concerned about *my* involvement,' says Charlotte.

Sébastien and Anna walk along the driveway, still talking. His head is lowered, either in deference or resignation. Anna's hands wave in the air, possibly in anger, or perhaps dispensing absolution. She can't tell.

Charlotte picks up a basket of mulch and moves it closer to Edith, all the while keeping her gaze on the distant figures. They're now standing beside the Begijnhof's battered Citroën, his hand resting on the rusted blue hood. Any moment he'll beckon Charlotte over with a wave.

Anna points at the back tyre of the Citroën, looks at her wrist, her gestures expansive. Sébastien opens the hood, unclips the spare tyre, heaves it onto the cobblestones. Clearly they're not discussing her infraction.

Edith pokes mulch around young cauliflower plants. 'Order more straw,' she mutters, 'arrange flowers ...'

Charlotte listens to Edith's ramblings while watching Sébastien loosen the Citroën's back wheel, slide it off the wheel hub.

'... change altar cloth, order candles ...' Edith's voice becomes insistent, louder. 'Ceiling leak will get worse if ignored. Need more help, since Léa left and now Petra ...'

She begins listening to Edith more closely. Anna had mentioned that one of their longest-serving *begijnen*, Sister Léa, had left the order and returned to her family in Arlon near Luxembourg. Losing two *begijnen* so quickly – one leaving, another dying – must have left a gaping hole. Not only has Edith lost her closest friend, but also another colleague who eased the burden of work. Edith is grieving in multiple ways.

Remorse washes over her for placing Edith in such a difficult situation. She regrets agreeing to her suggestion that she smuggle the portfolio box from the Begijnhof. She should've considered the consequences. She should've shown the portfolio box to Anna. Should've discussed everything with Sébastien right from the start. Should've. Should've. Hindsight, useless now.

Everything has been turned on its head. A day ago, she was convinced Sterck was the perpetrator, Miles her ally, while Sister Anna and Dean Mulder were oblivious bystanders. But now, Sterck has become her strongest advocate, Miles has dropped her like a cold fish, Anna has bared her teeth in a surprising show of authority, and Dean Mulder is ready to expel her from the university. Added to this tension is the realisation that other people, nameless and faceless, are aware of her search for the *Pandoras* and closing in. She's been thrown off balance.

Edith stands up straight, rubbing her lower back. 'Anna asked if I let you take the portfolio box from the Begijnhof. I wasn't going to lie, was I?'

'Of course not.'

'Proverbs chapter eight, verse seven says that wickedness is an abomination to my lips.' Edith directs her words to the swaying branches of the plum tree.

'I hope–'

'Petra said we should always speak the truth.'

'I'm sorry for getting you involved,' says Charlotte in a rush, trying to finish her apology before another interruption.

Edith smiles softly at the sky. 'Sometimes things have a strange way of working out. Everything has changed, but it's all going to be fine.'

The car wheezes into life, trundles along the cobblestones. Its hood and roof are covered in more rust than paint. As it lumbers past the garden, its exhaust emits a belch of smoke. Hunched over the steering wheel, Anna peers through the dirty windscreen.

'She has a meeting with the Diocese.' Edith's tone is wistful. 'Trying to resolve the budget.'

The car turns out into the road. Sébastien walks towards them.

'I need to arrange the flowers.' Edith picks up the basket, hurries across the garden, heading for the chapel. Her pleated skirt puffs around her as her pace increases.

Sébastien peers after the retreating figure of Edith. 'Is she okay?'

'Overwhelmed with work.'

'Anna has a meeting—'

'Yes, with the Diocese. I'll have to speak with her another time.'

'She said to leave the portfolio box in her office.'

As they enter the building and climb the stairs, Charlotte can't decide whether she's relieved or dismayed her meeting with Anna is postponed. She removes the portfolio box from the gym bag, placing it on Anna's desk.

'Did she say to leave it here?' Surely it should be placed somewhere secure, under lock and key.

'That's what she said,' replies Sébastien.

She takes another look at the battered portfolio box. It should've been handed over to Sébastien, surely, given it contains historical documents relating to his family, given he is its new owner. He's deep in thought, staring out the window, fiddling with his cufflinks, the furrows between his brows deeper than ever.

The building appears deserted as they retrace their footsteps, the corridors empty of people, devoid of noise. They walk across the courtyard, taking the same measured steps, hands buried in pockets.

Sébastien waits until they reach the street before turning to her. 'When you arrived at Villa Wouters yesterday, did you say there was a tyre iron on the bedroom floor?'

'Yes. Why?'

'It was difficult changing the tyre on Anna's car. The tyre iron was missing.'

79

As they head towards the university, rain mists the air, turning the cobblestones slick and shiny.

Charlotte pulls up the hood of her jacket. 'How long have you known Anna?'

'I met her for the first time at a history symposium last June.'

Preoccupied, Charlotte steps in a puddle. All she can think about are two vintage Citroëns with pale blue rusted paintwork. Despite the popularity of the French vehicle in Belgium, and the prevalence of the model and colour, it's too much of a coincidence, surely.

'How long has she been at Sint-Catharina's?'

Sébastien turns up the collar of his coat. 'About twenty years. Before becoming a *begijn*, she was a researcher at Brussels City Museum.'

'Explains her interest in historical documents. As a researcher, she'd have contacts. Former colleagues working in history, art, conservation, document analysis.'

'What are you saying?'

Stopping at a street corner, she focuses on the little red figure on the traffic light. *Wait*, the two-dimensional figure seems to warn, *don't jump to conclusions*. But her imagination flares: Anna parking at Villa Wouters, smashing the glass of the back door, using the tyre iron to pry apart the *kast*. Spotted by neighbours, the police would've been alerted to the distinctive vehicle, confusing Anna's battered blue Citroën for Karl's. A case of mistaken identity.

'I'm not sure ...'

'Talk to me,' he says.

The signal changes to green and they cross the road.

'Maybe Petra showed Anna the map folio and portfolio box. Maybe Anna saw Antonia's documents, returned them to their hiding place and, not understanding their significance, sent the map folio to the university, hoping someone would inadvertently point her in the right direction.' She's grasping at straws, desperate for an element to link the seemingly unrelated events.

He slows his pace. 'You can't think Anna …'

'You've only known her for a few months. People can be full of surprises.' Charlotte notices his dismayed look.

They turn down a side street, and weave through a vintage market, dodging shoppers.

'Anna saw the lawyer's letter from 1982,' she continues, 'which mentioned the Gistel property. Maybe Petra spoke to her about Villa Wouters and the antique furniture. When Miles and I searched the antiques at the Begijnhof, Anna realised we were looking for something significant among the family's possessions, so she drove to Villa Wouters and got there before us.'

'I can't picture Anna doing this.' His conciliatory tone has turned gruff.

'I'm playing devil's advocate.' She waves her hands in the air, excited to be back on the hunt for the missing *Pandoras*, although she knows the ideas spouting from her mouth are wild. 'Anna is desperate to find something of value, an injection of capital to save the Begijnhof from being closed.'

Passing under the red-brick archway, they enter the near-deserted faculty courtyard. Only a handful of teachers and students, completing weekend work for end-of-term deadlines, are on site.

'All conjecture,' he says. 'We have no proof Anna is involved.'

'I know, damn it, I know. I can't imagine her doing any of this.' Charlotte stops, jams her hands on her hips, frustration welling. 'I keep going over everything and coming back to the same common elements.' She stands on the central point of the courtyard where the cobblestoned patterns meet.

The geometric design of intertwined circles is like a Venn diagram, each circle representing an individual problem, the areas of overlap showing their connection. Three places ransacked. The campus attacker, the looter and Anna all desperate for information. A tyre iron among the splintered shards of the *kast*, a tyre iron missing from Anna's car, a tyre iron used to threaten the students. Fragments of the puzzle, somehow interrelated.

She spins around to face him. 'The victims of the campus attacks ... weren't they threatened with a tyre iron? Was it from their own car or the attacker's?'

He exhales white mist into chill air. 'Only one of the victims reported being threatened with a tyre iron. Do you honestly think there's a link between the campus attacker and Anna's missing tyre iron? Next you're going to suggest the attacker was Anna. All the victims said the attacker was a male, wearing a ski mask.'

'I'm just pointing out the common elements. The attacker was intent on stealing the laptops, but maybe it was the *information* on the laptops he was after. Whoever destroyed my apartment, the office and Duval's office was also desperate for information. As for Anna? Isn't she also after information to solve the financial problems of the Begijnhof?'

They continue across the courtyard in silence.

As they climb the stairs, Sébastien checks his phone. 'I still haven't heard from Miles. He hasn't replied to my messages. I don't mean to pry,' he continues tentatively, 'but was your misunderstanding more of an argument? Did he slink off because of a quarrel?'

She remembers the angry words she'd fired at Miles, her decision to distance herself. *I'm here if you want me*, he'd said in the letter, but when she'd reached out to him, he wasn't there. Her calls and texts remain unanswered. Nothing makes sense.

'We had an argument, but he would've returned my calls by now. Unless he's forgotten to charge his phone.' As soon as she voices the excuse, she knows how feeble it sounds.

'Check your messages again. I'll call my assistant.' Sébastien talks hurriedly into his phone.

She checks her phone. Still no response. How did Miles return from Oostende? Did he call a friend, or find a taxi willing to drive 120 kilometres in a storm? Is he in his apartment, aloof and brooding, or did he hear about the accusations levelled against them and is doggedly trying to resolve them? Aloof and brooding doesn't sound like him. He'd be doing everything in his power to find a solution. He wouldn't give up. Unless something – or someone – has stopped him.

Sébastien ends his call. 'Miles didn't arrive for a ten o'clock meeting scheduled for this morning. His students weren't notified it was cancelled.'

'That's not like him.' He's often disorganised – misplacing his phone and keys, leaving the office in a mess, rushing to get to meetings on time – but he always turns up, always lets people know if he's delayed, always stays in touch.

Something is terribly wrong.

Her concern grows. What if Miles isn't ignoring her messages? What if he's unable to contact her?

'Miss Beulen had a call from campus police,' says Sébastien. 'The woman who was attacked two weeks ago has been seeing a psychologist to help with the trauma and she's beginning to recall details of the attack. She contacted the police yesterday and gave them information that could help identify the attacker.'

'That's good news, right?'

'Yes.' Sébastien hesitates, his expression grim. 'But now I'm wondering if there's a connection between the four victims and Miles.'

For a moment, she's unable to speak. Her insides twist with fear, then she galvanises into action. 'We need to check the most likely places he'd be on campus,' she says, forcing herself to stay calm, 'and check his apartment.'

'If we split up,' says Sébastien, 'it won't take as long.'

They rush along the corridor, pausing only to connect their mobile phones using a find-your-friend app. *Just in case we want to quickly locate one another*, Sébastien had explained. They agree to contact each other when there's something to report.

'I'll see if anybody's in Admin. Maybe someone's seen him,' Sébastien calls out as she speeds past.

'I'll check our office.' Panic surges. Heart racing. She's jolted back to a memory from earlier in the year. Her mother had disappeared on a winter's night in the early stages of her illness. A neighbour had found the front door wide open, no hint of foul play. Filled with foreboding, Charlotte had cruised her car along snow-covered streets, slowing to check alleyways and front yards. The police found her mother two hours later, wandering around Palmerston Park in a stupor, wearing only a nightgown, skin blue with hypothermia. By the time Charlotte arrived at the hospital, her mother was asleep under layers of blankets, her body temperature slowly returning to normal, oblivious to the panic her disoriented wanderings had caused.

Charlotte senses the same fear now: someone she cares about is in danger.

80

Janneke and I were at the market, wrapped in extra layers to withstand the morning chill, when a voice boomed across the square.

'Miss Antonia!' A gentleman strode towards me. Broad-shouldered, handsome, smiling as if he knew me, he wore a dark woollen doublet, fashionably slashed and puffed, and a black cloak with crimson lining.

After doffing his elaborately feathered hat, I recognised the dark curly hair and lively eyes. Here was my teacher from the mixing table in the Rubenshuis studio. His lessons in smalt, ultramarine and lead-tin yellow came rushing back. I recalled the tangy scent of linseed oil, the sound of the grinding stone.

'You have returned from London a young lady,' said my admirer, his stare brazen.

'Meneer Barzetti,' I said, eyeing his elegant clothes, 'you dress as a gentleman.'

'What? So formal? You no longer address me as *dear Santo*?'

I couldn't help but smile at his boldness. 'I do not recall ever addressing you in such familiar terms, Meneer Barzetti.'

He offered his arm. 'No matter what you say, Miss Antonia, we are old friends and I shall address you as such. Let us stroll the square and you can acquaint me of your doings these past years. You must be at least seventeen now, or perhaps eighteen?'

'I am fifteen, Meneer Barzetti.'

'Surely not. You look much older.'

'I am often mistaken for being older due to my height—'

'And your mature appearance and grown-up conversation, no doubt.'

I blushed furiously, realising he had noticed my curves. Earlier that week, Janneke had handed me a pair of Mama's boned stays, telling me my figure had grown enough to wear them.

We walked along the edge of the square with Janneke following closely behind. I ignored her grumbles.

'Mixing paints is no longer my role at the Rubenshuis.' His chest inflated, matching his puffed sleeves. 'I am chief assistant to Meneer Rubens and accompany him on his travels. We have recently returned from Paris, where we held diplomatic discussions at court while securing a new commission from Marie de' Medici.'

Santo was nine years my senior, a witty conversationalist. I soon relaxed in his company.

'In what ways has Antwerpen changed since you have been away?' he asked.

'The unrest with the Republic has increased, with Marquess Spinola's mercenaries causing havoc along the northern border.'

'Did you know Marquess Spinola was born in my hometown of Genoa?' Santo beamed with pride.

A lively discussion ensued in which we bandied the merits of Spinola's mercenaries and the Hapsburg forces, followed by likely successors to the ageing, childless Archduchess and her recent acquisition of a map folio by the famous cartographer Abraham Ortelius.

'I have seen his *Theatrum Orbis Terrarum* with my own eyes.' I excitedly described how it had inspired me to become a cartographer.

Rather than scoff at my dreams, Santo responded with sincerity. We debated the differing techniques of cartographers, the use of Latin rather than local dialects in maps, and my own map creations and study of foreign languages.

'You are attempting to master six languages?' he asked, his tone incredulous. 'You are a remarkable scholar despite your youth and ...' His voice trailed away.

'Despite what?' I asked, emboldened by our growing rapport. 'Despite being a woman?'

'Forgive me, Miss Antonia. I meant no offence.' He offered a contrite smile. 'As a gesture of atonement, and to demonstrate the high esteem with which I regard you, I would be honoured if you would accept my services as your teacher of Genoese.'

'Genoese?'

'Genoese is from the Ligurian region and a Western Romance language. You will find it easy,' said Santo. 'You are a gifted linguist, like your father and Meneer Rubens.'

I hesitated with my response, eager to accept his offer, but keen to avoid any obligation or impropriety. 'Thank you, Meneer Barzetti. I will consider your offer and let you know my answer in due course.'

Our farewell bows were formal, but my heart sang in the most carefree manner. Janneke's scowl could not dissuade me from my happiness.

'He's too bold for my likin',' said Janneke.

'Bold, but attentive and gracious,' I replied.

I had discovered in Santo someone who appreciated my passion for learning and my desire to become a cartographer. Perhaps my dreams could be achieved by having a compassionate husband. After all, the accomplished still-life painter Clara Peeters was married, achieving the dual roles of artist and wife. Signora Anguissola was encouraged by her husband to accept commissions and enjoyed a generous pension from the Spanish court as a portraitist, while also a wife and mother.

I recalled my previous unfavourable thoughts about marriage, my disdain at Betja's decision to marry so young, my yearning for a life filled with academic studies and mapmaking, my eagerness to be free from the restraints of marriage and motherhood. Then my thoughts lingered on Santo's attentiveness and spirited manner, his empathy and kindness, those sparkling eyes and charming smile. Goodness, I was acting like a besotted maid.

Before Papa demands I accept the hand of an unknown suitor, I would be wise to secure the affections of someone who holds me in high esteem, applauds my dreams and fills my heart with happiness.

81

When Charlotte enters their office, she is surprised to find Karl standing in the middle of the room, scanning Miles' desk.

'How did you get in?' she asks. 'The office is always locked.'

'It was unlocked when I arrived. Where's Miles?'

'I was about to ask you the same question.'

'He called from Oostende last night about my car.'

'Last night ... yes ...' She's momentarily dazed; the details of the past twenty-four hours are blurring.

'He said you were catching the train back to Antwerp,' continues Karl.

'Trains were cancelled because of the storm. We returned separately.'

'How did he get back?'

'I'm not sure.'

'He's not answering his phone. I visited his apartment and he didn't answer the door. I was worried, so I asked the building maintenance fellow to let me in. Miles wasn't there,' says Karl.

'He's not at his apartment?' Her anxiety grows.

'Did you guys have an argument?'

She tugs off her jacket, hangs it on the coat stand. 'Why do people keep assuming that?'

'It's no secret he fancies you.'

She pushes up the sleeves of her jumper then tugs them down again, restless, agitated. Desperate for her fears to vanish.

'The police called me,' says Karl. 'Asked why my car was parked in front of a deserted house in Gistel. The back door of the house was smashed. What do you know about that?'

'I ... I think it was someone else's car, similar to yours, though

I don't have any proof … yet.' She wants to reassure him, make it right, but can't say any more.

Karl spreads his hands wide. 'What do I tell the police?'

'I'm not sure, but right now, I'm more concerned about Miles. He's been missing for nearly fourteen hours.'

'The police won't do anything until someone's missing for at least twenty-four hours. I'll make some calls. There's a pub he often goes to with hockey mates. I'll swing by there, take a look. Text me if you hear anything, okay?' He disappears down the corridor.

She stands in the middle of the office, absorbing the quiet. Turning in a circle, she takes in the bookshelves, the corner stand draped with coats, a row of upside-down tea mugs on the filing cabinet, desks with neatly stacked files.

Something isn't right.

She moves to the heavily draped coat stand. Most of the coats are hers: lightweight taupe jacket, black neoprene for cycling, down-filled puffer. She spots his coat: navy duffle, wooden toggle buttons.

Miles was wearing it when they visited Gistel. *He's been here.*

She spins around with a tremor of panic, realising why the office feels peculiar. It's too neat. The precise row of clean mugs. His desk with tidy stacks of paperwork, devoid of the usual apple cores, empty crisp packets, mugs with dregs of tea. Why so neat? With so much on his mind, he wouldn't tidy. Was there a struggle? Has someone cleaned up the evidence?

The lowest drawer of the filing cabinet is ajar. She tugs it open. His backpack sits inside. He had it with him in Gistel. He never keeps it in the filing cabinet. Always tosses it on the floor near his desk.

Unzipping the outer pocket, she finds his phone. Battery dead. Her hands begin to shake.

She plugs the phone into a charger, and after several agonising minutes, it flickers to life. Thankful it's an old phone without sophisticated security, she scrolls through dozens of incoming messages, reads his last outgoing message.

Need huge favour. Stuck in Oostende. No car. No public transport.
Urgent business on campus. Can't wait until tomorrow. Can you pick me
up? Will pay petrol and lifetime supply of beer. Please help. It's serious.

Miles sent it to an unknown number at 21.53 last night. Red words next to the text – *Undelivered* – show it was never received. The storm meant text messages weren't getting through.

She checks the call history. Dozens of missed calls from herself, Karl, Theo, Sébastien. She scrolls to the last call he made – *unknown number* – at 21.56 last night. When his text was unsuccessful, he must have phoned someone, managed to get a signal. But who? Work colleague? Mate from hockey? Drinking buddy?

The sound of the photocopier filters along the corridor.

She finds Filippo Donati standing at the photocopier, watching papers spew into a tray.

'Filippo, have you seen Miles?'

'Mmm.' He smooths his silk cravat. 'Saw him walking across the courtyard early this morning'

'*This* morning?'

'*Sì.*'

'What time?'

'About seven-fifteen. I had an early meeting and–'

'Was he with anyone?'

'A man. I recognised Miles from his blond hair and dark blue coat. The one with those awful wooden buttons.'

'Who was he with?' She knows her bluntness is rude, but she's desperate.

Filippo taps a bundle of pages together. 'Not sure. He had a hat pulled down low. Couldn't see his face–'

'You're certain you don't know who?'

'It was dark. The courtyard lights are dim.' He tilts his head. 'What's this about?'

'Have you seen Miles any other time today? Somewhere else on campus? Maybe with the same person?'

'You're getting me worried, Charlotte. What's happened?'

'Please phone me if you see him.' She hurries away.

Pausing on the stairs, she scans the near-empty courtyard. He was here early this morning, but now he's gone. On a campus this large, where are the isolated corners?

82

'Theo? It's Charlotte.' A sliver of light shines beneath the door. She knocks again, impatient to be out of the basement's deserted corridors, where every echo and shadow sets her pulse jumping.

The door opens. Theo peers out.

'Is Miles here?'

Theo shrugs, a mixture of indifference and irritation, before sitting at the bench and squinting through a microscope. 'Everyone's looking for Miles,' he mutters.

She enters the room. 'Have you seen him today? Heard from him?'

Theo shrugs again, looks into the eyepiece.

'He was last seen crossing the faculty courtyard early this morning with an unknown man.' She keeps her voice steady, but inside she's seething. 'I found his phone in our filing cabinet. His last message was to an unknown number last night. Do you know anything? Has he contacted you?' She's on the verge of screaming at Theo's apathy. *He's your friend, for god's sake*, she wants to yell, *and he's missing*.

Theo shifts his gaze from the microscope. A muscle flickers along his jaw.

She forces her tone to soften. 'Wait, what do you mean *everyone's* looking for Miles? Who else–'

His steely gaze stops her. 'It would be easier to ask who *isn't* looking for Miles.'

'Okay,' she says gently. 'Can you at least tell me if he's been in contact with you recently, or if you've seen him?'

'Don't think I want to divulge any information to you, Charlotte.'

'Divulge?' Her voice climbs. 'What do you mean *divulge*? I'm trying to help–'

'Really?' Theo glares. 'Help him be investigated for unlawful entry? Help him be questioned by the Faculty Board for concealing knowledge about certain people sneaking into high-security areas? Help him get suspended like you?'

'Who … who said …'

'Campus grapevine.'

She adjusts her expression, masking her frustration at Theo's knowledge of her suspension.

'Miles doesn't need your sort of help,' says Theo.

She forces herself to relax her muscles. Lowers her shoulders and head, a show of acquiescence, hoping it will ease Theo's anger. She doesn't blame him. Theo isn't apathetic about finding Miles. He's doing what any true friend would do in a crisis: identify potential threats, close ranks, offer assistance only to those who can be trusted.

'I need to go.' He slips on his jacket, holds the door open. With a flinty stare and a cursory flick of his wrist, he ushers her from the room.

Theo closes the door, shields the keypad with his body as he activates the system. Security has been upgraded, a code now required.

Theo stands in a pool of fluorescent brightness. 'Best not wander around here on your own,' he says tersely, then walks away.

She stands motionless as his footsteps fade. The sensor light flicks off, enveloping her in a darkness so thick it wraps around her like a blanket. The basement is silent. *Forget Theo's insinuations, ignore the past, push aside the mistakes*, she tells herself. Calmness descends, easing away regrets and fear. *Trust yourself*.

As she walks along the corridor, lights flicker on one by one. Turning on her mobile phone's torch, she holds it aloft at the entrance to each aisle, peering into corners. Some units gape wide apart, others barely ajar. Her eyes strain in the gloom, searching for something out of place.

She recalls Sébastien's speculation about a connection between the four attack victims and Miles' disappearance. The victims were all post-graduates – senior students involved in unique projects, all striving to make a name for themselves. Academics caught within a dog-eat-dog system. Perhaps someone has taken their struggle one step too far, desperate for a fast track to success.

Possibilities flit through her mind. Maybe Miles somehow identified the campus attacker and now he's been seized. Maybe it's two assailants working together, one identifying potential objects to steal, another attacking anyone who interferes. Maybe the perpetrators are not just targeting highly coveted objects, but unique ideas. Multiple attacks, multiple targets, including intellectual theft.

After reaching the end of the main corridor, she continues along the most isolated part of the archive. Rows of mobile shelving units disappear into shadows.

Her imagination is running in circles, each wild theory feeding her confusion. 'Doesn't make sense,' she whispers. 'None of this is linked to the Begijnhof.' A flashback of a blue vintage Citroën with Anna's obdurate face behind the wheel.

She spies a lumpen shape at the end of an aisle, and rushes forward. Her foot connects with a large misshapen box. Inside, metal shelf dividers. She checks the remaining aisles, retraces her route, dejected.

She hears the *tap-tap* of slow footsteps. Echoes bounce off floors and walls, making it impossible to tell if the footsteps are approaching or retreating.

As she ducks into the nearest aisle, she turns off her phone's light. She slips in between shelves, sidestepping along the aisle until she reaches the concrete wall at the end. Surrounded by blackness, wedged into a coffin-like space.

The footsteps approach. Two figures walk past her hiding place, oblivious to her presence.

She clenches her jaw. All this talk of attackers and victims has clogged her head.

Creaking sounds fill the air, wheels grinding along tracks, metal screeching on metal. A handle being cranked.

Run! She stumbles along the narrow aisle, bashing her shoulders against moving shelves, desperate to reach the safety of the corridor.

Someone is turning a handle, widening one aisle while closing others. She'll be crushed if she doesn't get out. Has the attacker followed her to the archive? Does he plan to scare or hurt her, snatch her satchel, just as he stole from the other victims?

She staggers out of the aisle, skids into the corridor and crashes against the wall. Cold concrete against her cheek.

'Hey,' a woman's voice rings out. 'You shouldn't be here by yourself. Haven't you heard about the attacks?'

Charlotte glances over her shoulder at two women standing thirty metres away, their hands on the wheel of the compactor. They are students, working late on a project, their faces filled with surprise and concern at seeing her sudden escape from the compactor.

'I'm fine. No harm done,' replies Charlotte, moving hastily towards the green-glowing exit sign. She wrenches open the door, rushes up the stairs, berating herself for letting her fears take over her common sense. With each step she curses her poor judgement. Her inability to trust others has made others mistrust her. Most of all, she's angry at herself for pulling Miles and Edith into her deceptions, allowing them to become embroiled. Everything is spiralling out of control.

83

July 6, 1624

'I can't be traipsin' about the market after you two,' said Janneke, 'when I should be home cookin'.'

'We walk for only thirty minutes,' I replied, 'which is as much time as you spend gossiping with other maids.'

'One of these days a neighbour will notice you walkin' with yer sweetheart,' said Janneke, 'and yer papa will find out—'

'Our neighbours should keep their noses out of other people's business,' I interrupted, 'and I've told you before, Meneer Barzetti is not my sweetheart.'

'You look at him as if he were,' muttered Janneke.

I ignored her and turned from Eikenstraat towards the market.

Having accepted Santo's offer to teach me Genoese, we conducted our informal lessons as we walked around the square, with Janneke remaining two strides behind. Sometimes we paused by the cathedral steps to read from one of Santo's Genoese books, other times we rested by a water trough to discuss difficult phrases.

'You are a natural linguist, Miss Antonia.' Santo was quick to praise.

'And you a natural teacher,' I replied, hiding my smile beneath a low-brimmed hat.

Our conversations sparkled with a shared wit and intellect. We laughed easily, engaged in debate on all manner of topics, listened to one another with mutual esteem. Santo good-naturedly accepted my teasing of his untidy handwriting, and accepted my offer to help improve his penmanship.

Whenever we peered at a book together and our hands touched, a warmth spread along my arm, to my neck and face. I'm sure he wondered about my foolish behaviour, noticing my fierce blushes and stammered replies, the times I jumped like a startled rabbit when he stood too close. I took long breaths to steady my racing heart, ordered myself to remain calm, but he surely guessed I was falling under his spell. Not that I would admit my infatuation to anyone, especially Janneke. If Clara were here, how she would laugh and roll her eyes, mock me with imitations of my earlier vows to reject marriage and become a spinster mapmaker.

I was maturing. Circumstances had made me wise to the way a person's heart could change as quickly as the toss of a die.

Santo and I sometimes reflected on our shared memories from the Rubenshuis. One day, he pulled from his pocket a familiar booklet.

'Do you still record information about all the Master's artworks?' I asked, touching the ochre leather cover.

Santo fanned the pages. 'The Master's works are extensive.'

We stood side-by-side, reading descriptions of *Adoration of the Shepherds, Three Graces, Pandora, Perseus Freeing Andromeda, Portrait of Archduchess Isabella*. Page after page described every artistic genre from Classical legends and Biblical stories to allegories, portraits and landscapes.

Despite the way in which I believed Meneer Rubens had impeded my friendship with Clara, despite the antagonism between him and my father, I couldn't help but admire his artistic skills. I had gazed at the ceiling panels in the Jesuits' church, and marvelled at the Master's imagination and artistry. It was impossible to remain unmoved in the presence of such brilliance.

I could not imagine my father's cast-off drawings being catalogued with the same care. Why, the shelves of Papa's oak cabinet were filled with drawings he believed inferior, and he happily allowed me to use the reverse side for my own work.

I pointed to an entry halfway down the page. 'What became of these?'

'*Seven Pandora drawings lost, early July 1621,*' he read aloud. Frowning at first, his eyes lit up with recognition. 'King Felipe commissioned a painting of the Greek legend Pandora. The Master prepared some drawings, but by the time I discovered they were missing, King Felipe had changed his mind and asked for a painting of the Three Graces.'

The Master's creations were so prodigious that one artwork could easily be replaced by another.

Our conversation was cut short by Janneke grasping my elbow. 'We be leavin' now, Miss Antonia.'

She pulled me through the crowd, her grip so tight I was unable to break free. We finally stopped on the far side of the square.

I twisted from her grasp, filled with fury. 'What compelled you to behave with such rudeness?'

'You be so enamoured with yer sweetheart you didn't see Mevrouw van Helst standin' three paces away, starin' at the two of you with her eyes as big as moons.'

My stomach twisted, remembering our nosy neighbour's reputation as a gossip. If she believed Santo and I were behaving inappropriately, the rumours would reach my father by nightfall.

Our city is filled with people who believe it is their duty to know everyone's business.

84

Charlotte leans against the brick wall of the gatekeeper's shelter, its coldness seeping through her coat. Clenching and unclenching her hands, she tries to compose her thoughts, but her insides are twisted. She doesn't want to be here. She wants to be at the university, helping search for Miles. But Sébastien has convinced her to return with him to the Begijnhof. Her instinct to spend time with him – to gain his approval, nurture their fragile relationship – has ebbed and flowed throughout the day, leaving her emotionally exhausted, tense, irritable. An elastic band stretched to snapping point.

'Anna needs our help,' Sébastien had told Charlotte, after she returned from the basement archive.

'Anna?' Frustrated over her failure to locate Miles, the last thing she wanted was to be dragged into helping Anna.

'She just telephoned. She's found a document in her filing cabinet she's never seen before, and she says it's critical.'

'What's it about?'

'I don't know. She became upset, couldn't explain, but asked us to come to the Begijnhof urgently.'

'Me?'

'She specifically asked for you, but didn't say why.'

They had walked in silence to the Begijnhof, Charlotte suppressing the urge to grumble, trying to push aside the image of Anna sitting behind the wheel of the battered Citroën, and instead, reflecting on the stress Anna is facing. The pressure of managing the dilapidated Begijnhof, juggling limited funds and escalating costs, grieving over Petra, offering comfort and guidance to her fellow sisters, dealing with *begijnen* who want to leave – one stress mounting upon another. Charlotte imagines such endeavours may be a spiritual calling for the mother superior, but it could also be a tremendous and, at times, overwhelming burden. Does Anna know about the secrets inside the map folio or antique *kast*? Did she drive to Villa Wouters? Does she know anything that could help find Miles?

Four clangs reverberate around the courtyard, then the chapel door swings open. Two rows of women, dressed in grey-pleated skirts and thick coats, descend the steps. They break their tight formation and disperse in different directions, some grouped in twos, most solitary, all walking with purpose.

'I can't see Anna,' says Sébastien.

'Maybe she's still inside.'

Entering the chapel, they spot Anna kneeling near the front. Sébastien indicates a pew several rows behind her. They sit silently and wait.

The stained-glass figure of Saint Catherine stares from her position on high, eternally trapped above the altar. Clutching the spiked wheel on which she was tortured, her expression is more aloof than serene. Charlotte wonders whether Anna will be aloof when she listens to her apology. Will the mother superior hold back her anger, or rebuke her?

Anna makes the sign of the cross, rises to her feet, turns. If she's surprised to see them, she hides it well.

'Please join me,' says Anna, inviting them to the front pew. The spider veins on her cheeks are florid, her eyes shadowed, the lines on her face more pronounced.

Charlotte remains standing. 'Anna, before we discuss anything else, I want you to know how very sorry I am for taking the portfolio box. I should've spoken to you first and asked permission.' Her words are rushed. She wishes her voice sounded stronger, less like a wayward child shamed before a headmistress.

'Please,' Anna says gruffly, indicating for Charlotte to sit. 'We can talk about the portfolio box another time. Right now, we need to discuss this.' She draws an envelope from her pocket, passes it to Sébastien.

He unfolds a sheet of paper from within the envelope, and reads the handwritten page. He drops his hands to his lap, the page crumpling between his fingers. 'This changes everything.'

Anna clutches the pewter cross hanging around her neck. 'I found this document in a folder of maintenance invoices, inside my filing cabinet. Petra's original will was lodged more than a decade ago with her lawyer in Gistel. It's our policy at Sint-Catharina's for the *begijnen*'s legal documents to be placed on file with us, as well as with their lawyer. I keep all the wills in my filing cabinet, but this document is new. Let me emphasise' – Anna's voice wavers and she pauses before continuing – 'the *begijnen* are free to do whatever they wish with their estate on their passing. They are under no obligation to leave anything to Sint-Catharina's.' Anna flaps her hand at the page. 'This Last Will and Testament is recent, signed two months ago, and the bequest is completely different from Petra's previous one.'

Anna's final words hang in the air.

Sébastien turns to Charlotte. 'It appears that six weeks before her death, my half-sister changed her will. The Begijnhof is now the sole beneficiary of her estate, not me. They will inherit my family's antiques, portfolio box, Villa Wouters, the lands, which are extensive, and also' – he pauses for emphasis – 'any items inside the villa.'

Light-headed, as if disembodied, Charlotte stares from Sébastien to Anna. Items of immense personal value may be sold to strangers, Sébastien's kinship summarily dismissed with the bang of an auctioneer's gavel. Santo's priceless booklet, sold to the highest bidder, spirited away into the private collection of a Rubens fanatic, keen to hoard it rather than share it with the world. The *Pandora* drawings, assuming they are found, could be sold, also disappearing into private collections.

Anna's gaze flits around the chapel like a butterfly, shifting from Charlotte to Sébastien to the altar. She clasps the cross to her chest, squeezing it tightly, her composure dwindling.

Charlotte watches Anna closely. The mother superior is clearly distressed, but Charlotte can't tell if it's because she considers the Begijnhof's sudden new bequest to be ill-gotten gains and undeserving, or if she's overwhelmed with remorse. Did Anna suggest to the ailing Petra that changing her will would benefit the Begijnhof in their time of financial need? Having encouraged Petra to write a new will, did Anna locate the missing drawings at Villa Wouters and stash them away in case Sébastien challenged the new will? Is her distress a calculated performance, designed to illicit his sympathy? If Anna is genuinely upset and surprised about the new will, Charlotte can't help but wonder whether the mother superior is also a little relieved the Begijnhof will receive this windfall. Their financial troubles will be over.

Anna takes a long breath, trying to calm herself, and turns to Charlotte. 'When you searched the Begijnhof for the portfolio box, did you find anything inside the box or a document somewhere else that could explain Petra's new will?'

Charlotte recalls the Vorsterman family papers, each one declaring the importance of preserving their heirlooms from one generation to the next, while Petra's new will is a total about-turn of this family tradition. She shakes her head. 'There wasn't anything in the box related to Petra's new will.'

'What about Dr Thornton? Can you ask him if he saw something related to the new will?' Anna is persistent.

'When I see him, I'll ask,' says Charlotte quietly.

'Didn't Edith also help with the search?' asks Sébastien. 'Perhaps she may have spotted something?'

'I believe Edith may be running errands in town at the moment. I'll ask her when she returns.' Anna clasps her hands together, thumbs kneading her knuckles. 'Edith's behaviour lately has been …' The mother superior shakes her head, looking up at the stained-glass saint.

Charlotte and Sébastien remain still, waiting for Anna to collect herself.

'… uncharacteristic,' she continues. 'She's been late for prayers, neglecting chapel, barely speaking with anyone. Last night, I found her scrubbing the floors and walls of Petra's bedroom, which she'd already cleaned after Petra's death.' Anna's voice quivers, eyes blinking rapidly, trying to keep the tears away. 'I'm worried about her. She hasn't been herself.'

'She's grieving over Petra—' says Charlotte.

'It's more than that,' interrupts Anna. 'Her behaviour started about six weeks ago, around the time Sister Léa left the order.

Léa said she wanted to spend her final years with her family, but her departure was unexpected. She told me in the morning and left the next day. We were shocked. She'd always been so happy, but suddenly ...' Anna wrings her hands. 'I'm sure it has something to do with Petra's new will.'

'What could Petra's will have to do with Sister Léa?' Sébastien rustles the paper in his hand.

'I'm concerned that it was written and signed without Petra's consent or full knowledge. Look at the signatures.' Anna's voice quavers.

Sébastien scans the page before handing it to Charlotte. His mouth tightens.

At the bottom of the page, is Petra's clear signature, so different from the wobbly writing in her garden journal. Alongside it are the names and signatures of two witnesses: Edith Rutten and Léa Loman.

Anna's hand shakes as she points to the date. 'Sixth of September this year ... the same day Léa told me she was leaving Sint-Catharina's.'

85

September 16, 1624

Mevrouw van Helst's gossip reached Papa's ears by nightfall as I predicted and I was swiftly punished for the disgrace I had nearly brought upon our family. I was forbidden from meeting Santo.

Two months on, Papa and I settled into a reconciliation of sorts, courteous yet distant. The bitterness that once filled me whenever I looked upon his face eased. I became adept at lowering my gaze, offering murmurs of agreement, my countenance a mask of obedience. Maintaining this deference, I completed my chores, then scurried away to my attic workroom and surrounded myself with maps and drawings. In secret, I wrote letters to Santo.

Papa's plans for my future exist in the silence between us. He is desperate to find me a suitable match, someone so highly esteemed that the union will lift our family from the middling ranks to the heights of the illustrious. A connection to a grand family will enhance his name. Colleagues from the Sint-Lucas Guild will treat him with greater deference, while the doors of new patrons will be opened to him, having hitherto remained closed. No longer will he do the tedious work of a copyist; instead, he will be able to create original engravings of his own designs and be lauded as an artist in his own right.

I had finished recording the weekly household expenditure in the ledger and was planning to retreat to the attic when Janneke burst into my chamber, red in the face, huffing with exertion.

'Quick. Visitors be waitin'. Yer father wants you downstairs.' Janneke rummaged through my clothing *kast* and pulled out a dark green gown with ivory underskirt.

I was slow to put down my quill. 'Has my aunt come to call?'

Janneke ignored my query, too busy struggling me into the bodice and fastening the skirt. She brushed my wild curls, securing the top strands into a chignon, allowing the remaining tendrils to drape my shoulders in the current fashion. 'It'll have to do,' she muttered. Making one final tweak to my hair, she pushed me out the door, urging me to make haste.

Dressed and dispatched at such speed, I was halfway down the stairs before I realised something was afoot. A welcoming party of strangers stood in the foyer, watching my descent. Too late for me to retreat.

'Here is my lovely Antonia,' Papa's voice boomed.

A middle-aged woman peered at me through a pair of spectacles, like a tortoise extending its neck. A ruddy-cheeked older gentleman swept me a bow. Beside them stood a young man of five and twenty, his droopy eyes and forlorn mouth reminiscent of a Basset hound.

'Meneer and Mevrouw Kappel and their son Edwin are visiting from Brussels,' said Papa.

I recalled Papa mentioning Edwin Kappel would be a desirable match. Despite knowing my disinterest, Papa had tricked me into being presented to the young man and his parents as if I were a prize sow at market. While I may look and sound older, Papa knows I am only fifteen. Far too young to be betrothed to a stranger with whom I have nothing in common.

Mevrouw Kappel dominated the conversation, darting from one topic to the next: the court's patronage of Jan Brueghel, the restoration of the long gallery at the Brussels palace, the Archduchess's preference for dressing as a nun.

I found it difficult to apply myself to the conversation. Inside, I fumed at Papa's trickery.

Mevrouw Kappel lifted her spectacles to scrutinise me. 'Have you inherited the artistic accomplishments of your father,' she asked, 'or are your abilities more musical in nature?'

My gaze drifted to the *spinetten* in the corner. I had the perverse idea of offering to entertain our guests with a cacophonous rendition of a fugue, made more deplorable by singing in a different key. I smiled sweetly. 'I have been practising a piece by Pieter Cornet—'

'The court composer,' interrupted Mevrouw Kappel. 'We would be delighted to hear you play, wouldn't we Edwin?'

'The piece is not ready for performance. Isn't that correct, Antonia?' Papa gave me a stern look, guessing my ruse.

Edwin and I sat mutely in the corner while the conversation flowed around us. His parents silently appraised my appearance and youth, my capacity to bear children, my willingness to be a compliant wife for their son. Edwin's demeanour suggested an insipid disposition, easily controlled by his domineering mother. I imagined she would rule the household, declaring academic studies and mapmaking unsuitable pursuits for her daughter-in-law.

Despite having been in one another's presence for less than an hour, I knew Edwin and I were incompatible. Ours would be a marriage of misery, certain to be as dismal as the mood within my Eikenstraat home.

86

By the time Charlotte returns to the university, twilight has descended like a grey velvet curtain. Rectangles of light dot the building façades, most windows in darkness. People cross the courtyard in ones and twos. The campus will soon be deserted, and she's no closer to finding Miles.

Sébastien had been sympathetic when Charlotte explained she was going back to the university to continue searching for Miles. 'I've spoken to the campus police and told them he's missing. There's not much else we can do.'

She shook her head. 'The more people looking, the better.'

'I'll stay with Anna for a little while, see if I can offer some support, then I'll come to the university. Call me if you need me sooner.' He squeezed her arm. 'Be careful.'

She couldn't decide if she appreciated his show of concern, or if his familiarity overstepped the mark. They've spent one day together, tiptoeing around the boundaries of their new father–daughter relationship, and already he's acting like a worried parent.

Charlotte stands in the middle of the courtyard, scanning the façade. She locates the brightly lit window of their office, remembering she'd forgotten to turn off the light when she rushed to the archive. Her eyes scan higher, coming to rest on a row of dark dormer windows on the floor above. What had Sébastien said about the top-floor renovation? The final fit-out was in limbo, waiting for the floor to be varnished. Could Miles be there?

She races for the stairs, and reaches the top floor within minutes. The renovation spans the length of the building. The steeply pitched attic has been stripped, rewired and formed into offices, a hallway running down the centre. A heavy plastic curtain is tacked across the entranceway to keep dust from escaping into the rest of the building. No voices. Silence.

She flicks on a switch. Light spills from the hallway into shadowy side rooms. Against the walls lie coiled electrical cables and plastic conduit. The space smells of sawdust and fresh paint.

'Miles?' She's unnerved by the eerie sound of her voice. Walking down the hallway, she glances inside the rooms.

Her phone rings.

'Sébastien?'

'I've just spoken to the police officer investigating the campus attacks.' He talks quickly, phrases running together. 'The fourth victim, the woman attacked two weeks ago, is remembering more details. The attacker used certain words that show he's familiar with campus procedures. He's possibly a student, or someone from the university.'

In the distance she hears a thump, muffled and indistinct. Perhaps a door closing?

'I have to go,' she whispers.

'Wait! You shouldn't be alone. Let the police look for Miles. Where are you?'

More thumps. Regular. Possibly footsteps.

Panicking, she ends the call and mutes the volume. She's terrified her voice or the ringtone will announce her presence.

There it is again. Intermittent. Too random to be footsteps.

She creeps through the next three rooms, searching.

More thumps. Louder this time.

She follows the sound into a small room at the end of the hallway. Pipes protruding from the wall show it will become a kitchenette. Twenty or more boxes of tiles are stacked against a wall.

The thumps are stronger. The boxes shudder.

Working quickly, she hefts the boxes away from the wall. Pushing and shoving, she finally reveals a low door that provides access into the eaves. There's another thud; the door shakes.

She wrenches it open. Two legs bound with cable ties kick out at her, thrashing, and she topples backwards.

'Miles!' She cries out with relief.

With his arms twisted behind his back, he lies on his side in a cupboard-like space under the eaves.

She drags him free. Eases gaffer tape from his mouth.

He blinks slowly, licks cracked lips. Dried blood smears the left side of his face; there's a gash on his forehead sticky with congealed ooze. 'Found me …' he whispers, then closes his eyes.

Inspecting his wrists, she tries to wriggle the cable tie loose, but it holds fast. She scrabbles across the floor, searching for something sharp she can use to undo the ties. Her fingers find a crooked nail. 'Talk to me, Miles,' she says, desperate to keep him awake, realising the deep gash on his head may have caused a serious injury.

His eyes flutter open, then close again. He gives a muted groan, pain and relief merging as one.

She inserts the nail into the tiny hole of the cable tie, then bends the tie's loose end backwards. 'Years ago' – she makes her voice bright, anxious to keep him from slipping into unconsciousness – 'I learnt this from friends.' She pushes the nail down to pry apart the one-way fastener, jiggles it open.

Another groan from Miles as his wrists are freed. He tries to bring his arms to his chest, but the weight of his body pins his lower arm to the floor. His limbs refuse to move, contorted for hours, circulation sluggish, joints rigid with pain.

Wrapping her arms around him, Charlotte hauls him into a sitting position. He slumps against her. 'You're going to be okay,' she murmurs, rubbing his shoulders to encourage circulation. On the side of his head is a lump the size of a golf ball. Hair matted in clumps. Blood soaking his collar.

'Students attacked' – his voice slurs – 'work stolen.'

She gently lifts the hair from his forehead. The gash is nearly three inches long, purple and swollen. The surface bleeding has stopped, but the injury could be serious. At the very least, he is concussed. He needs to go to hospital.

'He'll come back,' whispers Miles.

'Who's coming back?' She releases the cable ties from his ankles.

He blinks rapidly, sensing freedom. 'Need to go.'

She tries to haul him up, knowing they must leave, find help. 'Put your arm over my shoulder and lean against me.'

Eventually, standing with arms locked around one another, they sway like slow-dancers in a drunken stupor, moving across the room and down the hallway. It's no use urging him to hurry. He can barely walk, feet shuffling, leaning heavily on her.

'Can you remember what happened?' she asks.

He mumbles unintelligibly.

'Who did this?'

A grumble from the back of his throat.

She readjusts his arm across her shoulder, tightens her grasp around his waist. His movements are weak, knees buckling.

Halfway along the hallway, they stumble. Miles drops to the floor, slumps against the wall, closes his eyes. She's unable to support his weight anymore. Fumbling for her phone, she tries to remember the number for emergency services in Belgium. Her hands are shaking so much she can barely scroll. Panic surges. Her vision blurs.

Footsteps approach. She hears the crinkle of plastic being pushed aside at the entrance to the hallway.

'Charlotte?' a voice calls out. A man comes into view, holding the plastic curtain aside. He stands still, assessing the scene. 'You found him.'

Arnold hurries towards them, kneels beside Miles, peers at his face. 'Is he unconscious?'

'Arnold, thank goodness you're here. Miles is hurt and needs an ambulance ...' Her voice falters. She begins shaking all over, on the verge of tears, overwhelmed to see a friendly face and know that help has arrived, still terrified the attacker may return at any moment.

Arnold touches Miles on the shoulder. 'He's breathing.'

'We also need the police. Can you call them?'

'Let me call the ambulance first.' Arnold's hands are trembling as he pulls a phone from his pocket. He fumbles, taking several minutes to make a connection. Eventually, he speaks into the phone, gives their location, ends the call.

Arnold hurries to the door at the end of the hallway, nearest the kitchenette, jiggles the handle, muttering under his breath when he finds it locked. He rushes from one dormer window to the next, scanning the courtyard below, craning for a better view. 'They may not find us up here. I'll go downstairs. Meet the paramedics.'

Miles groans, tries to push himself up from his slumped position against the wall.

Charlotte kneels beside him, easing him into a sitting position. 'It's okay,' she murmurs. 'We've called the ambulance and they're on the way. Arnold is here and he's helping.'

Miles turns his head from side to side, his eyes wild, breathing ragged. 'No,' he gasps.

Arnold backs along the hallway. 'I'll just let the paramedics know–'

'Him!' Miles calls out. Raises his arm, pointing at the retreating figure.

There's the sound of footsteps running up the stairs.

Sébastien bursts through the plastic curtain.

87

February 25, 1625

Six new prospective suitors have visited our house in the past five months, each one duller than the last, each one meeting the same fate as the hapless Edwin Kappel. I have discovered that the eagerness of even the most steadfast suitor diminishes when I roll my eyes intermittently, stare mutely at the floor for the entire visit, or suggest I am a spendthrift. If Papa brings home another one, I may announce to them that I am barren.

Papa has grown more furious with each visit, curtailing my privileges one by one. I was forbidden to visit the marketplace, then neighbours, then friends. Papa warned I was close to being sent to the Begijnhof Sint-Catharina as their newest novice.

'You act the fool before these suitors,' said Papa, having summoned me to his workroom. 'You have presented yourself as dreary, lazy, half-witted, wasteful ... the list goes on. You have done yourself and our family a grave injustice.'

'While some girls at sixteen are ready for the responsibility of betrothal,' I said meekly, 'I would benefit from having several more years to prepare.'

'Several more years?' he sputtered. 'You have already discouraged half a dozen suitors who would make worthy husbands. We are running out of suitable candidates. News travels fast.' He paced in front of the fireplace, raging at my irresponsible behaviour.

I knew only too well how gossip flows through this city, like winter fog rolling in from the Noordzee. I stared at the floorboards, silently cursing my innate desire to remain loyal to him, while recognising a desperation within myself to avoid marriage to a dullard, bully or braggart at any cost.

'Your actions have damaged our good family name.' His voice was loud with frustration.

I winced at having to listen to Papa's well-worn pronouncements. Our family's upstanding reputation was more important than anything. Maintaining our good family name was his obsession. All he talked about was securing commissions to establish his renown as the city's master engraver, and forming connections to advance the Vorsterman name.

'Perhaps when I am older, I will be more responsive—'

'You should be more responsive *now*,' he shouted.

I glanced at the floor, hoping the girlish dress and hairstyle I wore would remind him of my tender age. In two weeks I would turn sixteen. Although most ladies did not marry until they were at least eighteen, many became betrothed at sixteen and waited several years for marriage. A two-year betrothal would not turn my disinterest to desire. I could not bear the thought of being bound for a lifetime to someone for whom I felt loathing or indifference. But if my betrothed was Santo ...

'Your mother was sixteen when we married.' Papa's voice faded.

While he stared out the window, I studied the twisting vines carved into the oak *kast* and recalled the shelves filled with etched copper plates which had built his reputation as an engraver. While I admired his skill and commitment, secrets existed within Papa that I did not comprehend, causing misgivings to fill my mind. I owed him my gratitude and loyalty, yet something inside me – my ingrained stubbornness, whispers of doubt, a yearning for independence – stopped me from fully submitting to his will. How can I remain loyal to my family and stay true to myself?

We achieved a temporary truce, of sorts, that day. I was permitted to continue mapmaking, but could only leave the house to attend church with the family. Papa agreed that he would not bring home any further suitors until after I turned seventeen, whereupon I must submit to his choice of bridegroom. I had a year to convince Papa that Santo would be a worthy son-in-law.

'Furthermore, you will no longer consort with that painter's assistant from the Rubenshuis.' He fairly spat out the words with disdain.

'But Santo Barzetti—'

'I do not care if the man has a knighthood from King Felipe. You will have nothing to do with him.'

I paused with my hand on the door, thinking of the numerous letters I had written and coaxed Janneke to exchange with Santo since my ban from the marketplace. Dozens of letters in which we declared our love.

Papa's next words were delivered with a menace I had never heard before. 'If you ask Janneke or any other servant to carry a letter to that man, they will be dismissed without a reference, and *you* will be responsible for the disgrace and hardship they will endure.'

'Yes, Papa.' I croaked out the words in a horrified whisper, and fled the room before he could see my fear.

88

Arnold swings around to face Sébastien. 'I've called the ambulance,' he says in a rush. 'I'm just going downstairs to meet them.'

'No need,' says Sébastien, his voice cool. 'Karl is downstairs. He'll let them know where we are.'

Arnold edges towards the stairs.

Sébastien puts up his hands. 'Stop.' His voice is sharp. 'The police contacted me, Arnold, and told me that the latest victim has remembered key details about the night she was attacked.'

Arnold is rooted to the spot, his face ashen. His eyes dart from Sébastien to the exit. He takes another tentative step.

'I said stop!' Sébastien shouts. 'There's no use trying to run. The police know it was you.'

Miles slumps against Charlotte's shoulder. 'Arnold. It's Arnold,' he mumbles into her neck.

Her insides turn cold, her heartbeat races. Sébastien's words repeat in her ears: *it was you.* She's unable to move, her legs suddenly heavy, as if glued to the floor. She wraps her arms tightly around Miles, instinctively trying to draw him closer, keep him safe.

Arnold glances from one end of the hallway to the other. Takes a step towards the far end.

'The police will be here any minute,' says Sébastien.

Arnold takes another step.

'You can't escape, Arnold,' says Sébastien, his voice rising, 'so don't bother trying. The door at the far end is locked. And if you get past me, you'll have to contend with Karl and the police.'

'Wasn't supposed to be like this,' says Arnold, his voice high-pitched. He pushes his glasses over the bump on his nose, shifts his weight from one foot to the other. Crosses his arms over his chest, jamming his hands first into his armpits then onto his hips, then back to his armpits. Wipes sweat from his top lip. His gaze flickers from Sébastien to Charlotte, then to Miles. He takes a few steps along the hallway, then turns back. He's like a caged animal, bewildered, unsure of his next move.

'You picked up Miles in Oostende,' says Charlotte, desperate to make sense of the chaos of the past twenty-four hours. 'Drove him back to Antwerp, didn't you?'

Arnold stares at his feet, looks at her then away, unable to meet her gaze. 'Miles texted me. Said it was urgent. While we drove back to Antwerp, he blathered on about your apartment and his office being trashed. I realised he was close to finding out.' Arnold's voice wavers. 'Research funding is tighter than ever. It's harder to get articles published. It's a dog-eat-dog world in academia. Started off with some soft tactics to scare a few inept post-grads, spooking them late at night to get hold of their research. I took their ideas from mundane to brilliant. Received rave reviews when my articles were published. Dean Mulder was impressed. Guaranteed funding for my research.'

Charlotte sits in horrified silence, struggling to comprehend the numerous ways this man has hurt others to advance himself.

Arnold closes his eyes for a moment, then resumes talking, more to himself than anyone else. 'They were incompetent. Couldn't do justice to their research. They ran away, scared. Except the last one. She started asking questions.'

Charlotte realises he's talking about the fourth victim, the student attacked two weeks ago, who stayed in Antwerp, stood her ground.

A siren wails in the distance.

Arnold peers out the window, emits a growl of frustration. Then in one sudden movement, he punches the wall with such force his fist smashes through the plasterboard.

Charlotte jerks with fright, her muscles rigid. She tightens her grip around Miles, who is barely conscious.

Arnold draws his hand back out, shaking plaster fragments onto the floor. His knuckles are gashed, streaks of blood mixing with white plaster dust. He clenches and unclenches his injured hand, then slowly turns and glares at Charlotte. His face is tight with fury, skin flushed, nostrils flaring, the veins at his temples bulging. 'My plan was working just fine until you arrived.'

'What did I do?' She recoils from him, stunned to have his anger directed at her. This is a new Arnold that she has never seen before: full of resentment and unbridled rage, the complete opposite to the laid-back colleague who met with her to discuss lectures.

His face is twisted with bitterness. 'The budget had to be stretched to cover the appointment of Dr Charlotte Hubert from Toronto, so my new research grant, which the dean had *promised* me, was sidelined. When I heard rumours you'd found something special and sent it to Duval for analysis, I decided it was the perfect quid pro quo for losing my grant.'

'You wrecked my apartment?'

'It was easy getting the key from Beulen's desk.'

'And our office.'

'Even easier.'

'And Duval's office?'

He shrugs.

'You called the Begijnhof, saying you were a cartography scholar–'

'A simple phone call.'

'You broke into Villa–'

'It was never supposed to get this bad.' He cuts her off, voice cracking. 'Things got out of control.'

Sébastien stands still, glaring at Arnold.

Charlotte doesn't move, relieved to feel Miles' steady breathing as he leans against her. *The paramedics and police will be here soon*, she tells herself. The nightmare will soon be over. Arnold will be taken into custody. He obviously hadn't counted on Miles stumbling on to his scheme. She imagines it led to a fist fight, Miles overpowered and dragged to the attic, and Arnold has been panicking ever since, trying to work out what to do next.

'That was you at Villa Wouters, wasn't it?' she asks quietly.

Arnold lifts his chin, curls his lip, then tilts his head.

She waits for him to reply, sensing his need to explain, even continue boasting about, his actions. Yet he appears distracted, as if his mind is filled with too many competing thoughts.

He shakes his head, then continues: 'Thought I was onto
something when I searched your apartment and office, then Duval's
office. But you're delusional.'

'Delusional?' she repeats, confused.

Arnold shakes his head. 'You think some amazing jackpot is
going to fall into your lap, simply because you've inherited the
genes of your genius academic mother? You're not so special.'

Blue lights flash through the windows. The siren eases to a
moan.

Arnold leans against the wall, then slides to the floor. 'What have
I done?' he whispers, his anger spent, smugness gone. Wretched.
Dazed.

Charlotte hugs Miles closer. Glancing at Sébastien, she realises
the irony of connecting with him via a find-your-friend app, after
weeks of wanting nothing to do with him. He had stepped in when
she needed him the most.

89

April 13, 1625

'What do you make of Adriaenssen's *Still Life with Oysters?*' asked
Papa.

Papa's guest cleared his throat. 'He's included oysters and lemons,
both of which symbolise affluence ...'

Their voices were clear, easily overheard from my secluded
position in the passageway. I continued folding the linen, eager to
listen, starved as I was for intellectual conversation.

Papa flaunted his knowledge of the Classics. 'Greek legend says
Aphrodite was conceived in an oyster shell and thus the oyster is
considered erotic–'

His guest interrupted, guffawing loudly. 'Adriaenssen was referring
to the dual pleasures of wealth and flesh ...'

Their discussion continued, interspersed with lewd comments.
They remained oblivious to my eavesdropping. While I had once
witnessed the furtive rutting between a drunken man and a strumpet
in a shadowy laneway off Grote Markt, I would never have admitted
such knowledge to my father.

I have learnt to hide my true feelings behind a mask of obedience,
and sometimes feigned ignorance. It has become a part of my nature,
allowing my thoughts to remain my own even if my actions, words
and demeanour are often at the command of others.

Don't we all wear masks, either to protect ourselves or to deceive
others? Even Greek goddesses wore masks, whispering half-truths.
I recall visiting the Rubenshuis years ago and seeing drawings of a
charming woman dressed in clinging robes, who displayed a mixture
of innocence and passion. When Papa discovered me looking at
them, I was ashamed, as if viewing something immoral. I learnt to
wear a mask, to hide my thoughts.

Papa also wears a mask, hiding the truth of our flight to London, the truth behind his conflict with Meneer Rubens, the truth behind his desire to lift our family into the higher tiers of society. Papa lives in perpetual fear his mask will slip, our good fortune and reputation will vanish, and the world will discover the man behind the mask.

I cannot understand his continued anger at Meneer Rubens. Haven't enough years passed for him to let go of his frustration? Is he so filled with jealousy that he has lost all sense of reason? Has he become so obsessed with striving for fame that he believes he can outdo the Master? Papa's bitterness and jealousy will eat him away like a worm coiled inside him.

I have also turned to deception to ensure my forbidden love will survive. My dear Santo's name is forever tainted by his affiliation with Meneer Rubens. Whenever the name of Rubens is mentioned, Papa's features become tight. Whether or not Papa attacked the Master with a knife remains conjecture, a rumour that occasionally circulates around the market like a fickle summer storm. But the animosity between the two men is clear, and Santo, who is blameless, is guilty by association. Is it any wonder I keep my love for Santo hidden?

Although Papa demanded we cease communicating, Santo and I have successfully exchanged letters for two months with Janneke's help.

When night descends, I re-read his letters. They are filled with news of the studio, court scandals and political intrigues. I relish his accounts of cartographers and artists, including the continued efforts by Clara Peeters to be admitted into the guild. I study his Genoese book, gifted to me last Christmastide, and am working hard to master Genoese by the time we are wed.

The paragraphs I examine until my eyes blur with tears are Santo's entreaties that I remain steadfast in the pursuit of my dreams. *I uphold your desire to become a cartographer*, he writes, *and together we will change the guild's opinion to allow female artists to become members in their own right*. He understands what brings me happiness, acknowledges my hunger for knowledge. *When we are married*, he writes, *we will instil in our children a desire for learning, and you will be lauded as Antwerpen's premier cartographer*.

'Antonia Barzetti,' I whisper as I practise writing the name on scraps of paper.

Tonight, I am creating a map for Hendrik's thirteenth birthday. Displaying a bird's-eye view of the Eikenstraat house, it includes Roman numerals along the borders. I will present it to Hendrik with a list of coordinates, which will provide him with clues to discover the pocket knife I purchased for his birthday from a visiting peddler.

I imagine my future with Santo, creating similar maps for our children in celebration of their birthdays. I have eleven months in which to convince Papa that Santo is the perfect husband for me. Eleven months to dissuade Papa of his alternative choice of groom.

90

Charlotte squints at her reflection in a stainless-steel cabinet. Deep shadows beneath her eyes, face pale. She tries to recall last night's altercation with Arnold, but the details are a blur, all thoughts now on Miles.

She turns to him, lightly touches his hand, careful not to wake him. His nails are caked in dried blood, knuckles scraped raw. Blond stubble covers his chin and a purple bruise extends from jaw to cheek, his left eyelid grotesquely puffed. Stitches hold together the gash on his forehead.

Since finding him gagged and bound in the storage cupboard, she's remained at his side. Travelling with him in the ambulance, watching over him in the emergency room, listening to his disjointed ramblings as he flitted in and out of consciousness, dozing at his bedside. Throughout the night, she followed the steady rise and fall of his chest, studied the familiar lines of his sleeping face, recalled the lightness that filled her whenever they were together. During the night, when the sky reached its blackest, she realised with an abrupt certainty that he was the only one who had ever made her feel so content and fulfilled, so light in spirit, despite the chaos in her life. He is the only one who understands her past without knowing every detail, recognises her inner drive without asking for explanations, knows her flaws and loves her because of them, not in spite of them.

He mutters in his sleep, grimaces, reliving the terror of the past thirty-six hours. She longs to stretch out beside him on the bed, wrap her arms around him, rest her head against his chest and hear the reassuring thud of his heart. But he's covered in so many bandages and monitoring devices, she's nervous of hurting him or dislodging a wire.

She enfolds his hand between her own and rests her forehead on the bed. Tears slip from behind her closed lids.

He's safe. That's all that matters. The tension and fear that has wrenched her insides for the past thirty-six hours is fading, leaving her with an overwhelming sense of relief. She's relieved the authorities will handle Arnold, and the police will chase down the stolen drawings. She's content for Sébastien to sort out Petra's new will and handle the bequest. At this stage, she's almost beyond caring about her suspension. When the time comes, she'll deal with it. Right now, all she cares about is Miles.

Breathing deeply, she searches for his distinctive scent – a memory of woodsmoke aftershave, black tea, red wine – but the smells of antiseptic and blood are too overwhelming.

A medic enters the room, moves to the monitor, and clicks buttons. Leaning over Miles, he adjusts the nasal cannula, checks the flow of oxygen, tightens the blood pressure cuff. He catches Charlotte's attention with a reassuring smile. 'He's doing well. You should go home and sleep.' His rubber-soled shoes squeak on the linoleum floor as he leaves.

She tightens her grip on his hand. She has no intention of leaving.

Miles stirs, opens his eyes. 'You're still here,' he whispers.

She squeezes his hand. Rests her chin on his arm.

He shifts in the narrow bed, plucks at the blanket. His voice low, words jumbled. 'Should've guessed it was Arnold ... two of the four victims ... Arnold was their mentor.'

'Mmm,' she murmurs.

'While stranded in Oostende, one of my students contacted me ... warned me about accusations of you entering the conservation room without permission and my possible involvement. I tried talking to Theo, but the storm was getting worse ... phone kept cutting out. Theo knew something, mentioned Dean Mulder, I tried explaining, but it was no good ... he couldn't hear clearly. I had to get back to Antwerp ... sort out the mess. You didn't answer when I knocked on your door. I managed to reach Arnold and he agreed to pick me up in Oostende.'

'I wish I'd answered the door,' she whispers. Everything would have turned out so differently.

Miles continues his scrambled recollections. 'I didn't explain to Arnold the reason I needed to get back to Antwerp ... less people who knew the better. But by the time we arrived at the university ... when I mentioned your apartment and our office had been upended, you should've seen his face. He was bug-eyed, but it wasn't with surprise. It was guilt and fear. Nobody else knew about the ransackings, but as soon as I saw his face, I realised it was him. Told Arnold I was calling the police. He ranted about work pressures, said he only meant to scare people ... got outta control ...'

She brushes the hair back from his forehead.

'You were going to be his next victim. When I confronted him, he lost it. Started screaming at me. Dunno what he hit me with, but it did the job. Must've dragged me up to the attic and dumped me. Where is he? Where's Arnold?' His voice grows panicked, terror returning.

'It's okay,' she soothes. 'The police have him in custody.'

'He's got the *Pandoras*. Must've found out about Gistel and arrived before us ...' His voice fades; his eyes close.

She holds his hand, watches him sleep, remains silent. Throughout the night, while dozing in the chair, her semi-conscious brain had replayed the day's events, weaving together Arnold's confession, Miles' accusations, and her suspicions. But now she remembers the look on Arnold's face after he'd bragged about rifling through her apartment and the offices. When she mentioned Villa Wouters, Arnold's smugness had disappeared, replaced with confusion. The information he could have gleaned from the copy of her mind map and the stolen documents in Duval's office would have been insufficient to track the drawings to Gistel. He needed more information.

Arnold knows nothing about the *Pandoras*. Of that, she's certain. So, who took them?

Still grasping Miles' hand, she sits back in the chair, tips her head back and closes her eyes. Rest for a few hours, she tells herself, then try to untangle this mess. Within seconds, she's asleep.

91

December 9, 1625

'I warned you!' Papa's voice thundered from the kitchen.

Janneke's high-pitched cry ended in a wail.

By the time I reached the kitchen, her words were coming out in convulsive sobs. 'Please ...' Tears coursed down her cheeks.

'Leave now!' Papa flung open the door to the courtyard, letting in blasts of chill air.

I stepped in between him and the door. 'What is happening?'

He brandished a piece of paper in his fist. 'She was carrying this letter.'

'It fell from my basket,' said Janneke, whimpering, 'when I arrived home from market.'

'How dare you defy me?' he shouted, his face scarlet, eyes bulging. He flung the letter in my face.

I flinched. The letter fell to the floor, the wax seal broken. Santo's handwriting was reduced to unreadable scribbles, blurred behind my tears. Private words intended only for me, now revealed to others.

Janneke crept down the steps into the rear courtyard, ignoring her cloak hanging on the peg. She turned and fled through the gate, oblivious to the freezing temperature.

Scooping Santo's letter from the floor, I held it behind my back. 'Surely you cannot mean to throw Janneke out on the street. She is hard-working, loyal–'

'Loyal?' Papa sneered. 'She disobeyed me and carried letters between you and that man. I hardly call that loyal.' His voice dropped to an ominous calm. 'I told you to have nothing to do with him, yet you disobeyed me. You have brought dishonour on our family by consorting with someone beneath our rank.'

'I cannot stop loving Santo simply because you order me to.'
I lifted my chin and glared, but I was no match for Papa and soon
dropped my gaze.

'You don't understand love,' he said, hissing with contempt. 'A
successful marriage is based on shared beliefs and respect, not idealistic
passions. I have tried to find you a suitable husband, but you have
ignored my advice ...' His tirade continued while I studied the floor.

Papa's interest in rank is an obsession. When I was younger, he
was proud of my academic accomplishments, but since reaching
marriageable age, he is preoccupied with my mastery of wifely
pursuits. I am compared to other girls using a measuring stick of
trivialities. How I long to be appreciated for my mapmaking skills.

Papa paced around the table in full rant. 'All I have ever wanted
for you, Antonia, is to be successful and happy as a wife and mother.
I had hoped you could trust me to choose you a suitable partner ...'

His words resounded in my ears. All Papa has ever wanted is to
be lauded as Antwerpen's favourite engraver. His ambition and pride
have seen him set aside the happiness of his family.

Footsteps ran across the courtyard. Standing in the doorway,
with his chest heaving, was my beloved Santo. Pulling off his wide-
brimmed hat, he attempted to bow towards my father, but in the
confines of the doorway it appeared clumsy.

Janneke squeezed past him and crept to my side.

Papa turned to Janneke, his face a frightening shade of puce. 'How
dare you bring this man into my house. You have defied me for the
last time. Get out!'

Janneke crouched on the floor, hiding behind my skirts.

'Papa, please ...' I began.

Santo stepped forward. 'Sir, may I speak?'

Papa turned a steely gaze on him. 'You cannot impress me with
your smooth talk and flamboyant dress. You are no more than scum
dragged off the streets.'

Santo placed his plumed hat upon the table and straightened his
brocade jacket. 'You may despise me for my humble origins, sir, but
I have worked hard and displayed complete loyalty to my Master.'
He took a step towards my father and lowered his voice. 'The same
cannot always be said of you, sir, in your dealings with Meneer—'

'Do not speak that man's name in my house,' interrupted Papa, his tone icy.

Unperturbed, Santo took another step towards him and lowered his voice further. 'There are certain facts I know about you, sir, which you may prefer to discuss in private.'

Silence descended.

Janneke rose from her crouch and whispered, 'Let us leave the men to talk.'

I motioned her aside, irritated that meekness was expected of me even from a servant. I addressed Papa and Santo. 'As you will be discussing my future, I wish to be present.'

Papa looked straight through me as if I did not exist. With a nod, he indicated for Santo to follow. As I had not been told otherwise, I trailed behind them into Papa's workroom and leaned against the oak *kast*. The men ignored me. I was invisible to them.

Without being invited, Santo sat in a chair and rested his hands on the carved arms.

Papa stood with hands on hips. 'Get on with it.'

A faint smile passed Santo's lips. 'Do you recall a day in the Master's studio, five summers past? The apprentices had retired for the evening. Only you and the Master remained. I had withdrawn to the anteroom to check a delivery.'

'How the devil am I supposed to recall a particular day five years ago?' asked Papa.

Santo tilted his head. 'This was an exceptional day, sir, one which you would never forget.'

Papa's face was a mask of stone.

'You and the Master were so intent on your disagreement you didn't notice the door ajar.' A grin twisted the corner of Santo's mouth. 'I witnessed everything. The Master was angry you had mentioned the ownership of the engravings. An argument ensued. He declared he would never cede operating privilege to you. You became furious and did more than shout and threaten.' Santo's half-smile curled into a sneer.

Papa took a step back and steadied himself against the worktable. Spots of red appeared in his cheeks.

Santo toyed with his beard. 'Your secret is not such a secret after all. The rumours of your knife attack spread.'

I looked from Papa to Santo, bewildered their discussion had taken such a turn. Where were Santo's pledges of love and loyalty, his declaration he was a well-suited match for me? What of his accusation of Papa attacking the Master with a knife? I had always hoped the rumours were false. Not my papa. For all his conceit, surely he wasn't a criminal. Of course, he wasn't perfect. He had made mistakes, but he couldn't be guilty of such a horrendous crime. It was a lie.

I had wanted to bury the rumours, but they had been re-opened like a festering wound, and by none other than my darling Santo. For him to say he had witnessed the attack and kept such news from me, while professing his love for me, was the worst kind of betrayal. Cruel and intentional.

Any second now, Papa would declare it to be all lies. The ugly rumours would be quashed forever. And Santo ... I couldn't think of what would become of us.

Papa sat heavily in a chair. 'What do you want?'

'You already know what I desire.' Santo's gaze flicked over me as I stood rigid against the *kast*.

Papa turned his head, as if seeing me for the first time.

Bile rose in my throat.

Santo leaned forward in his chair. 'I never understood why Meneer Rubens suppressed your knife attack. You slashed apart his waistcoat with such force, if the fabric had been thin silk, you would have done more than draw blood. His life would have ended and you would have swung—'

'Enough.' Papa's face blanched.

'Lucky for you, the cut was superficial. Lucky for you, the Master decided to show compassion, misguided as it was. Lucky for you, he hushed it up, let you flee, otherwise ...' Santo spread his palms wide.

'Otherwise, you would not be sitting in my house at this moment, attempting to blackmail me. Otherwise, you would not attempt to marry my daughter with the aim of lifting yourself out of the gutter.'

They sat in silence, oblivious to the object of their negotiation standing less than two yards away.

I was being used as a chess piece, manipulated by the men in my life. My father had allowed his past to haunt him, to dictate the future, imposed it upon me. Santo had revealed his true nature, causing me to mistrust his intentions, to realise his love for me was not pure.

No longer would I stand mutely by and let others decide my future and control my life. The only person I could trust was myself.

92

Charlotte stands in the Begijnhof courtyard, surrounded by step-gabled buildings silhouetted against the faint glimmer of a pre-dawn sky. A slivered moon offers scant light.

She stretches her neck from one side to the other, the muscles aching after too many hours resting awkwardly in the chair next to Miles' bed. She had woken in the silence of early morning, and slipped from the hospital room, tugged by an invisible thread to the Begijnhof, hoping that Anna or Edith held the key to understanding the mayhem of the past week.

Squinting at the screen in her hand, Charlotte re-reads Sébastien's message, sent last night while she slept in the hospital room: *Edith is missing. I'll talk with Anna and keep you posted.*

Charlotte is one step ahead of him.

A light flickers on in an upstairs window of the main building, illuminating the pot of begonias on the window ledge inside the mother superior's office. A figure walks from one side of the office to the other, then back, pacing. Like Charlotte, perhaps Anna has woken early, assailed with a multitude of unanswered questions and concerns.

Edith is missing. Charlotte repeats the message to herself as she crosses the courtyard, climbs the worn steps and enters the *Kantoor*. The linen press stands sentinel in the corner of the foyer. No need to wait for Sébastien, she tells herself, as she slowly ascends the staircase. She has a long list of questions and is desperate for answers.

Charlotte knocks softly on the office door, and Anna's voice calls out for her to enter.

Anna indicates for Charlotte to be seated, and eases herself into the adjacent chair. The dark shadows beneath the mother superior's eyes suggest she has not slept. The women exchange subdued greetings, the silence heavy between them.

'Sébastien tells me you can't find Edith,' says Charlotte gently. 'When did you last see her?'

'Yesterday afternoon, I saw her walking to the chapel as I drove out of the courtyard for my meeting with the Diocese. Nobody has seen her since.'

Charlotte is surprised to realise that this was also the last time she saw Edith. So much has happened since she stood in the garden, watching Edith spread straw over the cauliflower seedlings. The *begijn* was last seen fifteen hours ago, she calculates. 'Was she in her bedroom last night?' asks Charlotte.

'She didn't attend yesterday's evening meal or vespers or compline, and her bed wasn't slept in last night.' Anna's fingers work the pleats of her skirt, folding and refolding the fabric.

'Is it possible she's gone to visit a friend?'

'All her friends are here.'

'When I last spoke with Edith, she mentioned Sister Léa. Perhaps she's gone to visit her?'

'Léa lives in Arlon, which is four hours away by train. Edith's only friends are in the Begijnhof,' repeats Anna, 'and she never takes a day off without first checking with me. Besides, two days ago she asked for the afternoon off at the last minute. She said she wanted to visit the Schone Kunsten Museum in Ghent and asked to borrow the car.'

'Edith drove to Ghent on Saturday in your Citroën?' asks Charlotte. 'During the huge storm?' A fluttering sensation begins in her chest.

'Thankfully she returned before the storm broke,' says Anna. 'She's not an experienced driver.'

Charlotte remembers seeing the turn-off to Ghent while driving to Gistel with Miles. More disconcerting is her recollection of a student recently complaining to her about the Ghent museum remaining closed to visitors for another month due to its delayed renovation. Edith can't have visited the museum. She'd lied.

With unnerving clarity, she realises that Edith used the car because it was the only way to reach Villa Wouters. Located on the outskirts of Gistel, on the other side of Ghent, the villa cannot be reached by public transport.

Edith has vanished. The drawings have disappeared.

Anna brings her hands to her face, covering her eyes, all composure gone. She leans forward, shoulders shaking, and emits a series of wrenching sobs. Deep and drawn out, the sounds fill the room.

Charlotte falls to her knees beside Anna and draws Anna's crumpled frame into her arms. Resting her head on Charlotte's shoulder, Anna cries until she is exhausted and spent.

'It'll be okay,' murmurs Charlotte, rubbing the mother superior's back, suddenly aware of the woman's frailty and the burdens she has been carrying for so long. She's filled with remorse for having thought Anna could have had anything to do with stealing the drawings.

Anna mops at her cheeks with a handkerchief Charlotte offers her.

'I'll help look for Edith,' says Charlotte, squeezing Anna's shoulders. 'The Begijnhof is her home. She wouldn't have gone anywhere else.'

Anna nods, unable to speak, snuffling into the handkerchief.

Ten minutes later, with Anna nursing a mug of sweet tea, and the women having discussed Edith's possible whereabouts, Charlotte slips from the office and returns to the courtyard.

The sky is aglow with approaching dawn. Soon, the bell for lauds will chime, and the chapel will resound with voices murmuring in prayer.

A faint sound echoes around the courtyard. *Plink. Plink.* Charlotte turns in a circle, straining her ears for the location of the strange sound, while speculating on Edith's whereabouts.

Edith's words from their visit to the Plantin–Moretus Museum return: *After the orphanage, I went from one foster home to the next, one job to another, until the Begijnhof became my family.* She senses Edith is terrified the Begijnhof will be closed due to financial cutbacks and she'll lose her home, just as she lost one home after another during her childhood. Edith wouldn't be anywhere else. This is her home. She's here, somewhere, doing whatever she needs to save it.

There the sound is again. A soft clunk.

She tries to home in on its position. It's coming from somewhere up high. Her gaze travels up to the stepped gables.

After crossing to the chapel, she tugs at the latch, but the door is locked. Stretching her head back, she focuses on the top of the belfry. The muted clunk again, a faint scraping noise, small objects being moved.

Checking the door to the *bibliotheek*, she finds it unlocked. She climbs the stairs to the attic, ducking to avoid cobwebs, edging in between broken chairs, hat stands, a cracked mirror. She remembers her first visit to the attic, Edith telling her about the narrow door in the far wall: *for the bell ringer to access the belfry via the bibliotheek.*

The door opens smoothly. A rush of cold air hits her face. The clunking sounds are louder now. Along a short passageway, she finds herself at the top of the belfry's square tower. Suspended in the centre are three massive bells, huddled under a steeply pitched roof, ropes descending through holes in the floor. The top floor of the belfry is open on all sides, surrounded by brick half-walls.

Glancing around the bells, she spies a shadow moving in the corner. A familiar figure stoops to the floor, picks up an object, rests it on the half-wall.

Charlotte retreats into the shadows, needing a moment to calm herself, to plan the next step. She taps out a text message: *Found her. Top of belfry. Bring Anna.*

She sidesteps around the bells. 'Edith?' she calls quietly, trying not to startle her.

'Oh!' Edith steps back, her elbow bumping a loose brick. It topples from the half-wall, plunges through air, smashes against the chapel roof. Terracotta tiles shatter, crashing to the cobblestones far below.

'Anna is worried about you,' says Charlotte. 'Are you okay?'

'Yes, I'm fine,' says Edith, her tone hesitant. Holding an empty dustpan, she waves it in the air as she speaks, her face becoming animated. 'I've been tidying. Getting ready for when the builders return to finish the renovation.'

The floor is littered with debris. In the corner are wooden crates of new bricks, hessian sacks half-filled with rubble.

Edith uses a wire brush to sweep brick fragments onto the dustpan, before tipping them into another hessian sack.

'It's so cold up here,' says Charlotte gently. 'Why don't we go downstairs? I can make us some tea.'

'There's still so much to do,' says Edith. 'I'll come down when I've finished.' Her tone is lively, unaware of the worry she has caused.

Charlotte walks around the bells, taking a closer look at the crumbled half-wall. A section is missing, more than a metre wide, its uneven lower edge like a row of broken teeth. Beyond lies a four-storey drop to the cobblestones. She shivers, realising if she or Edith lose their balance, they will plunge to their death. Edith appears oblivious to the danger.

'Perhaps I can help,' says Charlotte, keeping her voice steady, desperate for Edith to move away from the gaping hole. The *begijn* has been missing since yesterday afternoon. Surely she hasn't been up here, clearing rubble, the entire time? It would've been too dark to work through the night, and terribly dangerous.

'Edith, have you been here all night?'

Edith empties more rubble into the sack. 'I've been doing odd jobs here and there. I had a rest in the chapel and fell asleep. Don't tell Anna. We're not supposed to sleep in the chapel.' She smiles sheepishly.

'I won't say a word,' replies Charlotte, returning the smile. She imagines Edith curled up on one of the pews, fast asleep, unaware her fellow *begijnen* were searching for her.

'By spring, the tradesmen will finish repairing the belfry,' says Edith, talking quickly now, her tone cheerful, 'then they'll fix the chapel roof and upgrade the electrical wiring. Then we'll set up the second-hand clothing shop and finalise our plans to be financially independent. Petra knew the repairs were necessary. When she was sick, she became preoccupied with the idea that objects were trivial and worthless, but she came to realise the objects would help Sint-Catharina's survive, for the good of everyone.'

The skin on the back of Charlotte's neck prickles, recalling Petra's self-condemnation for neglecting her duties, being lured by the distracting evils of *Materialism and Man-Made Beauty*.

'Petra didn't realise at first how she could help, but once I explained that we each have our role to play, she understood. She knew it was better this way. They can finally be put to good use, for everyone's benefit.' Edith's voice is high-pitched with excitement. She bends to scoop up another load of rubble, depositing it in the sack with a flourish.

'I'm pleased to hear that,' says Charlotte, even though she's more concerned than pleased. She has no proof that Edith drove to Gistel to retrieve the hidden *Pandoras* or changed Petra's will, but she senses Edith is hiding something from her, just as she concealed from Anna the true reason for wanting to borrow the Citroën. Wherever Edith drove on Saturday, it wasn't to the Schone Kunsten Museum.

She recalls the words Edith had used in the garden yesterday – *sometimes things have a strange way of working out ... everything has changed ... it's all going to be fine* – delivered with confidence and self-satisfaction, a hint of proud defiance.

Whenever she had spent time with Edith, the *begijn* had always been subdued and pensive, often shy, sometimes despondent, especially when reflecting on Petra and the financial troubles of the Begijnhof. Something drastic has happened to shift the *begijn*'s mood.

93

'Where did you find her?' whispers Sébastien. He stands beside Charlotte in the shadows of the *bibliotheek* attic.

'At the top of the belfry,' she replies, her gaze fixed on the far end of the attic, where Edith and Anna sit on a battered tin trunk.

Anna rests a hand on Edith's knee, talking softly, her voice too low for them to hear. Edith sits with bowed head, leaning towards the mother superior, listening. Every so often she shakes her head, murmurs a few words.

In hurried whispers, she gives Sébastien an account of her time with Edith in the belfry. 'I've never seen her so animated. She's very excited about the renovations, which are apparently going to start soon.'

'Exactly how does Sint-Catharina's suddenly have money for renovations?' he asks.

'Edith didn't explain, but she did say *they can finally be put to good use.*'

'Did she admit to finding the drawings?'

'She didn't admit to anything,' whispers Charlotte, 'but I'm certain she was the one who drove to Gistel.' Leaning closer to Sébastien, Charlotte shares with him the mother superior's revelation that Edith borrowed the Begijnhof's old Citroën on the same day as the huge storm.

Anna places an arm around Edith's shoulders, speaking quietly.

Edith shakes her head, her voice rises. 'No, I was helping! Petra showed me everything. She no longer cared for her possessions. Preferred a life of prayer and service. Said her possessions were trivial and worthless.'

Anna talks gently.

'She didn't agree at first,' says Edith, her voice insistent, 'but once I explained Sint-Catharina's was running out of money and would close, and we'd have nowhere to live, she understood.' Edith nods eagerly. 'She understood everything.'

Anna pats Edith's hand, trying to soothe the younger *begijn*'s growing agitation.

'I couldn't go back to having no home or family.' Edith pulls a handkerchief from her pocket, begins winding it around her fingers. 'All I did was point out that if Petra no longer wanted her possessions, they could be put to good use in helping Sint-Catharina's. I didn't do anything wrong. It's what Petra wanted.'

'I'm sure it was with the best intentions, my dear,' says Anna, her voice carrying across the attic. 'But, Petra's memory wasn't very reliable in the last few months. She often had periods where she was forgetful and confused, didn't understand simple tasks. It was the dementia. She certainly didn't understand complicated documents like a will.'

'But I explained everything to her.'

'How much help did you give Petra with her new will? Did you explain the consequences?' Anna pauses before asking the next question, her tone gentle. 'Did you write the will for her?'

Edith sniffs, her voice quavering. 'Petra could barely hold a pen. Yes, I wrote the will for her.'

Anna pulls a familiar envelope from her pocket, unfolds the will on her knee. She points at the bottom of the page. 'Edith, I need you to look at this signature.'

Edith looks quickly at the page, then at the floor. She blots her eyes with the handkerchief, scrunching the fabric in her fist.

'Did you sign Petra's name on her will?' asks Anna.

Edith sits motionless for nearly ten seconds then she moves her head, a faint tilt up and then down. 'Yes … yes, I did,' she says, before emitting a small cry. She clamps the handkerchief to her mouth, stifling sobs.

Charlotte glances at Sébastien. His face is controlled, mouth tight. She hasn't had the opportunity to speak with him much about his half-sister and their relationship. She imagines he's trying to make sense of what they've heard: his confused, ailing

sister cajoled, even pressured, into having a new will which she
didn't understand or approve, leaving her considerable fortune to
others.

Sitting rigidly on the trunk, Edith shakes with sobs, her wails
filling the air. Anna wraps her into an embrace, murmuring
comforting words. Edith presses the handkerchief to her mouth,
hiccupping and shuddering, trying to get her sobs under control.

'Léa and I … witnessed … the will,' says Edith.

'Was Léa happy to witness Petra's new will?' asks Anna.

'You know Léa … meek as a mouse most of the time,' says
Edith, 'but occasionally she quibbled.'

'Did Léa question you about Petra's will?'

'I told her to have faith. Told her it was for the best. She didn't
understand that Sint-Catharina's was falling apart around us, and we
would lose it. The Diocese wouldn't extend our budget, and with
such a small number of sisters, Sint-Catharina's was sure to close.
We'd have no home, no family, nowhere to go. I couldn't let that
happen.' Edith sinks in her seat, head hanging low.

'Was Léa agreeable to being a witness to Petra's will?' repeats
Anna, more firmly this time.

Edith is silent, staring at the floor. At last, she shrugs. 'Not really.
She signed her name, but came to me afterwards and said … she
said … she didn't think it was right. We argued, and then she said
she was leaving Sint-Catharina's. Said she didn't want to stay if this
was how she would be treated in her old age.'

Anna shakes her head. 'And that's when Léa announced she was
leaving Sint-Catharina's, after being part of our family for more
than thirty-five years.'

Edith flinches at the word *family*. Wraps her arms across her
stomach, as if in pain, and slowly stands. She looks down at Anna,
then across the attic to Sébastien and Charlotte. Walking towards
Sébastien, she opens her mouth to speak and a half-strangled
whimper emerges. When she begins talking, her voice is feeble,
then grows stronger. 'The family treasures belonged to Petra. I saw
the two of you together, in the foyer and at the museum, and she
was angry with you. She wouldn't have wanted you to have her
treasures. She wanted to give them to Sint-Catharina's. When I

read her old will in the filing cabinet, I realised she was leaving everything to you. I had to do something.'

Sébastien purses his lips, remaining silent.

Edith turns to Charlotte. Offers a half-smile, the shyness still there, her desire to please evident. 'You helped me fix everything. I'm so grateful.'

Charlotte winces.

'I'd already seen the map folio,' continues Edith. 'I often looked at the contents of the portfolio box while Petra was elsewhere. She was such a private person, didn't want to talk about her family, but the portfolio box was like a treasure trove. All those wonderful family mementoes, the genealogy charts going back generations, all the way to Lucas Vorsterman. So special to have family like that.'

She takes a step towards Charlotte, her face alight, words streaming together with excitement. 'You helped put all the pieces of the puzzle together. When Petra started fussing about getting rid of her family treasures, I was worried she'd do something awful, maybe destroy them. I couldn't let that happen. So, I sent the map folio to the university. I encouraged Anna to let you and Dr Thornton search Sint-Catharina's for the portfolio box when it went missing. I was worried when I saw Professor Sterck arrive; I thought he would take it away. When I found out you were going to Gistel, I remembered Petra telling me, years ago, about her family's country estate. I realised there must be something special at Villa Wouters, so I drove the Citroën to Gistel, broke in and found the drawings. They can be put to good use now. At long last. Everyone at Sint-Catharina's is going to be fine now, thanks to you.' Edith beams, clasps her hands to her chest, smiling steadily at Charlotte.

The attic is silent.

Charlotte is breathless, as if all the air has been sucked from her lungs. A coldness hits her core, though her face feels flushed. The *Pandoras*. Edith has found them. They are real. After all this time, after centuries in hiding, they exist.

Anna is the first to break the silence. 'My dear, we have so much to talk about. Let's all go downstairs.' She stands and places her arm around Edith.

Sébastien moves to the stairs, shines his phone's light down the stairwell. The two *begijnen* walk side-by-side, the elder helping the younger, arms around one another.

Charlotte remains rooted to the spot, staring as the figures cross the attic in the grey light of morning, as if watching a scene in an old silent movie.

Part of her wants to reassure Edith that everything will be okay. Wants to wrap her arm around the woman, help her down the stairs.

But the rest of her is silently screaming. *Where are the drawings? What have you done with them? Have you left them crumpled somewhere, in the boot of the car or under a bed? Do you understand how fragile they are? How carefully they need to be looked after?*

Sébastien walks ahead, holding the flashlight of his mobile phone to illuminate each step.

Charlotte shakes herself from her stupor, follows behind.

'We've endured so many struggles at Sint-Catharina's,' says Edith brightly, 'wondering if we'll be closed, but we won't now. Everything will be fine. We may renounce the trappings of marriage and materialism when we become *begijnen*, but it's impossible to completely reject materialism. There will always be possessions in our lives to help us achieve our calling.'

Charlotte moves slowly down the stairs, her chest aching with sadness at Edith's naïvety. The *begijn* is euphoric, honestly believing she has solved the financial problems of the Begijnhof and secured her future and that of her fellow sisters. It may take hours, even days, before she acknowledges her wrongdoing.

'When I was a child,' says Edith, 'I was sent from one home to the next, but not anymore. Sint-Catharina's is my home. It will always be my home.'

94

April 17, 1686 – Antwerpen, Spanish Hapsburg Empire

I have caught myself daydreaming of late, reminiscing when as a girl I bounded up the stairs to my attic chamber, impatient to sharpen a quill and continue working on my latest creation. My aching bones may not allow much bounding these days, but I still approach my worktable with the same eagerness as my youth. Especially now, since I am seventy-seven and time marches swiftly along.

As twilight falls, I have a clear view from the gabled window, of rooftops and spires. I adjust my spectacles and light another lamp to stave off the gloom.

I am never alone. Lex burrows his wet muzzle into my palm. I remember my first *Kooiker* spaniel, a hazel-eyed bitch called Lieve, gifted by Papa on my nineteenth birthday after I returned from the convent.

'She will keep you company while you draw your maps,' he said after I solved the cryptic puzzle and discovered her yelping with excitement in an empty barrel in the courtyard.

It was love at first sight as I collected her into my arms, a mass of wriggling softness and waggling tail. We were inseparable for twelve years, and I sobbed when I found her cold body beneath the table one morning. The void in my heart was filled with another spaniel, a mischievous puppy called Lars who chewed my slippers and knocked over ink pots, but whom I adored all the same. Droopy-eyed Loek followed, then sweet-tempered Lotte and finally Lex, who will be my loyal companion 'til the end.

Flickering lamplight picks out gold embossed letters on the green leather cover of the folio lying on my worktable. *Nova Europae Descriptio*. I open the cover. Seven maps are bound within. The frieze decorating the first map is spellbinding, each picture hiding a secret.

Terracotta rooftops and stone bridges, figures in ermine cloaks and glittering crowns, lapis-lazuli rivers winding through malachite hills.

My requirements for the map folio were so rigorous I feared the mapmaker would refuse the commission. We communicated back and forth, Meneer de Wit confirming he would add pictures of certain cities and rulers in the frieze, leave all maps free from geographical markings, include blank spaces for my own title cartouches for the six country maps.

'Is it necessary to include a Borghese crest on the surplice of the Pope?' Meneer de Wit had asked in one of his letters. 'Surely a generic image of the Pope in his triple crown will suffice?'

Frederik de Wit was endlessly patient, accepting the stringent conditions for the commission and sending the completed folio to Eikenstraat. I paid him well for his skill, his assurance of confidentiality, and his promise the original plates would be destroyed.

For the past two months, I have been embellishing De Wit's maps with my own touches. Highlighting certain letters with blue ink, heavier lines and dots. Creating a miniature crest, tilted on its side, within Portugal. Hiding numerals amongst the cross-hatching in the border of the first map. Writing verses in six languages in the borders of the six country maps. Drawing geographical lines. Here and there, I cannot resist touching up a coastline with ultramarine, mountains with verdigris. Keeping my hand steady is a challenge.

I have just finished drawing Roman numerals along the border of the first map, using a powerful magnifying glass. My nephew Gerard, an accomplished geography student, will be puzzled to discover something unexpected about my maps. 'Geographical coordinates are never drawn this way, *Tante* Antonia?' Gerard will mutter to himself.

I call them *my* maps, but of course they are not. The real creator is Frederik de Wit, master cartographer and printmaker, owner of *Witte Pascaert* in Amsterdam. Although I have practised cartography for decades, my own skills are no match for such masters as Blaeu, Hondius, Mercator, Ortelius and De Wit. I have created hundreds of maps for family, friends and acquaintances, but my skills were insufficient to create the special map folio which I will bequeath to Gerard on my death.

Gerard will find De Wit's name and mark on the first page. He will spy my name inside the crest within Portugal and my secret signatures inside the title cartouches, and no doubt smile at my use of the acorn, symbolic of the *eiken* that fall from the oaks every autumn along our street. My hidden signatures will suffice as credit for my embellishments and cryptic clues.

My eyes smart with tiredness. I should snuff out the candle and go to bed, but the books on my shelf always capture my attention. When I feel mournful, I turn to Ogier's witty plays or Donne's sonnets. For inspiration, I open one of the map folios gifted to me by Papa, Hendrik or Gerard. The green leather of the Vasari, the book which ignited my curiosity as a child, stands out in the row of earthy spines.

Sliding the Vasari off the shelf, I am soon lost in memories. When I was young, Papa and I often disagreed as to which path in life I should follow. On that dreadful day when Santo attempted to blackmail Papa, my anger at their treatment of me culminated in my decision to sever ties with them both.

Papa was appalled, days later, when I announced my acceptance as a *postulantem* in the cloister of the Zwartezussen. I farewelled my family, donned the black habit, and promised obedience, poverty and chastity as I ministered to the poor and sick. But days spent in solitude and silence, entrusted with tasks far worse than working a linen press, did not suit my disposition. I was miserable and lonely, my mind starved of intellectual activity, my creative spirit yearning for ink and quill, my heart longing for my family. For two years, I stubbornly held onto my Zwartezussen vows until the mother superior called me into her office.

'Your decision to join our convent, Antonia, does not appear to have been a spiritual calling,' said the mother superior, 'but rather a desire to escape your family.'

I handed back the robe, coif and cincture when I departed the Zwartezussen, and arrived home with a newfound understanding of sin and forgiveness. Saint Paul's teachings to the Romans became ingrained on my heart, admonishing me of everyone's sins, myself included. My psalter often fell open at Psalm 32, reminding me of God's forgiveness and how I should do likewise. When I re-entered the front door of Eikenstraat after a two-year absence, Papa welcomed me with open arms. Together we moved forward with humility, forgiveness, trust and love.

Night has descended. I return the Vasari to the shelf. Embers glow in the fireplace, while a blanket warms my knees. Lex snuffles in his sleep. I murmur a prayer of thanks for my comforts, the love of my family.

My family's good fortune has afforded me many privileges. When I returned from the convent, I decided not to marry. Instead, I chose to manage the household, spend time with books and maps. When Hendrik married Sara, I happily passed her the keys and surrendered my position as housemistress. I relished my role as spinster aunt to Hendrik and Sara's growing brood, encouraging my nieces and nephews to learn French and Spanish, read Molière in the original, write poetry, and play *verstoppertje* with the neighbourhood children.

When Hendrik succumbed to fever only six years after Papa's passing, my nephew Gerard adeptly took over as head of the family, encouraging me to perfect my mapmaking techniques. At first, he called it my hobbyhorse. 'An activity going in circles,' he said with a smile, twirling his finger in the air. 'A suitable diversion for an unmarried lady to occupy her days.'

My diversion was a business. First Papa, then Hendrik and Gerard secured commissions for me, allowing me to build a reputation as a cartographer worthy of patronage amongst friends, neighbours and associates. I was forever grateful for the steady supply of work directed my way over the decades.

My old resentment occasionally returns when I recall my denial of membership into the Sint-Lucas Guild due to my gender and lack of formal apprenticeship. Although I may not be permitted to accept coins for my maps, being paid in kind is splendid recompense. Fine vellum from Krant Stationers, pigments and ink from Goedman Apotheek, books from Plantijn Press are payments which allow me to enjoy my creativity and independence.

Occasionally I poke at the old wound of injustice, recalling bygone discussions about female artists and their failure, like me, to be accepted by their male peers. But I determined long ago that dwelling on bitterness is not for me. I have set aside the demons once plaguing me, and made peace with my past.

I turn to the *Italies* map, pick up my quill and draw the first words of the Italian verse on the border. Not Italian, I correct myself, but Genoese, the weakest of the languages I understand. My hand trembles, my mind wanders.

'Santo,' I murmur.

Discarding my quill, I pull Santo's Genoese book from the shelf and flip through the pages, disturbing dust and dreams. My sadness over refusing his marriage proposal has eased into acceptance. I am content with the choice I made. Regret is futile. But, like tonight, my long-ago heartache returns to scratch at my memories.

On the shelf sits another small volume, bound in ochre leather, with the initials *SB* stamped on the cover. I was surprised to receive the booklet, knowing the effort Santo had spent filling its pages. Opening the cover, I pull out the final letter Santo wrote me, dated May 30, 1640, written in his blotched scrawl. *Today, Meneer Rubens breathed his last, surrounded by his children and wife Hélène.*

Santo's letter continued with words of regret.

> *I cannot look upon this booklet without recalling the disrespect I showed your father and the pain it caused you. Please accept this booklet as my feeble attempt to apologise for the wrong I caused. Look upon it as a reminder of a relationship which may have flourished if not for the arrogance of your once admirer, Santo Barzetti.*

I push aside my spectacles to wipe away tears.

Lex whimpers, sensing my sadness.

''Tis fine, boy.' I stroke his velvety head. 'Memories are precious, even if they bring tears.'

Returning Santo's books to the shelf, my fingers brush against Papa's red felt hat. The edges worn, the tassel frayed, a scuff mark recalling the time Gerard played with it as a child.

I pick up a brush, dip it in pigment and hover it over my *Italies* title cartouche. The figure on the cartouche is seated on a wooden bench, dressed in a brown doublet, breeches, suede boots. With a dab of vermilion, I transform the drab cap into red, highlighting its brilliance against the sombre attire of the tiny bearded figure.

Resting my brush on a dish, I stand and stretch. I imagine the eyes of the tiny character following me, looking with bewilderment, wondering why I have painted manacles on his wrists and ankles, puzzling over his depiction as a common criminal while he is dressed as a gentleman.

'I'm sorry, Papa,' I whisper, 'but 'tis for the best.'

I lift the corner of the *Italies* map and inspect the pastedown of the inside back cover. The marbled paper remains open on one side, just as the pastedown of the inside front cover remains open. When the maps are finished, I will slide a sheet of vellum into each cavity, dab glue along the edges and press down the marbled paper. Papa's secret will be hidden, awaiting Gerard's discovery.

As I lie in bed that night, listening to the night-time creaks of the house, my memories carry me back to eleven years ago when I sat at Papa's bedside, holding his hand, listening to his last words and his final breath.

95

'Thank you for your patience and kindness during this difficult time.' Anna brings a hand to the small cross hanging around her neck, looking from Sébastien to Charlotte then Miles.

They sit in a circle in the foyer of the Begijnhof's office building. Subdued, lost in reflection. Charlotte squeezes her hands together, struggling to find the right words of reassurance to offer the mother superior. She can't imagine what Anna is going through, heartsick over the misguided actions of one *begijn*, a second one having abandoned Sint-Catharina's over the trauma, a third deceived before death.

'These past few days have been challenging,' continues Anna. 'Forging a will is a serious criminal offence, so the police have been interviewing Edith and Léa, examining the documents and visiting Villa Wouters.'

Sébastien offers a comforting murmur. 'Must be difficult to make sense of everything.'

'For you, too, with Petra.' Anna softly tuts. 'I can't take it in.'

They stare at the checkerboard floor, shifting awkwardly in their chairs. Sébastien straightens his tie in a gesture Charlotte now recognises as unease. Miles distractedly touches the livid bruises along his jaw.

Charlotte recalls the conversations she and Miles have shared since his release from hospital. The victims of the attacks and Arnold's theft of their research have been uppermost in their discussions, along with Charlotte's meeting with Dean Mulder to explain her unauthorised access of the conservation room. Their names may have been cleared by the Gistel police regarding the break-in, but a final decision has not yet been made by the dean and

board of governors over whether she will be asked to resign. She
has lost their trust. Only time will tell whether she will be allowed
to stay, to try and earn it back.

Anna clears her throat. 'Edith is distraught ... and in denial. She
still believes she was making the right decision to help the Begijnhof
in this way. It will take time for her to comprehend the severity of
her actions. I've tried speaking to her about the missing drawings,
but she's not cooperating.' Anna's hand tightens around the cross.

'I'm sure she'll reveal their location when she's ready,' says
Charlotte.

Anna shakes her head. 'I keep going over our conversation in
the attic. There's something she said that I can't ignore. She said,
although we renounce the trappings of marriage and materialism
when we become *begijnen*, it's impossible to completely reject
materialism.'

Leaning back in her chair, Anna's features soften. 'When we gave
tours of the Begijnhof to visitors, Edith often volunteered to show
them around. She was familiar with the history of Sint-Catharina's,
proud of its heritage. She wrote a spiel for us to use, which we all
learnt and shared with visitors.'

Charlotte remembers meeting Edith for the first time. She had
offered to show them to Anna's office and, as they crossed the
courtyard, provided snippets about Sint-Catharina's. She'd launched
into a commentary – explaining the difference between a *beguinage*
and *begijnhof*, pointing out the names engraved along each lintel – as
if giving a prescribed tour.

'Sint-Catharina's is filled with beautiful antiques and objects,'
continues Anna, 'but several became symbolic of what we set aside
when we become *begijnen*. An antique marriage bed, inherited
by Petra from your mother' – she nods at Sébastien – 'was hardly
suitable for the bedroom of a *begijn*. It was disassembled and stored
in the attic. But there was another piece of furniture, symbolic of
our renunciation of the trappings of marriage and materialism.' She
looks at Charlotte and smiles. 'Do you remember the day we met?'

'The linen press,' says Charlotte, suddenly filled with a sensation
of lightness. Standing, she turns towards the peculiar item of
furniture in the corner of the foyer.

Anna motions for everyone to follow. 'While we were in the attic, Edith repeated the exact words from our tour – *the trappings of marriage and materialism* – which we used to explain the importance placed on having beautifully pressed linen in a woman's trousseau.'

They cross the foyer and stand around the press.

'As I repeated Edith's words to myself,' says Anna, 'I wondered whether she had inadvertently let slip where she placed the drawings.'

Sébastien runs his hands over the polished timber. 'Have you looked inside?'

Anna shakes her head. 'I wanted you all to be here.'

'Miles, you're the tallest,' says Sébastien. 'Would you mind?'

'Let me help,' says Charlotte.

Standing opposite one another, they grasp the handles and in perfect sync, turn them two revolutions. The wood groans as the box rises from its base, gaps appearing in between each plank. They continue turning the handle and, as the spaces widen, collectively hold their breath.

Charlotte sinks to her knees, eyes level with the gaps, oblivious to the noise and movement around her. A smile spreads across her face. Speechless.

Resting on each plank of timber is a large sheet of paper, layered with lightweight yellowed paper, then covered in clear archive plastic, protecting each drawing. Seven pages. Earth tonings barely visible through the translucent, gossamer-thin paper. Charlotte recalls Santo's description: *seven preparatory drawings, pen and brown ink on paper, one by one-half Flemish ell .. lost, July 1621.*

Miles continues twisting the handle, Charlotte keeping her eyes on the drawings. When the press is fully open, she stands by Miles, reaches for his hand. Fingers entwine. No words needed.

The drawings are finally revealed, each one carefully wrapped.

Bless Edith, murmurs Charlotte to herself. For all her crimes, she had at least recognised the importance of protecting the fragile drawings with archive plastic.

96

July 20, 1675 – Antwerpen, Spanish Hapsburg Empire

At the height of spring, when the oaks were lush with growth, Papa was set low with a cough. It filled his chest and racked his body, bringing on a fever. The physician was called, bloodletting administered, salves applied, and although the fever abated, the cough remained. By the end of June, he was too weak to leave his bed.

I spooned bone broth into his mouth, fed him slivers of Seville oranges, enticed him with honeyed syllabub, a favourite from our time in London. The grandchildren visited, eager to coax a smile from him. When he complained of insomnia, I eased his mood by reading aloud. Surrounded by the sweet scent of beeswax, I paced the room with a book in my hand, spectacles perched on my nose. Together, we explored Huygens, Molière, Montalbán and Donne, changing from Flemish to French, Spanish to English.

Despite our best efforts, Papa sank into a deep melancholy which would not shift. He barely ate, became indifferent to visitors and my reading. He could barely lift his head from the pillow, but his voice remained strong.

One evening, as the summer solstice approached, he grasped my hand.

'I have been an arrogant fool,' he said. 'My obsession with trying to elevate our family above our station caused me to make decisions that hurt my family. *Mijn liefje*, please forgive me.'

'We spoke of this years ago, Papa, and put it to rest. No more forgiveness is required.'

'Santo saw my weakness and tried to take advantage–'

'Hush, Papa, it is in the past and forgotten.' I massaged the back of his hand.

'I asked the Master many times for ownership of the engravings, but he refused. He was awarded privilege. I was angry ... jealous.'

'Please, Papa.'

'I became incensed with rage ... could not see the consequences. I barely remember picking up the knife and before I could think, I was waving it in the air, yelling about injustice, slashing at him.'

I stroked Papa's hand, trying to ease his distress.

'The Master showed forgiveness to me, which I did not deserve. He tended his wound himself, bound the cut, tossed aside the slashed waistcoat, all while calming me. After the red mist cleared from my eyes and I yielded the knife, I was astounded to hear him declare that the details of my attack would not leave the room.'

'You worked in his studio for many years. He must have felt affection for you—'

'He told me I must leave,' Papa interrupted. '*Pack up your house, take your family and leave*, he said. *You can no longer work for me or stay in Antwerpen.*'

Papa and I sat in silence. He gazed at the ceiling as if it were the screen in a confessional box, while I stared at the blanket covering his body. He wanted to relive the anguish of yesteryear, while I wanted to brush such painful memories aside.

'The Master gave me a chance to redeem myself by allowing me to move to London, but I was arrogant.' Papa squeezed his eyes closed, then opened them to stare blindly at the ceiling. 'While in London, I maligned the Master's good name, and word got back to him in Antwerpen.'

My heart was heavy with sorrow. The anger I once felt towards Papa and Meneer Rubens for severing my friendship with Clara had melted away years ago. Still, the old wound smarted.

Papa began coughing. I rolled him onto his side to ease the congestion in his chest, then held a cup of honeyed water to his lips.

His voice was weak when he resumed talking. 'I was jealous of his success and patrons. I looked confident, *mijn liefje*, but lived in fear of being discovered.'

I didn't try to silence him, but allowed his memories to pour forth.

'You cannot know the regret that has filled me all these years, and now, I cannot leave this world without letting you know every detail of my wrongdoing.'

My heartbeat quickened.

'Before the knife attack, I did something worse ... I am ashamed to admit ...'

The heaviness in my chest moved to my stomach. Papa gazed so intently, I forgot for a moment he saw only shadows through his cloudy irises.

He cleared his throat. 'I took seven drawings created by the Master, rolled them within a sheet of waxed cloth and walked out of the studio with them hidden beneath my cloak.'

Silence filled the room.

I hoped he was too exhausted to continue. He was speaking to me as his confessor, eager to unburden himself of his crimes. But I wanted ignorance. He must wait until the priest arrived. I could not provide absolution.

'I took the drawings without thinking,' he whispered. 'I did not think what I would do with them ... sell them, destroy them. Days later, when I argued again with the Master and he ordered me to leave ... it was too late to return the drawings. I took them to London. I couldn't risk the drawings being discovered when we returned to Antwerpen, so I had a secret compartment made within my cabinet.' Tears filled his eyes. His voice broke. '*Mijn liefje*, I am sorry to leave this burden with you.'

A weight, like a stone, sat within me. Papa had carried this burden for decades and passed it to me.

'Now you know the truth, I can make my peace.'

I made to rise. 'Let me call for the priest.'

Papa reached for my hands. 'Wait with me 'til daybreak, then call the priest.'

I murmured soothing sounds.

'If my secret becomes known, dishonour will befall our family,' he whispered.

'Hush.'

'Antonia, you must promise me ... never reveal where the drawings are hidden.'

'Close your eyes and rest.'

'Promise me, Antonia. Promise now. For as long as you live, you will protect our family ... say the words.'

The candle on the nightstand flickered.

His grip tightened around my fingers. 'No dishonour ... for our family. Promise.'

I leaned forward and with tears coursing down my cheeks, I touched my forehead to his. 'I promise, Papa. I promise. As long as I live, I will never speak your secret.'

We rested against one another until his breathing calmed.

I sat back and studied the woollen blanket covering his body. His chest, once so expansive but now diminished with age, continued to rise and fall. Candlelight shadows wavered across his closed lids and parted lips. The droop of his moustache and white beard, his long nose and high cheekbones, his broad forehead, every feature familiar and yet strangely unfamiliar, as if we had just met.

Here lay my papa and yet somehow he was a stranger to me, dressed in the numerous ghosts of his past. Artist, engraver, linguist, guild member, husband, father, grandfather. I could add deceiver and criminal to the list of his roles, but I will not. I refuse to acknowledge his failings or speak of his crimes. Not tonight. Not yet. They can wait for another day. When he finally breathes his last, my grief can take hold and I will vent my heartache, condemn him for his crimes, rage at him for the burden he has passed to me. When he finally passes from this world to the next, I will be overwhelmed, transformed, weighed down with sorrow.

But only for a brief time.

At this moment, let me think only of his vitality and spirit, his loyalty to our family, his passion for life and art, his conscience that lifted him so high yet brought him so low, his tenderness and humour, his resilience and love. In the days after his passing, although his confession and my promise may cause my adoration to waver, it will be brief. My adoration will return, stronger than ever. Our love is true and unceasing. He will always be my beloved papa.

The dawn birds begin their chorus. Soon, I shall send for the priest.

Let me hold your hand, Papa, one last time.

97

Sébastien guides Anna to a chair. Karl and Willem lean against the bench, talking with Theo and Oscar Duval. Charlotte and Miles talk in whispers, catching the occasional words floating around the conservation room.

'Hidden for nearly four hundred years …'

'Seven drawings …'

'Worth millions if they're Rubens …'

'The map folio may not be entirely by De Wit … a female cartographer … Antonia Vorsterman …'

Miles slides a tray holding the seventh drawing onto the table. He catches Charlotte's gaze. A tilt of his head, crooked smile and it's enough to calm her racing heart and steady her hands. *You've got this*, his smile conveys. *Take your time, enjoy the moment.*

Charlotte looks from one face to the next. Only one person is absent. Her mother played a role in this journey, albeit an oblique one, encouraging her daughter to accept the position in Antwerp. Rachael's lies have merged into the background of Charlotte's memory, not denied, but a part of her existence. She wishes she could be here.

Sébastien moves to her side. 'Which one do you want to start with?' he asks, indicating the seven trays on the table, each containing a drawing covered in archive plastic. The drawings had been carefully transferred from the linen press into document cases, transported to the conservation room in a van.

'This one.' She slides the nearest tray towards her. The archive plastic and the yellowed paper obscure the details.

'Miles, can you please help?' she asks.

They tug on nitrile gloves. Each holding a corner of the archive plastic, they fold back the protective layer.

A hush falls over the room.

Translucent paper comes into view. Yellowed with age, the flimsy paper flutters as they lift it aside to reveal the first drawing.

Monochromatic earth shades, pen and brown ink on cream-coloured paper. Ochre smudges, cross-hatching in sepia and terracotta, delicate lines of white. Sinuous outline of high forehead, Roman nose, parted lips and pointed chin. Coiled braids nestle among curls, tendrils falling in wisps at the nape. Grey blends to black, highlighting pale iris against dark pupil. A woman's head captured at the moment of turning, glancing over a shoulder, beguiling the viewer with subtle all-knowing eyes and smile. Teasing seduction. Feminine charm personified.

'There she is,' says Miles. 'Pandora.'

'She's more beautiful than I imagined,' whispers Charlotte.

She recalls the adjectives used by Rubens to describe the duality of his Pandora: *innocence and delight, guile and misapprehension .. hint of indifference, even disdain on her pretty features.* Fickle, he called her, a mixture of surprise and confidence. She is all that and more, brought to life with the ink strokes of a genius.

'What do you think?' asks Anna, her voice ringing out across the room. 'Are they definitely Rubens?'

Sébastien touches Anna on the shoulder. 'Let's wait until she's had a chance to see them all.'

Ignoring the voices, Charlotte concentrates on the drawing. The background chatter about their authenticity, their monetary value, can't detract from this moment. She's dreamt of this.

She peers through a magnifying glass. Despite it being a preliminary drawing, the execution is first-rate, the style exceptional. Clean lines, controlled proficiency, a master's touch. Expert blending of light into shade. Chiaroscuro at its finest.

The second drawing shows Pandora swathed in clinging robes. Curve of buttocks and bare shoulders, diaphanous fabric skimming over full, rounded breasts, a gentle swell of belly. Fertile and feminine. Curves and plumpness artfully displayed in a glorification of womanhood. Rubens' *Pandora* is shapely and well nourished, the embodiment of the voluptuous seventeenth-century woman, the antithesis of the lean athleticism of the nineteenth-century *Pandoras* depicted by Waterhouse, Alma-Tadema, Perugini and their contemporaries.

'The pose ...' begins Charlotte, her eyes following Pandora's stance.

Miles leans closer. 'Does it remind you of other paintings?'

'*Perseus and Andromeda*, painted in 1621 by Rubens. Pandora's pose is the same as Andromeda's. The way the fabric flows over the hips and thighs, the turn of her head ...'

'Demonstrates a consistent style,' says Miles.

'... and the Three Graces in his *Education of Marie de' Medici*, also painted in 1621 ... the hairstyles are identical to Pandora's. Twisted braid set high on the head ... wispy curls ...'

He encourages her to take her time, understanding the importance of examining each detail.

They peel back the protective layers covering the next drawing. Everyone praises the artist's skill, admires Pandora's beauty, the close-up of her face and hands.

Charlotte is transported to her visit of a Pre-Raphaelite exhibition two years ago in London. Standing before Waterhouse's *Pandora*, she had been mesmerised by the artist's depiction of the invisible gifts escaping from a burnished golden chest. The ancient poet Hesiod's original account of the Pandora legend described the gifts being stored in a Greek *pithos*, but the jar transformed over the centuries into a box. Had Rubens chosen a jar or box for his *Pandora*?

Miles and Charlotte lean in for a closer look. Pandora's hand rests on a Greek-style *pithos*, the fingers of one hand curled around the handle, her other hand lifting the lid.

'Look ... it's signed in his preferred Italian.' Miles indicates a signature in the lower corner. A familiar scrawl: *Pietro Pauolo Rubens*.

She beams at Miles. He is quick to return her smile.

Sébastien lowers his voice so only she can hear. 'Are they his?'

'We'll need to organise tests to confirm age and origin, but yes, they're Rubens. Unmistakable.'

Every drawing is executed in the same masterful style, each depicting a different aspect of the beauty. The seventh drawing has a large corner missing, a jagged tear, Pandora's heel severed.

Charlotte retrieves a small tray from a side bench, which contains the triangular scrap of paper that she rescued from the antique *kast*. Tucked inside a plastic sleeve, the scrap displays the same well-worn paper and delicate lines as the *Pandora* drawings. Charlotte carefully holds the scrap above the seventh drawing, matching up the torn edges. The curves of the heel and ankle are perfectly aligned.

Charlotte and Miles swap smiles of total understanding. No words are needed for them to remember the day at Villa Wouters, and to know that conservators will decide how best to reattach Pandora's heel.

Charlotte rests her hands on the table, enjoying the sensation of lightness and happiness within. The *Pandoras* are safe, unveiled in all their beauty after four hundred years in hiding. Whenever she anticipated this moment, she imagined feeling euphoric, giddy with excitement. But she is calm, serene, as if she always knew the *Pandoras* would be found.

She gazes at Pandora. Smile meets smile.

Author's note

The Engraver's Secret was originally published as *De Graveur* in the Netherlands and Belgium in February 2022. Multilingual readers may notice that this edition is slightly different from the Dutch-language version. I'm always looking for ways to tweak and enhance my book, and this only stops once the manuscript is sent to the printer. These edits are a common occurrence for books that are first published in translation, before being released in their original language. I hope my multilingual readers enjoy spotting the differences.

Part of this story is set in the beautiful Begijnhof in Antwerp, which was founded in 1544. Today, if you enter the main gates, you will not encounter any *begijnen*. The last *begijn* in the world died in 2013 at the age of ninety-two, having served as a *begijn* for seventy-one years in Kortrijk. I was so enchanted by the Begijnhof in Antwerp that I was determined to place my fictional characters of Edith, Anna and their fellow *begijnen* within its walls.

Although the Antwerp Begijnhof has not housed *begijnen* for many decades, and the buildings have long since been converted into private housing, the exteriors have changed very little in the past century. The step-gabled, red-brick buildings still surround a cobblestoned drive and garden of mature trees. A small church, dedicated to Saint Catherine, still sits in the northeastern corner. The belfry was created from my imagination because the story was begging for a belfry. If you wander through this tranquil corner of Antwerp, please respect the privacy of the residents and their peaceful environs.

The buildings and streets of Antwerp provided me with enormous inspiration while writing this book, including the Rubenshuis, Plantin-Moretus Museum, Sint-Jacobskerk, Brabo fountain and the Wapper. The city is a mixture of winding lanes and grand thoroughfares, imposing step-gabled façades and narrow townhouses. It is a lively city where it is easy to imagine the historical figures of Peter Paul Rubens, Lucas Vorsterman and their peers walking through Grote Markt on an errand, relaxing with friends in a tavern or attending church with their family.

Vorsterman and Rubens had a complicated relationship. Born two decades apart in nearby countries, they moved to Antwerp as children and became accomplished artists, proficient polyglots and members of the Guild of Saint Luke. Rubens' star had ascended by the time Vorsterman arrived in the well-established studio of the older artist to be employed as his principal engraver.

As a diplomat who frequented the royal courts, Rubens proffered the printed engravings as enticements to the likes of King Philip of Spain, King James of England and Marie de' Medici of France. When diplomatic discussions were set aside for the evening and wine flowed, I imagine the conversation turned to plans for decorating the walls and ceilings of the monarch's latest architectural extravagance. I imagine Rubens pulled from his pocketbook an engraving of *The Lion Hunt* or *The Four Rivers of Paradise* and showed it to King Philip, offering to create something equally grand for a room in the Palacio Real in Madrid. The engravings were a marketing tool for Rubens, a means to showcase his considerable talent and procure commissions.

Few details are known about the real dispute in 1621 that severed the relationship between Vorsterman and Rubens. Several historians called it violent; others said Rubens petitioned the authorities for a protection order against the young engraver. The dispute resulted in Rubens being granted exclusive rights over the reproduction of his artistic creations. The relationship between the engraver and the painter must have been adequately reconciled by 1624 when Vorsterman reportedly asked Rubens to be godfather to his son Lucas the Younger.

Although this story deals with the issue of copyright, this term was not used until 1729. The term 'operating privilege' was used in the sixteenth and seventeenth centuries to refer to our modern understanding of the term 'copyright'. Rubens and Vorsterman both struggled to secure their author privilege, establish their artistic credo, and protect their livelihood.

The Engraver's Secret attempts to imagine the frustration Vorsterman may have experienced when he fell out with his employer and subsequently lost his position in Rubens' studio. Scant historical details exist on the life of Lucas Vorsterman. Even less is known of his daughter Antonia. Art historian Theodor Levin (1888) stated that Lucas Vorsterman, having lost his eyesight fifteen years prior to his death, lived opposite the cloister of the Swertsusters where one of his daughters was a nun. Levin did not name the daughter, but she reportedly cared for her father until his death in 1675.

Several details of Lucas Vorsterman's life have been altered to fit the timeline of this story. The theft of seven drawings, painted by Rubens, was created from my imagination. To the best of my knowledge, Rubens never painted the legend of Pandora. Maybe she is out there, waiting to be discovered.

Acknowledgements

My heartfelt thanks to my agent Amanda Preston from LBA Literary Agency for being my biggest champion. Thank you for your astute editing suggestions which added depth to my story, your clarity when I had doubts, and your insights into the publishing process. Also, huge thanks to Clare Forster from Curtis Brown Australia, who championed my writing and worked so hard to find the perfect home for my book in Australia.

It was a delight and honour to work with the exceptional team at HarperCollins Publishers Australia. Roberta Ivers, thank you for believing in my story and my writing from the start, and encouraging me to look at the plot and characters in new ways to help it shine. Rachel Cramp, thank you for your amazing editorial skills, your sharp eye for detail, and juggling so adeptly the numerous tasks involved in bringing a book from manuscript to market. Vanessa Lanaway, thank you for being the ultimate continuity expert, for noticing tiny details that needed tweaking and larger issues that needed resolution. I am so grateful to every member of the talented HarperCollins Australia team, who have worked tirelessly to help realise my dream of bringing my book to readers in my homeland of Australia, and further afield.

Thank you to my fellow writers, course participants and teachers from the courses I have attended, especially Curtis Brown Creative, Arvon Foundation and Jericho Writers. Your support and insight have been immense. The members of the KBO writers have a special place in my heart, and I am forever grateful for the shared laughter and optimism that has spurred us on to keep writing. Special thanks to fellow writer, Julie Holden, for clearing away the fog and allowing me to see the potential story lying within.

Huge thanks to my extraordinary Poldark crew – Emma Moore, Linda Bosma-Malley and Shuna Atack – for your unwavering enthusiasm, even when the writing of this book stretched from one year to the next and beyond, seeming little more than a pipe dream. You always believed in me.

My warmest thanks to my cheer squad in The Hague – Jen van Ginhoven, Carolyn Wiersum, Wanne Sinterniklaas, Sabine Miesen, Mary Bentham, Rada Yakova, Sana Bardawil and Thérèse O'Connor – for surrounding me with positive vibes and keeping me laughing through the rollercoaster journey of writing and getting published. And on the other side of the world, my sincere thanks to my Melbourne cheer squad – Heather Hausler and Danyelle Cawood – for your wisdom, encouragement and humour.

Thank you to my dear friend Rebecca Clarke, for your steadfast encouragement, and for accompanying me on that first train journey to Antwerp all those years ago. It was such an inspiration to visit the Plantin-Moretus Museum together and wander around the streets of the old town, past the Rubenshuis, Brabo fountain and chocolate shops galore. On the train journey back to The Hague a seed began to grow.

Thank you to my incredible parents, George and Frances Hams, who always inspired me to believe in my dreams and work hard to achieve them.

Most of all, my deepest thanks to my family. Thank you, Alex, for reminding me that the creative journey can be wild and unpredictable, and to enjoy the ride. Thank you, Natasha, for your wit and wisdom, and for keeping me firmly grounded. To my darling Stan, thank you for always being an enthusiastic sounding board, for happily joining me for another trip to Antwerp, for photographing scenes to inspire my writing, for sharing this journey of life, for the laughter and love. Life is amazing because of you.

Questions for Reading Group Discussion

1. Was the strength and determination displayed by Antonia when she was a girl and, later as an adult, realistic for the seventeenth century?

2. How does Charlotte justify her choice of stealing a keycard and sneaking into the conservation room without permission? Do you think her behaviour can be excused under any circumstances?

3. Did you agree with the advice Rachael Hubert offered Charlotte about being cautious about trusting others, and not revealing your full hand until ready? How did this contribute to Charlotte's hesitancy in trusting Miles and Sébastien?

4. Which of the two settings – modern-day Antwerp or seventeenth-century Antwerpen – did you prefer and why?

5. How did the themes of intellectual theft and ownership manifest in both timelines?

6. Did Rubens treat Vorsterman unfairly over the ownership of the engravings? Should Rubens have allowed Vorsterman to make copies of the engravings and sell them?

7. How does the book explore the core themes of ownership, jealousy, family commitment, loyalty and trust?

8. Do you believe that once trust in a familial relationship is lost that it is impossible to gain it back?

9. What surprised you most about the story? Were there any questions left unanswered by the end of the book?

10. If you promised a loved one to never reveal a secret, under what circumstances would you break your promise?